Also by James Haydock --

Stormbirds

Victorian Sages

Beacon's River

Portraits in Charcoal: George Gissing's Women

On a Darkling Plain: Victorian Poetry and Thought

Searching in Shadow: Victorian Prose and Thought

Against the Grain

Mose in Bondage

A Tinker in Blue Anchor

"How keenly green was that man's yesterday!"
– Blue Anchor Citizen

A NOVEL by

JAMES HAYDOCK

authorHOUSE®

AuthorHouse™
1663 Liberty Drive
Bloomington, IN 47403
www.authorhouse.com
Phone: 1-800-839-8640

Published by AuthorHouse 04/21/2014

ISBN: 978-1-4969-0665-6 (sc)
ISBN: 978-1-4969-0664-9 (e)

Contents

Gratefully I dedicate this book to Victoria,
my Dulcinea del Cisne Blanco.

Prologue

My name is Isaac Brandimore. I am writing this in the spring of 1863. I am not a young man. I passed the bloom of youth sixty years ago but remain spry and active in a solitude thrust upon me after my friend Seth went to his rest only hours after becoming a free man. He died in 1860 before the worst war in human history began. Even though I wanted him to live long enough to enjoy his new-found freedom, maybe it was a blessing he departed when he did. I live on as the war rages, and I suffer as all persons in our village suffer, even as thousands of young men on the battlefields of this divided nation are slaughtered like cattle. I am told they run with abandon into the jaws of hell, and they die in agony as their loved ones pray in vain for their safety and survival. It is my fervent hope that anyone who happens to read this will never experience such horror.

Now as spring looks forward to summer, the American Civil War as people in the North are calling it, or the War Between the States as we Southern folk call it, has dragged on and on with no end in sight. A turning point is bound to come soon, a major battle with a decisive outcome. The South has fought valiantly against superior forces, but I fear the North will celebrate a resounding victory before this year is over. The Southern states cannot win this war. Of that I am certain. Even so, although the prospect of a crushing defeat weighs heavily upon me, I am not here to talk about the war.

I prefer to talk about Seth, my companion from youth to old age. He was my servant but also my friend, and I miss him. I would like to trace the events of his long life and record its climax, the high-water mark of his existence, the night he was given his freedom. That's when he became young and strong again and with great dignity conversed with men as an equal. Perhaps I will speak of Seth when summer comes, but for now I wish to lay out on paper the life of another remarkable man in our village who has served us well but now faces an unknown destiny. Leo Tamasin Mack is the name of this proud Irishman. He is my age or maybe a few years younger. Nonetheless, it is certain the toll of the summers he will count on his knobby fingers will never again reach beyond another decade.

I've known the man for at least a dozen years. He came to live in this village when he was sixty or more, and though he grows thinner and more angular with each passing year he never seems to age as much as other folks. He makes his living as a traveling tinker, going from one isolated farmhouse in the outlying fields and forests of Blue Anchor to the next. In the early years he had a mongrel dog named Sparky that trotted at the wheels of his old wagon. An old horse pulled the wagon, and the old dog lay beneath it whenever it stopped. No one ever saw the dog riding in the wagon.

At present Leo visits my cozy little house more often than necessary because he believes I live in loneliness and isolation. Though I am not as miserable he thinks, I am always glad to see him and hear him talk as he works on a pot. You might think an unschooled man such as Leo would have little to say to a bookish old recluse like me, but not so. Even though he never says much about himself, a person can depend on him for a wide array of news, some good and some not so good, but uttered with an amazing depth of understanding in slow and clear articulation.

Always when he comes to my house he makes a beeline for the kitchen, trundling through my study, and turning up his nose in displeasure the instant he smells my leathery books. He loves the scents that greet his nostrils in the kitchen but has no use for the little room I call my study. He said to me once as we spoke of Lincoln's inauguration and the pressing issues of the day, "Isaac, you and your kind think you've examined all them thorny questions inside and out, but it just ain't so. You scholars with brains and books always think you get to know every visible part of everything, and even the shadow of every part, but maybe not. I really believe you miss a lot. Now me, I never examined anything but the bottom of a pot, but I have a good head on my stringy shoulders and a good store of commonsense, and so I don't need to read all them books you got in that room you call a study. What does *study* applied to a room mean anyway? I'm a tinker, Isaac, not a thinker."

He looked at me slyly when he said that, his head cocked to one side and chuckling to himself. I could see he was taking pleasure in the witty rhyme he had made, but maybe he was thinking too that I would see his remark as an insult and be offended. When I assured him he had more than his share of commonsense and a good helping of brains and humor to boot, he fell to his work with that crooked smile of his and a twinkle in pale blue eyes. He never got very far in school, and so I believe without training in logical thought he can't summon the clearest kind of thinking, and yet I do know his wit can match that of anyone. Every person in our Quaker community agrees that he's one of our best talkers when he's in the mood to talk.

Leo prides himself on being a bringer of news. For him it's always important news, now that a brutal civil war is killing our country. He tells me he's a tinker first but also a messenger, and his customers in solitary places always get their money's worth. When he mends a pot he gives us more than just his work, he says. He gives us news and the will to endure and maybe hope. Well, I believe most of us love him for that and for his honesty as well.

But maybe I exaggerate. I can't really say anyone in the village truly loves the man. However, if he died tomorrow or went somewhere else to live, all of us would sorely miss him. We'd realize that over the years, as the seasons came and went and time moved on, he slowly became a fixture in our community. We depend on Leo Mack. We know he will gather the news of the day, digest it as best he can without distortion, and bring it to us as long as this terrible war endures. When it ends, if it ever does, maybe Leo (and his customers too) will rest. In the meantime he will work, as we all do in hard times, to put food in his belly. He will labor to pay the landlady who feeds him and keeps a roof over his head.

He lives in a boarding house and eats at Ida Crabtree's table with the other boarders. He's been there for as long as I can remember. Some people say when he first came to Blue Anchor he lived in an old run-down house on the East Road, the one that goes into the swamp. He was there all by his lonesome for at least a year, they say, and then moved into the Crabtree place. He was a tinker even then, but didn't own a wagon or even a horse, and how he made ends meet I don't know. I do know he spent a lot of time in the swamp, the famous Great Dismal Swamp, and fed on the game he trapped.

Also he did odd jobs now and then for David Kingston and other people, and saved enough money to buy a horse at a good price and later a wagon to hold his equipment, and before long he was in business. Then one day he found old Sparky sprawled in the road hurt and full of worms, and when the dog was well again they were inseparable. I do believe Leo loved that dog better than any of us. When Sparky died years later of old age, no other dog seemed good enough to take his place.

I could tell you more about Leo's life in the boarding house, but right now I'd better move along to explain how I came to know him. As I said earlier, he almost never talked about himself when he came to do a job for me, but one day I invited him to go fishing. He smiled wide enough to show his bad teeth and a glittering gold tooth that seemed to mock the others. Covering his mouth with the back of one hand to hide his teeth, or maybe what he thought was bad breath, he said he would be glad to take an afternoon off and go fishing with me but where exactly. I told him about the small lake beyond the trees, the chinaberry trees in back of my house where we buried Seth, and said it was full of perch and other good-tasting fish. He smacked his lips when he heard that and said he couldn't wait. Right then and there we decided to fish on the first day that came with warm breezes and good weather.

The season was early spring, the month of April to be exact, and the weather in April in these parts is often wet and unpredictable. For two weeks it rained just about every day, and we had no hankering to sit on a soggy bank even if the fish were biting. Then when we were beginning to think the opportunity to fish in good weather would never come, a fine day dawned with clear skies and a bright sun. Leo lost no time getting to my house that day and away we went, the two of us with poles and a bucket of bait, to sit beside the lake and fish and talk and breathe the good air.

That's when Leo Mack relaxed in the warming sun and talked about himself, and that's when I decided to throw a noose around his story and capture it. In my study with all my books exuding their friendly aroma and giving me encouragement, I began to write it down. At times when I found Leo's story particularly interesting and when the good words came as if by magic to clothe and present it, I worked long into the night by candlelight. In a few weeks I put together the following account. I hope it's a faithful rendering.

Chapter 1

A Boy of Thirteen

The ceremony had ended near four in the afternoon, and the wedding party was on its way to the rented hall where a hundred people would dance and drink and frolic until the wee hours of the morning. Inside one of the carriages were the newly weds, Daniel and Katie O'Keefe, ready and eager to be the center of attention and the life of the celebration. Running behind the carriage, its metal wheels flicking sparks on the crusty bricks that paved the street, were several urchins shouting. One of these was a boy of thirteen, slim and tall with blonde hair and laughing blue eyes.

Though he hadn't been invited to the wedding or to the reception, he was certain the bride in her stiff white dress was a distant cousin, and that to his way of thinking offered him admission to the hall and to the food and drink he would find there. But if he dared to enter after the throng before the door had made its way inside, he would have to merge into shadow, taking care not to become a spectacle. Strong and brawny men were on the lookout for party crashers, and he knew if noticed they would toss him like a sack of potatoes onto the hard and wet pavement. The season was early June and a misty drizzle had arisen from the east.

Leo Mack watched with admiring eyes as the young woman made her way through the crowd to the entrance of the great hall. For a moment she stood in the doorway, surveying the crowd, breathless in her hour of ecstasy and fully aware that her friends and relatives were viewing her as a thing of beauty. From a distance Leo gawked at the girl, finding her happiness almost tangible and her joy something to be shared. Even in the half-light of late afternoon he could see a flicker of wonder in her eyes beneath drooping lids that trembled. She wore a white muslin dress, whiter than any cloud in the blue skies of a summer day, and a stiff little veil of white across her plump shoulders. On the gossamer veil were pink paper roses made bolder by shining green leaves. White cotton gloves covered her slender hands. In an overflow of emotion she laced her fingers together and twisted them. Leo could see the pain and the tremor of too much emotion. She was married now but only sixteen, not much older than himself, and beginning her life as a woman of means.

Beside her, tall and handsome in a dark gray suit and wearing a white flower in his buttonhole, was the groom. He was not a shy young man, and yet on this day he seemed as frightened as a hunted animal. His friends could see his mouth was so dry he was obliged to moisten his lips with a very red tongue before speaking to them in a voice that didn't seem his own. At eighteen, the groom was older than his fair and blonde bride and from a dark Irish family. Though both belonged to Leo's clan, and the blood that ran in their veins was identical to his, they had never claimed him as a relative. They called themselves Irish Travelers, Leo and all the others, and they lived in a small town in South Carolina called Kelly Junction.

When the festivities began, most of the onlookers drifted away. But Leo Mack and the boys with him hovered near the doorway until no one was watching and casually slipped inside. They were experts at doing this. They had done it before and they would do it again. Once when all of them were younger, they performed the same stunt at a Circus that had set up its tent on the outskirts of town. It cost money to go through the gate, money they didn't have, and so they had to find another way. Six of them crept behind the Big Top and while two of the boys gingerly lifted the canvas flap, the other four scurried under it and were followed by the lifters.

They found themselves under the bleachers but somehow managed to snake through a labyrinth of wood supports to reach a row of seats and watch the show. Two burly men seemed ready to pounce upon them at any minute, and yet all afternoon they sat high in the bleachers, laughing and hooting, taking in all the sights and delights the Circus had to offer. In the tent with them were clowns, acrobats, trained animals of gigantic size, trapeze artists, sword swallowers, tumblers and dancers on horseback, tightrope walkers, and jugglers. Because of skills developed early and carefully honed, getting inside the Ashland Avenue Dance Hall and filling their bellies with tasty food at a wedding feast was no insurmountable task for any of them.

They were in a cavernous room filled with active people dedicated to having fun. When they separated and his friends went off in different directions, Leo moved close to the wall in shadow. Directing his gaze to a little stage, he could see and hear four musicians hired to make music for the dancers. In the midst of a hubbub that made his ears tingle, they toiled heroically like warriors in battle. Two squawking fiddles were trying to conquer each other, and two instruments of lower register were backing them up. Leo smiled and tapped his feet as he listened to rhythms never taught by a music master.

The evening had just begun, and the musicians were already sweating. A blonde and buxom young woman in a white blouse and swirling skirt gave them heavy mugs of dark beer.

Two large tables laden with all kinds of food caught the boy's eye. He had never seen food of that kind at home, and cautiously he made his way in that direction. As he approached he could smell the aroma of roasted meats, baked bread, steamed potatoes with bacon, boiled rice with almonds, macaroni in a golden cheese sauce, sizzling sausages, succulent fruit, wedges of cheese, and platters of pastry. Some of the guests were already munching on the goodies, chatting as they ate and either unaware of the imposter or not caring so long as he caused no trouble. At one of the tables Leo bolted down cold ham, spiced beef, and fat sausages until his empty belly could hold no more. Then he drank half a flagon of beer and ate some fruit for dessert. No one bothered to notice.

He stuffed meat and cheese into a large golden bun, wrapped it in his soiled handkerchief, and quickly put it in his pocket to escape notice. At home in the middle of the night, or maybe the next day, he would eat it with gusto. Fully satiated and sipping his beer, he wanted to take part in the festivities, maybe even dance with some of the pretty girls, but resigned himself to watching. Not invited and not dressed for the occasion, he knew his appearance would give him away. His red shirt was soiled and ragged, his trousers baggy and frayed, and one shoe had a hole in it. Although he didn't belong to the wedding party and knew it, he made up his mind to have as much fun in the Ashland Avenue Dance Hall as anyone. His young senses thrilled to the sights and sounds around him. Living for him had never been easy, but for now he was alive and happy.

In a trice he forgets every pain he has ever suffered and immerses himself in the excitement of the present. He throbs with delight, his senses as keen as a tuning fork. Everyone around him, every man and woman, is laughing, singing, chattering in rising clamor and eating with both hands. The musicians are playing in a mad frenzy and a few couples in their Sunday clothes are dancing. It is the music that turns this barren room into a wonderland, a mansion in the sky. The person who leads this little band is a laborer by day but a poet and music-maker after the sun goes down. Donnelley is the man's name, and he has taught himself how to draw music from an instrument by practicing all night after working all day. His dilapidated fiddle is out of tune and with his bow he seems to be sawing the instrument in half, but from it comes raw and raucous music to stampede internal rhythms and warm the soul.

He stamps his booted feet as he plays, tosses his head, sways and swings with bleary eyes closed, and beseeches his companions to pick up the pace. Then as they remain on the stage he moves to the table where the bride and groom sit too excited or too uneasy to eat. A cry rings out for a fast and rhythmic tune to celebrate the beauty of the bride and the joys of young love. Standing now in front of her table, waving his fiddle-bow wand in her direction, Donnelly creates melodic strains that hang in the air and tug at the heart. The melody rushes forward on a siren note and conquers the girl. Tears come into her large blue-gray eyes and run down her cheeks. Her pallid face flushes deep and turns scarlet. In her very white wedding gown with its flowing veil she wants to run away, but this is her wedding day, her moment of glory, and her challenge.

5

When her closest friend stands on a little stool and begins to sing, a few minutes of respite come her way. The girl's voice is throaty on the low notes and unpleasantly shrill on the high ones. She sings a dolorous ballad of love found and love lost, and she almost chokes on her own love sickness as the musicians sweat to follow with foundation her emotional rendition. When the song is over and the applause dies down, the father of the bride comes forward to give a little speech and offer a toast. He is a man of middle age but looks older. His life among the Irish Travelers has not been an easy one, but now as he speaks he places all emphasis on the many good things that make any life worth living. In the past a man in his position took his speech from a book and learned it by rote, but Arthur O'Keefe is a poet at heart and delivers his own speech.

It is bombastic and boastful and downright embarrassing, but on the whole it's a bundle of warm and original congratulation and benediction. Even young Leo Mack draws near to listen, and some of the women wipe their eyes when Arthur touches upon the hardships of his life and expresses hope that such may never occur in the lives of his daughter and new son. Of late he has become possessed with the idea that he may not live much longer, and when he brings that into his speech the women begin to cry and even some of the men turn their faces to the wall to dab their eyes.

Then abruptly one of the guests, a fat and jolly little man only five feet tall, is on his feet to give a little speech of his own. He looks at life through rose-colored glasses, interrupts to say things may not be as bad as they seem, and paints a sunny picture of the future. He showers congratulations on the newly weds and predicts intense joy for them. He bases his prediction on particulars that delight the young men but cause the bride to turn her head away and blush.

The tables they take from the room, and the revelers pair up and dance as if competing in a contest. That's when the musicians really begin to earn their fare. As midnight approaches some of the dancers leave the floor and find their coats. Their long workday begins early and they must sleep off the festivity of the evening and gain some rest. The younger folk go on dancing, urging the fiddler to play fast and loose, but at length only a few remain and Leo by then is on his way home. He prances along in the middle of the street, dancing a little jig of triumph and joy. His evening has been better than he ever expected, and he is well satisfied. Stooping to pick up a rock as big as his fist, he hurls it fast and hard at the trunk of a tree. The sound of the stone whacking the wood pleases him. When he reaches his poverty-bitten house, he enters quietly and steathily.

Earlier in the evening his companions were identified as party crashers and brusquely removed. Alone and hovering against the wall, moving into shadow when anyone came near, Leo was more fortunate. Yet in a crowd making merry the boy was more cautious than merry. He told himself he was one among the group laughing and dancing and having fun, but somewhere deep inside he knew he wasn't. Even though he shared with these wedding guests the same blood and traditions brought to these shores from the Emerald Isle, Leo's poverty and personality as well separated him from them.

Like his father and brother, he was accepted as an Irish Traveler despite a difference in attitude. For reasons he couldn't understand he had developed a moral sense that was lacking in most of the men in the village. Though he was able to steal into a party or a circus and avail himself of food and drink, he didn't see himself as a thief or swindler, or a person who took advantage of others. While his father and brother often bragged about cheating others, their stories never impressed him. In Ireland where his footloose relatives had lived for centuries, the establishment labeled them Irish Gypsies or Traveling Tinkers. In no way related to Romany Gypsies, they were nomadic by choice and necessity and grew to like their way of life. They preferred to travel from town to town and living on the edge rather than putting down roots in a specific place. Their way of life caused others to see them as strangers, petty swindlers, and drifters.

Home for Leo Mack was some distance from the Ashland Avenue Dance Hall. He lived with his obtuse and abusive father, oppressed and silent mother, a worthless older brother who was always teasing him, and a younger sister losing her eyesight. The family owned a cat named Merlin and a dog named Jude. Both were long and rangy, feeding only on table scraps and anything else they could fasten upon outside. The cat was a good mouser and sometimes dragged dead mice into the kitchen. The rented house with two bedrooms, a sitting room, and kitchen was dilapidated and much in need of repair. The outhouse or privy stood in back over an open pit that attracted biting flies in summer. Its door cut with a crescent moon had begun to sag on its hinges when the outhouse tilted to one side.

The family home was not big enough for five people and two pets, but Papa Mack declared once a day they would be moving before the week was out. Liam was a restive man, always on the move, never wanting to settle down in any one place for any length of time. He was one of those typical Irish Travelers who somehow had found their way in a huge and confusing country to South Carolina. He was also a drinking man and found it hard to keep a steady job. He didn't like someone else telling him what to do, and so in a tizzy he would quit a well-paying job with its boss demanding diligence and attempt to work for himself. However, none of his schemes turned out well, and more than once he found himself in trouble with the law.

The authorities didn't like Liam Mack, were in fact intimidated by his size and manner. His eyes, like those of a pitiless judge, seemed to pierce all persons who let their guard down. Calmly he read their feelings and thoughts, assessed any weaknesses, and drew conclusions. He delighted in mocking law and order as if some acidic grudge against society rankled him, as if he were hiding something the authorities would soon discover. And though he called himself a Catholic and often crossed himself in times of stress, he didn't like the church either. To his mind members of the one Catholic Church in Kelly Junction spent too much time conversing with God, didn't work for a living, and were nothing more than parasites.

The Mack family seemed unable to climb over the obstacles that life placed in their path, and so instead of prospering they grew poorer with each passing year. Liam and the older boy Luke were now traveling through the countryside in and around Kelly Junction to offer their services to farmers. The son was a roofer and the father was good at repairing farm equipment. Leo was still a pupil in the one-room schoolhouse, but now that summer had arrived he was expected to learn carpentry and landscaping and help with the roofing. He wanted to remain in school and do more with his life than either his father or brother, but the vagaries of circumstance had other plans for him. I remember he once said to me, "You know, Isaac, school was never all that hard for me. I wanted to stay in school, I really did, but life kept getting in the way."

Leo opened the unlocked door and quietly went to his sleeping room. His little sister was curled up on a narrow cot in the corner, the cat snuggled against her on one side and the dog on the other. His hulking brother who often teased the animals to cause them to keep their distance was sprawled in his underwear on the barren bed the brothers shared. Though the room's door was wide open, the one window was closed and the air was stale and musty. A scent that reeked of uncleanliness made Leo's nostrils flare. Before dropping his pants and crawling into bed, he opened the window with a noisy squawk of damp and swollen wood rubbing against similar wood. Jude the dog woke with an audible growl and pointed ears but quickly went back to sleep. Lena and the cat didn't stir.

The boy's side of the bed was against the wall, and the wall was grimy with layers of dirt and grease from the time the house was built. He lay there smelling the grime and the fishy odor that came from Luke's sweaty, unwashed body. In his usual loutish way he was claiming most of the bed. Tired from the hours of standing and from his long, high-spirited walk homeward, despite the fragrance surrounding Luke and the odor of urine that came from the lumpy mattress, Leo drifted into sleep. With Merlin the cat and Jude the dog, he had no trouble breathing the tainted air. Sleeping with Luke was a hardship that repeated itself every night, but on this night the merriment he had seen and heard allowed him to ease into deep and undisturbed sleep with no trouble whatever.

———◁◍▷———

An hour later his sister Lena tossed in her cot, mumbled a few words out loud, pushed the dog onto the floor, and went back to sleep. She was ten years old, skinny, and almost blind. For two years she had been losing her sight. Her mother had persuaded a doctor in another town to examine her, but he found no cure for her malady.

"These things just sort of happen," he said. "Some children are just unlucky that way. They get a lazy eye and the good eye works harder than it should, and their eyesight gets worse and blindness sets in. It's not a painful condition, thank God, and so most people can live with it. Maybe your daughter will go entirely blind in a year or two, but maybe not. We just have to wait and see."

"Can't you fit her with spectacles, Doctor?" Sarah asked, her thin face showing deep concern. "Anything at all might help a little. Please do something. My little girl don't really deserve to go blind."

"Well, I guess anybody can say no child deserves to go blind. But sometimes there's very little medical science can do about it. Trying to treat what's wrong and trying to prescribe eyeglasses would cost more than your family can afford, and I'm not sure spectacles would help her much anyway. It's something more than just poor eyesight."

In those days the science of optics was not so well developed as today in 1863, and so the girl had to go without proper care. If the family had money to spend, solicitous attention (though not a cure) would have been easily available. If Sarah and her daughter had arrived in a carriage instead of a rickety wagon, the entire staff would have greeted them at the door. For enough money the medical establishment would have tried to work miracles, but in the very act of trying they could have made matters worse.

The doctor in the town not far from Kelly Junction believed pressure on the optic nerve could be causing the problem.

However, he had no way of knowing if that were true and certainly no way to correct it for any amount of money. So day by each day Lena Mack made her way through a yellow-gray fog that grew steadily thicker. She struggled against a fate I would never wish upon any living soul, and yet most of the time in a broken and misty world she was a chirpy, engaging little girl. Though her beaming face was not always clean, Leo told me that day we went fishing, it was somehow as fresh as a frosty morn in autumn.

Morning came with a rattle of dishes in the kitchen. Merlin was looking for milk and had jumped on the table. Sarah swatted him off with the kitchen broom. Instantly a male voice bellowed a malediction as a fork whizzed through the air, barely missing the squawking cat. Leo heard it all and knew another day in the turbulent Mack household was beginning. His brother was already up and gone to the outhouse. His sister was lying in her cot looking at the ceiling. All she could see on the water-damaged ceiling were shifting patterns, and she imagined they were white clouds in a crystalline sky. Leo felt sorry for the little girl and would have done anything to make her condition better but knew he was helpless. He mumbled a few words, which he hoped sounded cheerful, and left the room. She lay there smiling inwardly to herself and didn't get up to meet the day until her mother called. In summer she lived in a faded gingham dress that covered her from her chin to well below the knees. In winter she wore a coat over the same dress, and after several seasons it was becoming threadbare and tattered. Every other week or so she washed the dress to keep it clean, and she wore a ribbon in her hair.

Breakfast at the Mack house was not as good as the food on other tables in the village at that hour. Some of the Irish Travelers ate well and lived high on the hog while others barely made ends meet. The Mack family fell into the latter category and was eating a mush of cornmeal flavored with bacon grease. With the mush each person had one egg, a cup of strong coffee, and a glass of milk. In better times they had grits instead of mush and bacon with their eggs instead of just the grease. Also on some occasions Sarah made fat and fluffy country biscuits the family ate with thick gravy. On this day, in a noisy hubbub of chatter, they washed the spare meal down with milk Liam got from a farmer who said it was going bad. Except for Sarah, who had turned inward to survive the vicissitudes of life and Lena who was in no mood to chatter, the others at the breakfast table were talking at the same time. Liam with an emphatic warning shout called for peace and quiet.

"Listen up you buggers! Today we gotta make some money. Me and Luke are gonna go out to the Wilson farm to do some work. Leo, I want you to come with us. Wilson has a big barn out there needing a new roof. If we can find some good cheap roofing panels, maybe we can get the job and do it in a couple days. I'm gonna base my estimate on the cost of the panels and of course the labor and charge as much as I can, but Wilson ain't no fool and so I gotta be careful."

"I gotta better idea, Pa," Luke added. "Why don't you let me go and price them panels. I can meet you and Leo later at Wilson's."

"You know good and well I can't do that. First of all, Leo don't know a thing about installing roofing panels. Second, you wouldn't bother going anywhere 'cept maybe fishing down by the creek and then lie about it. I can't trust you, Luke, nobody can. I have to keep my eye cocked on you all the time."

Luke was sputtering milk and laughing. "Well, we are Gypsies, Papa! Irish Gypsies! And we gotta live up to the name!"

Liam launched a saucer at the boy's head. It spun across the table, narrowly missing its target, and shattered against the nearby stove. "Wal, bog myn away frum thu taddy!" he yelled in the Cant he often used. "Oh God Almighty, deliver me from evil and stupid young 'uns! How many times I gotta tell you, boy? We ain't Gypsies! Now get that through your thick skull. We're freeborn men of the traveling people! We're Travelers, damn it, and don't you forget it! We trace our roots back to oldest Ireland. The country people hereabouts call us Irish Travelers and there in Ireland they call us Tinkers, but only the ignorant call us Gypsies! We like to move about like they do, but our blood is different. I swear this boy don't have sense to come in out of the rain. No use trying to tell him anything!"

Sarah as the meek and dutiful wife Liam insisted upon was moving away from the table to pick up the pieces of pottery. She knew if she didn't do it, no one else would and Lena, half blind and barefoot, would cut her feet on the shards before the sun went down. She and Leo glanced at each other, looked downward at their plates, and said nothing. They could see their father was in a tizzy over nothing. It had happened before, and it would soon pass.

After breakfast, riding in their wagon with Jude trotting at the wheels, the males in the Mack family went out to the Wilson farm. It was four miles from town, and they chatted as they went along.

"Now when we get there, don't neither one of you say nothing," Liam cautioned. "I'm the daddy here and the leader, and I'm the one that's gonna be doing the talking."

"I ain't gonna mess nothing up," Luke replied peevishly.

"You always mess up anything and everything you touch, boy. But this time you gonna get a whuppin if you so much as open your mouth. Just keep quiet and let Wilson see you're willing to work, and the same applies to Leo."

As they pulled into the yard, Liam put on a long face and drew the farmer aside to tell him how his family was struggling just to pay the rent. Hard times had come to them and they would be much obliged if Wilson could find it in his heart to give him and his boys that roofing job he needed. Luke was known far and wide as an expert roofer with strong hands, and any soul needing a roof couldn't go wrong hiring him. And Luke would have helpers too, and the job could be finished quickly without dragging it out all summer.

Wilson listened to Liam's persuasive prattle but shook his head. Some of his neighbors had hired the Travelers to do work of that sort only to regret it later. The Irish Travelers of Kelly Junction had come out to neighboring farms with shoddy materials, had done a sloppy job as fast as they could, often not even finishing it, and had left with the money they demanded before starting the job.

One or two unhappy customers had tried to recoup their losses in court but to no avail. The lawyers found it difficult to prosecute persons with fictional names on bogus contracts that made no sense. Even when a lanky Traveler was brought into court and identified as the culprit, it was his word against that of his accuser and nothing happened. What did happen was for the Travelers to gain a reputation in the community so negative as to require them to travel in order to find work. Wilson was privy to all this and didn't allow Liam and his sons even to go near his barn. However, he gave them work to do in a potato patch for the rest of the day. They spent a couple hours breaking clods with rusty hoes, complained of blisters on their hands and sore backs, and went home with a few coins.

Also they got from Wilson, a generous and good-hearted man, some turnips in a sack, a slab of salted pork with streaks of lean and fat, and a small bag of onions. At home again, Liam roared with laughter, exclaiming they didn't get the roofing job from Wilson but weaseled some goods from him that would make a good supper.

"That Adam Wilson ain't the smart man I thought he was. In fact, before the day was over, he showed himself a damn fool. We didn't do no work in that potato patch, and yet he gave us all this stuff plus a few coins. Well, they say the world's made up of two kinds of people, givers and takers, and I guess we're the ones that take. Don't hurt my conscience even a little."

Luke snickered, nodded his head vigorously, and slapped his younger brother on the shoulder. Leo knew he would be cussed and even kicked if he didn't go along with his daddy's little joke, but somehow he found the courage only to smile. His father gave him a hard look, seemed poised to say something more, but turned on his heel and walked away. Sensing he had left the room and would not be returning anytime soon, Lena crept into his chair, held Merlin the cat on her lap, and gently stroked his fur. Blank of face and saying nothing, Sarah fell to preparing supper.

Chapter 2

Gypsy Caitlin

Years passed and the family went on in its stubborn way, living from hand to mouth and somehow getting by, and then came the time for Leo to marry. His marriage to a local girl was nothing like the ceremony of Daniel and Katie O'Keefe. They had united in holy matrimony in the village church and had produced a festive and memorable reception in the fashionable Ashland Avenue Dance Hall. A crowd of friends and relatives had attended the occasion with hired musicians and good food. That wedding, as everyone knew, had cost a lot of money. But the Macks had very little coin to spend on anything, much less a fancy wedding.

So at eighteen Leo married Caitlin O'Hara, a blossomy girl of fifteen, in a private ceremony with few attending. The marriage took place in the open air in May on the edge of the woods the two had often explored together as children. Caitlin's family came with a dowry of food and clothes and several bottles of red wine. Since they were as poor as the Macks, they could add no money to the dowry. Proud of her son and beaming, Sarah attended the ceremony and so did his sister Lena. His father and brother, Liam and Luke, were on the road at the time moving northward. They were not expected to return to Kelly Junction until late fall. In a clean, well-starched gingham dress and new shoes that made her feel special, Lena held on to her mother's arm for guidance. She was now almost blind.

Liam and Luke with several other Irish Travelers had left early that spring in wagons they could live in while on the road. Trailing behind them were a dozen horses and mules they expected to sell to farmers as they made their way to the north and west through Tennessee and Kentucky to Illinois. Their plan was to spend the spring and summer traveling, selling livestock, and working at odd jobs. Then finding themselves somewhere in a northern state with the weather falling apart near the end of summer, they would think about returning home to South Carolina. It was not an easy life for any of them. Often because they were in the habit of fleecing the inhabitants of every town they visited, they found themselves in trouble with the law. It was their chosen way of life, however, and the life of their ancestors, and a custom in their blood.

When he was married four months, Leo rented two rooms above a barbershop in the village and moved in with Caitlin. Until then he and his bride had lived in the cramped Mack house and later in a camp they set up in the woods. They liked the free and open camp and how it brought them close to nature. He often smiled at the image of Caitlin lying in a hammock, swinging gently back and forth, and listening to the birds chirping in the trees overhead. She could identify many of the birds just by their songs, and she could imitate a bird call with her girlish vocal chords and get a response.

It was a pleasant time for them both, but in late summer with fall coming on and knowing his pa and brother would be showing up soon, Leo knew he would have to find a more permanent place. Already his young wife was showing signs of poor health. She was a pretty girl with clear skin and long blonde hair, but thin and undernourished and lacking energy. He worked at whatever odd jobs he could find to put food on the table, and often he cooked it himself when Caitlin seemed too weary to get out of bed. But jobs in the vicinity were scarce, particularly for a young man living as an Irish Traveler in the village of Kelly Junction.

With most of the men on the road at that time of year, the women and children did the necessary work in the neighborhoods of the town. A man of eighteen, unless newly married and trying to set up a household for the large family he hoped to create as the years passed, was expected to be on the road with the other men of the village. The children who went to school were now out of school for the summer. Kelly Junction could boast only the one-room schoolhouse that Leo attended when younger. Any additional schooling the children got was in a nearby village or at home. Even though the community was tight-knit and everyone knew everyone else, were in fact related by blood or so the joke went, some families were affluent while others were poor. Families more fortunate sometimes helped those in need, but often stubborn Irish pride stood in the way.

The small Catholic Church with its one priest and two nuns was the only agency in town attempting to help people in need. Often the efforts of clergy and well-meaning church members didn't extend far enough to aid those who really needed help, and so people in dire poverty were known to exist. Though his family was poor, Leo as a young man didn't place himself in that category, didn't see himself stricken by poverty. He had said he was fully capable of making his own way and caring for the wife who depended on him. At the time he married he said he would never accept charity of any kind, and he lived by that rule all his life. That first summer of their marriage, in love and feeling the joy of first love, he and Caitlin went hungry at times but never suffered from hunger. It worried him that she went to bed with an ill-defined emptiness under her navel, but she declared it didn't matter. To him it did matter. He could lose some weight if it came to that, but his bride could not.

In their sitting room she nestled her head against his shoulder and murmured she would love him forever and forever. He laughed at that, saying forever is a long, long time. She made a little face and said they would live each day as a special gift and cherish every moment of every day even when work and food were scarce. She would adore her young husband without restraint even if she had to wear the same dress for a year. Leo assured her she would have good clothes to wear even if he had to steal them. He loved the doll-like girl with the rapture of first love, and it generated strength within him. That emotion he had never felt before, and it delighted him. He told himself he would look after his fragile wife with deep and unswerving devotion. She would return his love many times over, would eventually give him children, and would be the only companion he would ever need in the long life he expected to have with her.

Their new living quarters, two rooms rented from the O'Keefes who had prospered since their marriage five years earlier, were clean but barren. The smaller room had a bed and dresser but needed a tallboy and wash table. The sitting room, doing double duty as the dining room, had an old couch by the window and a small table with two chairs. In the little alcove that served as the kitchen stood an old black stove that worked well enough to heat simple meals and would heat the rooms in winter. It didn't matter that the place had battered furniture, no carpeting, a tiny niche in the wall for a kitchen, and only two dingy windows fringed with bedraggled curtains. When the candles burned low they could always go to bed, and they could live with the roar of laughter, banter, and cursing that often came from the barbershop below. Even the barking dogs in back didn't matter, nor the odor of decaying fish that wafted up from the alley any time they opened the rear window. They were two against the world now, and that for them was all that mattered.

Morning came and the happy couple awoke to the clanging of a bell. Leo in high spirits threw off the counterpane and jumped out of bed. Caitlin sat in the middle of the bed with only a pillow in her lap. Her long blonde hair flowed like a waterfall over thin shoulders, and she looked very white and clean. Her big blue eyes darted doe-like around the room and settled on her husband beside the window. Leo was looking at a bakery cart making its way past the building. It had rained during the night and the unpaved street was muddy. The vendor was pulling the cart slowly through the mud, calling out bread and pastry for sale. Leo jumped into his trousers, scooped up some pennies lying on the table, and ran downstairs. Barefooted in the warmth of the morning, he picked his way through the mud to reach the vendor and bought two gigantic rolls with little tubs of butter. When he returned, flaunting the golden rolls as a captured prize, Caitlin in a pretty summer dress was heating water for coffee. They ate the buttered bread at the old table in their sitting room, washing it down with black coffee, laughing and making jokes, and delighted to be in the company of each other.

As they began to talk about the future, the morning sun slipped through the windowpanes and cast a pattern of black bars on the bare floor. The shadow, stark in its outline, caught Leo's attention.

"I'm gonna find you a carpet to cover this dirty floor," he said, "something you'll like. And I'm gonna get new curtains for them windows. I don't wanna see you waking up every morning and seeing bars on the floor. We're not gonna live with bars of any kind."

"Oh, don't you bother with that, Love. The bars are made by the sun and quickly disappear. We have to think of more important stuff, just the bare necessities right now. Any luxuries like a fancy carpet will have to come later. Maybe when we're sixty?"

He laughed at her light-hearted reaction and got to thinking how she might look at sixty. Would she gain weight and become matronly? Or would she remain slim and trim in her sixties and beyond? He was scanning her delicate fifteen-year-old face, and it seemed even younger than fifteen. Leo remembered it looked exactly that way when he first became friends with her at twelve. Maybe at sixty she would look only forty. Even at eighty she would appear to be only fifty. She returned his gaze, giggled musically for a moment, and pouted. He leaned across the table and kissed her forehead.

"I feel so light and limp this morning!" she exclaimed, sipping her coffee. "Limp as a wet noodle and sort of lazy like. But I do want to go romping through a meadow today and gather some wild flowers. They would look so pretty in the vase my mama gave me."

Leo lost the reserve his bully of a brother had branded upon him in years gone by and burst into a great bellow of laughter. The sudden eruption startled the girl and she almost dropped her cup.

"Hush!" she cautioned. "You'll disturb that old barber down there below us. If he complains to the landlord, we might have to find another place."

"Roaring laughter and noisy chatter, even singing and chanting, often come from his shop," countered Leo. "So why can't we give him back a little of what he sends up to us? It's only fair."

"Shhhh," she cautioned, putting her index finger across her full but pale lips. "Now, please, Leo Love, no more of that."

He was in love with her nubile face and the blonde hair that surrounded it and the way she walked and talked. When his sister Lena emitted a high-pitched giggle, most of the time depending on his mood it annoyed him. But Caitlin's giggle was throaty and pleasant, even amusing. He could see she was not altogether perfect, but she was young and fresh and alive. She was also lovable and funny, and she was his. He ceased his laughter, seized her tightly in a comical bear hug, and kissed her mouth gently at first and then hard.

All night long in the amber light of a sputtering candle they had made love. The release he felt when the tryst was over was engaging, relaxing, expansive. Now this girl he adored was saying she felt limp and lazy even as she wanted to romp in a meadow. He understood, and he wanted to tell her she had made him feel limp and lazy too but more than that. He couldn't put it into words, but somehow he felt complete. Perhaps no words were necessary, for in that one vivid phrase she captured not merely her own feelings but his as well. Then her mood changed even before they left the table. She complained of a headache and wanted to lie down.

He put his arm around her waist, almost lifted her from the floor. How light she was, how lacking in substance, no heavier than a parched leaf in autumn. He led her to the unmade bed and placed her in it, pulling the sheet and counterpane over her smooth flesh. She lay in bed still as a statue while he ran errands. As soon as he was home again, they sipped cups of sassafras tea, ate bowls of thick soup flavored with filé, and planned their future together.

Early the next day Leo went looking for work. Caitlin remained in bed till late in the morning. Then rising hungry and looking for something to eat, she found on the shelf behind the stove half a loaf of brown bread, a rancid dollop of butter, and some stale coffee. She nibbled the buttered bread, hoping it would curb her hunger, and thinking her husband would return late in the day. He would be exhausted from all the walking with nothing to show for all the searching. Not having found any work at all, he would be in low spirits but would assume a cheerful air, kiss her lightly on the back of the neck, and ask about dinner. How could she tell him they had no dinner? How could they get through the night without food? Could he rise the next day with his belly empty and go looking again for work? She couldn't stay home and wait for a miracle.

Somehow she would have to find a way to make some money to buy food. She knew women and girls in the colony had ways of earning money, and she told herself she could do it too. She would never sell her body as some had done to bring disgrace on themselves and their families. That was out of the question. She would starve before doing that, but why not try her hand at fortune telling? Her mother had taught her the art of reading palms, had required her to memorize what to say when tracing the creases of the mark's hand, had even taught her when to look into the person's face with deep compassion and concern and offer words of comfort.

As a little girl, breathless and fascinated, she had watched the woman read the cryptic lines and foretell the future. The ritual went far back in time and was always the same. It followed an arcane formula tested by time, and her mother had passed on to her the carefully guarded knowledge. All she needed now was the signature costume of the fortune-teller, a colorful red and black skirt and a scarf to cover her head. The clothing was in the yellow pine chest where she kept most of her things. She found it, put it on, and looked at herself in the mirror. In minutes she had become a bona fide fortune-teller, a bit too young for the trade perhaps but genuine.

Some distance from town, half a mile from the main road and set deep in a thicket of tall cedar trees, stood a sprawling stone mansion. A retired chandler known as George Harris owned it, having inherited the property from an uncle. He had lived in the vast, dark entrails of the house for several years and rarely went outside except to walk in the garden near evening. Everyone in Kelly Junction knew of his existence but had seldom seen him. Word was out among the women in the village that he was a very wealthy man but eccentric, reclusive, and miserly. He was an old man, they said, who took no interest in anything at all that didn't directly concern him.

Well, didn't his future concern him? Caitlin's husband wanted to know what the future held for him. Didn't every man want to know that? She convinced herself the man in spite of his age wanted to have his fortune told. She had heard he lived with many servants who kept the rambling old house in order and lived their lives there much as they pleased. Someone had said Harris wasn't always in his right mind, and the older and feebler he got the more power the servants gained. It was thought that in time, should the man die without a secure will stating his wishes, and with no relatives to turn up on his doorstep, the help would take ownership of the place.

These stories piqued Caitlin's curiosity. She wanted to learn more about the chandler while entertaining him, and she hoped the old man would be generous with payment for her special attention. It was a long walk to the mansion, but shortly after the noon hour she knocked on the massive door and waited for a response. She knocked again, bruising her knuckles on the ebony wood and drawing her hand back quickly. Again no one answered the door, and she could hear no one moving about inside. Then she saw mounted on the heavy door a bronze apparatus for sounding a very loud knock. She lifted the ball-shaped knocker and pounded it against the plate. It made an elaborate, resonant sound like a huge tuning fork. In the quiet of the countryside the knocker created an echo among the hills, and Caitlin stood surprised at what she heard.

Immediately a heavy woman in gray and white answered the door, opening it wide enough for Caitlin to see her face and dark dress with its white collar but little else. Uttering not a word, she seemed to be asking with supercilious impatience, "Who are you, Missy, and what do you want? Why have you come so far off the road to bother us here? Are you trying to sell us something?"

"I wish to see the master," Caitlin began, summoning inward strength to appear resolute and remain composed. "I am here to have a private meeting with him."

"The master does not see anyone," the woman replied, a note of cold contempt creeping into her voice to emphasize the scornful gaze that surveyed the girl from head to foot. "You must go away now. The master does not see anyone, and certainly not the likes of you!"

"You assume incorrectly, Madam. George Williston Harris will see me. It is a matter of grave concern for him as well as for you and your comrades in service. Please announce my arrival and allow me entrance." The words came from Caitlin's mouth as from an oracle, and the housekeeper looked stunned. She had found his full name in a newspaper.

"Wait here, please," she mumbled after some hesitation. "He's sick in bed and may not be able to talk to you or to anyone, but I will send a girl up to check on him."

"Show me the way to him instead," Caitlin demanded, leveling her eyes upon the woman's bemused face. "He will talk to me even though I will do most of the talking. Do not require me to wait."

"You're one of them Gypsies in the village, ain't you? I can tell by the way you're dressed and by the way you talk. Master Harris has no use for Gypsies, my lady. Now go away."

"I will say this once more and only once more," said Caitlin, her voice calm but insistent. "If you value your position here, you will allow me entrance at once. You will take me to George Harris as fast as you can walk. I will not argue with you, Mistress Housekeeper."

———◉———

Defeated, the woman reluctantly opened the door, gathered her skirts on one arm, and walked briskly down a long and gloomy hallway with Caitlin close behind. At the end of the hallway they ascended a barren staircase that led to a room meanly furnished. On a narrow, rumpled bed pushed up against the wall lay an exhausted old man. Though his eyelids flickered when the two women entered, he said nothing to acknowledge their presence.

27

"This young woman claims you will see her, sir. She's one of them Irish Gypsies in the village. Shall I send her away?"

"Eh? Eh? What is it you say? Gypsies?"

"I am not a Gypsy, Mr. Harris. I am an Irish woman newly married. You probably have Irish blood in your veins too. I belong to a nomadic people called the Travelers, and the country people who surround us in these parts confuse us with Gypsies who travel, but that is all we have in common."

"She is dressed like a Gypsy," said the housekeeper, "flaunting that red and black skirt and swaying them hips. I dessay she'll steal anything she can get her hands on if I leave her alone with you."

"Leave her alone with me? Have you not left me alone with you, Bessie, and for too long? You and your kind have already stolen everything I own, and so I believe this woman, this Gypsy or whatever she is, can find nothing here to steal. Go from me now and close the door on your way out. Have the cook send up my lunch and also lunch for the young lady."

"Of course, sir, if that's your wish," snapped the housekeeper, edging her way out of the room and descending the stairs.

Caitlin by now had made a turban of the colorful scarf and was assuming the pose of fortune-teller. But on hearing she would be having lunch with the owner of the mansion, she removed the turban to display her blonde hair and assumed an air of easy informality. In a vibrant voice with girlish overtones she spoke kindly to the old man, and he liked the sound of her. She propped him up on huge pillows. He looked at her with intense interest, smiling weakly. In the tired, flinty old eyes under shaggy brows, Caitlin could see a tiny, satirical glint that amused her.

"Are you a Gypsy?" Harris asked, forgetting in his dotage what had been said just minutes ago. "I want you to know I have no use for Gypsies. They make a living plundering people. I don't like Gypsies. They stole a wagonload of premium wax from me once and sold it to a competitor for half its worth. I was a candle maker in my prime, you know, and a damn good one too if I do say so."

"I know, sir. It's well known in the community, but listen to me. I am not a Gypsy, sir. As I said to you earlier, I am Irish. My skin is fair and my hair is blond. My eyes are blue and I speak a fine Irish brogue. Gypsies, as you must surely know, are dark of skin and eye, swarthy. They have black hair and speak gibberish unknown to me and my people. Their blood differs greatly from ours."

"Yes, yes! Now I see all of that clearly. You are young and pretty. You speak with a soothing and musical sound. I give you permission to entertain me if that's your desire, but let's have luncheon first."

A maid came clumping up the stairs with a large tray, placed its dishes on a bedside table, and left. It was a generous lunch of sliced cold ham, biscuits, fruit, and buttermilk. With no vestige of an appetite, Harris nibbled on a morsel but Caitlin ate her fill. The biscuits were fresh from the oven, and the ham was expertly seasoned. The thick buttermilk with flecks of butter on the surface had a tangy taste and quenched her thirst. No longer hungry and thirsty, Caitlin felt alive and happy and was hoping her husband had eaten well too. The visit with George Williston Harris was turning out better than she had imagined. He was lonely and sick and needing kind attention, and she gave him that. Far from rejecting her, as the housekeeper fervently wished, he found her entertaining and charming.

"Take this key and unlock the drawer of my dresser there," he said to her when they had chatted amicably for more than an hour. "If the servants in this old house didn't pilfer the key while I slept, you'll find a wad of money in the drawer. I want you to take it, all of it. If you don't, they will in time, and I want you to have it."

"But I've done nothing to deserve it, Mr. Harris. I came to tell your fortune, hoping to earn a small sum of money by doing that, but when you said you didn't like Gypsies I decided against it."

"I will say it again. I don't like Gypsies, Missy, but I do like you. The air in this little room is fresher because of you. They moved me here from the master bedroom, I don't know why. Now take the money, please, and go with my blessing. I feel just a little weak from the excitement of your company. I want to rest now."

Caitlin left the old chandler's mansion with enough money to buy provisions until summer's end. Also there was money for the rent and for new clothes. Three days later she learned that George Harris was dead. All the servants were driven away by the authorities, and the mansion he had lived in almost as a prisoner was put up for sale by the county. Before that could happen, however, a nephew with papers to prove it took over the estate and hired a caretaker to look after it until it could be sold. The nephew found no will, no legal papers of any kind, but on the bedside table was an unfinished draft of something that might have become a will. Barely legible and almost lost in a smudgy paragraph of legal terms scrawled by hand were two words: *Gypsy Caitlin*. The document was ripped to pieces and quickly forgotten. It was only a scrap of paper and of no consequence. It was unsigned and bore no legal weight.

Chapter 3

When Spring Comes

While Caitlin was entertaining the old chandler, showing kindness and concern when all the hired people living on his bounty were cold and indifferent, Leo was looking for work. He scouted the village hoping to pick up an odd job or two, anything at all that might bring a few pennies, but in Kelly Junction in summer no work was open to a man not on the road. Had he known his pixie wife had conquered George Harris with her femininity and good will, he might have asked the old man for a job. The house had too many servants, but maybe there was work to be had outside. The estate, however, was no longer a farm, and Harris was dying.

Trudging along Chestnut Street, his shoe leather becoming thinner with each step, he noticed a woman washing clothes and hanging them on a line to dry. He could do that. He could take in washing and return it all dry and folded the next day, and his wife could help him. Residents in that neighborhood could pay to have their clothes washed, and why couldn't he do it? When he mentioned the idea to the woman, she laughed and shook her head. No male Irish Traveler to her knowledge would ever do such a thing. Washing clothes was woman's work. Of course a man could do it, but no man she had ever known would even think of doing it.

In late afternoon Leo found himself in the country looking for work. He knew country people looked at Travelers with a jaundiced eye, but he would tell any farmer he met that he was there to work for him and not to cheat him. That's what he said to Adam Wilson, but Wilson had turned him and his father away on more than one occasion because he didn't trust the men who lived in Kelly Junction. He remembered the time some years ago when the Macks wanted to put a new roof on his barn. Wilson needed a new roof but had to turn the trio away for fear they would cheat him. He felt their work would be shoddy, their materials inferior, and their fee exorbitant.

Now Leo was saying if he couldn't paint the Wilson barn, he would clean out the stalls and clear the barnyard of dung. The yard was thick with cow piles and the waste of several goats. One couldn't walk from the barn to the gate without stepping in something. Wilson loathed removing animal dung and seemed ready to hire Leo. Then after a pause to think it over, he said he couldn't afford to pay someone to do it. The times were hard, and people more fortunate were too poor to hire those less fortunate. Leo left the farm with some turnips and a cabbage, but with no job. He was up against negative impressions carefully carved in stone over many years.

He returned home in a blue funk, tired and hungry and worried. His delicate young wife would be waiting for him, and she would smile wanly on learning that while he had earned no money, he had brought home something for supper. She would take the vegetables and wash them and make a soup of them. They would have no meat for the soup, but chunks of cabbage could take the place of meat. When he entered, Caitlin was sitting by the window looking down at the street. He went

A Tinker in Blue Anchor

over to comfort her, to assure her they would not go hungry that night, and he kissed the back of her neck.

She turned around with her face glowing. Laughing that special laugh he liked so much, she pointed to the table on the opposite side of the room. It was covered with a crisp and clean tablecloth, and on the pale yellow cloth were several dishes filled with savory food hot and ready to eat. Two candles, tall and tapered, were in the middle of the table among the dishes. She lit the candles and invited him to dinner. Astounded by what he saw but mute, Leo quickly rolled up his sleeves, washed his hands, and sat down.

———⊰⊱———

Until the end of summer Leo and Caitlin had few worries. When late fall came, the men of the village, proud Irish Travelers, came rolling into town again with money in their pockets. They had sold their mules and horses at prices beyond their worth and had made a good profit. They had sought and found itinerant labor in the towns they visited and had worked rapidly at the jobs they were expected to do. Most of the time they left each town in a hurry when the citizens realized some of them had been duped. Before the summer was out the Travelers had racked up a long list of consumer complaints.

A widow was told the wooden siding of her house was full of termites and would have to be replaced and painted at considerable cost. Two men patched some of the holes in the old siding with plaster and painted over it. The plaster dissolved in the rain and the watery paint quickly lost its luster and looked worse than the original paint. Even though the widow complained to the sheriff, the men by then were in another county or state. Always they were a day or two ahead of the law, and always when they contracted to do a job they demanded payment up front before the job was done. They claimed they needed the money to meet their expenses on the road and to buy supplies. They returned to Kelly Junction richer than when they left and capable of getting through the winter without working.

In the midst of the traveling men were Liam and Luke, the father and brother of Leo Mack. They swaggered about the village for several days, boasting of their exploits among the country people and telling everyone their season of work had been a good one. Now they could relax and take it easy and live high on the hog through the winter. In early spring they had plans to be on the road again, fleecing as many people as they could find and taking care to be one step ahead of the authorities. They wanted Leo to come with them and maybe the women too, but Sarah Mack was in ailing health, Lena Mack was almost blind, and Caitlin was fragile too. Leo suggested he might have to remain in Kelly Junction to look after the women. With a curse and a frown, Liam was adamantly opposed to that.

"When a boy gets to be a man, Leo, your manhood demands you go on the road and work for a living. It's something us Travelers have done for a long, long time and will go on doing. We lived that kind of life in the old country and we live that way here, and we expect our sons to do it after we're gone. It ain't fitting for a strapping young man like you to stay here in the village all summer like a little girl. The women can take care of themselves. You need to be with men, not hanging around a bunch of women."

"When I married I promised my wife I would care for her any time she needed care. She's not in the best of health, Pa, and she has no one but me. And if I have to do look after her come summer, I guess I'll do it. I owe her that much."

"The women can take care of themselves," Liam asserted with finality. "You're still my son, you know. Even though you're married now and likely to be a papa yourself soon, you still have to listen to me. That's the rule that goes way back. Traveler families stick together, and it's because they do what the head of the family tells them to do, and I'm the head of this family."

"I know that, Pa, but I got my own family now."

"That ain't so, boy. You got only your wife. And I don't have to tell you that's not a family. You don't have a lot of schooling, Leo, and you never learned much arithmetic, but I don't have to tell you three Mack men can make more money than two."

"I know that too, Pa. Also know you jerked me out of school."

Liam's temper was beginning to rise but he put it down. "When spring comes, I want you on the road with us as you ought to be."

"Well, I won't object to going on the road, but . . ."

"I won't listen to excuses, Leo. Caitlin can live with Sarah and Lena, and she'll be just fine with them."

"I was gonna say I'll go, but I won't be stealing from nobody. I heard some of the men last time out took advantage of a poor old woman, a widow living alone, and bilked her out of her savings. So what is she gonna live on now all by herself?"

"Who knows? She'll manage, they always do."

"Maybe she won't manage, and you know it. I don't have the stomach for that sort of thing, Pa. I'm Irish and a Traveler and I'm proud of it, but I ain't gonna be no criminal. I got a young wife to support, and I can't be doing no time in jail."

35

"Don't you worry about jail, boy. You're worse than your old ma when it comes to worry. Now I'm sure you know every single one of us came home again this season, and nobody went to jail."

"What about last year? Maybe half a dozen got arrested last year and two I know of are still in the pokey way up there in Indiana."

"Well, that all started when they got too rowdy in that bar. The boys always say they work hard and play hard, but sometimes they play too hard and that's when they get in trouble."

"You forgot to say the two up there in the jailhouse cheated a farmer real bad. Sold him a mule that dropped dead when a plow was hitched to him. The old farmer chased them down and complained, and they laughed in his face. The sheriff threw them in jail to await trial, and they got five years."

"That's what happened, boy. You got a good memory and you got it straight and I ain't gonna say otherwise. Now about that wife of yours. Sarah backs up your story when you say she's kinda sickly, and I'm gonna say I'm not against you looking after her, but I do want you on the road. The men in this village don't treat their wives as good as they should, but most feel a need to look after them, and that's why we leave this place when spring comes and go looking for work through the summer. This time you gonna be with us."

The winter that year was cold for South Carolina. In November came frosty winds and rain. In December came a mix of sleet and rain. The snow came in January and lasted three weeks. Melting, it left the ground wet and muddy. Leo and Caitlin got through the winter with no hardship whatever. They ate well on the Harris legacy, as they called it, and they didn't have to blow on their fingers to warm them for lack of firewood. But as the cold and humid days dragged slowly toward spring, Leo could tell his young wife was paler than usual and bothered by a persistent cough.

She told him it was nothing more than a cold, but one morning as they were sitting down to breakfast she was seized by a violent spasm of coughing. When it ceased after several minutes, and when exhausted she looked into her handkerchief, she saw to her dismay an undeniable blotch of red. She quickly thrust the handkerchief into an apron pocket, but the telltale blotch haunted her. It was late in the afternoon before she could summon the courage to reveal her discovery to her husband.

"I think I must see a doctor," she said to him, looking upward into his face with sad eyes. "I seem to be coughing up some blood. I'm sort of weak but don't feel sick. I'm not in pain but even a little spot of blood in my handkerchief is a worry."

Leo knew exactly what she was talking about and was careful to control his alarm. In his short life he had known several people, two of them cousins, who died of tuberculosis. It was an awful disease that gnawed away their lungs until they could no longer breathe. Caitlin had the symptoms: cough, fatigue, shortness of breath, and weight loss. But she was losing weight before she began to cough, and the mucus that came from her throat and nose seemed the product of a bad cold, yellowish green with no blood. Now even with bloody mucus her symptoms didn't have to point to consumption as the disease was called in those days. Perhaps the condition was nothing more serious than bronchitis or pleurisy or a bout of pneumonia. He reasoned she had caught a cold in the damp of winter and it grew worse. Nothing more than that. She would get over it.

These thoughts raced through Leo's mind before he spoke. He wanted to calm her and reassure her, and so he made an effort to sound cheerful and to smile.

"It can't be anything real bad, sweetie. All you need is plenty of rest in a good warm bed. I'll look after you and give you liquids to drink and nourishing food too. Then if you don't improve we'll find a doctor, I promise. A doctor just as soon as spring comes."

"You are so good to me, Lovey, and I know you'll do all you can to help me all you can, but what if I get worse instead of better? What if I have to take to my bed? Then what? And what's gonna happen when spring comes and your papa wants you to go on the road with him even when he knows I'm sick and Sarah sick too?"

"If it gets worse we'll find a doctor. We'll find a doctor even if we have to go to Columbia or Charleston. We'll find someone that can tell us exactly what's wrong. And the old man? Forget him! He don't matter any more. I won't listen to him."

"And where do we get the money? My family might help a little but we both know they're just as poor as your family, and the money that lovely old man gave me is gone already."

"I can get you there in a wagon or cart and that won't cost much. Then when I find out how much the doctoring is gonna cost, I'll find a way to pay. I'll work something out with the hospital. I'll scrub the floors and empty the bedpans and do the hard and nasty work sixteen hours a day if I have to, and you'll rest and take your medicine and get well."

"You're a jewel, Leo Love, and you dream big and I love you for that. You know I love you more than life itself, and I know you dearly love me. If I get sick I'll be in the best of hands."

"If you're sick when spring comes, and I sure hope you won't be, I won't go on the road. I'll stay here and look after you and Mama and Lena. I know it's hard going against my old bulheaded pa, with my brother standing there snickering, but I'll do what I have to do, sweetie. Now I want you to go back to bed. I'll bring you in some lunch when noon time comes."

She kissed him on the cheek and went to bed. When noon came he went to her with a bowl of hot soup he had made himself. He expected her to sit up smiling and eat the soup, but she appeared to be sleeping. He nudged her shoulder gently, but she didn't respond. He decided to let her sleep and serve the warm soup to her when she awoke. Or maybe she could skip lunch and eat a good supper and feel strong and refreshed. In the afternoon he went out to buy oysters for supper. Oysters were cheap and simple to prepare. In chowder they were her favorite dish. When the meal was ready he went to her bed again. She was awake now and leaning against a pillow. All the blood had drained from her face and she was very white.

"Supper is ready, sweetie. And you'll never guess what we're gonna have. Fat oysters in a thick and creamy chowder. Steamy and tasty! I made the supper myself!"

"Do you mind if I eat the chowder in bed? I seem to be sort of weak at the moment, and I feel guilty letting you prepare supper, but I'm not feeling good."

"You'll feel better with food in your belly," he called from the little alcove that served as a kitchen. He was ladling the steaming chowder into a bowl and brought it to her on a little tray. She supped a little chowder, chewed on an oyster, and smiled.

"It's good, Lovey, real good. But I'm afraid I can't eat much right now. I'll eat a little and rest and then eat some more.

Is that all right? Thank you so much for the supper and for looking after me."

She ate very little, sipping the liquid from her spoon and chewing an oyster a long time before swallowing and trying another. She smiled wanly, leaned back on the pillows, and struggled to speak.

"It's so good, Lovey," she repeated. "But I feel more sleepy than hungry. Do you mind if I sleep through the night? I'll be up with the sun and fix you a good breakfast and we can talk. I'm worried about your mother. She's complaining of pain in her joints and she's not all that old either, and you know as well as I do that your papa never offers to turn a hand around the house."

He covered her with the colorful quilt his mother had given them as a wedding present and made her comfortable. When night came and he crept into bed beside her, she was sleeping soundly. In candlelight he glanced at her face. Her lips were curled in just a bare semblance of a smile. When morning came and he expected her to be wide-awake, perhaps up and about while he continued to doze, he found her sleeping still. He nudged her and she didn't move. Gently he shook her by the shoulders and then gently slapped her very white cheeks. Always a tender slap on the cheek got her attention. He remembered when he did that she would always giggle and slap him back. This time she didn't move. She was dead.

Caitlin Mack died two months short of her sixteenth birthday. Her death caused a rippled in the community but didn't come as a big surprise. In those times the medical arts were not so advanced as they are now, and so before the bloom on their cheeks had time to fade numerous young girls died of tuberculosis or cholera or dysentery. When Leo revealed that Caitlin's coughing had left a blotch of red in a white handkerchief, the old crones in the village quickly marked her a victim of consumption as they called it. No doubt about it, they were saying. They had seen scores of girls die of that dread disease, and coughing blood into a handkerchief was one of the first symptoms.

Growing up in the midst of hardship had left Leo with a stoical attitude toward life. Caitlin was his first love and he had loved her intensely. Now he suffered losing her just as intensely even while concealing the full range of his misery. Losing his bride after so little time was the most painful incident of his life and the most difficult to bear, but he decided he would work through it alone and come to terms with it. Yet in what manner could he possibly overcome so terrible a blow? It dissected him. It shattered him. It left him in a thousand little pieces, each of them seething with anger.

No loving God could possibly allow such a thing, he told himself. No God of any kind, loving or not, could stand by and see the life of one so innocent and so young cruelly wrested from her. Father Murphy speaking at weddings or funerals in the church on the corner had spoken nonsense. All his grandiose claims of a beneficent God loving his children were reduced to babble when Caitlin died. For half a century or more there was no place in the mind and heart of Leo Mack for the God the Irish Travelers professed to love. He had lost his faith and no longer believed. At nineteen he felt like an alien in a world without any power to succor.

When spring came, Leo went traveling again with Liam and Luke. The activity might help him forget the pain of losing Caitlin, and maybe he could think about his future. Liam

41

expected him to live all his years in Kelly Junction, but he had other plans. Irish Travelers prided themselves on traveling, but this Traveler wanted to see more of the world than just the South and Midwest. Caitlin had known him better than anyone else, and she had called him when she was prone to wax poetic a dreamer, a rider of rainbows, the wind behind a painted ship upon a painted ocean. Well, maybe she was right. Maybe he could dream of doing something different.

Chapter 4

The Traveler Travels

They were on the road all summer, and Leo liked what he was doing. It was good to move along with a group of vulgar, joshing, loud-talking, swaggering men and see new places and do new things. The Mack trio traveled in a caravan of five wagons and camped beside the road when evening came. Each day near five in the afternoon they began to look for a suitable campsite, and when they found it they circled their wagons wide enough to make room for their animals in a small stockade. With that arrangement no prowler could run off with the livestock, and only two men stood watch. Some of the Travelers had mules and goats for sale, and they were placed away from the horses. Some had brought their wives and children, their entire families, and that irritated Liam.

"Them children should have stayed home," he complained. "They sure don't work, and they clutter a campsite and make it so noisy a feller can't hear himself think. The wives ain't gonna be no real asset either. All they ever do is stand around and chatter and gossip."

"Them happy little children have just what you see there in front of you," one of the men replied. "They have nothing more than a wagon with a canvas top and that's their home summer and winter. They don't have nothing back in Kelly

Junction 'cept too many kinfolk. At least you have a house and they don't. So go easy on 'em, Liam, and show a little charity."

"Well, I got as much charity as any of you blockheads," Liam grumped, "but it's hard to be kind and tolerant to a bunch of noisy kids when yer trying to think about tomorrow and what you gonna do to make a living."

Among themselves they spoke English, but when a sheriff or his deputies began to pester them they spoke the Cant. It was a pidgin language using a simplified grammar and a vocabulary of Gaelic and English. Sometimes early in the morning one could hear an Irish voice ring out, "Slum hawrum!" Or after sunset when the camp was quiet and the Travelers were getting ready for bed, a man on the way to his wagon might say, "Slum dorahog ant muni kon." No outsider hearing these phrases would know they meant good morning, good evening, and good night. The lilting patois, made musical on the Irish tongue, was old and traditional and ready for use when needed.

Liam, Luke, and Leo Mack traveled in a covered wagon with MACK painted in black on the white canvas. They slept, ate, and relaxed in the wagon when not working. Its living space was cramped, messy, and smelly in mid-summer, and yet somehow comfortable. A gentle dun mare pulled the wagon, and trailing behind it was a small cart where food and water for the horse and various supplies were stored. The group left South Carolina near the end of April and began to make their way westward as far as Arkansas. It was a cold spring that year, and the weather determined their destination before turning homeward again. Instead of going into the Midwest, their route took them across the northern parts of three states – Georgia, Alabama, and Mississippi – to the central region of Arkansas.

Along the way they worked as roofers, carpenters, tinkers, well diggers, and even road builders. In the hot sun, they labored at many jobs when summer finally came. While some of them did good work and even received compliments, others did not and got complaints. Despite Luke's mockery and ridicule, Leo took care to do an honest job for an honest wage whenever he could. And because he worked hard to keep their jobs honest, even daring to warn his crusty old papa of punishment if he cheated, the Mack kinsmen escaped becoming the targets of sheriffs and their deputies. Some others in the caravan were not so lucky.

When fall came the little band of Irish Travelers slowly made their way back to Kelly Junction. Because an accident had damaged a wagon beyond repair and the horse that pulled it had to be shot, the original five wagons were reduced to four. It happened this way. As they were traveling down a country lane at night, a fox attempting to cross the road jumped from the underbrush and spooked the horse. The fox managed to cross to the other side, but the horse rose up on his haunches, snorted in fright, and began to gallop. The road was dark and uneven and within minutes he turned a hoof on a stone and went down. The driver jumped from the wagon as it began to turn over, rolling on top of the stricken horse. It rolled over at least three times and shattered to pieces. Members of the band searched well into the night for items thrown from the wagon and strewn along the road. The owner of the injured horse, shaken and not in full command of his senses, asked another man to shoot the animal. They dragged the carcass into a ditch and went onward.

As they were skirting the borders of a huge plantation in Mississippi, the authorities detained three of the men on misdemeanor charges of chicanery and petty theft. Though loudly protesting their innocence, the accused men were not allowed to travel any farther than the county jail. Their relatives took over the wagon they had to vacate, and when a nip was in the air the caravan pulled into Kelly Junction glad to be home. Leo Mack was with them but in no mood to celebrate. He felt a nagging pang of remorse and misery as he remembered the untimely death of his pretty young wife, and he was beginning to believe he couldn't live in the village much longer. He told himself he didn't want to forget Caitlin, but at the same time he didn't want to be reminded of her wherever he went in Kelly Junction. He decided to spend a few days at home with blind Lena and his ailing mother and leave without notice.

———◈———

Even though his mama was in constant pain and finding it difficult to move from room to room, Leo knew his father and brother wouldn't turn a hand to assist her even when she began to shiver and ask for a sweater or a coat. As for doing any of the housework, that was out of the question. Traveler tradition defined all work inside the house as "woman's work," and that the men shunned consistently. Leo knew himself to be different and risked being ridiculed for helping his suffering mother. Yet even as he attempted to help he knew he was doing very little to improve her life. Even so, his show of concern made her burden lighter, and he could see that in her worn face and sad eyes. Although he had no mind to stay longer than necessary in that odious house, her gentle appreciation was his reward. As the days passed, however, a strong desire to travel disturbed him. It seemed to him that all his life he had lived as a barnacle in a murky sea, clinging to anything stationary. Now even more so than in the summer he felt it was time to move out.

Where exactly he would go he wasn't certain. He knew only that he had to get away from Kelly Junction and the roots of

46

his childhood. He felt he no longer had friends in the village, probably because as they grew older they eagerly embraced time-honored traditions while he seemed to be in rebellion against them. They became immersed in the popular culture of the Travelers even as he seemed to be moving away from it. And so gradually, scarcely without knowing it, Leo became a loner in Kelly Junction.

Now the time had come when he knew he had to get away. He had to find a steady job and perhaps discover new things about himself as he gave all he had to the job. He wanted to make money and send money to his mother who needed medical attention. Yet he hoped the job would offer him more than mere wages. Working from morning to night would give him a sense of purpose and direction, and that he needed. But where would he start and what kind of job could he take? Were any jobs at all available to a youth with little education and little experience in the world?

At best his schooling was rudimentary. He had been taught to read and write, and he liked to read. He was also given a smattering of basic arithmetic, but little beyond that. No business that required accounting or any skills based on using mathematics would hire him. The worlds of business and finance were therefore closed to him, but not that of a common laborer. He was strong and he could work with his hands in the open air. As he had done all summer, he could work with horses in a livery stable or if he had to, in a factory making items rich people would buy. Thinking it over, he quickly dismissed working in a factory. The hours were long, the labor was mechanical and exhaustive, and the pay was barely enough to keep one alive. Also the thought of working inside a stuffy building thirteen hours a day was not to his liking. Then he thought of going to sea. Why not? He was young and fit and the open sea offered adventure. He really believed he could make a good seaman.

In November the weather in South Carolina is often damp and chilly though not very cold. However, on the morning of Leo's departure a bone-chilling mist had arisen and frost lay in the gullies beside the road. He dressed as warmly as he could, had a spare breakfast of biscuits sopped in brown gravy, and left as soon as Liam and Luke were out of the house. He knew if he revealed to them what he planned to do, he would face severe objection from his father and cackling derision from his brother. So he remained mum and spoke only to Lena and Sarah. The girl put her thin arms around his neck and hugged him tightly, murmuring what he took to be a benediction. The mother hugged him too but looked deep into his eyes with question marks in her own. She didn't want him to move out of her life. He was her favorite son and she would miss him.

"I don't want to see you go, Leo," she said in mounting tones of sadness. "I want you to stay here in the village and find another young woman and live happy with her and give me grandchildren. I want you near me and Lena when we might need you, and I want to be able to help you any time you need me."

"I'll write to you, Ma. I'll write and let you know how things are going with me every so often. I feel I have to leave this place, have to go. They call me a traveler but I never saw much of the world at all."

"If you feel you must go, then do it, son. But try to remember your raising, where you came from, and the folks you got to know here. I'm aware you don't get along too good with your papa and brother, but they'll miss you as much as me and Lena. So remember us and write to me when you can."

Experience had taught Sarah Mack that a young man had to make his way in the world. Unlike his older brother, Leo had moved out of his father's cramped little house to marry and set up a place of his own with plans to raise a family. Then providence, fate, or the devil had slapped him down and stomped on him. When his beloved child-wife died before her time, he wanted to die too. He wanted to throw in the towel and call it quits after losing all he valued so completely. Now after gathering strength he was up for a second round, and Sarah admired him for that. In her gravelly voice she whispered her blessings and gave him a few dollars she had saved. He didn't want to take her money, but she thrust it into his shirt pocket. With tears in her eyes she demanded he take the money and write to the family whenever he could. Holding him tight once more, Lena wet his face with kisses and tears and clung to him as he moved away.

Leo went first to the livery stable in Kelly Junction. He had no horse and no wagon, only a knapsack on his back and tough walking shoes. His plan was to travel northward and make his way to the coast and look for work in a seaport. He was aware that hawkers, traveling salesmen, often stopped at the livery stable. If he could be lucky enough to find one moving north, after refreshing his horses, he might be able to hitch a ride with him. The hawkers or hucksters in those days went from town to town selling their wares, but sometimes a man would take on cargo to be delivered to a distant city. That person would move at a steady pace mile after mile through towns and villages and along country roads. Although it would not be a rapid transit, for the roads were deeply rutted and generally in bad condition, there would be no long delays. So that kind of peddler Leo hoped to meet at the livery stable. He was willing to wait a few hours for the right man to arrive, hoping the man would like a little companionship. He was willing to take a chance, for life itself was a gamble, and there in time he met Quentin Sadeye.

Sharing a common bond, they soon became friends. Both were young men in the prime of life and trying to survive in a world indifferent to their needs. Both were also outsiders. Sadeye was a Cherokee Indian beginning to earn his living as a hauler of goods after his parents had died in a fire. Leo Mack was a struggling Irish Traveler hoping to become a seaman. The white folks of the region, Anglo-Saxons claiming to be Christians, looked askance at both of them.

People in those days were more wary of the Indian population than now. Some believed a cock-and-bull story that thousands of Indians had mated with blacks and were conspiring to undermine white authority and rule the region. The white establishment also had little tolerance for nomadic Irish Travelers, equating them with Gypsies and often condemning them as thieves. Exchanging stories, the men soon discovered they were aliens in their own land, pariahs through no fault of their own. As they traveled northward on the spring seat of Sadeye's heavy wagon, they found another common denominator they had no trouble sharing. It was poverty.

All the time they were growing up their families had battled nature and the social system merely to live. Now they too were struggling to survive. That in a sense made them brothers. When Leo slyly offered the peddler a dollar for helping him on his way, he refused to take it. In a couple of days, Sadeye said, he would have money in his pocket too. Already a man wrestling with sorrow but able to function in spite of it, he was going to a place in North Carolina called Blue Anchor. There at the general store he would deliver an assortment of goods carefully packed under a tarpaulin to protect them from the weather. Later he would fill his wagon with dry goods to be transported southward. On the road he prepared scanty meals for himself and slept under the tarpaulin. He assured his passenger there would be room for him in another corner of the wagon, and there the traveler adjusting to a hostile world and the seeker looking for a world better than any he had known slept well.

———◆———

Leo spent nineteen days in Blue Anchor before moving eastward to the coast. It was a pleasant little village with its easy, slow way of living and he liked it. Many of the inhabitants were Quakers, and they didn't shy away from him as some in the villages near Kelly Junction had done. In fact, the good people of Blue Anchor invited him into their homes, fed him well, and talked openly with him of their hopes and fears and beliefs. They were deeply religious people but casual and friendly and open-minded. Unlike some of the people he had known in his own village, Leo quickly learned the Quakers didn't harbor an insincere piety that allowed them to raise hell on Saturday and sanctify themselves to reach heaven on Sunday.

Secure in a faith that went back many years, they were not at all dogmatic. In earlier times they had broken away from the protestant church to worship in their own way and to pursue a different creed. They had nothing good to say about Methodists, Baptists, Episcopalians, or Roman Catholics, but at the same time they had nothing bad to say about them either. While Leo viewed himself as possibly a Catholic (his mother was devoutly Catholic), he was not religious. Pleading poverty as he was growing up and too poor to tithe, with the exception of Sarah his family rarely went to church. In Kelly Junction he had known only the Catholic Church on the corner where two main roads met. He learned in the years he was growing up very little of the church's doctrine, and so it didn't stand in the way of his tendency to admire Quaker doctrine.

Living in Blue Anchor was costing him almost nothing, and he was slowly adding to his small accumulation of money. The proprietor of the general store gave him a job arranging goods on the shelves, sweeping the floor, and dumping the trash. The store was a rich depository of all kinds of things he had never seen before. It catered mainly to farmers but also to housewives and even children. Spanking new posters on the south wall caught his attention. They advertised in gaudy colors remedies for upset stomach, palpitation, sore throat, fatigue, scrapes and cuts of the skin, grippe and pneumonia, diarrhea, constipation, joint pain, and poor eyesight. Other posters praised in urgent and flowery language ingenious farm implements and machines for the home. One was a colorful portrait of a woman wearing a flamboyant hat with flowers. She was sniffing a medicated snuff to relieve headaches, dispel melancholy, and shrink hemorrhoids. Unable to determine the accuracy of the posters and disposed to believe all he read, Leo Mack glowed with wonder.

One day curiosity set his tongue wagging and he asked how and when the village got its name. Two Quakers sat him down near the pot-bellied stove in the store and told him the story. A farmer plowing a field not many years back had snagged a rusty anchor embedded in the soil. It incited curiosity, for no one could explain how the anchor was miles away from the sea in a field recently cleared of woods. The plowman scraped off the rust, painted the anchor cobalt blue, and displayed it in front of his cabin. People passing through couldn't help but notice the blue anchor and talk about it, and in time the hamlet came to be known as Blue Anchor.

Later, when four hundred people, farmers, tradesmen, small professionals and their families, began to live in the area the name became official. A separate list recorded the names and ages of slaves that worked a plantation northeast of the village and slaves on the smaller farms as well. A third and growing list had the names of slaves once owned by Quakers but given their freedom. Nestled in the midst of fertile farms bordering the Great Dismal Swamp of North Carolina, little Blue Anchor for Leo was a place of undeniable charm. Its memory would lure the traveler back in later years to earn his living there as a tinker.

Quentin Sadeye was on his way southward again when Leo Mack was moving toward Virginia and Norfolk on horseback. Without explaining in too much detail, I should tell you how he got the horse. In a way it was a stroke of luck. If bad luck had visited him in the past, now as he traveled farther and farther from Kelly Junction toward a wide ocean he had never seen he was having some good luck. Wherever he went in Blue Anchor fortune seemed to favor him. Getting a horse for nothing, one past her prime but able to take him all the way to Norfolk, was one of those rare lucky breaks that didn't come to him very often. And yet he acted at the right moment, and that had a lot to do with it.

When he heard of an aging mare that would have to be put down because she was no longer able to perform the chores her owner expected of her, Leo Mack came forward in haste to inquire why that was necessary.

"Why kill the animal?" he asked the planter, "simply because she don't have the strength any more to pull a heavy wagon?"

"What else can I do?" the planter replied. "I can't feed and stable an animal that can't work. About the only think I can think of doing with her is maybe sell her to the glue factory."

"I'll take her off your hands, sir. She's a gentle sort and still good for riding and I don't weigh much. I'll look after her and feed her. I'm a traveling man with not a lot of money, but if this horse can get me to where I wanna go, I promise you I'll care for her and find a good home for her later. She still has a lot of worth left in her."

"She's yours," said the laconic planter. "She never gave me much service even in her prime, and so I'm glad to be rid of her."

———————

As soon as the horse was his Leo fashioned a makeshift saddle, bridle, and stirrups and spent a day or two learning to pace her for a trip. His family owned a dray horse, but in all the years he was growing up he had never ridden a saddle horse for any distance. Liam had told him that in the old country any man who rode a horse was seen as a gentleman of wealth and class. Now, believe it or not, he was the owner of a handsome though aging horse, and proudly he rode into Norfolk on horseback. A street boy saw him sitting tall in the saddle and hooted as he passed. He created a look of haughty disdain, gestured to the cheeky boy as though he were a potentate blessing his minions, and rode on. Asking a pedestrian how to get to the waterfront, he went there to rent a room and see the harbor. He had seen pictures of sailing ships but never a real one.

Several graceful ships were berthed at piers waiting to load or unload their cargo. Silhouetted against the darkening sky, their masts seemed ten stories tall and their spars huge. Their sails were carefully furled and he tried to imagine the ships in blue water with all sails working. He had heard it said that in all the world there is nothing more beautiful than a frigate under full sail on the deep blue sea, a galloping horse kicking up clouds of dust, or a woman in scanty dress dancing and swiveling her hips. Of the three he preferred the first. In his mind's eye he could see a triple-masted square-rigger flaunting an abundance of white sails, scudding across a dark blue sea under a bright blue sky. His imagination transformed the ship into a bird, a gigantic and gorgeous bird, lifted into flight.

But these ships in Norfolk harbor were moored in half-light with their sails furled and their sleek hulls half hidden against the wharf. To study them as daylight was ending was not the proper time. Their beauty deserved more than a cursory glance in poor lighting. He would have to return and see them in sunlight, but for now he had to find a place to spend the night and a place for his horse to rest.

The next day, leaving his mare in the livery stable, Leo sauntered down to the docks. The morning was cold and misty but later the sun came out and the weather turned mild. He went to the berth of a handsome ship and asked if he could come aboard. A man wearing a red vest, a short blue jacket, and baggy trousers called slops, sternly denied his request. He said his job was to stand watch and prevent strangers from boarding the ship, and if he let even one unauthorized person come on board he could lose his job.

"I'm only a common sailor," he said with an accent that sounded British, "but I'm here to tell you no bloke boards our vessel without permission from the captain or maybe the mate."

"I'm looking for work," said Leo. "I want to become a sailor. How did you get your start? You don't look much older than me."

"Ah, me lad," he said, "if I only had the time I could tell you tales you'd never believe. I been at sea more than six years and for half of them years I never had two farthings to warm a pocket. All I got for loads of hard work was blisters on me hands, grub not fit to eat, and a moldy place to sleep a few hours. You don't want this kinda life. Go find something else."

Leo got the same response from other sailors he met at the docks. There was no money to be made as a seaman, and the life was hard. A man could be flogged within an inch of his life for not obeying an order, or for behavior that endangered ship or crew. On some ships able-bodied seamen lived in squalor and servitude and couldn't leave even when they tried. On others, however, the salty life was good. It was the luck of the draw, the way the wheel turned. Hearing this from several men, Leo decided he would make no hasty decisions. He would try to find work as a stevedore and learn more about ships and seas working close to vessels on the water.

He was thinking if he could work on the waterfront till spring or summer, he could possibly move northward to another port and find a ship willing to take on an able-bodied man willing to learn the ropes. With that in mind he rented a room nearby and found a job that taxed his strength but prepared him for what he thought would be a harder life at sea. His work as a wharfie, as sailors on arriving and departing ships called him, made him more fit than he had ever been, but at the end of the day he was too tired even to eat. He knew he couldn't do the job for long; he wasn't made to be a wharfie.

The muscles of his legs and arms ached every hour of the day but adapted to the hard work and grew strong. In those days there was little machinery to move and load cargo. Expending every ounce of muscle as they worked, even the best of the dockers lost strength and were replaced after two or three years. The wages were low, the hours long, the bosses hard, and the working condition dangerous. Also in southern seaports a wage earner often worked side by side with slaves who labored before the light of early dawn until dark to enrich the pockets of their owners.

Leo found out that thirty slaves on the docks were owned by a black man who rented them out as carpenters, mechanics, stevedores, messengers, and whatever job the boss demanded. Each slave wore a thin copper tag on a leather string around his neck. On the tag was the name of his owner. Leo had lived all his life in the South and thought he knew all about slavery even though it didn't exist in Kelly Junction. The town was an isolated ethnic community inhabited primarily by whites with blue eyes and blonde hair. It had its own language even, a secret argot called the Cant or Gammon by the Travelers but Shelta by scholars who studied it. The mix of English and Irish Gaelic, as I have already said, was spoken mainly when outsiders, and particularly the authorities, were present. It occurred to Leo as he worked that no Traveler had ever been a stevedore.

When spring came, Leo went to his boss, a single-minded man of crusty disposition, to say he was quitting and going to Baltimore.

"You can't quit now," the boss complained. "The busiest season of the year is coming on now and we need you. We need all the men we can get. Ships from all over are coming in every day. It's my ass if I don't get them unloaded fast. Quit when winter comes."

"I'm sorry to say it, Mr. Ledbutter, but I really do have to go now. This is Saturday and you owe me for a week's work. I won't be coming back on Monday."

"You didn't read the contract, boy. It says any man that quits without notice gets no pay. I have it right here in writing."

"But I'm giving you notice right now, Mr. Ledbutter. You owe me for sixty hours of labor. It don't come out of your pocket. So be a good sport and pay me. I need that money."

"I think maybe you don't hear so good, son. I said you can't quit now. I said you gotta give notice, two weeks' notice. It's in your contract, so read it and come to me two weeks from now before payday."

"Today is payday, Boss. I want my money."

"Nothin' doin', buddy boy. Now get the hell outta here, or do you want me to call a brawny lout and have him throw you out?"

"I want my pay, Mr. Ledbutter!" Leo's eyes were blazing now and his boss was hearing quite clearly the hard edge of his demand. The man stared at Leo for a moment, fumbled in a pocket, brought out a gold coin, and flipped it in his direction.

"Take it and get out of here and don't come back," he said.

"Well, something is better than nothing," said Leo, stooping to pick up the coin and losing most of his anger.

He left the grubby office with half of what he had earned during six grueling ten-hour days. The other half would go into Ledbutter's pocket. He had heard of this happening to others, and now it was happening to him. There was something in the contract about "curtailed pay" for situations such as this. He could fume and fret, but there was little he could do about it. By accepting the coin he had given up his legal right to claim full payment. He thought he might storm out of the office cursing Ledbutter in Gammon, but why bother? He was a man now, not a recalcitrant boy, and it wouldn't do to curse a man who wielded power, not even in a secret language. Before coming to Norfolk the world had taught him how to handle disappointment. Then it made him hard and aware of evil but told him nothing of trust. When Ledbutter tossed the coin for him to scoop up from the floor, he learned a new lesson.

Chapter 5

Leo Becomes a Sailor

In Baltimore the weather was soft and fine. Leo sold his horse for more than he thought he would ever get and boarded a sea-going vessel for the first time in his life. In Kelly Junction when he was thirteen, he and a friend had gone fishing in a rowboat. When the fish didn't bite, they rowed the little boat around the shores of the small lake and then across it. He liked the feel of being in a boat, even a clunky little boat that could barely hold two people. He wondered what it would be like to climb into a sailboat and trim the sails and go flying off with the wind. On more than one occasion he had seen the O'Keefes sailing gracefully along in their own sailboat. Kevin O'Keefe, an Irishman but not a Traveler, lived in a big house and earned his living as a manufacturer of furniture.

On Sunday afternoons in summer and well into the fall of each year the O'Keefe family could be seen in the extravagant act of sailing their own boat. The sight was the envy of every person in the village. People often stood on the banks to watch. One breezy day when Leo was hunched over in his friend's boat trying to catch a beguiling fish, the speedy sailboat came whooshing in close and almost capsized the smaller boat. It seemed to be moving fast and it was leaning far over, and his friend told him the boat was heeling in the manner of all sailboats. Now Leo was on a ship and wondering if it too would lean way over under sail. He had come from a tiny rowboat to walk gingerly and with some misgiving on the deck of a ship.

The expression "money talks" was coined a long time ago. When people in faraway places ceased to barter and began to pay for goods and services with shells or beads or gold coins, they learned quickly that currency has power as well as value. Leo Mach was learning that money often speaks with greater fluency than the human tongue, and now when he hoped to sail from Baltimore to New York it spoke loudly for him. For several months he was paid for his labor, and he saved as much as he could. Though a greedy, dishonest boss had wrested from him half a week's wages in Norfolk, he had added to his savings by selling his horse. That placed in his pocket enough cash for a sea passage to New York with some left over.

Quickly he found himself on the deck of a ship with the name *Endeavor* on her transom. A sailor in canvas trousers and a striped shirt was speaking very fast, almost too fast for his Southern ear to comprehend. For a reasonable fee, the sailor told him, they could take him aboard as a passenger, but he would have to spend most of his time on deck or in the common room. He had come late, and the few cabins they had for paying passengers were already occupied. Leo paid an agreeable reduced fare and looked forward to strolling near the rail in balmy winds. Should the weather turn sour, he would roam the ship below decks to explore.

It was a new adventure for him, a novel experience to walk on a surface constantly moving and tilting under his feet and driven by an invisible but palpable natural force. It was a valuable learning experience, too, for it would tell him conclusively whether he could tolerate months at sea. Sailing for the first time in his life on a huge vessel, he could laugh at the puny little sailboat the O'Keefe's boasted of owning. Within a day he awoke to the ship and the sea, to the sky and mist above it, and the wind. He marveled at the wind, that invisible and mysterious force that either pushed or pulled the ship like fine horses. It was the one thing a sailor could never ignore, the machinery of propulsion coming now from the southeast.

On board that ship and walking on its deck, he almost forgot he was on his way to find work as a sailor on another ship. He ate his lunch with the crew in the forecastle, fo'c's'le they called it, and joined in their laughter and chatter. He asked many questions and learned from them. He could have used the fancy dining room where passengers and officers ate better food, but he preferred the company of common sailors. They were workingmen like himself, and he felt comfortable among them. Also when they began to talk they told him all kinds of things he needed to know.

In the late afternoon when the wind was building a rougher sea, he began to feel a sickly queasiness in his stomach. A joshing deckhand, smiling broadly, said it was the first sign of seasickness, a common ailment among landlubbers and even among seamen until they got their sea legs. He was affable and helpful and advised Leo to take the sickness in stride.

"You don't have nothin' to worry about. Just find a chair on deck and sit by the bulwarks. You'll probably puke yer guts out for a couple of hours, but then you'll feel a lot better right afterwards."

"Won't I be too weak even to walk after all that?"

"It hits different people different ways, but when you feel better just go and rest somewhere. Let plenty of fresh air can hit your face. Later you wanna fill yer belly with something good to eat, something starchy and salty. Ask Cookie for some hardtack."

A fresh breeze was heeling the ship ten to fifteen degrees and the seas were lumpy. The sleek vessel was sailing now with a bone in her teeth. Leo got to the lee rail as fast as he could. Then the vomit came gushing up and out and overboard, blown away by the wind. As the deckhand had said, he got over his misery as soon as the retching stopped. He began to feel well again but hungry. That evening he filled his belly with salted fish. Except for one day when a storm blew in, he had no trouble with seasickness for the rest of the voyage.

In New York Leo rented a cheap room for several days within walking distance of the sprawling harbor. It was poorly ventilated and smelled of unwashed bodies coming and going. Though the weather in late spring was becoming warm and pleasant, the swollen window frame could be opened only inches from the sill, and the panes had several layers of winter dirt on them. All he could see when he looked out was the blurry brick wall of another building. The dirt and grime didn't bother him because he was gone most of each day and returned to the stuffy little room only to sleep. The bed was a narrow cot. It had a good pillow but a thin and dirty blanket that didn't ward off the night chill and a mattress with urine stains. The cot was smelly and too lumpy to be comfortable. Leo managed to ignore all that because walking and waiting and standing in the open air during the day brought on fatigue that welcomed sleep.

Early each misty morning he was up and out and headed for the waterfront. His mission was to find a ship and find a job. The sailors on board the *Endeavor* had said it shouldn't be difficult to hire on as a common sailor if the captain was planning to cross the ocean. On voyages of several weeks, some members of the crew would become sick and to hire an extra man or two before the journey began was a common practice. It was common too for sailors to get drunk the night before departure and not show up for duty the next morning. So they advised Leo to hang around the docks and be seen as departure time approached. He went looking for ships that would be leaving for Europe, hoping he might sail on one for England or Ireland and thus have the opportunity to see the homeland of his ancestors.

On the fifth day he was beginning to think he had made a mistake coming all the way to New York to acquire work for which he had no experience. It was the first of many questions asked of him. "What is your experience, Mr. Leo Mack, and what ships have you sailed on? What is the name of your most recent vessel and where is she now? Why do you want to sign on with us?" When he answered the first two questions honestly, he was abruptly dismissed before he could answer the third one. One interviewer, older and kinder than the others, patiently explained why.

A sailor had to know what he was doing. His safety and the safety of others depended on it. Of course he could swab a deck without training, but what about night watch, or work in the rigging, or steering the ship? What could he do in stormy weather when squalls hit hard and fast, and every person had to fight against time to secure the ship? An untrained sailor would be in the way, a danger to himself and others. Possibly he might obtain work as a cook (if he knew how to cook) or as a helper in the galley if he had plenty of stamina. When hope was fading, an old salt suggested he talk with the captain of a vessel called the *Sea Cloud*. The ship was docked at a landing in the East River and would be sailing in a few days for Italy.

Just about every day when he was growing up Leo heard talk of Italy. Some older women in Kelly Junction had gone there with their husbands before immigrating to America. They had lived in Italy for only a short time but spoke of the country and its climate with soft and appealing nostalgia. As a child he clung to their knees and listened to their stories of gondoliers in Venice and Saint Marks's Cathedral and the Vatican in Rome. In the streets of Naples one could hear music all day long, buy very good wine at a good price, and enjoy colors so vivid they dazzled the eye. The women spoke of the warm weather in southern Italy and the good food and how cheap the wine was, but seemed to have little affection for the people.

They wanted to stay and buy wagons and travel the length and breadth of the country as their kinsmen were doing in Ireland. Their husbands consulted with officials who told them it would be difficult to gain citizenship in Italy and eventually they would have to go. The Italians were free-spirited people but didn't encourage nomads, Gypsies or otherwise, to move from post to post in their country. So in time the small group of fair-skinned Irish Travelers reluctantly returned to Ireland and later crossed the seas to America. That was their story and it lingered in the imagination of Leo Mack into young adulthood. Now he might have a chance to go to Italy, that favored place he had heard so much about as a child.

Early Saturday morning after eating a spare breakfast with black coffee to wash it down, Leo walked several blocks to visit the *Sea Cloud* at the East River wharf. The weather near the end of October was misty and cooler than usual and his jacket was thin, but the hot coffee warmed him with energy. He noticed as he walked that the soles of his shoes were wearing thin. He had heard that sailors wore their own special clothing, and so perhaps the new job would come with new clothes and shoes. His little store of cash was running low, and he had to think about getting the job above all else. He put his hand behind his back and crossed his fingers, a common gesture in his family, as he spoke to the sailor at the bottom of the gangplank. The fit and sag of his clothes sang unmistakably of the sea, and for a moment Leo wanted desperately to be in his shoes.

"I'm looking to work as a seaman on your boat, sir. I will sign on for as long as you need me and do any kind of work you want me to do. I'll work hard and not give nobody any trouble."

"Oh, don't call me sir, feller. I'm not an officer. I'm just a deckhand on this tub. I'm not even sure the galley boy is below me in station. All I do is help sail the boat and keep her clean and stand here to keep stowaways, like you maybe, from sneaking on. In a place like this hooligans are always trying to climb aboard."

"Will you let me come on deck, please? I won't try to stay if your skipper decides he can't take me. If you let me talk to someone in charge I'd be much obliged."

"Again I gotta say I can't help you. I'm not the captain and not the first mate, not even the second mate, and so it's not my call to let you go up this plank. Even if I did open this gate, nobody on board would hire you. That has to be done by the firm that owns the ship. Here, I'll give you my map. Their office is right there where you see the X and only a few blocks from here."

Leo looked at the crude map of the streets of New York near the waterfront drawn by hand and named. The location of Bolt and Winchester, owners of the vessel, was clearly marked with a large black X inside a circle.

"I'll go there right now!" he exclaimed, running his fingers over the map to get his bearings. He shook the man's hand and thanked him. "Maybe if all goes well I'll be seeing you again. I sure hope so!"

"Maybe we'll be shipmates!" the mariner laughed. "Good luck!"

The office was in the commercial district of the city and more than a few blocks away. With one eye on the map and the other on the streets, Leo walked briskly at first and then slower. An hour or so later he stood before the severe brick building that housed the offices of the shipping company and entered. As he was sitting in the waiting room, someone speaking the name of the ship he was inquiring about caught his attention. He looked across the room and saw a tall and lanky man leaning across the counter and making inquiries of the clerk. He was older than Leo but looked strong and fit though quite thin. His voice was a confident baritone, and his well-chosen words hinted that he was a man of some education.

"I wish to ask you a few questions about the brigantine *Sea Cloud*," he was saying, his dark eyes riveted on the clerk. "I understand the ship will be sailing from this port in three days. Am I correct as I make that assumption?"

"Yes, sir," said the young clerk, "absolutely correct. The ship will sail in three days. She'll be leaving New York with the noontide on Tuesday. We expect her cargo to be fully loaded by Monday."

"Where is the destination? I presume a country in Europe."

"Oh, she'll be going to the south of Italy, sailing to Naples to deliver her cargo. Manifest says barrels of alcohol for the wine industry. Ports of call are Gibraltar, Genoa, and Rome. A new cargo of fruit to be loaded in Naples."

"How many crew members will she carry?"

"Seven at present, sir, perhaps two more to make nine."

"And will she have passengers too?"

"The manifest says room for three passengers. The captain is sailing with his wife and child, and so the ship can take only one more."

"Put me down as the third passenger, please. I desire a comfortable cabin with all the amenities including a private water closet. The expense is no concern. My name is Delgado. Marvin Delgado."

"You will have to share the WC, sir. The ship has only two, one for passengers and officers and one for the crew. She's not a big vessel, you know, not luxurious."

The water closet or toilet on a small vessel, called "the head" by sailors because it was located near the bow, was nothing like the kind one could find in a good house on land. It was hardly more than a box with a toilet seat on top. The box was securely mounted over a twelve-inch hole in the cabin sole above the waterline. Human waste fell through the hole into the sea. On most ships the head for the crew was on either side of the bowsprit in the forepeak and could be used by two men at the same time. The head for the captain, first mate, and passengers was a similar device but more private and more carefully made. It was located near the transom, or aft section of the ship, which displayed her name and hailing port. Some vessels bigger than the *Sea Cloud* had private heads in staterooms, and passengers were expected to pay considerably more for the convenience.

The clerk was thinner than his customer. He was a pimply young man in a starched shirt with a high collar. His hands were very white and the nails of his fingers very blunt. With a flourish he filled out a form and gave it to Delgado to sign. As Leo listened he grew hopeful at first and then excited. He had heard the ship could use two more sailors, and maybe one of the vacant slots would be his. The clerk directed him to an inner office where after answering some questions he signed his name to some papers and left the office with a job as an ordinary seaman on the *Sea Cloud*. His pay would be three dollars per week, but when promoted to able-bodied seaman – able to hand, reef, and steer – it would increase to four and later to five.

The next day, a Sunday when most of the crew had the day off, Leo went to the ship to meet the captain and make arrangements to be on board when the *Sea Cloud* departed New York. Edward Spooner was a bluff and hearty man with a decisive air of command but also a fair-minded captain displaying an easy, congenial manner. He was known to be religious with strict habits and with no acceptance of alcohol on board his ship in any form. Leo found it intensely ironical when later he learned the ship's cargo was many barrels of raw alcohol destined for Italy to fortify wine.

Captain Spooner examined Leo's papers, found them in order, reminded him to buy a sea chest for his personal effects, and explained the rules of behavior on his ship. As an ordinary seaman Leo was expected to perform with dispatch any job the captain or the first mate ordered him to do. He would also take orders from the second mate. He would not be working all the time but would be on call twenty-four hours a day and ready for any emergency. He would keep himself clean and free of odor, knowing he would be living in close quarters with other sailors. And a final requirement: since the captain's wife and child would be on board, he would watch his language at all times. Salty expression commonly employed by sailors on most ships was forbidden on this one.

Not wishing to break any rules and thereby place his dream of becoming a sailor in jeopardy, Leo carefully noted all these requirements. The captain went on to tell him he would have enough to eat but should know that seafaring food is not always the best. He would be allowed to smoke but never below deck or near the cargo. He would consume no alcohol of any kind, nor bring any aboard. At all times his behavior would be governed by calm self-control. Captain Spooner hoped that with a good crew and good luck he might reach Gibraltar in three to four weeks, and by then Leo would know the ropes. There the sturdy vessel would rest for a day or two and sail eastward to Italy. As they parted, he asked Leo to come to him for assistance if he should run into trouble while gaining his sea legs. The would-be sailor left the ship with a good impression of the man. He seemed a good and capable mariner with a steady temper and all the qualities of a good leader.

———◈———

On Monday, October 26, Leo packed all he owned in his newly purchased sea chest, hoisted it to his shoulder, turned in the key to his rented room, and walked to the *Sea Cloud*. There he met his fellow crewmembers, including Eugene Hawkins, the man who had steered him in the direction of the company office. Eugene took it upon himself to show him around the ship and help him get settled in that part of the vessel called the forecastle by landlubbers but the fo'c's'le by sailors. Located in front of the mainmast and below the deck, it was that part of the vessel closest to the bow. Underway it received the full brunt of the sea in any weather. Sailors went to sleep and woke up to the sound of the bow cleaving the water. In his bunk or hammock in the fo'c's'le, Eugene said, a sailor can often read the speed of the ship by the vigor of the bow wave, and he can know also the condition of the seas.

The tight little space was the crew's living quarters. Leo soon discovered it was dark and cramped, poorly ventilated, smelly, and often noisy. He found an empty bunk close to the hull of the ship and put his chest in the special clamps under it. Securely clamped, if the ship rolled on her beam-ends the chest would not go flying. In his innocence he didn't know he had chosen the wrong bunk. Any sailor trying to sleep "against the wood" as the crew called it, felt every little movement of the ship. Every morning for more than a week Leo woke up dizzy and dazed, the whoosh of the bow wave running through his head. It was not a good place to rest or sleep, and in time he found a better place.

Editor's Note. *Now that my friend is eager and ready to embrace a new life at sea, I will let him record his adventure as I found it in the journal he gave me to read. His account is a logbook kept with day-by-day entries until ending abruptly. I have taken the liberty, with the reader in mind, to divide the document into chapters. On the whole Leo expresses himself well, though on occasion I have found it necessary to alter his language for the sake of clarity and propriety. Though quite colorful and perhaps exaggerated in places, the accuracy of his account speaks for itself. In these initial entries, he gives the reader a vivid impression of his first days at sea. – Isaac Brandimore*

October 27, Day 1 — It was nearly two in the afternoon, 1400 in sailor language, when we eased away from the wharf and ran into the bay. We set every sail to catch the wind and skipped along at nine knots with a brisk southerly breeze off our starboard side. The captain wanted to leave with the noontide, but as we prepared to cast off he discovered three of his most dependable sea dogs were missing. They were steady, experienced men who had shipped with him on other voyages, and their failure to show for this one puzzled him and made him testy with disappointment. At the last moment he had to take on a couple of rough characters, sailors or would-be sailors, who happened to be on the wharf to watch the vessel depart.

Eugene wasn't pleased with their looks. He called them "wharf rats" and said the whole crew would have to keep an eye on them. We didn't want to live and work with strangers chosen at random, but we knew we couldn't go against the captain who insisted he needed more men. All we could do was to keep our distance and see to it the two worked hard. In time if they proved worthy and caused no trouble, the crew might accept them. If they did cause trouble, Hawkins confided with a grin, on a dark night with no moon they could end up visiting Davy Jones. Well, I understood what he meant and wanted no part of that business. So I hoped for the best.

The wharf rats replaced the men who probably got drunk and got stabbed or shot in a brawl the night before. Both admitted they had never been to sea before but were willing to learn the ropes and work hard. So maybe they will turn out to be good sailors, maybe not. Time will tell, and time I'm told by people who know moves slowly at sea. So the *Sea Cloud* is now on the open ocean with a crew of seven instead of eight. Also on board is the quirky passenger, Marvin Delgado. He seems a little shifty and could be running from something. I don't know but expect to garner something about him when I have a chance to talk with him. The remaining people on board are the captain, his wife and little child, and the first and second mates. I will have more to say about them later.

Now what concerns me is the lack of good, well-seasoned sailors on this brig. When only seven men, including a new recruit like me, have to work a two-masted ship of one hundred feet, 282 tons and a long bowsprit, replacing experienced mariners with greenhorns like me can be a problem. That means any one of the three new hands can take a spell at the wheel or swab the decks or stand watch, but how much use are we gonna be in rough weather or coming into a tight berth in port? Our cook says not to worry. The first rule of the sea is to take things in stride. But the cook keeps to the galley and don't have to take much in stride. He's a jolly black man always laughing. Eugene says his laughter at times seems forced. And that sounds almost like a warning or bad omen, but I don't know of what. Delgado stayed in his cabin all day.

October 28, Day 2 — On this second day of our voyage the sun broke from the eastern horizon bright and clear, and the ship came alive with crew and passengers enjoying the good weather. Captain Spooner is a handsome man and well liked by the crew, but spends all his time to weather of the first mate on the quarterdeck. Only the second mate has the full run of the ship and seems to be one of us though we call him Mister. The captain's young wife appeared on deck this morning with their little daughter. Her name is Sophie – I don't know her mother's name – and she is able to toddle with the aid of a helping hand. She is now beginning to talk and say "Mama" when she wants to be in her mother's arms. Mrs. Spooner is an energetic and pleasant young woman with a soft persuasive voice. She didn't appear condescending as she walked the deck from stem to stern, but I noticed she didn't get chummy with any of the deckhands either. I guess she didn't want to interfere with their work. She paused to say a few words to Mr. Delgado who was standing by the rail. He smiled and bowed stiffly.

The weather is most desirable and I hope it continues that way. We have a fresh breeze from the south-southwest, and I'm told it's off our starboard quarter. The vessel is moving smoothly in mild conditions, so smooth in fact we hardly know she's moving at all. Then we look up and see billowing white sails with full bellies, and that tells us the wind is fresh even though we can't really hear it. However, we do hear the bow wave and see it too and see the wake behind us. Also we hear the rigging sort of whining and see a long, white lane in our wake. She is moving fast, this well-named *Sea Cloud*, but how fast I don't know. A practiced eye can clock her speed even without tossing the log, but for accuracy the second mate trails the log now and then to read the speed. It's only a weighted piece of wood attached to a knotted line but does the job.

Today is only my second day at sea and I'm learning the language of sailors and how to make myself useful. At present I can swab the decks and do necessary chores, but the first mate tells me that before long I will stand my watch day and night like all the others and even steer the *Sea Cloud* by day and also by night. Already I know how to read the compass, but exactly what the helmsman does to keep the ship on course is still a mystery. Before we've gone a thousand miles, the second mate informs me with a chuckle, I'll be risking my neck in the rigging. He wants to see me running like a squirrel up the ratlines to perch like a parrot on the crosstrees. I'm not looking forward to doing any of that! I didn't tell him I'm afraid of heights.

Chapter 6

In a Wooden World

Editor's Note. *Leo Mack recorded the events of his sea voyage in a thin book with blank pages that he must have had in his possession on boarding the* Sea Cloud. *It became his personal logbook comparable to the ship's log but with a good deal more detail for each entry. As the editor of his remarkable narrative, I have attempted to divide it into chapters with sections for easier reading. I am obliged to manage my friend's account, editing and polishing when necessary, while interrupting as little as possible. Making his daily entries, he speaks as a "green hand learning the ropes," the seasoned mariners say, but in time he becomes a seasoned seaman himself. I am fond of the sea, have wanted to go down to a ship as he did, and so I envy him. – Isaac Brandimore*

October 29, Day 3 — Nate Rawlings is one of the older sailors on board and prides himself on being an able sailor. The officers and men place high value on his knowledge and experience and say if he really had to do it, he could sail the ship alone through a gale. I'm of the opinion they exaggerate, but I guess they really like the man. He admitted he has pain in his back, and the odor that came from his feet last night was . . . well, I won't go into that. I didn't complain but another man did, and Rawlings put a blanket over his feet, and that helped a little in cramped quarters. Now I'm beginning to see that living in a wooden world too close to others can be a problem.

I'm told the fo'c's'le is always smelly and stuffy, and so I'll have to get used to it and not complain. Happily, while some of us are sleeping other sea dogs are standing watch or steering. The ones on duty at night grab a few winks by day but never on the job. A sailor can be flogged for sleeping on the job, though I doubt Captain Spooner would go that far. The fo'c's'le is dark most of the time, even in the daytime, and so sleeping comes natural there. By contrast the cabins for officers and passengers are small but comfortable with lanterns after dark and at least one watertight window called a porthole. I peeked into a cabin my first day aboard and saw oak and mahogany panels on the wall and what looked like a settee covered with velvet. I know for a fact that money can buy a vastly different world, and yet it remains a creaky wooden world for fancy passenger and earthy seaman alike. The ship moans at night.

Eugene with a chuckle explains she has seen her lover go to sea never to return, and it's out of loneliness that she moans. She wanders lonely as a cloud that floats on high, he says in that nasal twang of his, quoting from a poem he read somewhere. Well, she is a cloud and she floats and so his description fits. Eugene is a clever man and very capable. I believe he has salt water in his veins instead of blood. He loves ships and the sea, and he would have no life anywhere else. The little things that bother some of us, and that includes boredom, he don't even notice. Though not a jolly fellow like the cook, he takes his life at sea as he finds it and makes the most of it.

Well, I was about to say all of us, regardless of station, have chosen to live behind wooden walls for several weeks. But hastily I must add sailors live in the open air too for weeks and weeks, and the air that sweeps across the deep blue sea is like no other. That is why men at sea never worry about dying of respiratory trouble, but I won't talk of that. When the sun goes down and night moves in and the crew retires, the silence comes on heavy. One who has never been to sea will never know the silence a sailor knows. At first it seems oppressive, like when you're in a stuffy room and it's hard to breathe, and you wonder if you can stand it, and then you begin to like it. I guess if he has to, a man can adjust to anything.

This morning I gathered some snippets on navigation. That is the one big mystery that seems beyond my understanding, especially what they call celestial navigation. The first mate, a well-seasoned man named Coates, uses an instrument called a sextant to calculate latitude and a chronometer to read longitude, and the charts showing the line of dead reckoning tell him our approximate position and how far we've gone. At noon he looks through the sextant to measure the angle between the sun and the horizon to find our latitude. The instrument is complicated and can be used even on foggy days, but the noon sight is the most common. Like the chronometer, it's kept hidden away in a weatherproof case and handled with care.

As the days passed I learned more about nautical instruments and how important they are on a ship at sea. The first mate has them always under his eyes and tells me with total conviction he can't do without them. Not only do they indicate position and direction in the middle of the ocean, but they also forecast the weather. The thermometer tells the crew how hot or cold is the day as they swab the deck. The barometer measures the weight of the air and foretells changes in the weather while the hygrometer marks the dryness and wetness of the atmosphere. The magnetic compass, of course, is probably the most important instrument because it guides the ship on its course, but the sextant, chronometers, spyglasses, charts, and sailing directions are also important. Several times a day Mr. Coates must consult complicated tables in thick books in small print. Aids for effective navigation he calls them.

I'm told since leaving New York the ship has sailed more than two hundred and twenty miles, but ahead of us we have many hundreds of miles. As evening was coming on, the wind shifted more to the south, and that put us on a beam reach and caused the vessel to heel. The first mate ordered reefs in the topsails and the top-gallant sails, and the men who did it looked like monkeys swinging on vines in a jungle. I was amazed at how sure footed they were in the rigging and how dangerous it must be without sure footing. We were expecting a windy night, but after midnight the wind diminished to no breeze at all and for four hours we lay becalmed. To my surprise, in the stuffy fo'c's'le I found it hard to sleep in the calm.

October 30, Day 4 — The second mate, an Irishman like myself named Doyle, said the barometer was falling and that could mean rain, high winds, and bad weather in a day or two. In that kind of weather, he said, a man scanning the horizon will see petrels flying close to the water, their legs dangling beneath them as if they are walking on the water. They delight in wind and rain and range hundreds of miles from shore. Well, the barometer is an instrument that measures atmospheric pressure, and the ones who know how to read it always keep an eye on it because it can forecast the weather. A man's life at sea is always governed by the weather, and keen eyes must constantly observe the weather. On a good day everyone hopes the good day will last forever, but it never does. The weather at sea, as everyone knows, is given to sudden and unaccountable change. It can be delightful one day and deadly the next.

I'm hoping our voyage will not be a rough one. I have my sea legs now, I think, but I'm not ready for gale-force winds and thirty-foot waves. I like to see the ship leaving a good wake on a fair day with porpoises sporting in her wake, but that rarely happens. At night the sailors tell their tales of wild storms they endured. Always they make them worse than they actually were, and I'm convinced no barometer could measure the ferocity of their fictional storms. I am not a timorous man, but I quake in my bunk when I hear some of those tales. However, I don't fear the storms that may hit us on this voyage. I'm confident the captain will know what to do, and his vessel, though not as big as some I've seen, is sturdy and seaworthy.

Now as I write about storms we are drifting becalmed in a greasy sea. Catspaws here and there ruffle the surface, but our sails hang lifeless from the yards. All the men are saying no wind is worse than too much wind. With too much wind we can reef the sails and move along at good speed and with full control. In calm the riggers have to run up and furl them. Later they will have to shake out the furls when a breeze comes up. I will have to ride the rigging soon, and I hope I can do it without falling. The old salts tell of riggers plunging to the deck from sixty feet up. They grin like the devil describing the sound a man's heavy body makes when it hits the deck. Immediately the lowest ranking sailor must clean up the blood and guts, and the man is buried at sea, and there is nothing on earth after his possessions are auctioned for anyone to know he ever lived. It's not like dying on land where you get a tombstone, and your loved ones can visit your grave and remember you when you were alive. When a rigger falls into the sea it usually means death too. Rarely does a man get plucked to safety. When he kisses the hard water, it knocks the breath out of him and he can't yell for help, and he sinks into the depths never to be seen again. All this is gory, I won't think about it.

The captain is grumbling about his chronometers. That's a word I didn't even know before I came aboard this ship. I found out it's a very accurate time piece and keeps perfect time in spite of motion and variations in temperature, humidity, and air pressure. But now Captain Spooner is saying the three of them don't show exactly the same time, are not synchronized to use his word. Mr. Coates, explains the chronometers help him and the captain read longitude. The sextant helps with latitude and the chronometer with longitude, and the point where the two meet is the ship's position. It's the science of navigation, and I wish I learned it in school but didn't. Coates was not able to get a noonday reading because of the haze and clouds. But his dead reckoning, another term our navigator uses, shows we've come a hundred and sixty miles in twenty-four hours. Dead reckoning requires tracing our course on a chart with parallel rules and dividers and calculating our current position using a previous position or fix. You advance the position based on speed, elapsed time, and drift caused by the wind.

But enough about instruments. The crew was wondering what happened to the seasoned sailors who didn't show when the ship was ready to sail. Captain Spooner sent a wire to the owners of the vessel, explaining what happened and asking if they could look into the matter. He waited for several days and learned the men got involved in a drunken brawl and were thrown in jail. He believed the wharf rats who replaced them would prove of little worth as seamen, and he was right except for one fact. They know how to steer, and they do it in all kinds of weather, and they even do it at night. Both are able to keep the ship on course, and that leaves the more experienced men to work the deck and rigging. What they are capable of doing in a gale and a strong head sea no one knows, but I'm sure all of us will find out before our voyage is finished. I'm told that in these northern latitudes storms are more common in the fall than any other season. So I guess we can expect a few.

I'm a new hand but I carry my share of the load and I'm learning as I work. I help the laughing cook from time to time as a galley boy. No one seems to know his full name, but we call him Dan. He's a big fellow and sweats in the heat of the galley and smells to high heaven, but I have to admire him. Every day he cooks for a dozen people in a tiny hole of a kitchen we call the galley where pots and pans are always swinging on their hooks. In a blow, he tells me, they fly all over the place. He cooks for the captain and the captain's wife and maybe even the toddler Sophie. Also he prepares meals for the crew, no small chore, and the one paying passenger we have. How he does it I'll never know. I don't envy him his job but he likes it. I should tell you he's more than just the ship's cook. In his own way he's a home-spun philosopher and a medicine man.

When he heard of my bout with seasickness, violent vomiting when the seas were rough and the ship rolling, he said this to me: "You won't get sick no more, my lad. That's because you're well cleaned out now. You don't have a drop of that shore swash aboard you, and now you're strong again and off on a new tack. Pitch any of that land food you brought aboard overboard and feed on salt beef and sea bread. That stuff is gonna stick to your ribs and quell your belly and make you hearty." Then he laughed and pushed into my hands a slab of salt beef and two biscuits wrapped in white paper. I can't describe the change the beef and biscuits quickly brought about. Now I have my sea legs and no more upset stomach, no more landlubber seasickness.

I will close this entry with mention of the whale we sighted just as the sun was breaking through clouds in the western sky and sinking behind us. A man clinging to the topmast crosstree saw it first and shouted, "Whale Ho!" Everybody went to the larboard rail and looked and it caused quite a flutter. I'd never seen a whale before, not even a picture of one that I could remember, and it was big. I mean really big. When it began diving under the water its fluke or tail fin was huge and powerful. It hovered above the water a while as if on display. Then it slapped the surface of the water with such force we could feel the spray two hundred feet away, and it slowly sank beneath the surface. Our passenger Mr. Delgado said it looked like a baleen whale, either a rorqual or a humpback.

Delgado seems to me a person of means with a good education. I want to learn more about him. I know for sure he has the best cabin on board, even better than the captain's. That cabin is cramped and has one berth for the skipper and his wife and a small crib for the child. It's fine for one person, the captain, but not for three. I sometimes wonder why he brought his wife and child to sail with us on this voyage 'cause it certainly cannot be seen as a pleasure cruise. Maybe Mrs. Spooner persuaded her husband to let her and the toddler come along because she wanted to see Naples.

———❦———

October 31, Day 5 – The weather continues fine but with a drizzle of rain. We have a steady wind in spite of the rain, and our vessel moves like a frisky horse running headlong to the barn. Eugene tells me she is one of the most responsive boats he has ever been on and has a life of her own. "You can feel her heartbeat when the wind is up," he says. "You can almost hear her speaking as the breeze rattles her timbers." He has a good imagination that causes him to mutter wild things at times, and that is a good example. I smiled when he said that and probably rolled my eyes but made no remark to belittle the man. He's imaginative, maybe even mystical, and yet I question his sanity when he tells me this sailing vessel made by old-world shipwrights in Nova Scotia lives and breathes like you and me. On the other hand, if I manage to sail for a time on the *Sea Cloud,* I could begin to think like that too.

I know this sea adventure will change me even though some of the old Irish Traveler traditions remain with me at present. My people have always loved the land and loved traveling from one place to another on land. But as far as I know not one in a thousand ever farmed the land, and not one in a thousand ever went to sea. They live by their wits traveling and working in the summer and returning home in the fall. Some – well, to be honest, many – are not entirely honest, but they are my kinsmen. So it seems the landlubber in me will have to go before I become a true seaman, but never the Irish and our fondness for green. To be a sailor, Rawlings tells me, I must have salt in my veins, not leprechaun milk he says with a sneer and a swagger, and speak like a sailor and think like one. Well, I'm learning the lingo as I do the work, and I'll speak it like any good Irishman with a twinkle in my eye.

I was yammering with Dan the Cook today for a few minutes after going off duty on deck. I asked him if he ever came up from the galley to walk the deck and get a bit of fresh air. He said he rarely did that, preferring to rest in his bunk after standing on his feet ten hours or more. Then rubbing his cheeks, he said, "See them cheeks? They're smooth as a baby's butt and that's the way I want 'em to stay. I don't like that leathery look them sea dogs get from working the ship in sun and rain." Of course he was laughing all the time he was saying this, but I think he was serious too. Then we got to talking about ships. It seems no sailor can resist talking about ships. I said in my ignorance I didn't really understand how a sailing vessel moved against the wind. Again he laughed and did a little dance and recited a poem he said he made up one night when he was young and green. I think it went something like this . . .

> One ship drives eastward and one to the west,
> And they both ride the same southerly wind.
> It's the set of their sails and not the gales
> Determining their direction, my friend!

He puffed up his chest and proudly claimed to be the poet that made the poem. He said he dreamed it up rhythm and all one night in his bunk when he couldn't sleep. I thought it pretty good and asked him to repeat it. Then I said he should write it down. He sort of hung his head and said he had never learned to read and write. So I decided to jot it down here in case he forgets it and for anyone reading this who might like it. I remember these lines when I remember Dan.

I should mention, too, that when night came and the moon rose full above the horizon, several of us sat on deck and smoked our pipes and sang Irish songs and spoke of Halloween. For centuries All Hallows Eve, was that time each year when ghosts and goblins of all shapes roamed through Ireland guided by a small lantern. Captain Spooner is descended from New England Puritans who never celebrated Halloween, believing it was pagan rather than Christian, and so he and his wife never prepare any spooks at the end of October to scare little Sophie, or perhaps instill wonder in her.

The evening passed with no Halloween pranks on board our ship, but one of us remembered the tale concerning the jack-o'-lantern. The folklore tells us it represents a soul denied entry into both heaven and hell. After a life of sin and hard drinking, Jack was refused entry into heaven. Also the devil refused to let Jack into hell and even threw a live coal at him straight from the fires of hell. But old Jack caught the flickering coal in his gloved hand, put it in a hollowed-out turnip to keep it burning, and then roamed the earth at night looking for a place to rest. Ah, we Irishmen love a good story!

November 1, Day 6 – I had the watch four to eight this morning. When I came on deck at four, all drowsy from not enough sleep, the sea and wind had gone down. The stars in a black sky were shining brightly and seemed so close I thought I could reach up and touch them. A warm and balmy breeze touched my face to make me feel awake and alive. I stood at the rail on the weather side viewing the gradual approach of dawn, a sight that few living on land are able to enjoy. To the east I saw the first streaks of light. They flashed into refulgent beams the moment the sun touched the horizon. There is something about those silver streaks of light, lying in wait for the rising sun and suddenly bringing color to the sea, that stirs one with loneliness. Maybe it's the darkness refusing to go, or the new day struggling to be born, that causes this sense of foreboding. You look around and all you see is nothingness, the murky water merging with dark sky and your tiny boat so small, but then comes the dawn with silver and the sun with gold and the sea day begins.

Just as the dawn was breaking I noticed a cloaked figure sitting on the lee side of the cabin house shielded from the wind and smoking a pipe. Because it was my watch, it was my responsibility to find out who the person was and make sure he was careful with his ashes. The man seemed to be singing some kind of song, and I paused to listen . . .

Oysters and rocks,
Sawdust and socks,
My grandpa could make clocks
Out of cellos!
Blow us a breeze,
Blow us a breeze, grandpox!
Blow us a breeze,
With your bellows!

I had never heard that song and thought it funny. I was chuckling when Marvin Delgado greeted me with a friendly hello. He said he woke early, couldn't sleep, decided to come on deck and smoke, and do a little thinking in the quiet of the morning.

We chatted for a while and I learned more about him than ever I expected. He said he took passage on our ship because he was told Gibraltar would be one of the ports of call, and that would place him close to Spain. His plan was to leave us there and find his way to Segovia where he hoped to meet with relatives he had not seen in many years. The family had fallen on hard times, he said, and he was taking with him a hoard of precious jewels and gold bracelets they would be able to sell for a handsome sum. It would allow them to live in comfort for the rest of their lives. He was glad to help them in that way because they had helped him when he came to America as a young man. He said he was not afraid to tell me all this because he had seen me in the company office, and his valuable collection was well protected in the captain's safe. Even so, I wondered why he could be so talkative with one of the ship's common sailors at a first meeting. An order from the second mate interrupted my thoughts.

"You, there! No time for lollygagging! Rig the pump and swab the decks and put things in order. Get some help."

Four of us – the carpenter, the wharf rats, and me – pumped water from the sea and began washing the decks. It's an operation performed every morning at sea, and it takes about two hours. When it was over and the pump put away and the cordage coiled, I sat down to wait for seven bells, the call to breakfast. Mr. Doyle, disliking my lazy posture, again spit out an order.

"You, there! Check the rigging of the mainmast. Royal masthead downward. Look for any worn stay or shroud and be quick about it."

I was hungry and my empty stomach was aching, and I wanted to ask if I could do the dangerous job after I ate, but I knew I couldn't disobey an order from this man who refused to call me by name. So up the mast I went, and the higher I got the more the vessel rolled until it seemed to me I was on the end of an upside-down pendulum swinging back and forth, back and forth. It was quite a ride! And what a sight! From the masthead I could see a tiny white spot far out on the horizon. Because of the curvature of the earth – now I know for certain the earth is round – only I could see the object from my great height. Forty minutes later when breakfast was done we heard the official cry from a seaman replacing me aloft, "SAIL HO!"

Having completed my watch, I was off duty by then but went on deck to see clusters of sail approaching slowly. Two ships larger than our brigantine were moving westerly. It was the first time I had seen other vessels at sea at such close range, and it seemed to me an artist had carefully painted them to exceed in beauty anything the human mind can imagine. They passed to leeward of us and out of hailing distance, but Captain Spooner using his glass could read their names when their sterns hove into view. They were both out of Boston and headed home. I don't like to admit it, for I've been told a sailor must have no regrets when on an outward voyage, but I wanted to be with them. I was beginning to think that maybe I loved the land more than the sea after all. The homeward ships were things of beauty and moving fast. Within minutes, or so it seemed to me, they had come and gone. That strange feeling in the pit of my stomach must have been a longing for land.

Chapter 7

Man Overboard!

November 2, Day 7 – Last night the wind came up fast and blew hard enough to build a steady four-foot sea with some waves measuring maybe six. I was in my bunk but could hear the crew on deck scurrying about, reefing the sails, and taking orders bellowed by the second mate. I could feel the roll and pitch of the ship and knew we were in for a blow, but there in my bunk I had no feeling of seasickness. I slept well through the heavy weather, and this morning the sun rose clear and bright. We had a moderate wind and performed the regular duties of sea life with good humor and a good deal of banter. It was the usual routine broken only by a storm, a sail, or the sight of land. The captain believes this spell of good weather will last for several days, and that means less work for the crew. It's a good time for me to describe in more detail the people on board the *Sea Cloud*.

Captain Spooner. He is the lord of the ship. He stands no watch, comes and goes wherever and whenever he pleases, and answers to no one while at sea. On shore I guess he must answer to the owners of the vessel and maybe the companies that insure our cargo but not here. He takes no orders, but any order from him must be obeyed without question and quickly. That includes the two officers under him as well as the crew.

He has the power to make or break an officer. By that I mean he can demote the chief mate or the second mate and send them to the fo'c's'le as ordinary sailors if necessary, but from all I know he gets along well with both and well with the crew too. Because his wife and child came with him on this voyage, he chose his crew carefully and they seem to respect him as a levelheaded, experienced mariner. We respect the officers too, though Second Mate Doyle seems more like one of us than an officer.

The First Mate. Just below the captain who may exercise supreme power whenever he chooses is the chief mate who conveys orders from the captain to the crew. He is comparable to the Vice President in Washington, for if the captain should fall sick or die, he would take the man's place. First Mate Coates is one of the most active seamen on board. At breakfast each morning or on the quarterdeck, the captain tells him what has to be done and he sees to it that it gets done. We call him Mr. Coates when speaking directly to him, but among ourselves we call him just Coates or the mate. He keeps the logbook to show later to the owners and insurers, and with the captain he helps navigate the boat. Also he keeps an eye on the cargo and dines with any passengers that happen to be on board. I've heard that he and Marvin Delgado sometimes play a friendly game of pinochle or poker after dinner, and some money exchanges hands. If Delgado's tale is true, he has money to burn. I've been told that Coates and the captain keep nothing from each other and constantly share what they know about the life of the ship and what goes on among the crew. That's important because no captain wants a disgruntled crew surprising him with a mutiny.

The Second Mate. We address the second mate as Mister too, but instead of calling him Second Mate Doyle it's always Mr. Doyle and just Doyle among the men. The captain expects him to maintain dignity and enforce obedience, and yet he's obliged to work right along with us as we operate the ship. He must go aloft to reef and furl the topsails and be on deck nearly all the time. His job demands that he be young and fit and not easily tired. He is little more than an able sailor like Rawlings even though his wages are twice those of Rawlings. Doyle sleeps in a cabin and not in the fo'c's'le like the rest of us, but he eats at the second table after the captain, first mate, and passengers are done with their meal.

Dan the Cook. On the lowest rung of the social ladder, as far as I can tell, is our likable cook/steward. When he's not in the galley cooking for officers and crew, he's the captain's servant. He has full control of the pantry, and not even the mate may go there without permission. He keeps an eye on food supplies and drinking water. He cooks and serves all the meals we eat and works many hours each day. Though he sleeps in the fo'c's'le and chats amiably with the men when off duty, he is not seen as one of our number. Maybe that's because he does no work on deck and spends most of his time below and takes no orders from anyone except the captain. Because he works all day and stands no watch, he's allowed to sleep in at night and to remain in his bunk even during a storm. Dan is a big and burly black man, but no man on this ship seems to care about the color of his skin. I've seen Mrs. Spooner and her little daughter talking and laughing with him. Little Sophie in particular has taken a liking to Dan, probably because he brings her sweetmeats now and then, speaks kindly to her, and plays harmless little games with her like "here's the church, there's the steeple, open the doors and there's the people!" He does it with his fingers.

November 3, Day 8 – Fine weather with hardly a cloud in the sky. A fresh breeze from the southwest strikes our starboard quarter and sends us scuttling along in rolling three-foot waves that never break. The swell is a sign of heavy weather either passing us to the south or approaching. The mate has made it known we must be ready when the weather turns sour. Today begins the second week of our voyage. On leaving New York, the captain said he hoped with good luck to reach Gibraltar in only three weeks. That means the *Sea Cloud* sailing night and day will cross the wide Atlantic in two more weeks (if the weather holds good) despite the heavy cargo made fast in her hold. On making landfall and approaching the coast, the skipper's plan is to move through the Strait of Gibraltar before dropping anchor. It's wide enough (about eight miles at it narrowest between Spain and Morocco), and sailing vessels can get through its thirty-six miles even when tacking against a rare head wind. The plan is to remain in the English port of Gibraltar for two or three days. The ship will anchor in Catalan Bay before sailing on to Italy and to Naples.

In that port our cargo of 1,701 barrels of raw alcohol, intended to fortify Italian wine, will be unloaded and new cargo taken aboard. I'm hoping to spend some time on shore. I want to stroll through the streets of Naples and listen to the music and be dazzled by the color and maybe have some good Italian food with a good bottle of wine. It's sort of funny that with all this alcohol on board the captain is a teetotaler and does not allow on this vessel any spirits of any kind. Some of the crew are grumbling about that, saying we ought to crack open a barrel or two and find out if the stuff is drinkable. That's dangerous thinking in my opinion. Raw alcohol can be deadly. Also I've been told the cargo has more value than the ship and to tamper with it could be seen as mutinous. It belongs to the shippers, appears to be highly insured, and can't be touched except for a daily check to see that every barrel is tightly secure.

November 4, Day 9 – The heavy weather I spoke of earlier came in the night with a cry from the watch, "ALL HANDS, AHOY!" I was asleep all warm and cozy but had to clamber up with the other men to a wet and slippery deck, angry seas, and a howling wind. On captain's orders we hove-to and sat bouncing in the waves until the crew could shorten sail. We sprang aloft and double reefed the topsails and furled all the other sails. It's no picnic to climb a wet mast and wrestle with wet sails on slippery yards in a stinging rain and winds of thirty knots. I'm amazed we got through the ordeal without a man getting killed, but Eugene, Rawlings, and Dan only laughed at my concern and said every white-knuckle battle with the elements trims the monotony of sea life and makes a sailor a man. The storm went on all day, and before it finally moved on toward the northeast we were tired to the bone. Happily after sunset the winds diminished a little, and so maybe we can rest for a while. For supper each man rolled and rumbled to the galley and got a lukewarm and greasy stew in a pewter bowl and went somewhere to squat on his hams and eat it. There can be no dining at table in these conditions. I ate nothing and now my stomach feels queasy.

November 5, Day 10 – On this tenth day of our outward voyage the weather is not good. Another storm blew in from the southwest last night, and I'm told if we're lucky it will be only a three-day blow. The little ship wallows in huge waves and seems to be taking a beating, but the mate and the captain say there's nothing to worry about. Our vessel is as seaworthy as any that have sailed these waters, they say, and is capable of sailing around the world. We need only to brace ourselves and do our duty as best we can. We are told we must endure Mother Nature and let her whip us without whining. To be a sailor is to be a strong man but never stronger than nature.

The two men hired late and no longer called wharf rats manage to steer the boat quite well in these conditions, and so they are now fully accepted by the crew. The captain maintains his station on the quarterdeck in these wild conditions, but no one has seen his wife or daughter in days. The rumor goes that Mrs. Spooner is sick. It could be nothing more than seasickness though I don't know. With the help of the cook/steward, the captain must care for her and the child in addition to his nautical duties. We are now on short rations even though Dan assures us there is enough food in the pantry for a month or more. Until the storm subsides and conditions return to normal, the crew will eat sea bread and strong, cold, salt beef that makes us thirsty. Fortunately we have a good supply of fresh water stored in water butts on deck.

November 6, Day 11 – It saddens me to report that we have lost a good man. I am shaken by what has happened. This morning as the storm raged even fiercer than yesterday, Hans Huber was swept overboard. He was in the rigging at the time but not skylarking as seamen will sometimes do out of boredom in good weather. A fierce gust of wind must have knocked him into the sea. He's the older of the two German brothers on board. He performed his duties well but spoke in German most of the time. Only his brother Ernst could understand what he was saying, though Marvin Delgado, our mysterious passenger with a broad knowledge of many subjects, may know some German. In the midst of the storm two men ran like squirrels into the rigging to look for the man from a height, and the captain gave orders to heave-to and launch the tender, but on the surface of the riotous sea not a person could see a thing.

Many pairs of eyes could find no sign of the man whatsoever, and so reluctantly no tender was launched and we moved on.

Since Hans and his brother shared the same sea chest, there will be no auction of his belongings. It's customary when an unattached man is lost at sea to hold an auction but not in this case. Each one of us offered our condolence and support to Ernst, but maybe he didn't quite understand. The man was terribly shaken by the death of his brother. Who wouldn't be? My brother Luke had a nasty temper and teased me without end as I was growing up, but I wouldn't want to lose him in the way Ernst lost Hans. I think maybe our show of sympathy made him feel better but who can tell? He said nothing to anybody. Just sat clenching his hands and looking downward, his face frozen with sorrow. Until the end of my days I will never forget that awful cry: "ALL HANDS! AHOY! MAN OVERBOARD!" So today all the good souls on board the *Sea Cloud* mourn the death of Hans Huber. We remember him as a comrade and honor him. I will not write more about this. I cannot.

Editor's Note. *I said I would interrupt Leo's narrative as little as possible, but at this point it seems necessary to do so. Possibly because of the language barrier, Leo Mack and Hans Huber were not personal friends. And yet they lived together and worked together on a small boat in a big sea and were members of a close-knit family braving danger every day. Losing a member of one's family, as I know only too well, can be a terrible experience. When my friend Seth, my servant and companion of many years, died the morning after receiving his freedom, I was shocked and angry and suddenly lonely. But at least I had the luxury of selecting his burial place, attending the ceremony of a Christian burial, and erecting a headstone. However, when a man dies by accident at sea, none of that is possible. He is alive and well one moment, then dead and lost to everyone the next. Neptune has yanked him away from the world of the living and placed him forever in regions we can only imagine. The fatal accident was a new experience for Leo Mack and one he never quite got over. I know that for a certainty because my friend to this day speaks with sadness of what happened so long ago. His leathery face freezes with solemn remembrance, and he hears that awful cry once more: "Man overboard!" A man dies on shore and his body gives evidence of his death, but at sea he is near you, beside you, and suddenly is gone. Nothing but vacancy remains, and whether you knew the man well or not, you miss him. You miss him at every turn with no new face to replace him, and you remember him and mourn. – Isaac Brandimore*

November 7, Day 12 – The storm has moderated Mr. Coates is saying, but the bad weather continues with a cold spell. The air is colder than it was yesterday, and I have put on my thick woolen jersey and will need my peacoat when I stand watch. I'm glad I was able to purchase warm clothes before leaving New York. If I need them now, I will certainly have use for them during our return trip. The wind is raw and cold and even the captain keeps to his cabin, but probably because he must care for his wife and child. I've heard that Mrs. Spooner though not seriously ill is confined to her bed, and little Sophie plays contentedly with her toys on the bed and under it with no signs of seasickness or trepidation. Mrs. Spooner brought her sewing materials on board and was in the act of putting together a night gown for the little girl when illness struck. I do hope all goes well with them, and with us. One thing I've noticed in recent days is that Dan is no longer laughing spontaneously and loudly, as he often did in the early days of our voyage. I am not superstitious, at least not as much as some others I know on this ship, but I hope the cook's ceasing to laugh is not a bad omen.

November 8, Day 13 – The weather continues cold, and now comes a constant drizzle of rain. It stings the flesh and makes all aboard miserable. The captain has announced that we are to go north of the Azores instead of taking the usual route south of the islands. His instruments tell him another violent storm may be approaching from the south, and with a change of course we may be able to avoid it. But if the storm should hit us, we could take shelter in the lee of an island. Mr. Coates is saying that even though they don't offer a lot of protection, the waters near the nine volcanic islands are safer in a storm than in the open ocean. Owned by Portugal, they are located more than nine hundred miles west of Lisbon and more than a thousand from Gibraltar. We still have a long way to go, but to see land again will be a welcome sight for every soul on this vessel fraught with too many barrels of alcohol. The rumor is the sight of land will make the captain's young wife strong and well again. I have little doubt it will make us all feel good again.

On this 13th day of the voyage with a dim vision of land in sight (dark, shapeless forms in the blue ocean), some of the men are saying it's an unlucky day. I'm learning that sailors have many superstitions, and the number 13 foretelling bad luck is one of them. Our talk centered on 13 just yesterday. Eugene said the number of people embarking on the *Sea Cloud* bothered him. I didn't bother to count them, but he said the number was 13 and went through a list of crew, officers, and passengers to support the claim. Of course when Hans fell overboard the number was reduced to an even dozen, but the owners wanted more than 13 on board.

"So what are you saying?" Rawlings asked as we huddled to talk.

Eugene was quick to reply. "Hans might never have died had the number been more. Poor Hans became the scapegoat of a villainous fate because the captain was forced to sail with only 13 aboard. Look back at what happened. Three men didn't show and the skipper was forced to hire only two to replace them. If them three sons of bees had come to the ship as they were duty bound to come, we would've had a lucky 14 instead of an unlucky 13."

"Why, you can't even count, Hawkins!" Rawlings exclaimed. "Let's look at that number again. You say we have a crew of 7 but what about the cook? You can't call him a seaman, of course, but he has to be counted. That makes a crew of 8. Then you add the two mates for 10, the three passengers for 13, and the captain for 14."

"You can say that," Eugene replied, "but you can also say the infant has to be with her mother and so not counted as a person, and that brings us back to 13. Or you can say with the loss of Hans we are now 13, and that ain't good."

"What ain't good," said Rawlings in a half joking sort of way, "is bringing that woman on board. Oh, I know she's the cap's wife and all and a good woman, but every man that ever went to sea knows the old legends about how women on a ship bring on bad luck. So forget your numbers, Eugene, and think about that."

"Well, the legends also say a naked woman can calm a storm at sea. That's why figureheads show women with naked breasts. They touch the sea to calm it ahead of any other part of the boat."

And so it went. They were becoming bawdy when I brought them back to the subject. I made it known to Eugene that the *Sea Cloud* left New York with 14 people on board, and no shenanigans would make the sum less or more.

Eight crew, three officers, and three passengers including the little girl (not an infant) equal 14. But alas, the loss of Hans brought the number to Eugene's unlucky 13, and so how could we argue with that? Now with 13 souls on board, including a woman that could bring us bad luck, we are approaching the Azores and their uncharted shoals in bad weather at nine knots, trying to avoid a storm barreling in from the south.

We sailed to the north of the archipelago, being careful not to get too close. Eugene taught me that word. It means a group of islands such as these, or a stretch of sea containing many islands. On the whole the Azores stretch south-southeast, and the northernmost island (not very big at all) is named Corvo. We rounded that island and headed for the largest of the nine. Its name is Sao Miguel and it's shaped like a kidney bean. Captain Spooner issued orders to get behind that island, measure depth with the lead line, and drop anchor. It's the one island among them all that offers protection from winds blowing from the south or southwest. Just as darkness was coming on we put our anchor down in six fathoms in the lee of Sao Miguel. The wind was howling and the rain was constant, but the anchorage was fairly calm and the *Sea Cloud* rode peacefully all night. Every soul on board, save Sophie who didn't know what was happening, heaved a sigh of relief. Except for the wharf rats standing watch, every person slept like the dead.

November 9, Day 14 – I was jolted from bed to hit the deck at 0500 this morning. My usual watch is from 0400 to 0800, but at anchor I was allowed to sleep an hour later. The storm passed during the night, and the weather this morning promises a good day. Some land birds came and perched in the rigging, and that was a good sign. Also the cold passed with the storm and it appears we have a fine day ahead of us. Several people, including the captain and the mate, are now up and about. I could see Captain Spooner pointing toward the southeast, the course we must take when we move out. The southernmost island of this group, Santa Maria by name, is located just to the south of us. It will be the last bit of land we see after rounding the eastern tip of Sao Miguel and setting our course for Gibraltar. Everyone is hoping we have good weather all the way.

Our captain as an act of typical kindness has decided to remain here until noon instead of moving out early as we thought. We had many hours of storm with winds exceeding thirty-six knots and seas building to eight feet or more. The *Sea Cloud* took a beating and so did everyone on board, but the little ship brought us through it all and now we rest. Some of us would like to go ashore, but the one tender we have on board is tightly lashed and not easily launched. Mr. Doyle, our second mate, has the ornery job of checking every barrel of alcohol on board to make certain none of the 1701 barrels shifted in the storm. Ships have gone down at sea because their cargo shifted and left them off balance and lame.

That must not happen to us. However, if not adequately chocked, any barrel because of its shape will try to roll even in calm weather. Between now and the time we move out of here Mr. Doyle will check each barrel carefully and correct any problem he finds. The captain decided before the voyage began that only Doyle would check the cargo because helpers don't often observe carefully enough. At the time we dropped anchor, the German seaman Ernst with sensitive nostrils made it known to Doyle that a peculiar smell was coming from the hold. He was thinking some of the barrels might have slipped their chocks and broken open to release alcoholic fumes. Doyle didn't like hearing that because fumes of any kind can be dangerous in a tight, unventilated space like a ship's hold. He talked the matter over with the captain, who ordered all hatches opened and said the hold would receive plenty of air when the ship sails.

Chapter 8

Rumbling in the Hold

Shortly after the noon hour we weighed anchor and moved out. Mr. Coates was not able to get a noon sight with his sextant because, as he said later, a light cloud cover is common here throughout the year. So with dead reckoning he marked a southeasterly course on his chart and ordered Nate Rawlings at the wheel to look alive and steer as close to the course as the sails would allow. Even though the wind was light from the southwest, our ship under full sail left the Azores far behind in no time. I stood at the rail and watched Santa Maria get smaller and smaller until a speck of land merged with sea and sky. In the open sea the breeze turned colder. I went to my sea chest in the fo'c's'le to get my jacket. That's when I heard a rumbling in the hold and men shouting. Something was wrong . . .

Editor's Note. *This marks the end of Leo Mack's journal entries. Anything else he had to say about his sea adventure came from memory and was revealed to me in the spring of 1863 as we sat fishing in balmy weather with not a single fish biting. There is little chance he has forgotten or distorted the facts because, as he admitted to me, they are seared in memory for as long as he lives. As he went on talking in slow, precise recollection I could tell he was grateful for a listener.*

Perhaps for the first time in his life, because he was a very private person, he was telling another man about all the pain he had suffered and about important events he had witnessed. I liked the way he strung together moving sentences in that guttural voice of his, and I've chosen to continue his tale in his words with just a little editing for the sake of anyone who may read this later. – Isaac Brandimore

When I heard that rumbling and all that shouting I knew something was wrong. I wanted to run in the direction of the trouble to find out what was happening, but I guess instinct took over and self-preservation propelled me to the deck and the open air. On the quarterdeck, his wife and child beside him, the captain was commanding three men to wrest the tender from the doghouse and get it ready for launching. Then as most of the crew gathered in front of him, he explained that several small explosions had gone off like firecrackers in the hold, and he feared our cargo of raw alcohol might explode. He couldn't be sure what caused the explosions or what would come next, but thought it prudent to abandon ship and wait to see what might happen. Immediately we understood that we were carrying a volatile cargo that could explode like a ton of gunpowder at any minute and blow the ship sky high. Several men rushed to help the three struggling with the twenty-one foot tender, and within minutes with launching lines attached we got it over the side and into the water. Mrs. Spooner, Sophie, and Dan were in the boat as we lowered it. The rest of us were ready to follow.

Mr. Doyle received an order to grab a coil of heavy line from the lazarette and cleat it securely. The first person in the tender was told to tie its painter to the line. Then thirteen people would crowd into the small boat and be towed more than a hundred feet behind the ship. The plan was to wait at

a safe distance to see if she would blow. Because time seemed
to be running out, Doyle uncleated the long main halyard,
yanked it from the masthead, fastened it to a cleat on the taff
rail, coiled it quickly, and tossed it to Dan who tied it to the
painter. Methodically without any confusion at all, every man
on board slid down the launch ropes and found a place in the
tender. Dan was at the oars ready to row away, and I noticed
he was looking closely at the way he had tied the tender's line
to the long halyard. Maybe he was thinking the knot could
become untied in a heavy sea.

Our angular captain in yellow wet gear stood calm and tall
beside the ship's wheel. As we looked up at him, he seemed
the very picture of a Gloucester fisherman putting out to sea.
To this day I believe he had decided to remain on his ship, and
for an instant I thought he would surely go down with her. A
pitiable cry from his wife, beseeching him to hurry, caused
him to reconsider and join us. He threw off the launch lines as
he found his seat and grabbed an oar. I remember all this as
vividly as if it happened yesterday. The sky above us was blue
and the wind was light, but to the southwest dark clouds were
scudding low on the horizon. The *Sea Cloud* under short canvas
was moving slowly southward, and she was pulling thirteen
people behind her in a tender designed only for six and only
for protected water, not the open ocean.

At intervals the first mate called out the time for all to hear.
For an hour and twelve minutes our little boat bounced along
behind the ship that seemed to have a mind of her own. Not
a soul was on board and yet the *Sea Cloud* with two forward
sails on her bowsprit and two studdingsails aloft was moving
gracefully along at two to three knots. All eyes were on the
vessel and though running almost under bare poles, she was a
beautiful sight from where we sat. Also, and not so beautiful to

any of us in the crowded tender, we could see a storm brewing to the south and slowly approaching. We looked and waited for something to happen, waited a hundred and twenty feet away for the alcohol to explode, but nothing happened.

Then as Captain Spooner made the decision to draw in the towline and climb back on the ship with Mr. Coates to check her for safety before allowing the rest of us to board, a fresh wind filled her sails and she picked up speed. A squall line lay on the horizon and the storm moved in with winds so fierce we could do nothing but hold on with white knuckles as the ship and boat moved faster and faster. The tender quickly exceeded its hull speed and its prow began to rise and fall in building waves and even dip beneath the surface. As we crashed through the waves, seawater splashed over us and began to collect along the centerline. Dan with furious energy was bailing with his cap when the tender's towline broke short of the knot he had made. The long halyard trailed behind the ship for a few minutes and sank. We were adrift now in a dangerous sea, and our vessel was sailing on faster and faster beyond us. Rowing hard with over-sized oars, we tried to catch her. The little tender plowed into a wave and capsized when a ton of water came smashing down on it. Twelve adults and little Sophie in her mother's arms were thrown headlong into the water.

The boat turned turtle, floated upside down for a few minutes, and sank. I could hear the shriek of a woman's voice and a child crying. A calm masculine voice I took to be the captain's was entreating the woman to remain strong, but she was saying her clothing was like a leaden weight to drag her down. The captain tried to rip off the long skirt she was wearing, but she dipped beneath the surface and disappeared. He dove under the water to grope for her and save her, but

I never saw either one again. Dan the cook seized the child and tried to hold her above the water, but in her terror she squirmed out of his hands and sank like a stone when both were hit hard by a wave. A few human heads bobbed in water made rough and turbulent by gale-force winds. One by one they slowly disappeared, their frantic cry of confusion muffled by the wind.

I looked around and saw no one, heard nothing but the howling of the wind and the patter of heavy rain. Though not ready to die, I was in the lap of a very angry sea intent on killing me. Santa Maria lay to the northwest not more than ten miles away. That helped even the odds with the sea. It wasn't like being in the middle of the ocean losing hope and strength and waiting to die. I was near land in water almost as warm as the air, and I knew if I held on I wouldn't die of exposure. The wind and waves were moving in the direction of the islands. I kicked off my shoes and trousers and began to tread water while attempting to ride the waves. Then to my surprise I heard a man's calm voice only a few feet from me. Marvin Delgado with his many accomplishments was also a good swimmer.

He was holding in his capable hands the two large oars of the tender, but a wave hit one of them hard and it slipped away from him. When it came floating near me, I furiously swam for it.

"Are you wearing a belt?" he yelled over the turmoil.

"Yes! My wide seaman's belt. I never go anywhere without it!"

"Take it off and lash the oars with it! Lash them tightly together."

I did that and found the oars could almost support our weight. All I had to do after discarding my boots was hang on and kick just a little. Delgado was doing the same thing but appeared weak and drooping. Blood was streaming down the left side of his head.

"When the boat capsized, I was injured," he said quietly after the storm had passed on to the north of us. "Something sharp jabbed me in the temple. I'm losing a lot of blood and losing my strength with it. I may not be able to hang on much longer."

"Don't say that, Mister Delgado. You can do it and you will. Both of us are gonna hang onto these oars long enough to reach Santa Maria. The island ain't far from here."

"I'll try, old man, but if I don't make it I want you to have this."

Beneath the water he was pushing something against me. It was a bag the size of my head filled with the precious jewelry he was taking to his relatives in Spain. Early in the voyage he had said in a moment when his guard was down that he had valuable items in the captain's safe. Somehow before abandoning ship he had managed to take the hoard with him. Now he was saying if he didn't survive it was mine. The bag contained a fortune I could live on in comfort for the rest of my life, but I didn't want his wealth. I wanted only to escape the heaving ocean and feel the firmness of dry land.

"Hang on!" I shouted. "You have to get that bag to your kinsmen. You are gonna live to have them thank you for being so generous."

He did hang on through the remainder of the day and into the night. But when dawn came I found myself alone. Exhausted, I must have dozed in the darkness and didn't see or hear him slip beneath the water and sink with his treasure.

Even now, many years later, I sometimes think he might have made if he had not been weighted down by that sodden leather bag made heavy with water and jewels and precious metal. It brought no comfort to anyone and probably cost him his life. However, on second thought I believe the jagged puncture above his left eye was the real cause. In daylight his blood trickled into the water, turned it scarlet for an instant, and went on flowing. It must have done the same when I could no longer see him in the black of night. Marvin Delgado was bleeding to death. He silently let go the oars, sank downward, and drowned.

In the east the cloudy horizon gave way to a brilliant sun. Its path streaked across the calm water to dazzle my eyes. And then looking westward, I saw land! Conserving the strength I had left but kicking as I held onto the oars, I moved slowly toward a rocky shore. The surf wasn't kind as I tried to climb barefoot up and on and over the rocks, but somehow I made it to a pebbly beach and sprawled flat on my stomach. There I lay for what must have been hours, for when I awoke my shirt, coat, and underwear were dry, and the sun was low in the western sky. In the water I had kicked off my shoes and trousers, and the sun had burned my hands, neck, legs, and bare feet. My sunburn was deeply red and painful to the touch. Even so, I was lucky to be alive and in the Azores where the sun filters through a thin cloud cover. Because of that I had no blisters on my skin.

———◈———

Now, Isaac, you are probably wondering how I managed to save my journal, the document I turned over to you some weeks ago for you to read. Before I left the ship I found a large piece of oiled paper in the galley. Dan was wrapping some meat in the paper, and I grabbed a piece of it to wrap around my logbook tightly in several layers. Then I thrust it deep in one of the inside pockets of my pea jacket. When I checked it after waking on the beach, I found it damp with seawater but not unreadable. So the scribbling I had done on board before things went bad was saved for you to read later. As the journal was drying in the sun I realized I was sitting on the pebbles of a barren, uninhabited beach and weak from hunger and exposure. It was an effort merely to stand, and so on my hands and knees as the tide went out, I searched for shellfish and found a few. I cracked open the shells and sucked away at the salty flesh inside and though I was still hungry I began to feel a little better.

Later walking painfully on the beach, I found some rocks left exposed by the retreating tide. On the slippery rocks were clusters of mussels tightly attached. Bivalve mollusks and bigger than shellfish, I found if I tapped on their shell with a flat rock, I could pry it open and get to the gooey gray meat inside. Even though the mussels had a bitter and salty taste, they were better food than the shellfish. Then looking toward the ocean, I saw gray rocks in the water with limpets on them. I waded in to get them. They were clinging so tightly to the rocks I couldn't pull them off with my fingers. With a thin rock used as a blade, I scraped them off and ate my fill of them. The raw seafood restored my strength but left me thirsty. Later before the sun went down I trudged along the shore until I saw people in the distance. A kind fishermen gave me a pair of old trousers.

As for the ship, I think you know what happened to the *Sea Cloud*. She sailed into the storm, turned her nose away from it, and began to make her way northerly under almost no sail toward the islands again. When the storm passed and the winds shifted to the north, she fell off on a westerly course. Then about two weeks later another ship, the British brigantine *Gilded Swan*, found her abandoned and seaworthy but with quite a bit of water in the hold. The cargo of many barrels of alcohol had not exploded and was still intact. Every person on board the *Sea Cloud* had quickly abandoned the ship because we thought she would blow at any minute. I felt awful when I learned nothing at all had happened. We had acted in haste hoping to save ourselves, and as fate would have it all aboard except me were lost. The first mate of the British ship with two sailors to help him sailed the *Sea Cloud* to Gibraltar, hoping to salvage her. They were brave and competent sailors. An inquiry was held in the Admiralty Court there, and the rest of the story you know from the news.

"As you well know, my friend, your harrowing experience happened a long time ago. All I know is what you've told me. I'm a lonely man living in a lonely place, and I rely on you to bring me the news. But I do remember reading something about a great sea mystery that no one, not even the best seafaring minds, seemed able to solve, and now I know a lot more about it."

"Well, Isaac, you may be a starchy old scholar, but I've always tried to do the right thing by you, and bringing you the news was just part of my job. You're correct when you say it was a great sea mystery. It was the mystery of the American brigantine *Sea Cloud*, the ship I sailed on in my youth, and the one on which I hardened my hands to become an able seaman. In the years that followed I served on other ships, but none had the heart and the soul of the *Sea Cloud*. I regret to this day that we lost her, and particularly I regret so many lives were lost, so many worthy people and one innocent child."

"Do you believe the captain made the right decision?"

"To this day I believe he made the right decision. He couldn't allow his loved ones and his crew to remain on board and be killed by a great explosion. He took the precaution of trailing the tender far behind the ship, and he planned to climb on board again when nothing happened. But then came the storm and Neptune played with us like a kitten with a mouse and all hell broke loose."

"It sounds to me like that ship was in the clutches of a terrible, unfriendly fate. Unfortunate describes everyone on board."

"You are speaking like one of them philosophers, and you know I'm no friendly with that kind of thinking. All I know is that limey court tended to blame the captain for the loss of so many lives, but I never blamed him. And no one who died with him would have."

"Were you called by the Court to tell your story of survival? Did they subpoena you to explain why the *Sea Cloud* was found abandoned though seaworthy and sailing serenely and properly without a single soul on board?"

"I wasn't called by nobody because nobody knew of any survivors. I'm telling the story now for the first time, and you are the only one to know. The islanders on Santa Maria asked me how I happened to turn up on their island, but I gave them some cock and bull story they half believed and soon went on my way."

"You've given me a taste of what life was like in your youth, Leo, and now I want to know more. I want to know how you lived when you returned from the Azores to the land of your birth. I understand that after your time at sea you became a traveling man, and I want to hear about that. I hope you will give me a full account of all the years of your life so I can write it down and perhaps publish it."

"I'll tell you what I'll do, Isaac. If you give me one of them blank books I saw in your study, I'll scribble in it when I find the time and turn it over to you when I get something in it, and you can do anything you wanna do with it. Also if you wanna take me fishing again when summer comes, I won't complain."

———————

I gave him the blank book and he began to write in it every evening after making his rounds as a tinker. Sometimes he scribbled into the wee hours of the night and didn't get enough sleep and felt dizzy and wobbly when the gray morning came. But true to his word he filled page after page in that book with neat but gnarled handwriting done with a scratchy pen. He seemed driven almost to tell his story in full detail and make it complete.

One afternoon when he was visiting me in my quaint little house off the main road, he rustled through his old canvas bag, found the book, and gave it to me with a flourish. Smiling to show his bad teeth, he said he would like to have it back later. He would pick it up the next time he came to work on a pot or kettle. Maybe I would have a rabbit in a pot that didn't leak and almost ready to eat. Once before we had eaten a boiled rabbit at my table and also potato soup. I was more than willing to fix him a hefty and tasty dinner for his story. I wanted to read it carefully, revised it a little if need be, and bring the project to a suitable conclusion.

Nearly every page of the book was covered with a neat, backward-slanting cursive quite readable but hard on the eyes, and my eyes I may have said earlier are no longer as keen as they were in my youth. Because summer had begun, I thought I would invite him to go fishing. Blue Anchor that summer of

1863 was quiet and peaceful, and the lazy summer days seemed almost ordinary. Not far away, however, it was a frightful and deadly summer for thousands. The Battle of Gettysburg raged for three days at the beginning of July, and the Confederates suffered a terrible loss. Then at Vicksburg in the west came another defeat, and so the South was shaken and reeling. Leo dutifully gathered the news and brought it to his customers.

He has been a busy person this summer but has found time to write in the book I gave him. We plan to go fishing one fine day so we can talk. I'm hoping the material he turns over to me and all he will tell me when we sit and pretend to be fishing, if he happens to be talkative that day, will bring his life's story to an end. Oh, I'm sorry to say it, but as yet we haven't fished and we haven't talked. I must say I've gone to my bed with a fever and a sharp pain in my abdomen, but I expect to be well again soon. People in the village are saying a disease like typhoid is careening through the air, and I may have caught it. My constitution is strong; in a few days I will shrug it off. My work is not yet done.

Editor's Note. *Isaac Brandimore, Blue Anchor's savant and scholar, died shortly after penning the words above. With Leo Mack's permission, I have taken it upon myself to complete his story as told to Isaac and later to me. My name is Emily Kingston. I am the daughter of Matthew and Catherine Kingston and the granddaughter of David and Rachel Kingston, respectable farmers and Quakers living and working on the homestead they founded long ago near the village of Blue Anchor in North Carolina. I am grown up now but as a curious child, about a year after the death of our village scholar, I was allowed to rummage through the attic of his house with my brother Ben. At first our play was a game of hide and seek but soon it became a quest for strange and unusual items stored in the attic. There I found behind a little door all* the books Isaac had owned neatly stacked and labeled. Rats had nibbled on the edges of some, but most were in good condition and ranged widely in subject matter. Except for their owner, no one had read the books. To get them out of the way Olga Hannaford, who then owned the house, had put them in the loft. The books with numerous marginal notes let me know something of Isaac Brandimore unknown by anyone else. And so from my childhood into adulthood I had a deep and lasting respect for the man. Now I feel privileged to pick up the writing project he thought he was putting aside only temporarily and finish it as he himself looked forward to doing. – E. Kingston

Chapter 9

Isaac and Terra Firma

As I said in the editor's note that concluded the preceding chapter, my brother Ben and I as children were allowed to rummage through Isaac Brandimore's attic. Crawling on our hands and knees to explore its nooks and crannies, we found his many books put there by his former housekeeper, Olga Hannaford. I was amazed to find extensive marginal notes on many pages of books on difficult subjects, thoughtful commentaries on the text it seemed to me, the gnarled script faded but legible. Equally amazing to my little-girl eyes was a manuscript of eighty pages setting forth in full and lucid detail the Old Testament story of Elijah and the Ravens. In the style I could see Brandimore at work, but the directness and simplicity of the language suggested he had children in mind as he crafted his story. I had no trouble understanding the story and was delighted by his rendering of it. When I asked my parents whether he had written other stories, they said he had never spoken to anybody about any writing he had ever done. He was a very private man.

That afternoon, after Olga served us lunch with big slices of watermelon for dessert, my brother and I went on searching through a welter of books and papers. In a thin book the size and shape of a ledger, I found a folded sheet of paper filled with handwritten words in black ink. Opening the crisp and fragile document, I saw at a glance that Isaac had bequeathed the house and land to "one Olga Hannaford, friend and housekeeper." The neat and readable handwriting – I learned to read at five and read well at nine – was the same as that of the manuscript and the marginal notes in his books.

For years the village notary had questioned whether the housekeeper had come by the property legally. By accident two curious children, rummaging in the loft to see what they could find, put the matter to rest. As a gesture of her sincere gratitude, Olga gave Ben the Elijah manuscript that has become a family heirloom. In a burst of generosity, she gave me the poems of Elizabeth Barrett Browning in three volumes. A man who loved poetry and one who tried to talk about it with farmers and tinkers and anyone else who would listen, Isaac Brandimore had collected them all.

He died only days after our Southern forces were defeated at Gettysburg and Vicksburg in July of 1863. He never got the chance to fish with Leo Mack that summer and hear him talk about those years in his checkered life that challenged his very existence before coming to Blue Anchor. He didn't live to use Leo's journal to complete the narrative of that worthy man's life, and the village of Blue Anchor never heard what his sentiments would have been regarding Lincoln's Gettysburg Address. Lincoln's reverent attention was on the Union heroes at Gettysburg, but the South as Isaac certainly knew had its heroes too. However, I firmly believe he would not have seen the rampant slaughter at Gettysburg during those three terrible days as heroic. He would have said it was horrific and mindless and would have added: "Let the world never be witness to that kind of promiscuous carnage ever again." My grandparents told me he mounted his stiff-legged horse, after alarming my grandfather with a few stark comments about the war, and rode off chortling. As they remember as he made ready to leave them, he was praising his loyal housekeeper. And in that dry, ironical tone that characterized his speech he spoke of fleeting, evanescent, fugacious youth.

"Women are often long on hair and short on sense," he was saying, "but not this one. So I will tell you this. If I were forty years younger, I would marry her. But we can't turn back the clock or the calendar. Of course I would like to return to those days when life was young and blood was warm, but my old brain tells me I can't."

Then he paused for theatrical effect, my grandmother said, and added in that clear, rich, orotund voice of his, quoting Tennyson to illustrate his point:

"All one can do is ripen to the grave and die."

That was the last my grandparents saw of their friend. A few days later he awoke feeling unwell. He asked his housekeeper to send for Robin Raintree (our medicine woman in 1863), but before she could reach his bedside he died of a fever. For some time there had been talk of typhoid in the neighborhood, but in those days few precautions were taken against the spread of infection. When a fever was suspected, nobody did anything but hope for the best and wait. Almost at once severe intestinal irritation afflicted several people, and one person, Isaac Brandimore, died.

The venerable old man suffered for a day or two but in the end went so peacefully to the other side it was like the blending of sea and sky in a soft and hazy ocean. He was probably thinking of Leo Mack bobbing in that ocean when he mumbled his last words. He spoke of tall ships in milky seas swooping and darting like phantoms in purple light. And then gently expiring, he murmured: "How keenly green was that man's yesterday!" It was probably the best tribute anyone could have paid to Leo Mack while the man lived. To this day I regret not passing on that compliment to Mack himself.

Editor's Note. *Using the journal given to Isaac in the summer of 1863, and perhaps embellishing it in places with conversations I had later with Leo Mack, it is my privilege to let the man speak again in his own voice. I intend to follow Isaac's lead and interrupt as little as possible. – E. Kingston*

⸺ ◉ ⸺

You wanted to know how I lived when I finally made it home again from the Azores. Well, for several months I did whatever jobs I could find and then went to sea again. I had a problem finding a good vessel because the owners always wanted to know all about any ship I'd sailed on earlier. I felt I might get in trouble if I told them about learning the ropes on the *Sea Cloud* and the captain losing the ship and me the only survivor. So I kept the most memorable experience of my life to myself and made up a couple of false stints with fictional ships, and of course they checked and found nothing and refused to hire me. Then when I thought I might give up and go back to my Irish Traveler roots, I got a berth on a brigantine headed for Buenos Aires. That was our destination, the skipper said, but we never got any farther than Rio. Anyway it was quite a voyage. The trip began in cold weather in Boston, and the farther south we got the hotter it got. At night, looking up at the stars, we couldn't see the Big Dipper or the North Star. The constellations were not the ones we were accustomed to seeing in New York or Boston. The Southern Cross glittered brightly in the black sky but no Big Dipper. Some in our crew couldn't understand why it was gone.

Some days the deck was so hot it burned a sailor's bare feet, and some days we were too lazy and languid to work but had to anyway. When we finally sailed into Rio for a cargo of coffee, some of the men jumped ship and found pretty women who wanted to live with them and even support them. I guess I was too dumb to do that, or maybe a haunting remembrance of Caitlin lingered with me, preventing that sort of thing. Anyway, except for two or three days of shore leave, I remained on the ship to stay out of trouble. On the return trip I got as far as Norfolk. The weather most of the time was good, more so returning than going down. We carried tallow and American clocks to the South Atlantic and a load of coffee beans and lumber on the way back. When the hold got hot near the equator, the whole ship smelled of coffee. Night and day we breathed the aroma of roasted coffee beans. These days I drink a mug of coffee now and then when I feel weary but can't stand the smell of it.

Another time I sailed on a ship called the *San Pedro* to Venezuela. We didn't cross the equator that time but ran into rough weather I'll never forget. In the Caribbean on our way to Caracas a hurricane clobbered us real bad. We tried to prepare for it, but it hit us so fast and so hard we didn't have time to shorten all sail and several got ripped to shreds. The captain ordered the helmsman and crew to heave to and we managed to do that, but the ship yawed and pitched so violently I thought she would turn turtle and spill her guts, including every living soul on board. The man at the wheel came very close to being washed overboard. I'm happy to say he had the presence of mind to wear a safety harness, and that saved his life. As for the rest of us, all we could do was go below and curl up against the ballast and wait for the worst to be over. We were a bunch of strong men and certainly no cowards, but no crew regardless how strong could handle the ship in conditions like that.

If she lived up to the captain's high opinion of her, she would ride out the storm on her own. If it proved too much for her and she capsized, we were dead. Gigantic waves and winds that took a man's breath away put her all the way over at least twice, but slowly she righted herself and waited for another blast. We were lucky to get all the hatches closed, and so we shipped only a little water compared to what could have happened. When the storm moved on, the pumps got the water out and we walked the deck again to check on the damage. As I said, we lost some sail, some yards and running rigging, but the masts stood solid. I survived that storm but decided I would never fall victim to another, and I didn't. It was the last of my seafaring days. I have some good memories of them but also some that haunt me when I'm restless in the night and can't sleep.

After my life at sea I became a traveling man. Well, you might say I was traveling even greater distances on the ocean than on land, but it's not the same. At sea it seems you don't really travel. All you do is sleep and eat, walk and climb and work on a floating object that's always moving and taking you with it and yet in a way standing still. It's sort of like being safe and secure at home but moving all the time and finally realizing you've come a long way. Travel on land, of course, is very different. At sea you can move a hundred miles and never know it, but on land you go only a couple of miles and know all about it. Well, truth be told, traveling on land is far less boring than traveling by sea. On land you observe all kinds of things, some made by man and some by nature and some by both, and some of the stuff you've never seen before. At sea it's only water and sky and birds once in a while and sea creatures that sometimes follow the boat. When the weather is good you have a blue sky and white clouds and a shimmering horizon, and a sailor gets to see day after day the most gorgeous sunsets ever.

Well, the sea does have its attractions, but I guess I have to admit I liked being an Irish Traveler again. I was much older when I bought my horse and wagon and hit the road, and I knew the world better. I decided I wouldn't go home again but do it on my own. I didn't want to dig up the old memories and get involved with a gang again, even with kinsmen. My ma and pa were dead by then and my brother in and out of jail, and my poor blind sister . . . Well, I don't really know what happened to her. The last I heard she was blind and not able to care for herself and went to live in some kind of home. I sent her some letters but never got a reply.

Anyway, I decided if I did any traveling at all I would do it alone. Now that's where I differ from my brother and kinsmen. They are social critters and can't stand being alone, and they sort of feed off one another and grow fat but never really expand their lives. When I started traveling again I wanted every trip to be a learning experience, but in reality it didn't work out that way. I had to rein in my dreamy Irish imagination and feel the sweat on my brow before I could learn a few things. I had to walk on solid ground and be realistic and accept the world as I found it. And then I learned it's a hard place we live in, harder for some than for others. Well, as I think about it, I can say with conviction I already knew that at thirteen.

I'm rambling here. You can strike all I just said if it don't make sense. You wanted to hear about my travels, where I went and what I did, and I will try to oblige. From Norfolk I went up the eastern seaboard by land to Boston. I knew the region pretty well and knew the waterfront of several cities along the way, but now with a sturdy horse pulling a good wagon I could move away from the water and see new things. I had some money to carry me through the summer. Even though sailors are poorly paid, they don't have a lot of places on a long voyage to spend their money and so can save it. Well, some blow it all on their first shore leave getting drunk and raising hell, and I did that once or twice but saved some of my wages too.

I had some money left over after buying my horse and wagon, but then it occurred to me I had to find a way to make a living. The Irish Traveler tradition meant working as I traveled or end up broke with no money for rent or food. My wagon had room for me to sleep in it in warm weather, but a luxury it didn't have was the covered frame we had when I was younger. It had a good tarpaulin to cover equipment, and so in time I bought the necessary tools of the trade and became a tinker. I didn't know the first thing about tinkering, I'm sad to say, but I learned as I went along. I learned the tinker's trade on the job, and while I don't care to brag I'm a damn good tinker even now. Not a person in Blue Anchor will say I'm not.

I guess you know my people, the Irish Travelers, were known in the old country as tinkers. It was a good trade for people on the move, and they were even more nomadic then than now. The Travelers in the old country were often confused with Gypsies, probably because they were outsiders moving from town to town and looking for work wherever they could find it. Also their equipment, their traveling accessories and habiliments as the elders called them, were much the same as for the Gypsies. Their clothing and their wagons were not as ornate or foreign-looking on them Irish roads, but some of the women and girls went into the fortune-telling business, and Mama often told me in the early days she was real good at reading the Tarot and made money doing it.

Tarot cards are very old, you know, going back centuries, and a woman that knows the science or the art of laying them out in the proper way and reading them can dig up amazing information to fit her customers every time. My old mama often said it gave her the shakes sometimes when the cards predicted a series of events that would bring bad luck to a paying customer. More than once it turned out to be true, and that's when Mama herself began to believe in the dark power of the cards. She had a good heart and didn't like predicting bad luck for anyone, and so in time she stopped reading the Tarot, and stopped reading palms too, altogether.

And of course the women among the Travelers read palms just like the Gypsies, but you don't see much of that these days. Anyway, that has nothing to do with me as a tinker, and so again I'm straying from my subject. I was going to say something about the tools of my trade. They are simple and known to just about anyone and so don't require much explanation or discussion, but I can say a little something about them. A tradesman is only as good as his tools, you know, and I managed to acquire some good ones.

I had in my wagon a heavy anvil, several good hammers of different sizes, screwdrivers and pry bars, solder, clay to make a tinker's dam, a brazier for heat, a wooden form or shaper, some rasps or files, and so on. After pouring the solder into the place to be mended, you throw away the dam. That's why people say something ain't worth a tinker's dam. Tinkers are known to cuss, particularly when they hit their thumb with a hammer, but "not worth a tinker's dam" has nothing to do with cussing, and so you have to get the spelling right. Often in good weather I worked in the open air with my tools. It was a good way to make a living. I liked it and still do.

———— ⁃◦⁃ ————

There's been a lot of negative talk about traveling people in recent months. I've been reading that the Travelers in Kelly Junction, South Carolina don't see themselves as good, law-abiding Southern people. Instead of going off howling and whooping to war, the young men in the village are making themselves scarce. Confederate recruiters swept through the place not long ago, a paper in Columbia said, and found not one male older than thirteen. But that's because the older men were on the road trying to make a living, trying to scam country folk some of the authorities are saying. I believe there's some truth in that because our ancestors believed God gave them the right to fleece country folk. In every society, they argued, there are givers and takers and our people living in poverty and watching their children grow extended bellies from too much hunger slowly became takers just to survive. So now people see us Travelers as shady con artists, swindlers and fraudsters targeting old people with substandard work and demanding payment in advance. Like the Gypsies, the Irish Travelers are said to have a dual set of ethics, one for us and a different one for the population that surrounds us, the people we call the country folk. To some extent that's true but not entirely.

I've been reading all about the Carolina Tool and Equipment Company supposedly run by Irish Travelers in or near Kelly Junction. They have a lucrative contract to make rifles for the Confederate Army, but the rifles are said to be unreliable and dangerous. The people in Richmond are saying some of these weapons explode in the shooter's hands and are seldom accurate. If all that is true, and if Irish Travelers are the culprits, I say close them down at once and throw the scoundrels in prison. If it ain't true, then throw the jackdaws spreading the rumor in prison.

I have no sympathy for crooks, even if I must call them my brothers. But one thing I want to make clear is this – all Travelers are not involved in crime. I for one have not committed any crime I can remember. At sea I could have stolen from sea chests but didn't. On the road before going to sea I could have fleeced a lot of people, as many of my kinsmen did, but I didn't. Traveling after my seafaring days I could have done some shady dealing to make money, but I didn't. I could have painted fences, houses, and barns with water-thin paint and could have asked the gullible marks to pay me ten times my costs in advance, but I didn't.

I could have used intimidation tactics like my brother was always doing. I can remember the last time I worked with him he got a job trimming trees on the farm of an elderly couple. He turned on the charm when making his pitch and quoted a very reasonable estimate for the job. Then after he completed it, doing fast and shoddy work as he always did, he claimed it was more difficult than he ever expected and so doubled his fee. When the couple refused to pay more than the original estimate, he applied pressure on the victims to pay up or maybe go to jail. Also my pa was there to egg the persuasion on, and the old couple paid.

Well, at least my brother Luke did the work. Some other Travelers walked away with a lot of money for work that was never done. They were seldom caught and punished because no Traveler will squeal on another. In that respect the Traveler code is almost as unbending as the one the Mafia has in Sicily. I've read they have an oath called omertà, which means you die if you spill the beans to the authorities. Well, I do know members of our clan never reveal anything when the sheriff comes snooping around. For their own health and safety they keep quiet, but that's all I'm gonna say about this. You wanted to hear about my travels and how I made a living as I went along. I will talk about that.

Before I left Norfolk I went up the road a piece to a secluded beach and did some shell fishing. I heard some people were making a good living collecting cockles, clams, and other shellfish from the seashore, and since it required no expensive equipment to get started I thought I'd try my hand at it. I found out that shell fishers are hard-working people. They collect the shellfish from below the high-water mark regardless of weather conditions. An entire family including the children often work year round, even in winter when the weather is damp and cold and windy. In fact, the best harvesting of shellfish comes in the winter, and so the fishers wear rubber boots and gloves and heavy coats and squat on the wet beach and dig into the sand with a metal fork or rake to find the mollusks and fill their baskets made of wire. It's a messy job and takes a lot out of a person, especially the young 'uns, but a worker can sell his catch most of the time for a handsome profit.

I worked at shell fishing three weeks. I would have stayed longer if not for the locals. They seemed to think I didn't belong there competing with them for a living. Also they were saying I had to have a permit to harvest shellfish in that area, and rather be pestered by the law I moved on. I tried it again on the Maryland shore, because I already had the tools, but the locals hounded me there too. So I sold my rake and basket at a better price than I paid and went on up the road. Collecting shellfish reminded me of eating raw and slimy mussels in the Azores. I did it to put down the raging hunger I had when washed ashore on Santa Maria Island. I was happy to be alive as the one survivor of the *Sea Cloud* disaster, but miserable too. It's a memory I would like to abandon, but I guess a person never forgets that kind of stuff. It gets seared into memory and just won't go away. Anyway, it didn't take long to get over my stint as a shell fisher. I went back to being a Traveler and was glad of it.

I kept close to the shoreline and didn't bother to go into Washington, and I stopped only for the night, sleeping in my wagon, until I got into Pennsylvania. There I read in a newspaper that a woman of Chinese descent living in Upper Darby had been swindled in a most terrible way by a Gypsy fortune-teller. Yin Wang met the woman all sweet and friendly in a grocery store. Her bizarre name, Wang told authorities later, was Kissy Peaches Teeny John. In her forties, she was flamboyantly dressed and claimed to be a palmist and a psychic. Peaches or John, or whatever her name, told the gullible Miss Wang that she and her family had a curse dating back to the building of the Great Wall of China, and the curse would forever make her and her family and anyone else close to her poor and miserable.

She volunteered to cleanse the curse for nothing but would have to take all the woman's money to a church, clean it with holy water to rid it of bad sprits, and return it to her. When Wang gave the Gypsy every dime and dollar she had, she was told to sell her house for more cash. In a short time the poor believing Chinese woman was robbed of everything she had worked all her life to obtain. Kissy John was later hauled into court, but by the time she went to trial Yin Wang's nest egg had disappeared entirely. To make ends meet, maybe simply to survive, she went to washing dishes ten hours a day in a Chinese restaurant. When she got to her bed at night, her feet and ankles were swollen and hurting, and her back ached with pain. The Gypsy got only four months in jail, was ordered to make retribution to her victim, but disappeared and couldn't be found and didn't pay her one red penny. A year later Yin Wang died a pauper.

So why do I bother to tell you this? It's because the Gypsies give the Travelers a bad name. Some Travelers bewitched by old wives' tales believe they have a license to swindle country folk, but their crimes are petty compared to Gypsy scams.

Chapter 10

Eastlake Penitentiary

In Pennsylvania I went from house to house doing good and honest work as a master tinker, work as good as any I ever did here in Blue Anchor after becoming a Quaker. However, and this part of my story I don't like to talk about, I ran into trouble. When I got near Philadelphia, I decided to work the rural parts of the state and went as far as Lancaster County where many Amish and Mennonites live and speak Pennsylvania Dutch. I didn't do business with any of them because they're self-supporting people and would be suspicious of an itinerant tinker anyway. I was told they keep to themselves and don't like outsiders, and so I went on to a large farmhouse away from their farms. It was sitting on a hill and looked well maintained.

I did some work there, mending some pots and pans and kettles, and the woman of the house, Rebecca Foley, liked my work so well she gave me half an apple pie, and I can tell you that pie was real tasty. Then before I got to the main road, three men on horseback came galloping up in a cloud of dust and accused me of running off with her silverware. Of course I didn't know what they were talking about it, but they claimed I stole the woman's silver when I took the pots back into the kitchen. And not just a few spoons and forks, mind you, but all of it for a dozen people. Well, they searched my wagon and found nothing. Then as I was about to go on my way they accused me of hiding the stuff and hauled me off to jail. In that closed, tight-knit community the sheriff sided with them.

I sat in a jail cell for several days before I finally went before a judge. I tried to tell this man who seemed to be lurking behind a bush of white whiskers, his little black eyes peeking over it, that I was innocent. But when I had to reveal my identity as an Irish Traveler, and they took it to mean just another name for Romany Gypsy, I lost my case outright. A band of Gypsy footpads had come through the neighborhood only a few days before I showed up, and in one afternoon they fleeced an old couple of all their savings. Even worse, they went to the same farmhouse I was unlucky enough to visit. One pretended he was a county official who needed to inspect their well, and while he had the couple outside looking at the well, the other rogue slipped into the house and probably stole their silverware.

Since the family didn't notice the theft until the day I was there, and probably right after I left, in their eyes I just had to be the thief. They found no silverware in my wagon but said I hid it somewhere. Now where in the world would a traveling man, a stranger knowing nothing of their neighborhood, hide all that stuff? I tried to explain all this to the judge, that man with the whiskers and black eyes, but he only smiled grimly, said I was lying, and delivered a thunderbolt. The sheriff's deputies had proof of the theft he said, pounding his gavel for emphasis. They had found three silver spoons embossed with the Foley initials in my wagon. If I confessed and revealed the whereabouts of all the other silver, then maybe he'd go easy on me.

Of course I was dumfounded. I couldn't understand how three initialed silver spoons got in my wagon. I had some spoons of my own, of course, but they sure weren't silver. So I began to believe the real thieves placed the spoons in my wagon to make me take the blame for their crime, and that's exactly what happened. I lost my horse and wagon and all my equipment, was ordered to pay $300 in restitution which I didn't have, and got four years in prison. It was a harsh sentence for something I didn't do, but the judge claimed I did it all right and he wanted to make a good example of me. When my case got reported in the newspapers, he loudly proclaimed that in his district transient tinkers would think twice before visiting a lone farmhouse to swindle the occupants.

They hauled me handcuffed and shackled out of the court. Two days later I was an inmate of Eastlake Penitentiary in Pine Grove. I answered to the number 4957. I could never understand why they gave me that number because the prison had only a few hundred inmates, not thousands. A little more than a year later Rebecca Foley's silverware turned up in a pawnshop in Philly. The thieves were long gone and were never caught, but I was eventually released. I had my freedom again but very little else.

I think at this juncture in my tale I should tell you something about that prison and the life, or lack of life, I had there. It's not a pretty story but if you're trying to understand who I am as branded and shaped by the events of my life, it has to be told. I guess you could call it a chapter in my book of life, but I intend to confine it only to a section and get through the section as fast as I can. It's a painful subject, and I don't like to talk about it. It's a narrative of loss, and when I think about it I'm forced to conclude that a main theme of my life's story is one of loss. When I was young I suffered the loss of my wife. I loved her maybe too much and it's not good to lose someone you love too much. Of course if you've read my story from its beginning up to now, you know all about that time in my life that was hard but happy, and I won't go into it again. Even so, I think about Caitlin every day. I think about her when I wake up in the morning and when I go to bed at night. I just can't help it. I bristle with anger when I think how unfair it was for her to die so soon. She was too young to die and too good, and I railed against any super power who might have decreed such a thing to happen.

Long after she was dead I had to train myself in Quaker doctrine to come to terms with my loss. I guess it's one of the main reasons I became a Quaker. I still can't believe a loving God could allow things like that to happen, but my Quaker friends (and you, Isaac, are certainly one of them) tell me it's not up to me to question the ways of God to man. So forgive me for even bringing it up. I will say nothing more about it. I will tell you about the months I spent in penal servitude, thirteen months or more, for a crime I didn't commit. I will tell you about a thug smashing me in the face with his fist and knocking out a tooth and how the prison dentist replaced it with this golden one up front. I will tell you about a lost year in the life of Leo Mack, and then I will go on to something more sunny than prison.

Anything is sunnier than prison, and I really don't want to talk about it. If you want to finish my story, Isaac, you'll have to gather the bits and pieces and jot them down maybe each time I visit your house. This journal thing is taking up too much of my time. I'm a workingman, Isaac, and have to make a living, and I never was very good at putting words on paper. Even so, I will tell you about that prison in just a few words. As I was saying, I sat in that grimy jail for more than a week before I got to see a judge.

Then old Father Time standing still for days on end with his hands in his pockets suddenly began to run at break-neck speed. Before I could sort through what was happening, I was tried, convicted, and sentenced. I had no lawyer in that court and no jury heard my case. Only the judge in his black robe and white whiskers seemed to be working that day. Of course any number of people were standing around or sitting on benches, but the ones standing were guards and the ones on benches were suspects waiting for trial. I was only one criminal on the court's docket that day, and I guess that's why the whole procedure took half an hour.

I heard the gavel bang loud and harsh. With its sound echoing in my ears, two burly guards grabbed me on either side and frog-marched me out of the place. I heard metal banging against metal and suddenly I'm back in my grimy cell. I'm sitting on my cot, as I remember, eating something they called a stew but looking like dog puke and with a strange metallic taste. A couple days later, when they led me to an iron cage on wheels outside, I couldn't walk like a man. With ankles shackled and hands bound, all I could do was shuffle in small steps and dance a somber little jig to keep my balance. Two laughing deputies, Irishmen like me but certainly not my brothers, lifted me by the elbows and tossed me into the wagon.

For five hours I bounced up and down on the hard floor of that cage. By the time the driver stopped to give me some bread and water, I was sick from the smell of urine and other disgusting odors. He snickered when I complained, saying: "When you hafta go, fella, you hafta go! This wagon don't have no latrine, and the low-life slobs we carry deliberately miss the bucket."

Late in the afternoon they hauled me into a waiting room that was almost as bad as the wagon. The dark and smelly room had only one window partly open and the day was hot. It had only two short benches against the wall where some men sat waiting. Two or three more were standing around and yammering in a thick Southern drawl. I never found out who they were or why they were out of their element way up north in Pennsylvania.

Another man of the Dutch country from which I had just come was talking with a thick German accent to the clerk. He was an official of the court, I guess, and not a wretch like the rest of us. The harried clerk with his head buried in papers was trying to process the men. His sleeves were rolled to the elbow and beads of sweat glistened on his forehead. He looked tired and bored, and his fish-like eyes blinked every time he looked up. He was an anemic little man moving without an ounce of energy and slower than a snail but with more than his share of self-importance.

I waited in that stifling room for at least two hours, and then a guard with short legs, a big belly, and a slack mouth behind a grizzled beard led me away. When the sun was low in the sky, he hustled me down a dark and rank corridor to a tiny cell. Then the cold reality of my situation began to flood my brain. I was in prison.

<hr />

I was an inmate in a penitentiary convicted of a serous crime. My freedom had been wrested from me, and no one loves freedom better than an Irish Traveler. We're famous for loving freedom, and there's nothing we won't do to preserve it or avoid losing it. Night came on fast and in the clammy darkness I lay down in a blue funk on the brick-hard cot. I tried to sleep just to escape my predicament but couldn't. All through the night I heard a doleful church bell tolling the hours. Midnight came and I counted twelve, then one and two and three. I was thinking of home and the happy days of my short marriage, and I remembered the sun in that tiny apartment casting a shadow on the floor that looked liked bars. I had returned from buying rolls from a street vendor, and Caitlin in a pretty summer dress was heating water for coffee. We ate the buttered rolls in high spirits, laughing, and talking, and delighting each other. Then we talked about the future, and that's when I saw that ominous pattern of black bars on the bare floor.

That remembrance in a strange place in the middle of the night, I can tell you, was hard to bear. That pattern was burning itself into my brain, and suddenly I knew what it meant. The bars on the floor predicted prison! I sat bolt upright trying to breathe the stale air and broke into a cold sweat. I will give you a bit of advice, my friend. It's no good to remember the happy past in a miserable present. It only makes the present even more miserable. As dawn was approaching I slept. Then the piercing cry of a klaxon seemed to break me into little pieces before jerking me awake.

Eastlake Penitentiary at the time I was there was as bad as any prison could be, and I doubt it's any better now. Well, on second thought, I've heard of worse prisons in Australia and Africa. And now we have Devil's Island in the tropics and prison hulks in the Thames, and I've heard when you go as a convict to either place it's like going to die as an oarsman on a French galley in the Mediterranean. Until the fleet was put out of business in the middle of the last century, the felons – galley slaves they were called – died quickly of overwork, disease, abuse, and starvation.

When a man slumped and ceased to row, his body was tossed immediately and without ceremony overboard. No one bothered to check whether he was breathing or not. So maybe that Pennsylvania penitentiary was a sanctuary compared to some other places, but if I live to be a hundred I don't want to set foot in it again. The place was infested with mosquitoes in summer and miserably cold and damp in winter. It brutalized every inmate unfortunate enough to be there regardless how strong he happened to be. The prison was over-crowded even then and reeked of putrid odors.

Some of the guards but not all were savages who really enjoyed beating a man senseless. And always they did it in front of the other inmates to teach them a lesson and keep them in line. It seemed to me they never chose a strong man for a beating. It was always the weak and cringing and helpless little man who got the lashes while the rest of us had to look on. The sound of a beating, the agonized cry of terror and pain beyond endurance, was as ugly as the sight of it. Some of those cries still ring in my ears even as I write this. For reasons I don't understand, because a man didn't have to offend to get a beating, I was never beaten. I was struck in the face with a fist once or twice and lost a tooth. I was walloped on the back with a baton but never endured a severe beating in front of other prisoners. Some of the old hands, winking as they spoke, said it was because I looked strong enough to exact revenge.

Well, I'm not one to scheme and plan revenge. I never got in the habit of doing that. Even when as children my big brother would slug me and taunt me and steal my stuff, I never thought of revenge. And I sure didn't go looking for revenge in prison. Maybe one reason is the longer I stayed there the less strong I became. I lost weight as all of us did, and my strength gradually ebbed away even though I'd been sentenced to hard labor and had to work in the blazing sun in summer and the cold in winter. The rations could not sustain a man, and so gradually everyone in the prison grew weaker and weaker.

The food in that place was coarse and poorly prepared and lacking in nutrition. It cut the lining of your stomach and gave most of us bloody stools and diarrhea, and to make matters worse the sanitary system was crude. In every corner of the place, except the warden's office and mess hall, the stench of human waste struck a man's nostrils like a slap in the face. There was talk of building a new sanitary system, and inmates were chosen to work on it, but one delay after another stymied the work. I left with the job unfinished, and I doubt they have a new system even now. Maybe they felt it was part of a convict's punishment to breathe the filthy air.

Men got sick there and died fast, leaving behind their disease as they went. I was told that every hour around the clock at least one skeletal wretch in the horrid place lay dying. And did they throw away his grotesque prison garb when he died? Not on your life! They stripped the corpse of that ugly costume and required new prisoners to wear it. Maybe they washed it before issuing it again but maybe they didn't. Deliberately the warden wanted us to look exactly the same, like drops of water and with no more humanity than a drop of water. But any man trying to escape would stand out in those black and white stripes like a fish out of water.

——— ◦◉◦ ———

For months I languished in a tiny room with a hole for a window. I had to stand on the rickety cot and stretch my neck to look outside, and even then I couldn't see the ground except for a few trees in the distance. It was just as well because men were being treated like beasts of burden on the grounds of the prison, forced to do useless labor until they dropped, then beaten and carried on a stretcher to their cells if they were lucky. If not lucky, they were dragged by the heels and suffered burns and scrapes on their backs. When I began to work outside, I saw four men pulling a heavy cart loaded with machinery. One of them, a very old man, fell exhausted to his knees. The other three waited for a moment for him to get up and pull his share of the load. When he tried to stand and walk but couldn't, they beat him to the ground and left him sprawled in the dirt and bleeding. They were prisoners like him but no longer human. The old man walked in danger wherever he went because the brutes could sense he was weak. He had been assaulted more than once, even in the cell he shared with another old man, and they made his life a living hell.

The guards were often brutal in behavior but so were the inmates. I guess when you're treated like an animal, you begin to act like an animal. Living among dangerous men reduced to animals, I knew I had to be alert at all times. Hardened faces with unblinking steely eyes were everywhere, and yet I felt alone and lonely. I kept to myself and didn't go looking for friends even though I was told a strong companion, especially in the yard, was good to have. When not working I was confined to my cell. Most of the time when I tried to look through the hole that served as a window with no panes, I saw only a patch of sky and quickly learned to read the weather. Once in a heavy rain a bluebird fluttered to the opening. It cocked its head as it perched there and peered inside. Then it tweeted as though frightened and flew away. It was my imagination, of course, but

I'd swear the bird looked at me and shuddered before it lifted off that ledge.

As I had survived the loss of my wife and more than one perilous adventure at sea, I made up my mind to survive the prison stint too. I tried hard to adapt, counting the dreary days as one dissolved into the next, and then I gave up the count as a stupid thing to do. Each day was like the one that went before it. Every morning, just as the sun was coming up, I was rousted from bed by that hideous klaxon to stand in a line of unwashed and smelly men waiting to be seated on rough benches. In the mess hall I ate a watery breakfast that sometimes had the sour taste of spoiled food, and I washed it down with a mug of brave coffee. I can't explain it but even though I hated the smell of coffee, going all the way back to my seafaring days, the prison coffee was fairly good and never failed to jar me awake.

We were given twenty minutes to gulp down breakfast. Then the brawny guards with sticks to prod us hustled us into the work yard. If you poke me right there above the hip, I'll jump 'cause I can still feel the end of that stick in my lower back. In the yard I labored in the heat of the day, or the wind and cold when winter came, to build a new sanitary system with new latrines. But as I said earlier, we never finished the job for reasons I can't remember, or maybe just plain indifference. At noon I rested in the shade in summer or huddled against a wall in winter and drank a watery soup. Half an hour later I was back at work toiling until supper. Allotted half an hour for supper, I ate beans and rice and stale bread and returned to the hard labor of my sentence until I found release in darkness. Within days both hands were covered with blisters. We ate a lot of beans in prison, and they flavored the stale air with gut odors, but for all that I think the beans kept me alive.

I could bathe in the river once a week but couldn't eat as much as my body demanded. The food was greasy and starchy and sometimes tasted of raw fish, but the work made me hungry and I knew if I didn't eat I would sicken and die. I knew also I could die without rest. So I sought comfort on that hard and narrow cot, and because I was dead tired when evening came I had no trouble sleeping. Yet with every day that passed I could feel myself losing weight and becoming weaker. Those around me were suffering the same predicament. Some would vomit soon after eating, unable to keep the rough food down long enough to benefit from it. Others suffered from galloping diarrhea but somehow managed to work, knowing if they didn't they would endure a beating.

Some with bulging, bloodshot eyes and swollen stomachs were not able to work. Too far gone to be beaten, they were skin and bones, cadaverous and confined to their cells waiting to die. Sometimes a kindly inmate, feeling sorry for them and willing to risk a beating, would bring them food and water snitched from the mess hall. The guards were on to that, however, and so most of the time the poor wretches were ignored. The guards paid little attention to any of them until one by one they had to be shuttled out into the yard and tossed into a shallow trench beside the wall. They had come to Eastlake healthy and swaggering in the prime of youth. Their journey ended in a mass grave beside the prison wall.

For an entire year I endured all this, and then one morning when I was eating breakfast in that sullen silence imposed upon us, a guard approached and tapped me on the shoulder with his baton. That's what they called the stick, and they enjoyed poking prisoners in the back, ribs, or buttocks with it.

"The warden wants to see you," he said. "Finish your grub and I'll show you how to get to his office. In fact I gotta take you there."

He wanted me to speak, to break the rule of silence, but doing that meant direct and immediate punishment. I nodded and wolfed down something spongy on my tin tray, wondering how I could have come to the warden's attention. I walked in the guard's direction where he stood leaning against the wall near the door. He pushed me ahead of him down a corridor to the warden's office. We stood in the open doorway, waiting for permission to enter.

The warden, Joseph Bauer, sat behind a spacious desk cluttered with the business of the institution. Saying nothing, he motioned me to come in and signaled the guard to leave. I had seen the warden in his daily rounds but had never stood before him in his office. Prison scuttlebutt had it he was a moody man, and whether he treated you well or miserably depended on his mood. For what seemed a long time he did nothing more than shuffle papers on his desk. Then he looked over his wire-rimmed spectacles and muttered something I didn't understand. I didn't ask him to repeat it. He was silent again for a long time and then spoke clearly.

"I have in front of me," he said, "an order to release you. The jewelry you were convicted of stealing was found recently in a pawnshop in Philadelphia and returned to its rightful owner."

"I hesitate to say it, sir, but I didn't steal no jewelry. I was accused and convicted of stealing a woman's silverware. Without anyone to represent me, I was quickly judged guilty and sent here to serve a sentence of four years. I'm now at the beginning of my second year."

"Well, then, I stand corrected," he replied gruffly but showing no anger. "One idiotic document says jewelry was stolen, another describes your offense as stealing silverware. Either way it makes no difference. The stuff was pawned for half its worth and the thieves never caught. Finding it proves you never stole it. So in a day or two you'll leave this place a free man."

I wish I could tell you my exact feelings on hearing that, but I can't. I guess it's because too many emotions began to swirl around inside me and create a fog of confusion and dismay. I went back to my cell, escorted by another guard, in a curious state of mind. I had heard that in a day or two I would see no more of Eastlake Penitentiary, and yet I wasn't inclined to celebrate the good news whatsoever. I recall I was more bitter than jubilant.

The state of Pennsylvania had convicted me of a crime, had robbed me of all my earthly possessions, had stolen more than a year of my life, and then in time had found me innocent. The question now is what did I receive as payback for all the losses I suffered? When I left that lovely prison, they gave me nothing more than some stiff new clothes, five dollars, and a promise to erase my conviction. I was expected to pick up the tangled threads of my life and weave them expertly into a durable new fabric but with no loom. I didn't receive an apology from anybody, either spoken or written. Even so, I was a free man again and that was no small thing.

Two guards, unlocking the front gate and walking me outside to face the world again, seemed happy to release me. I left that place like another Lot, without looking back even once.

"Go your way now and stay out of trouble," one of the guards said with a broad smile, "and don't go looking for three feet on a cat."

To this day I don't know what he meant by that remark. The other guard was more solemn and more sensible. He advised me to keep my shoes well shined and replace any worn heels, saying a man with good-looking shoes is well regarded in society.

Well, I was bitter for a while and didn't bother to take his advice and let my shoes run down at the heel. In fact the sole of one shoe got a hole in it and every other day or so I had to put a piece of cardboard in the shoe to cover the hole. But I had my freedom again and that was worth more than fancy shoes or new soles and heels. To be honest, it was worth more than a diamond stick pin in a fancy tie or even a thousand dollars.

Now I have this to say and will say no more. You don't really value your freedom until you lose it, and you can lose it when you least expect it. It wasn't a good thing to be charged and convicted of a crime I didn't commit. It wasn't good for an innocent man to waste a full year of his life in a stinking prison. But what happened to me later wasn't a good thing either.

Chapter 11

Into the Free World

Editor's Note. Here I must inform the reader that I, Emily Kingston, will now edit Leo Mack's narrative from notes recorded during numerous conversations with him. As a girl I wrote stories for my own amusement and learned something of the art, and so I'm not exactly a novice as I attempt to complete the work begun by Isaac Brandimore. He would have wanted me to continue the project and make it whole and would have said it's because nature abhors a fragment. I owe a lot to Isaac for doing so much, and so I feel obligated to guide Leo's narrative to a satisfactory conclusion. It pleases me to report that while Leo refused to record in writing the latter events of his life (claiming he no longer had the time to do so), he was willing to talk with me at length over a platter of good food and a mug of hot cider. We met once a week for our gab sessions, as he called them, and all he said in that husky voice of his I found absorbing. Diligently I jotted down his remembrance of things past and will let him go on with his story. – E. Kingston

When I left that dark and dreary prison, it was summer again and the sun was shining brightly in a clear, blue sky. A gentle breeze came from the southeast and birds were chirping. People passing me on the street smiled and nodded as they glanced at me in my new clothes. It was policy in the prison to give a man a new shirt and trousers in summer and also a coat in winter, for everyone knew a man couldn't go into the free world in prison garb. So they gave me a pair of tan trousers, a leather belt to hold them up, and a checkered shirt. Also in my pocket I had five dollars for room and board for a week but no promise of a job of any kind. It was good to be free to walk the streets again, or just sit on a bench and watch the people passing by, some carefree and some miserable. But again I had to make a fresh start, had to rebuild my life after another false start.

I had married early to have a good life with a pretty girl named Caitlin, and we were deeply in love and were happy for a time. I expected to find a good job, settle down in a good place to live, and raise a large family. That didn't happen, however, because my young and delicate wife died shortly after our marriage. Adrift in the community without her anchoring influence, I left Kelly Junction and all my relatives to make my way in a world bigger than I ever expected. For a number of years I was a seaman, returning home eventually with tales of high adventure. Then having saved some money while at sea, I was able to buy a good horse and wagon and finally enough tools to set myself up as a traveling tinker.

At that time I left Norfolk in early summer expecting to go as far as Boston before turning southward again. My plan was to travel the country roads and repair the pots and pans of farm wives along the way. For a while the occupation afforded me a good life. Then one bright day in summer, after completing an excellent job on the cooking utensils of a woman named Rebecca Foley, a job so good she gave me half a pie she had newly baked, I was accused of theft and arrested. Hauled before a judge in the Dutch Amish community of Lancaster County, I was quickly sentenced to four years for a crime I didn't commit. I languished in prison, growing thinner each day, for slightly more than a year. Then suddenly to my surprise, I was released with all charges dropped. The items, pawned by the thieves, were discovered intact in a Philadelphia shop, and that, of course, proved I had not stolen them. All of this you know already, every word of it, but a brief summary never hurt nobody. Now I'm thinking I have to tell you how I almost died of starvation in the city of brotherly love after doing my time in prison.

I had no money, no means of transportation, and no place to live. With little more than the new clothes on my back I wandered the streets of Philadelphia, eyes on the pavement most of the time but looking once in a while at well-dressed people who always seemed to be in a hurry. I could have rented a room for less than a dollar a night, but since it was summer I slept in the public parks and saved my five dollars for food. I didn't want to be arrested again, and so I always found a place away from the beaten path to bed down after dark and be up again at dawn. In a trash can one morning I found a large apple with only one bite from it. I could see clearly the imprint of teeth in the white flesh of the apple, and so I dipped it in a little stream nearby to clean it. I ate it to the core and then ate the core. The apple was sour but juicy and for a time satiated my morning hunger. I told myself I would have to save the few dollars in my pocket for a rainy day. That meant eating whatever I could find, and I soon discovered people visiting the parks with picnic lunches often threw away good food. For several days I lived on discarded scraps of meat and bread and even fruit like an orange now and then and a watermelon not ripe enough for refined tastes. My time in Philly was memorable for its discomfort, and yet at the same time I managed to survive. I was down and out but not dead.

All my life I've had to live with poverty, but any situation denying me a place to sleep or enough to eat had never occurred to me. It was beyond the range of my experience because in Kelly Junction the more fortunate Traveler families usually got around to helping those less fortunate. We viewed ourselves as one big, interrelated family and to some extent we were, being of the same blood and ancestry. That way, and living by our wits, we survived. And now my thoughts went back to the village. I can recall lying flat on my back on the green grass of the park and looking up at the blue sky and looking back at growing up in that community. People were not always kind to one another, and everyone in Kelly Junction took a few knocks in the school of hard knocks, but most of the time someone showed up to help a person who really needed help. I halfway expected that to happen in Philly. It didn't.

Even though they call it the city of brotherly love because its name in Greek means that, I didn't see much love of any kind in that place. The streets were full of bustling people, but indifference ruled the day. I was down and out and needed assistance but no one except the police seemed to notice. When night came I tried to sleep on a bench, but just about every night a policeman swinging a heavy baton rousted me and told me to move along. Sometimes in pouring rain I walked the streets all night. In the dim light of morning I sneaked into a park, crawled under some bushes, and slept the sleep of exhaustion even as the rain continued to fall. Days as long as weeks dragged slowly by, and I became weaker and hungrier than the day before. I felt ashamed for sinking so low even though I told myself I was the victim of a social system that cared little whether I lived or died. I even thought it might be better to be dead than endure the pain and humiliation of being destitute in a wealthy city and being forced to beg. But let me tell you this – as soon as the thought came to me I rebelled against it. I would not become a beggar and I wasn't ready to die either. Reason told me my hunger and pain wouldn't last forever. I had only one life to live and I would live it as long as I could. I would find a way to climb out of my distress.

———————

I still had a few dollars in my pocket, and for more days than I can count I lived on peanuts in the shell bought a pennyworth at a time from a street vendor. The man was tall and swarthy, thin as a rail, dour in manner and appearance, but talkative with an accent I couldn't exactly place. He said his name was Alexander Kouropoulos, and he came to this country from Greece and still had relatives in the old country. His plan was to sell his peanuts in the fine summer weather, and when fall came to find work in a factory or a restaurant. In one section of the city lived Greeks who owned and operated any number of restaurants catering to all classes. He would go to them, plead brotherhood in Greek Philadelphia, and get a job as a dishwasher. He really believed restaurants were eager to hire a good dishwasher, and so for him the future presented no worries at all. In summer he would live each day in the fresh air and sunshine, spit tobacco juice at the pigeons in the park, and enjoy being alive. When the change of seasons brought on problems, he wouldn't waste his time in worry but find a way to solve them. I hesitate to say this, but I believe I took strength from that man.

I'm not sure whether the strength came from his peanuts or from his staunchly resistant will, but somehow my casual friendship with that Greek made me stronger. When my darling Caitlin died so very young and left me alone, I had dark thoughts of self-destruction. That you know and maybe you know also I had similar thoughts when clinging to a pair of oars in a boiling sea in a violent storm. In the throes of the tempest the sea was lovely, dark, and deep. More than once I thought I might give up, slip downward, and sleep. But I didn't feel that way in Philly. In that city of history and culture, I felt only a dull ache in the pit of my stomach. When night came with no secure place to rest, I felt a leaden dread of the dark and what the next day would bring. I felt lonely and fearfully tired but with an insistent will to live and overcome. It was my secret weapon, I guess you might say, my way to survive.

One morning I managed to find behind a grocery store enough thrown-away food to stave off hunger. After gorging on stale buns and pastry and a cantaloupe that was over ripe but not spoiled, I walked with a bellyache into one of those grand neighborhoods that visitors to Philadelphia like to talk about. The street was wide and paved with bricks and even had curbs for water to run away in heavy rain. On either side of the street were sprawling elm trees almost touching each other in the middle of the street and making it look like a tunnel. And everywhere in the neighborhood I saw neat green lawns and flowers. I stopped in front of a very impressive house, summoned my will to act, went up to the massive front door, and knocked. A diminutive young woman opened the door just wide enough for me to see her face.

"I'm looking for work," I said. "I'm a good gardener. I can prune your trees real good, and they need pruning. I can clean out the weeds in your garden and make it look like springtime again."

"I'm only the maid here," she replied with just a hint of a smirk on her pretty face. "I don't know if Master needs a handyman, but I guess I can go and ask."

"Will you, please? He won't find a better handyman than me."

Well, to make a long story short, I worked all afternoon on Master Andrew's estate – I never learned his last name – and when night came I slept in a little room behind the greenhouse. At the end of the day's work I went to the kitchen for a fantastic meal and went to sleep with my belly full for the first time in weeks. I worked in the garden and yard for almost a week, had plenty to eat, and a comfortable cot to sleep in. By the time I left I was feeling like my old self again. I think they liked me in that place, and I know the little maid did. One day when no one was home she invited me to lunch. We ate smoked beef and cheese on warm and toasty bread, a tangy salad with berries and three kinds of nuts, and a tasty dessert. She had placed a finely carved bowl of purple grapes on the table, and they reminded me of the Italy I never saw when I found myself in the middle of a sea disaster that made headlines. I popped a big grape in my mouth, and instantly it put my tongue awash in juice.

Another day just before I left, the maid whose name was Dolly and who was dressed in a crisp pink and white uniform, urged upon me a heavy crystal dish filled to the brim with ripe strawberries. But that's not all. She had dipped the strawberries in melted chocolate, a rich and sweet chocolate. It was a treat I couldn't resist, and it was all I could do to eat only a few. She stood beside my shoulder almost touching me as I ate, and she gave me a tall glass of cold punch. I felt like kissing the girl for all the goodness she was showing, and I probably could have gotten away with it too, but I didn't try. She smiled sweetly when I thanked her and even bobbed a curtsey.

With vivid memories of that girl I went looking for a more permanent job and found one for the rest of the summer. A man named Conrad Barnes, a salesman of farm equipment, hired me to be his assistant. That's when I began to travel again, and that's when I began to feel good about myself all over again. The world looked a lot better just then because traveling is in a Traveler's blood. I had thought when I went to sea, the urge all Travelers have to get to the end of the road would leave me. It never did, and now I had a chance to travel in a wagon again. Barnes was a slightly built man with a large head and hollow chest. He seemed to have too much energy for his thin legs and was always moving even when sitting. We went to a tavern and ate thick summer sausages with beer and bread. The food was simple but good. We talked about the job I would do and all the particulars concerning the job.

"I won't be able to pay you even a living wage," said Barnes apologetically, "but I can tell you one thing, you won't go hungry."

"It sounds good to me. I'm down on my luck at present, and I'll gladly work for food and shelter and your companionship."

"Then I think we can work out a deal agreeable to both. So with a handshake we have an agreement. You won't regret it."

"In time I hope to get back to my roots in the South, but we can travel together. How long have you been selling farm equipment? I'm a tinker by trade myself. I used to have a good horse and wagon and a fine set of tools but ran into some bad luck and lost it all."

"I've had my losses too, friend. I've been doing this job for five and a half years. I had some bad luck too before I started, but slowly I found that work will numb the pain and help one forget."

"Oh, it sounds like you got hit as hard as I did, even harder."

"I don't like to talk about it. My wife and son died of diphtheria. It was not a good time for me but worse for them.

They suffered terribly. They couldn't breathe, couldn't swallow. And then came heart and nerve damage and before I knew it they were dead. We lived in Kansas. I sold everything but two horses and a wagon and got a job traveling for Dorchester Farm Equipment, and here I am."

"Your story, Mr. Barnes, is similar to mine but more tragic. I lost my wife too. We weren't married long enough to have any children. We planned on it, but things didn't work out the way we planned."

"They seldom do. Call me Conrad, my friend, everyone does. I'm sorry you've suffered, but what's done is done and we can't undo the past. Can't forget it either. Just have to live with it. Hey, you ate only two sausages. I've already had three. Take another and have some more beer. We got traveling to do and work ahead of us."

Before night came we were on our way northward. We traveled from town to town all the way to New England. Except for a few small samples, the wagon didn't carry actual equipment. So on rainy nights or any time we felt like it, we could sleep in the wagon. When nights were balmy and warm we slept in the open air among trees in a makeshift camp and ate a good breakfast each morning before leaving. Conrad had sketches of the equipment for sale and complicated paper work to fill out and send to his boss.

He saw to it that a farmer's order with part payment went to the company, and the firm would later ship it with an invoice for money due. He was good with figures, and I was glad of that because in Kelly Junction, though I learned to read and write pretty good, I never got very far with arithmetic before my papa said no more schooling. Every morning, regardless where we slept, we were up bright and early. I remember one morning Conrad sort of turned poetic as he rousted me from sleep. "Now, my friend, while the sun drinks the dew you and I must travel." I guess I liked that 'cause it stuck in memory, and now you have it here.

One thing I can say about Conrad. He went out of his way to feed me well. Later the man even paid me a small salary and bought me new clothes. We visited the homes of comfortable burghers in New York and parts of New England and got a number of good orders. I was able to eat meat and potatoes again, gain some weight, and save a few dollars. In September I said goodbye to Conrad Barnes and went into Boston. I had been there before, had sailed from the port of Boston, and so I knew the town had a lot of Irish residents to make me feel comfortable.

One of my shipmates had told me about a boarding house run by a woman named Helen Hawthorne. He said it was a good place to stay for a man to get on his feet. So I went looking for the boarding house, and a policeman who let me know he was Irish as soon as he spoke told me it was located in a quiet neighborhood within easy walking distance. I went there and signed on for room and board for seven dollars a week. In Philly room and board in a good house cost more. Also Mrs. Hawthorne proved to be a generous and caring woman. She said her boarders would have the best of care through the winter. I felt safe living there. Her sheets were clean and her food was famous for being as good as any in the city.

As soon as I was settled, sharing a room with a man who tended to repeat like a parrot what people were saying at table, I went looking for a job. I spent several weeks looking for work that fall, but with not a single stroke of good luck.

Then finally I got a job as a printer's apprentice. It was dirty work, didn't pay a lot, and stained my fingers something awful. At Mrs. Hawthorne's table I had to explain that my dirty-looking hands were not dirty at all but stained with ink. It was embarrassing to eat with blackened fingers in the company of other boarders, but what could I do? I'm glad to say they accepted my explanation cheerfully. There's one thing I can say about most of the people in Boston: they live and let live. I liked the job all right because it promised something better. I was thinking I would give up traveling, find another wife, and stay in one place.

If I could get past the training, I would have a job to provide me with security for years and years. I knew that a well-trained printer with sound credentials could find a job in any town or city big enough for a newspaper requiring a printing press. I liked Boston and thought I could make a good living there. I wandered through the Irish neighborhoods not far from the tenderloin district and felt at home even though on the weekends people got drunk and disorderly. And the city's business district, not far from the big houses of the rich, boasted broad and airy streets lined with shops that seemed to be flourishing. But in spite of all that promise, after living through the winter as a favored denizen of Mrs. Hawthorne's boarding house, I began to feel restless. After experiencing the approach of spring and feeling the sap rising in my veins, the relentless urge to travel again pricked and prodded me. Irish Travelers are restless people.

Before I leave the boarding house and get on the road moving southward I want to say something about the place. It was not a fancy house, far from it, but the food was abundant and I gobbled it down with gusto. As you know, I survived prison on short and starchy and greasy rations and came close to starving after I got out. Then Conrad Barnes fed me pretty good but nothing like the widow Hawthorne. For dinner we had many kinds of vegetables – squash, white potatoes, sweet potatoes, tomatoes, green corn, spinach, several kinds of beans, cauliflowers, and turnips. The servant girl loaded the table with meat, vegetables, fresh-baked rolls, cranberries, and fruit. We ate cranberries with our meat, and sometimes we had a sweet dessert. For breakfast we had meat and potatoes with fried or scrambled eggs, waffles, and coffee. Sometimes Mrs. Hawthorne put a pitcher of thick white milk on the table, and I always drank a big glass. She had about a dozen people living there, one or two not the prettiest puppies in the litter but all very pleasant.

One person in the house was a woman named Myra Medlock. I want to talk about her, but first I want to tell you about Susan Withers. She was Mrs. Hawthorne's black servant, or maybe just another worker in the house like the cook. She had come to Boston as a runaway slave and had come close to being arrested and sent back to her Virginia plantation. But some people calling themselves abolitionists pleaded with the authorities to let her come into their custody, and because Bostonians have always loved freedom and hated slavery, the abolitionists won their case and found a job for Susan. Not only did she work for Helen Hawthorne, but she lived there in safety as well. About the time I left Boston I heard she was trying to get her whole family off the plantation and out of slavery and into the free and easy life she enjoyed. I never heard whether that ever came about or not.

Now Myra Medlock. If I ever forget the woman, I will never forget her name. It sticks in memory. Myra was tall and plain with wispy dark hair surrounding a thin and pale face, but she had a nice smile. A year or two shy of thirty – I was already

155

in my thirties by then – she was the daughter of a city official and worked long hours in a milliner's shop. Her dark hair was parted in the middle and fell to the nape of her neck in ringlets as I remember. Her cheeks were colored and her eyes expressive but restless. Her sensual lips seemed to me a curious contrast to her straight and severe nose and her rather distant manner. She got her clothing wholesale and dressed more fashionably than the other lodgers and was better educated. To tell you the truth, she affected all the social graces most of the others didn't even come close to having. For some reason or other she took a liking to me and always tried to sit next to me at dinner. I guess she liked my blonde hair and clear skin and the way I talked with an Irish brogue but also with an echo of the Southern accent.

"I do believe you came of late from the Emerald Isle," she said to me one evening, tilting her head close to my ear and speaking in an undertone as if what she had to say was a secret.

I knew the expression Emerald Isle, of course, but somehow it seemed funny coming from her and made me want to laugh. I thought if I didn't concentrate on filling my plate with food I just might explode with laughter and sort of hurt her feelings, and I didn't want to get off on the wrong foot. So looking at a dish passed to me by another boarder, I asked in total and honest ignorance, "What in the world is this?"

I'm sure I heard a girlish giggle, and then she said, "Oh, that's succotash! It's a mix of corn and lima beans and sweet peppers and a some sugar and bacon for flavor. Try some! I think you'll like it."

I put some of the colorful stuff on my plate and passed it on to her. She smiled primly and placed just a little on her plate beside an ebony chunk of pot roast almost floating in brown gravy.

"I like succotash," she remarked, "but I never eat large portions of anything. I do believe a woman is more healthy staying slim."

I noticed she had plenty of meat on that big plate of hers but not many vegetables. I guess she favored meat over vegetables and so do I, and so right away we had something in common, or so it seemed.

"How long have you been in Boston, Mr. ----? Oh, you don't have to answer that! I'm being presumptuous."

"Oh, I don't mind answering any question you ask. My name is Mack, Leo Mack, and I came here only recently but not from the Emerald Isle. I came up from the South and went looking for work and finally got a job with a printer, but I'm a tinker by trade."

"A tinker! A traveling tinker! I've heard of those wonderful souls. It sounds so romantic, traveling from place to place in the fresh air without a care in the world! Tinkers are their own bosses, and they travel with their own tools and sleep in their wagons and do what they like in full control of their time. If I had a house with pots, I would call you over to mend them. I surely would!"

"Well, I'm not a tinker at present. My hands will tell you I'm a printer's apprentice and if I get to be a master printer, I'll probably give up tinkering. Also my tools and equipment were confiscated some time ago and without them I can't follow the trade at present even if I wanted to."

"Oh, that's too bad! I'm sorry to hear that, Mr. Leo Mack, but you'll get new tools and become a tinker again. I'm sure of that! In the meantime, enjoy our city. It's one of the finest cities in all of this country. We have everything that anyone could wish. Perhaps when the weather improves I can show you some of the sights."

"I'd like that, Miss Medlock," I replied, looking downward at my plate. All the talk was interfering with my eating, and already my slab of meat was cold.

"Oh, call me Myra. We don't stand on formalities here."

"Well, Myra," I asked. "What do you do for a living?"

"I am the assistant manager of Flora's Hats and Accessories in one of the new buildings situated on Elmhurst Avenue in the heart of downtown. It's a lovely job and I feel proud to have it. We sell women's hats and garments, and I spend a lot of my time in the shop designing hats and even shaping them into reality with my own fingers. At present our customers are looking for hats with wide brims and artificial flowers. Trends change just about every year."

She spoke with an enthusiasm that seemed a little forced, and I was thinking as I listened that someone had said she worked many hours each day in the milliners' shop. I think I said I'm glad to hear you like your job and then fell silent. She picked at her food, eating all the meat but leaving the vegetables, glanced at me archly for a moment, pushed her chair back, and rose to her full height. She looked down into my face for a moment and left. I didn't mean to do it, but I think I hurt her feelings by not talking more. The next day, however, she was as perky as ever. She spoke of Boston as a progressive city and said she would never want to live anywhere else.

When spring came, Myra Medlock left the boarding house where she had lived for three years and took up with a traveling man. He was a salesman of barbershop supplies, Mrs. Hawthorne told me. He traveled up and down the eastern seaboard by train and by whatever means he could find. In the beginning Myra went with him, but after a few weeks he deposited her in a cheap hotel room in White Plains and later in poor lodgings. She found a job in a shop and looked forward to his arrival once a month. Over time his visits became more and more infrequent and stopped altogether. Later Myra found a schoolteacher, Mrs. Hawthorne informed me in a letter, and married him. Though his income was small, they raised a family of six children. I was glad to hear her life turned out well.

Another boarder was my roommate, Orville Mucker. He never had much to say on his own but often repeated what others said at the dinner table and even when I tried to talk with him head to head. He was a good sort of fellow, as far as I could tell, but anemic and annoying and looking for work as a clerk of some kind and having terrible luck. Maybe no one would hire him because he appeared to have the brain of parrot. At table someone would say, "The President of this country is a confounded blowhard!" Orville would smile his sickly smile, glance around the table to be sure he was heard, and would say, "A blowhard! A confounded blowhard that man is, a blowhard!" He never repeated the words he heard exactly, and yet they always came out of his mouth with the same meaning as when spoken by the other person. I think in all my years of meeting people I never met anyone quite like him.

Still another resident at the boarding house was a freckled young man with copper hair named Alan Berkshire. He worked as a clerk in the Postal Service and seemed to wear the same dark and slightly greasy clothes all the time. He was very thin and his skin was very white, made even whiter by the dark clothes. If you got close to him you could smell a flowery aroma sort of mixed with natural body odor. It came to be known among the boarders as Berkshire's special scent, but no one seemed to know exactly what it was. At table Alan was known as a ravenous eater but never added an ounce to his slim and angular frame. His baritone voice had a way of startling people when they first heard him speak. His utterance seemed too strong for one so slightly built, but he was affable and agreeable and the boarders liked him all right. They found him amusing.

I liked him too, and when I was looking for work he tried to give me some help, but nothing came of it. Myra told me one day that he wouldn't be in the Postal Service for long. She said he was a very talented classical singer and hoped eventually to get to New York and make it big in opera. He was even learning Italian so he could sing opera. Because I left Boston as summer was coming and never went back, I never knew what happened to him. Mrs. Hawthorne wrote to give me all the news of her establishment, and she was chatty about any number of things but never said a word about Alan Berkshire. I thought I might see his name in print but I never did.

In that letter she did speak of Orville Mucker. She said she didn't really want to talk about, but felt I should know because he had been my roommate. And then she came right out and said Mucker died in his sleep one night. She and the maid washed all the clothing on his bed and made it spic and span and fresh-smelling but had a hard time getting a new boarder to sleep in it. It seems no one wanted to sleep every night in a bed where a man died. Also any time a new boarder came to the house, he or she always heard the story the owner was trying her best to stifle. It was all about how Mucker died all peacefully in his sleep but released his bowels and bladder at the moment of death. I guess that's why people thought twice about taking the bed, but things like that happen. People are flesh and blood, soft and squishy, with plumbing.

I never had a problem with Mucker all the time we shared a room. When he began to repeat what I was saying to him, I just stopped talking. I remember he had digestive problems like gas and heartburn, and that caused him to belch a lot, but I do a little belching myself from time to time, and so it didn't bother me all that much. His belching and passing wind were not pretty sounds but human. The doctor who examined Mucker said he died of "congenital heart disease," whatever that means, and went quietly.

I can't say I was sorry to hear of his death because I didn't know him very well. That applies to most of the people I lived with in the Hawthorne boarding house. They were pleasant and I liked their chatter at table, and I do remember most of them after all these years, but I never got to know any of them all that well. Anyway, it was a good experience living there, and true to her promise Mrs. Hawthorne looked after her boarders carefully all through the winter and fed us well. Then when spring came some of the restless souls, including me, made plans to leave and drifted away in different directions. That left her with empty rooms and with the expense of advertising for suitable people to fill them. At the time I left she was angry and frustrated, declaring that no woman in her position should have to suffer as she was suffering. Too many people had decided to leave at the same time and for no reason other than wanderlust.

Chapter 12

Urban Adventures

You are probably wondering why I quit my job and left Boston as soon as the warm weather came, and I will tell you. For one thing, the job didn't turn out the way I hoped it would. I was apprenticed to a leathery old German named Hugo Meyer. The man knew everything anyone could ever know or want to know about the trade, and he was a good teacher too. I liked working with him. He never talked much and when he did, it was only to mumble something half in German and half in English. I didn't understand much of anything he said, but when it came to teaching he talked with his hands. I mean he showed me exactly how to choose type and how to set it, and I was making good progress. Then one day he didn't come to work. The boss sent a boy to the tenement where Hugo lived, and the boy pounded on his door. When he got no response, he went back to the boss to say no one seemed home.

After lunch Boss Williams sent a couple men over to see if Hugo was sick. The landlord let them in with a master key, and they found him dead. He had died in his sleep just like Orville Mucker in my boarding house sometime later. I had never heard of people dying in their sleep before and never since. Maybe it was something in the water. It looked like he thrashed around in the bed quite a bit, maybe in pain, and then gave up the ghost and died. The company lost its master printer and a few days later I lost my job.

They couldn't keep me on at any kind of wage until they could find a replacement for Hugo, and so they had to let me go. I felt bad about losing that job. Built into it was the dream of becoming a master printer like Hugo and having nothing to worry about for the rest of my life. Well, it didn't happen that way and I felt bad that Hugo Meyer went so sudden like. But I guess he had a good life even though he lived alone and had no friends. I heard he was fifty-one when he died. His shoulders were hunched, his face pallid, and he walked with a limp. He looked older than that.

From Boston with enough money to last me through the summer I went on down to New York City. I'm a hick from the backwoods of the South and I know it, but I figured any number of people in New York were no better off than me. Also I knew about thousands of Irish Americans living there, and weren't they my brothers? There's an old saying among the Irish. It claims we are the children of one mother 'cause no other mother would have us. There's some truth in that 'cause everyone knows the Irish are an ornery lot. But all this puts me off track. I was about to explain why that big city called New York has so many of us. And Boston has many too.

Periods of famine brought thousands of Irish men and women to this country. By the time I was trying to find a steady job and maybe a female companion they made up maybe a third of the population of Boston, New York City, Philadelphia, and Baltimore. New York had the largest number, and so I didn't have any trouble at all blending in and finding a place to live in the Bronx. The city had Irish neighborhoods all over – in Brooklyn, Queens, and Staten Island – but I preferred the

Bronx because it's close to Manhattan. I didn't want to live isolated from other ethnic groups, and so in my spare time – well, to be honest, all my time at that time was spare time – I started exploring the city. It was summer and I'd leave my room early in the morning and walk mile after mile being curious and stopping to look at anything that caught my eye.

One day I went through the commercial district all the way to Mulberry Street in lower Manhattan. The street was listed on maps of the area as early as 1755, and in all the years it's been in existence it has teemed with people. It goes right through the middle of Little Italy, and walking that portion of the street I had to be careful not to bump into another pedestrian or step on someone's heels. In all my life I've never seen so many people, mainly Italians from Italy and Sicily, crowding the street and sidewalks. Most of the time I had to dodge wagons, carts, horses, dogs, goats, and children as I moved along. On the edge of the sidewalk were green grocer stalls tended mainly by women, and children of all ages were everywhere.

Scores of men didn't seem to be doing anything whatever except standing in the street with their hands in their pockets and talking about the weather. Every swarthy man I saw wore a mustache and a hat and dark clothing in need of a good cleaning. The women were all in short sleeves but wore long and colorful skirts with aprons, and barefooted children ran about in the street playing games. One little boy with long hair was running through the crowd chasing after a hoop rolling fast in front of him. He wore only a dirty shirt that barely covered his belly button and buttocks. Two young men were throwing pennies at a line in the dirt (a gambling game my ancestors played in Ireland), and two boys grabbed apples from a vendor's cart and ran with them. The street was noisy and congested with a hullabaloo of sounds and strange odors that came for all directions. I had to be careful not to breathe what I didn't know too deeply.

Another time in September I went to Mulberry Street to participate in the festivities surrounding the Feast of San Gennaro. The celebration began a few years back as a one-day religious ceremony. It was put on by immigrants from Naples to continue the tradition of paying homage to their patron saint. Then overnight it became a fair lasting three days and more. Mulberry Street was the center of the celebration, and it was closed to traffic for the occasion. The festival featured hot sausages with cheesy bread, parades honoring the saint, street vendors selling food and souvenirs, games and trinkets for children, Italian pastries that melted in your mouth, and other attractions. I was there to gawk at the Grand Procession that came near the end of all the festivities. In the colorful procession, the saint's statue was carried from one church to another down Mulberry Street. The faithful tossed coins in a container at his feet while others kissed his outstretched hand. I liked being there in the midst of all the activity, and I thought about the Naples I planned to visit when the *Sea Cloud* docked there, but as you know, the original crew of the ship never got to Naples. After the inquiry at Gibraltar, I heard some strangers formed a crew to take her there.

The southern end of Mulberry Street merges into New York's Chinatown, and of course I had to go there and spend a couple of days jostling the hordes of people on the sidewalk and soaking up the atmosphere of the place. I think I stood out like a sore thumb in Chinatown because of my height and fair skin, but the Chinese are polite people and made me feel at home. If they noticed me (and I'm sure they did) they didn't show it. They just went about their business and left me to go about mine as I looked at the buildings and window displays and all the street activity. Little eateries along the way were serving up scallion pancakes, wonton soup, fried dumplings, tapioca bubble tea, taro-filled sticky buns, candied crabs, and more. It was clear to me the Chinese love to cook and live to eat, and yet I didn't see fat women as I did among the Italians.

The street was crowded with green grocers, butcher stores, fishmongers, vendors of live animals like geese and goats, and above the street was an array of brightly colored signs in Mandarin. People on the pavement were speaking Mandarin or Cantonese or whatever, and I felt like I was in a foreign country. It was a noisy place and smelly but it dazzled my senses. I stopped to sample some of the food. It was cheap and good. Once or twice I got jostled and thought of pickpockets, but I had nothing they could pick and must have been a disappointment. I heard about the Lunar New Year Chinatown celebrates with eye-popping parades every February. An old man touched my arm and asked in broken English if I wanted to visit an opium den. I politely declined and made my way back to my room in the Bronx and slept like a stone from all the walking I did.

When September came, I had to think about moving on down to a warmer climate and finding a job. I liked being in New York for the summer and not having to work or worry about a thing, but now the money was running low. I didn't want to find myself somewhere in winter with no job and no place to sleep and nothing to eat. Just the thought of that, after almost starving when I got out of prison, made me shudder. So near the end of the month with all my belongings in a rucksack I hitched a ride on a military caisson headed for Washington.

With mention of that caisson, maybe you thought you didn't hear me right but you did.

They were a convoy of vehicles moving southward to the capital to participate in some kind of military exercise for the benefit of the politicians that like to be entertained at government expense. I was straggling along beside the road, struggling with the weight of my rucksack, and a soldier asked if I wanted a ride. Of course I gladly accepted his offer, and to keep a low profile I hopped on the back of the caisson. I didn't even know what a caisson was until they told me it was a cart for hauling ammunition. They bellowed with laughter and claimed it could blow at any minute. I took it to be a joke and didn't move an inch and got a free ride for a good long distance.

You probably want to know what I thought of Washington. It's a pretty city with a lot of imposing buildings but a bit too grand for me. And I never did have much use for politicians. They claim their only reason for living is to help the people they represent, but I'm pretty sure most are there to help themselves. I remember the local politics back in Kelly Junction and I know how nasty the wheeling and dealing got to be at times. Even in a place like that we had a cockalorum – that's a word my grandma taught me – who went about telling everybody else how they were to live their lives. Well, that wouldn't be so bad if you didn't have to pay money to be told how to live, but even in Kelly Junction we paid taxes.

The politicians were always into graft and corruption and just plain old greed. Oh, I guess you could say it was on a smaller scale than in a city like Washington, but it's still the same. As an Irish Traveler, I know for sure how some of them self-important little men, swaggering around in fancy clothes, fleeced even their own mamas and laughed about it. Oh, they lived high on the hog until someone smarter took them down.

It happened all the time in Kelly Junction and around the clock in Little Italy, and though I never learned much about the Chinese, probably in Chinatown as well. The politician's cast of mind just ain't the same as yours and mine.

But you wanted to know whether I liked Washington. I can't say I despised that well-planned city with all its fancy buildings that look like they were shipped over from ancient Greece, but I was glad to leave it before the weather got cold. However, instead of going on southward, I decided to do a little backtracking. I got to thinking I wanted to go back to Baltimore. I had been in that port city years earlier but never saw much of the place. On the waterfront when I was young and seeking a way of life other than being an Irish Traveler, I had sold my horse and wagon and boarded a ship for New York hoping to become a seaman. So maybe nostalgia took be back to Baltimore, or maybe I was feeling I needed a partner in life and could find her there. I don't recollect exactly what my feelings were at that time, but I do know along about then I was beginning to think I should settle down and maybe start a family.

And you guessed it, I was feeling kind of lonely too. In the midst of all the crowds in Chinatown and Little Italy I felt lonely. I was a solitary traveler enjoying myself but not sharing the good times with anyone else. All the people around me seemed to be in groups joshing each other with give and take and having fun together. I knew I didn't belong there with my fair skin and blue eyes and light brown hair, and all that sweaty being together made me feel even more like an outsider. I remember a funny little girl in Mulberry Street. She was dressed all in white and came running up to me and caught my hand and looked up into my face. Well, to judge from her reaction I might have been a monster or an ogre.

Suddenly aware of her mistake – I was not her papa – she let out a frightened, high-pitched little cry and scurried away like a rabbit. That incident was sort of painful and got me to thinking. Could it be I was wasting my life?

I've always liked children. So maybe I needed to meet a compatible young woman, settle down with her, and raise a family. I needed an uncomplicated person from the working class, but who would want to marry a drifter, even a good-looking one, without a job? And even if I could find her, how would I support her? I had to find an occupation before looking for a woman, and Baltimore seemed as good a place as any to begin my search. I really wanted to be a tinker again, but that's not a good job for a family man. You have to be away from home long hours every day, and also the city is not a good place for a tinker unless he has his own shop like a tailor or cobbler and shelter for his horse. Starting the trade in a city would mean finding a shop, buying equipment, and advertising with money I didn't have with the hope of getting customers.

So I got to thinking I would have to work for someone else. For an Irish Traveler that's really something to think about. For two or three centuries the Travelers have worked for other people but only for a short time before moving on to another job. And always the Traveler made it clear to his customer that he was self-employed and his own boss. That way he was sort of like a company performing a service and not a worker. Working for someone else meant doing it every day and following the rules, and the Travelers never did that sort of thing. Now it looked like I might have to break tradition and try to get work on a construction crew. New buildings were going up all over in Baltimore, and they were not sprouting on their own like spring flowers. Hundreds of men, day laborers mostly, worked with might and main to build them, and I was thinking I could be one of them. The pay was low, I heard, but the work was steady.

Every morning at daybreak, on the corner of Calvert and Conway, the men huddled in a crowd to be chosen by a straw boss for the day's work. I went there near the middle of October to be one of them. The mornings were already cold, but nobody seemed to pay much attention to the weather. A man stood on a wagon to pick the strongest-looking blokes, and day after day I stood and waited and never got chosen. Then just as I was ready to call it quits my luck changed. I went out to a construction site and worked hard all day at what they told me to do. At the end of the day the foreman called me aside and said if I didn't mess up, I had a job for as long as the project lasted. I had to find a room nearby so I could walk to work, and I stayed on that job all through the fall and winter. It wasn't easy working outside in the winter even in Baltimore. Some workers got frostbite and lost a toe or two, but it made me tough and I saved my wages and felt pretty good about the way things were going. I even had time to eye the girls in the neighborhood, particularly a waitress I met in early spring.

I was standing outside a shop on Barker Street on a Sunday afternoon when she strolled by with a girl friend. I could tell they were sort of looking at me as they approached, and so I tipped my cap to them and smiled. I guess they felt safe being together like that, and so they stopped to banter for a minute or two. They hoped to present themselves as clever young ladies trilling an avalanche of witty comments to impress a lonely Irishman. Well, I didn't mind playing their little game and so I went along with them. As they were casting sharp eyes on me I was looking them over too.

We talked for a while, they doing most of the talking, and I began to pay more attention to the tall and thin one. She said her name was Justine Ryan, and she looked to be near twenty. I knew right away she had Irish blood in her veins just like me. But unlike mine, they looked slightly blue under her thin and delicate skin. We hit it off pretty well and she even told me where she worked. In fact she was telling me so much about herself the other girl tugged at her sleeve as a kind of warning, and they went on down the street.

I didn't think much about that little meeting until several days later. It was just one of those things, I thought, between a guy and a couple of girls and one girl flirting while the other was advising caution. Then I remembered the one called Justine told me she worked in a small restaurant nearby. I thought it might be nice to drop in some evening for a meal and find her working. Maybe she could take my order, and then I would slyly speak her name and ask if she remembered me. It would be a hoot to surprise her that way even if she didn't remember me. Well, sad to say, I couldn't remember the name of the restaurant, couldn't remember she had even told me the name. But it had to be somewhere near the shop on Barker Street, and I asked the seamstress there if she knew of the restaurant.

"Of course I know," she said. "It's maybe the best eatery we have in this neighborhood coz the other one is mainly a bar."

"Will you tell me the name of the place? I have a fierce hankering for some good food and would like to try it."

"I won't promise you'll get good food there. I just said it's better than the bar where most of the men folk go mainly to drink. If they eat anything in that bar, they're probably too boozy to taste it."

"I'm not a drinking man, ma'am, and so I'm not interested much in the other place, just the one where a girl named Justine works."

"Oh, Justine! You know her? She comes in here to buy ribbons. Pretty girl, and works at Marley's. That's the name of the place, Marley's. It's on Third Avenue just a couple blocks from here."

I thanked the woman kindly and went straight to Marley's, but I got there too early for dinner and didn't see Justine. Later I had better luck, and she came to my table and before I could say a thing she said with that little laugh I noticed when I first met her, "I know you. We chatted one Sunday afternoon at the fabric shop."

Well, I can tell you I was surprised to hear her say that. I thought she would pretend she didn't know me even if she did. But she recognized me right away and chatted non-stop all the time she was jotting down my order on her little yellow pad. Then when she came to my table with food and a pot of coffee she smiled a sweet little smile and flounced away. I couldn't help but notice her skirt swirled gracefully from her hips, and I liked looking at her.

So I got in the habit of going there to eat my supper when work was over. Just about every day she was on duty. She saw me come in and knew I was there but pretended to be too busy to notice. I sat looking at her slender and pretty moving from table to table serving her regular customers. In time she came to me, holding that little yellow pad in long, tapered fingers and ready to write something on it. Even though she was sort of moody most of the time, she tried hard to be pleasant and a cautious flirtation got underway. When she took my order one evening, wetting her pencil to make the writing blacker, I mentioned how pretty she looked. She tossed her curls, smiled, and began to move away. I grew bolder.

"I'm wondering if maybe we can walk together when your shift is over. Do you think you might like a little stroll in the night air?"

"Why would you ask me that?" she demanded, attempting to show a mix of surprise and disapproval. "We spoke briefly on the street one Sunday afternoon when me and Alice were out for a bit of fresh air, and that's absolutely all I know about you. I see you here all the time, but I don't really know you from Adam!"

"You know I come here to eat the best food in town," I said with a chuckle, trying to flatter but not overdo it. "You know I'm a well-behaved fellow. You never saw me drunk or disorderly, and I never cause any trouble at all when I come here to eat."

"I really can't talk about personal things, y' know. It's against the rules in the workplace. My boss would fire me on the spot if he heard me talking to a fellow about personal stuff. Also my papa tells me never to get chummy with any of the men that come in here, no matter how good looking they happen to be. So I'm just gonna take your order and forget we talked."

As she was speaking she pretended to write something more on her little yellow pad. A beefy, bullet-headed man behind the counter was sort of glaring at her, and I took him to be the boss. I didn't want to get her fired or in trouble, and so I backed off.

"Well, it was just an idea. Just thought it might be fun to walk and chat. Maybe some other time."

I expected her to turn on her heel and walk away, but she spoke in spite of her boss. "You seem real nice but that's all I know."

"Then you'll walk with me to know me better?"

"I don't mind," she replied curtly. "I guess it can't hurt."

"When do you get off work?"

She was moving toward the kitchen and didn't answer. "I'm off at nine," she said as she returned with my supper. "If you meet me out front, we can walk and talk but I have to be home by ten."

Justine Ryan looked young and pretty as she moved from kitchen to table balancing bowls and plates on a big tray. I liked to look at her in motion, and though she spoke with a nasal twang I liked the way she talked. Maybe it was the natural instinct of a young man that made her so attractive, but that I don't know. I do know she had a warm and sensual quality about her that seemed to speak to me. Well, I was lonely and I liked her and we can let it go with that. I ate my food in silence, ate slower than usual I think, left a generous tip, paid my bill at the counter where her boss collected the cash, and left. Outside I waited for her in a steady drizzle and felt a little thrill of excitement when she finally appeared. We went to a small café near the park and talked for an hour.

"Oh, I must go!" she cried in a flurry as the clock struck ten. "Papa will be worried, and I just can't afford to get home late. He's a good man but has a bad temper and he can be very strict."

"Will I see you again?"

"Of course, silly! I have to work, don't I? And you have to eat."

Her slender fingers were fumbling with her coat. I helped her put it on. "You won't let on to the others we talked, will you? I mean the girls I work with? They can be so catty at times and they just love to gossip. If they really wanted to, they could get me in trouble."

Before I could respond, saying I wouldn't breathe a word to anybody, she threw her cloak around her shoulders and sort of melted into the darkness like shadows melt when a day gets cloudy.

I expected a backward glance from her, maybe even a fleeting smile, but that didn't happen. I went back to my place wondering if that hour with Justine was the start of something good or something not so good. In a way the lonely heart is a hunter.

Chapter 13

Justine and Merry

That's how the thing with Justine Ryan began. How the relationship ended you probably don't want to know, and I'm not sure I want to tell you. But now that I'm into it I suppose I can go on with it. When my friend at work – his name was Colin – heard I was prowling the streets to find a woman, he was certain I was going soft on my morals and looking for a whore. Colin is something of a skittish guy, high-strung you might call him, and so he came to my room to warn me to be careful. He said the ladies of the evening in Baltimore are famous for venereal diseases and no good for a workingman. I had to tell him right away that while I might have been looking for a bit of forbidden gratification, I was not and had never been in the market for a professional. He uttered a few words of relief and I made us a pot of coffee. We drank it hot and steaming beside the window and had some day-old muffins with it and chatted.

"So what's going on with you, Leo?" he asked. "It seems you're frustrated and lonely like half the men we know at work, but you gotta be careful, old boy, very careful with the girls in this town."

"I know I'm obliged to be careful, Colin. You don't need to tell me that. But the time comes when a man can't stand it no longer and has to rush out and speak to the first woman he comes across. Well, I didn't do exactly that but it's the gist of it."

"You met her on the street or in a shop? Where exactly?"

"I think it was outside a chandler's shop, but she said later it was a place that sold fabric mainly to women. It was a Sunday afternoon and she was out strolling with another girl, and I tipped my cap as they came near me, and they stopped to exchange a few friendly remarks. Flirty small talk, you know, and she did most of the talking. I found out she worked as a waitress in a little eatery nearby."

"And then you became her best and most generous customer!"

"Well, not exactly, Colin. But you're not totally wrong either. It's a cheap little restaurant catering to poor people, and so it didn't cost a lot to eat there. I went there to see her shortly after we met and was there a few days ago. I was feeling miserable, and so I asked the girl if she would care to walk with me when she finished her shift."

"And of course she said Yes. What else could she say to a handsome bloke like you?"

"She was defensive at first, said her father would disapprove and said she didn't cotton to walking in the rain. I said it was only a drizzle. She laughed and agreed to chat in a little café in another neighborhood. We were there an hour. She seemed to enjoy herself but said her father was very strict and required her to be home no later than ten. Then before I knew it she was gone in the night."

"So what happened later, Leo? Did you go back to the restaurant the next day? Did you decide to have all your meals there?"

"No, I didn't decide on nothing of the kind, but I did look into her background. I found out where she lives. I talked with

177

people who know her. They told me her mama is dead and her papa is a cobbler and she lives with him, just the two of them."

"So what do you want out of this?"

"All I want is a little female companionship. If it leads to something else, well y' know that's all right too. As the saying goes, a man can't live by bread alone, and I've been alone for a long time."

That was all I said to Colin about the girl, not because I didn't want to talk more about her but because the construction project ended and we went our separate ways, and I never saw him again. I was out of work for a while, but during the summer I got a job as a house painter. I worked first with a painting crew and found out it's mainly just hard work not requiring a lot of brains.

So I bought a painter's ladder and some brushes and started working on my own after advertising in the local paper. Because my estimates came in lower than the competition, I got all the work I could handle. Then after work me and Tina – that's what she wanted me to call her – began to see each other just about every day. By the end of summer she was hinting she might leave home and live with me if her papa didn't stop yelling at her. I didn't know at the time what she really wanted was to leave a job that kept her on her feet ten or more hours a day six days a week. I thought she was falling in love with me and wanted to be with me, but the job was the main reason. It was threatening her health.

One evening Tina came over to my place unannounced and not expected. I had worked hard all day and was tired and needed rest, but there she was. She had never been in my room before, had always refused to be alone with me. I gave her my address not long after we met and asked her to come around, but she always said her papa wouldn't allow it. Now when I opened my door she covered her face with her gloved hands and sort of squealed, "Hello, there! Guess who!" Well, I don't have to tell you no guessing was needed. Even though I couldn't see her face or even her body plainly, I knew her voice and the moment I heard it I was no longer tired.

She was standing in shadow in a dark gray coat that went to her ankles, covering her face and giggling. After work she had changed into a dress more suitable for summer than fall, and I could see when the coat was off it accented her slender frame and made her look real good. She wore some rouge to make her pale cheeks look more rosy, and her hair wasn't pulled back straight, like when she was working, but was all fluffy and abundant. Of course I invited her inside, making a joke I don't remember now. Her laughter was sort of shrill and metallic but not disagreeable, and all we did was talk. That was the beginning of the cozy evenings we had together in my room, but never more than two hours at a time.

After several days, when the talking dwindled down to almost nothing, we sat in front of the fire and just looked at the flames. Because it seemed like the right thing to do, I put my arm around her and tried to kiss her. Well, I didn't get very far. Later I think she took pity on me and allowed me to hold her gently in my arms. Then I got a kiss on the cheek, but anything beyond that was off limits. She told me she thought being intimate with a man was necessary to start a family, and maybe show affection in marriage, but any other time it was just plain indecent. She admitted she didn't go to church but labeled physical love out of wedlock as something animals did and downright disgusting. Pursing her thin lips and wearing a funny little frown, she cautioned me not to speak of such things in her presence. I really believe her papa had taught her well.

I wanted to meet her papa. I thought if I could talk with him and let him get to know me, maybe we could become friends. I'm Irish, I told her, and so is he. I'm a workingman and so is he. So where's the problem? Well, each time I brought up the subject she found excuses, saying he was a hard man to know and not likely to accept a younger man. She said he worked fifteen hours a day, always had dirty fingernails, and was always grumpy and tired. He didn't bathe often enough, wore the same clothes every day, and had a strong body odor and bad breath.

Also he ate spicy foods and beans and broke wind backwards. Well, she didn't say that exactly. She said primly, beating around the bush, "Well, you know about spicy foods!" He drank a little gin now and then, and that made his breath stink, she said in a dainty sort of way, even though he never got sloppy drunk. Well, after a few weeks I met Oliver Ryan in a public place, and he seemed to fit her description exactly. The meeting didn't go well. He bluntly said I was not welcome in his home. Yet for reasons I couldn't quite understand, he didn't object to his daughter visiting a man he despised.

In time we began to talk about marriage, and the more we talked about tying the knot, the more reluctant I became. I had decided to go looking for a girl to marry, thinking I might have better luck with a second marriage than with the first, but even though I liked Tina there was something about her that called for caution. I couldn't put my finger on it, but something just didn't sit right. She pretended to be an innocent girl swept off her feet by a handsome Irishman, but at times I caught glimpses of street knowledge that went beyond innocence. I believed she was listening to that cranky old man, her papa, and of course I couldn't blame her. He was a man of the world, a businessman dealing every day with people who tried to swindle or cheat him. He told his daughter to keep her treasure chest securely locked or risk having its contents spill into muddy water. I can imagine even now the instruction he gave her.

"Don't you dare give the key to nobody, not to any bloke that just wants a fling. You'd be plain crazy to do that, girl. If you're getting serious with that house painter, you gotta hold out for matrimony."

"Yes, Papa, you know I won't do nothing rash."

"You'd better not! If you do, I'll disown you right out!"

Well, summer came and went and the house painting went with it. Again I was out of a job and feeling anxious. I found a few odd jobs to keep me afloat during the fall, but they dried up when winter came. I was out of work again with no prospects. Maybe that's why I didn't want to think seriously about marriage but Tina persisted. In little ways she let me know she liked me, maybe even loved me, but if I wanted anything more than a kiss now and then I would have to think about marriage.

"No hanky-panky, y' know," she would say when I got a little frisky. "We can't do a thing without a wedding."

"Oh, come on now! Listen to your heart!" I would say. "Follow your feelings, pretty girl. I know you better than you know yourself. You are just as driven as I am."

"P'raps so, but little you know!"

Not about to cross the stern line her papa had drawn in the sand, she was determined to hold out for marriage. But even if I knew for certain I loved her, which I didn't, I couldn't marry without a steady job. I tried explaining that to her, but she didn't seem to understand. So after a few months we reached a stalemate and things between us sort of stood still, and though she said her feelings hadn't changed one bit she didn't come to my place very often any more.

You are wondering now how I got through the winter. Well, Tina talked to her boss at the restaurant, the beefy man with the bald head, and he gave me the lowest job in the house, washing dishes. Of all the jobs I ever had that one was the worst. They brought the dirty dishes in from out front and dumped them in a big tub. I had to take them out of the tub and scrape the crud off and drop them into scalding hot water. Then wearing rubber gloves I plunged my hands into the water and suds and scrubbed them with a brush. The next step was to put them in more hot water for rinsing and then on a rack for drying. I didn't mind the dishes all that much, except for scraping the crud off, but washing greasy pots and pans in a hot kitchen was a little more than I could take. As a tinker I loved working with pots and pans, but now I was beginning to hate the very sight of them. I didn't make enough to keep a bug alive, and any time I had a little spare time I looked for other work. The only good thing about the job was the food. It was certainly not the best in the city, and the workers never got the quality stuff like a good steak, but on my shift I had enough to eat and never went hungry.

When winter lost its hold and the weather warmed again, I went back to house painting. The kitchen boss, the chef as he called himself, was always nagging me to work harder and faster. After a while he got on my nerves, and I was glad to get out of there. Back to painting houses I could set my own hours and work in the sun and see Tina more often. On her one day off if the weather was good, we took long walks together. We talked and laughed and enjoyed a bottle of wine with good food as a special treat. She told me stories of her childhood, happy stories mostly though some were gloomy. She grew up on the south side of Baltimore in a rough neighborhood. Coming home from school, three boys tried to assault her. She managed to get away and told her parents, but they couldn't do anything about it. The police said it happened all the time, and it was just something a girl had to put up with until she got a husband.

At thirteen she was yanked out of school to work in the cobbler's shop. Soon afterwards her mother died of cholera, leaving her as the only assistant to the old man. At sixteen she wanted to become a ladies' hairdresser and cosmetician but her papa claimed the training was too expensive and wouldn't pay for it. So in a huff – she had a temper even then – she left his shop and worked for a time in a shop run by two women. Later she became a waitress, and that job she didn't like at all. It was hard on her feet and back. The hours were too long (often more than ten a day) and the pay too low. Customers would sometimes embarrass her or be rude to her, and the boss always stood up for them. And so it went on and on. She was naturally a very talkative person, liked to talk. But she could be quiet as a mouse at times, and I took that to be a good sign. Maybe she was more thoughtful than she appeared to be.

I married Tina at the end of August. In a brief civil ceremony with only her gruff and silent father attending, Justine Ryan became Mrs. Leo Mack. She had no money for a fancy wedding dress. Even in those days wedding dresses and all the stuff that went with them cost a lot of money, and her papa was too stingy to open his wallet. So even though she merited the symbolism of a flowing white gown, she went to her wedding in a pea-green dress she sometimes wore on Sundays. At the ceremony she was crispy clean, radiant, smiling, demure, and seemed happier than she had ever been. She squeezed my hand as we said our vows and whispered she would live her life for me. I believed her and nodded I would do the same. Back on the street and waiting for a cab, she wore white and pink flowers from dear Papa and a golden wedding band from me.

We drove to a hotel overlooking the harbor and had a festive wedding dinner. It was most enjoyable. The food was good and Papa relaxed and wished us well. He toasted us with his glass of red wine and even chuckled at times. Then Papa left us and for three days we remained in the hotel to savor our honeymoon. With eyes only for each other, we lived in a hazy dream world. It was raining most of the time, and so we had no reason to go outside. The harbor from our fifth-floor window reminded me of my days at sea. It was full of activity and color even on a rainy day. At night it was shiny and tranquil with night birds flitting across the water. In our room in the big and comfortable bed, we made love and slept until noon and rang for room service to bring us lunch.

The honeymoon over, we had to come back to the real world again and it was nothing like the world we had lived in for three days. The first problem we had to solve was where to live. In a working-class neighborhood of old houses, we found two plain rooms and a kitchen that would become our home for a year. Tina was guardedly pretty in the soft autumn light but soon began to look tired and worn. She confessed she was suffering from migraine headaches that came on without warning and robbed her of sleep. During the honeymoon with nothing to worry about they went away entirely, but now they were back and more painful than ever. It was a condition she had lived with for a long time, beginning shortly after she began work as a waitress. Because I thought I was doing the right thing, I assured her she could quit any job that was hurting her health and depend on me for support. I would work for the both of us, and she could stay home and be a housewife like other women.

She smiled wanly, kissed me on the cheek, and reluctantly went off to work. I spent the day painting my last house of the season. I figured it would take three days to finish the job, and then I would have to look for something else to do. Even in Baltimore, unless the season happened to be unusually mild, the climate wouldn't allow house painters to work through the winter. That's when I realized I was in a seasonal job and really needed year-round work. When I got home again, Tina was in the kitchen fixing supper. We had beef stew with carrots and potatoes and biscuits. I had to put some salt and pepper in the stew to spice it up a bit, but it was a good and tasty stew and filling. We ate it laughing and talking about our day, and I cleaned up afterwards. Then we drank the hot tea she had brewed and talked about how to make our lives good. It didn't matter the rooms had battered furniture, no carpeting, an alcove for a kitchen, and dingy windows fringed with stained curtains. We had each other and we thought we loved each other and nothing else mattered.

Tina quickly made friends with our landlady, giving her personal information just a little warped. What I mean is she gave the woman a fancy and false account of where and when we were married and what I did for a living. I could see she was inventing stories to tell, but if that gave her pleasure it was all right with me. She developed a keen interest in gossip and told me all about the woman who ran the house and the lodgers living in their rented rooms. I was glad to see my wife making friends with people near us but didn't care for the landlady all that much. She was a stout and coarse woman with a flat nose, bad teeth, yellow hair, and wrinkles. I guess she was about fifty but looked older. Justine didn't mind her looks and said she was interesting and helped her stave off boredom. Sometimes my new wife complained when I came home all sweaty and smelly, but seemed to like me just fine most of the time. However, she put her foot down and resisted when I began to experiment on how cheap we could eat without damaging our health. I will tell you about it.

First, I went to vegetarianism and discovered the lentil. It was high in protein and could be made into a rich and nourishing soup. Tina liked the taste of it, especially when boiled with onions, and for a time we made it a staple of our diet. Then I found I could buy a bucket of grease from a nearby restaurant for only a few cents, and later Tina brought it home from her workplace for nothing. We heated it almost to boiling, poured it into bowls, let it simmer in its own heat, and dipped chunks of tough bread in it. The bread soaked with hot grease had a meaty taste and filled the stomach. However, at times the dark brown grease had a metallic taste and flavors of fish, foul, beef, and pork all mixed together. Tina tried eating the greasy bread, liked it at first, but soon pronounced it disgusting. She preferred bread and butter, especially with a dollop of jam, but butter was expensive and jam was a luxury.

Coals were expensive too, and our little fireplace had only a feeble flicker throughout the winter. Sometimes we burned chunks of wood in the kitchen stove to stay warm, and sometimes we went to bed before bedtime just to get out of the cold. It was not a warm winter, and the New Year came in with a blast of cold air that rattled the old, ill-fitting windows. Though she complained of the cold and bad weather, Tina worked through the winter when I couldn't find work. I went out looking just about every day but couldn't find even an odd job. I began to envy the people with jobs, even the shoeshine boy and street sweepers. When spring came late that year, Tina quit her job and I went back to house painting. Even though I advertised in the local paper with money we couldn't afford, I found only one house to paint. Times were hard and getting harder, and my would-be customers didn't seem to have any money.

I don't want to lay it on too thick, but I can tell you we were just plain poor in the early years of that second marriage. In my first marriage we endured poverty and struggled to keep our heads above the water, and now in the second it was the same old grind. Just trying to make it from day to day was a burden. I went off to work even when I knew I would have little or no work. That way I could tell myself I was busy, and I could ignore the squalor of the slums – the noise, stench, and congestion that came from living too close to too many unwashed people. Yet Tina didn't seem to mind where we lived. She had grown up in a neighborhood very similar to the one we were living in, and so it seemed like home to her. Also she was more outgoing than me, I guess, and liked being around the same kind of people she had known all her life. I was an outsider in that neighborhood, an Irish Traveler. The people Tina saw as family the Travelers viewed as marks, as country people to be fleeced. My background wasn't the same as hers.

Of course the country people in Baltimore were city people and poorer than traditional country people. The lodging houses in that neighborhood were teeming with raw humanity. Also in just about every one of them an aggressive and raucous landlady was in charge to make the tenants tow the line. I could see that entire families were living in a single room, and most were at the mercy of a shrewd and unforgiving landlady who might dump them on the street any time she felt like it. They were desperately poor, even poorer than us, and with little hope for anything better. They were often drunk and disorderly, and foul language in the middle of the night was common. The flimsy walls didn't hide the shrieks of abused women and children and all the other domestic sounds. In the middle of the night we could hear male voices cursing, females crying or moaning, and children screaming in terror. We often wondered what was going on, and there were times when Tina insisted I go and tell them to shut up and be quiet. Well, I'm not a coward but I'm not a fool either. It's not good to dabble in the lives of desperate people. I told her that more than once, but instead of agreeing with me I'm pretty sure she thought less of me for not being her champion.

When the middle of September came with the promise of another severe winter, we moved out of the tiny apartment into a single room on Bushnell Street. Before we could hustle our meager belongings into the cheaper place, the landlady – squat and square with gray hair and a dry cough – laid down the law. She spoke methodically in a monotone as if from a list repeated many times and remembered by rote. We were not to have visitors other than "respectable people." If denizens of the underworld came to our apartment, we would be immediately turned out of it. We could not send out our washing or do it ourselves. It had to be done by a washerwoman in the basement at extra cost. We could have meals sent up to us on occasion but also at extra cost. We would have to respect the furniture and the walls and floor and damage nothing.

Once a month on schedule a cleaning crew would inspect the room. If they found it dirty, and they always did, they would go through the motions of cleaning it at extra cost. We had to be absent during the inspection but didn't worry about valuables because we had none. That slum house was not a good place to live and the grasping landlady was not a good woman. But it was cheap enough if one didn't take advantage of the extras, and we didn't. We managed to stay there through the winter but left as soon as we could. Despite cleaning the sordid little room once a month, and they did it whether we liked it or not, the old wood behind the faded wallpaper with its strange, unsettling arabesque design was infested with vermin. In warmer weather they came out of the cracks at night and competed with the bed bugs.

Chapter 14

Justine and Misery

"I f winter comes, can spring be far behind?" That's what the poet said, or so I've heard, and it seems a good line but I don't read poetry and so can't say anything about it. Even so, just like him, I've never liked winter and all my life I've looked forward to spring. And when spring finally came around, after we had lived with vermin in that awful little slum room all winter, we both went looking for jobs and found them. Tina got a job in a milliner's shop working with needle and thread and was able to sit as she worked. Her boss, a middle-aged woman, was the owner of the shop and treated her well. The pay wasn't much, but it was steady work and didn't depend on pleasing the public. It was a good job and Tina liked it.

As for me, and maybe you won't believe it, I applied for a job with the city of Baltimore and became a fireman. I can't explain exactly how it happened. Just luck I guess. I filled out a long application and turned it in and waited. During the winter some of the slums on the south side had gone up in flames, and the mayor decided the city would need several fire departments located in strategic places for more effective firefighting. So the hiring began and Leo Mack became a rookie fireman to be trained. The pay was rock bottom for as long as six weeks, but

190

when the training was over it was better pay than I had on any other job. Now with both of us working at good jobs we began to live comfortably again.

We rented an apartment this time in one of the old but still-fashionable neighborhoods of the city. It was a very comfortable place and made us believe our nomadic way of life was coming to an end. For a few months we lived better than ever before in our lives. Tina was happy and became less acid of tongue, more open and honest. No longer did she smell indecency in every little joke I made, and no longer did she beat around the bush when talking about the facts of life. She had no religious scruples to overcome, having never gone to church, and as far as I could tell she had no restrictive moral code to stand in the way either. So we got along fine in the bedroom, and I found myself feeling genuine affection for my second wife. I didn't love her with the passion of first love, as with Caitlin. But until the time Tina became pregnant, I think we got along as well as most couples and treated each other kindly. Even when she was pregnant she cooked for me and washed my clothes and went on long walks with me. She was young and alive and eager to please her husband, and of course I liked her for that. Also she even went out to work again, and that surprised me.

However, as the months of her pregnancy dragged on and on and she had to quit her job, she became fat and round, grumpy and lazy. The friendly climate we had tried so hard to maintain between us grew cooler with each day. Then one night her water broke and I had to run to a hospital calling for a doctor to come quick. After what seemed an eternity, I finally persuaded a medical person to leave his post at the hospital and come to our rooms. When we got there my wife was sprawled in a bloody bed writhing with pain and sweating. The man had come too late and we lost the baby.

191

We cleaned up the birthing scene, and he gave her something to make her sleep. A few days later the hospital sent us a hefty bill "for services rendered." It claimed the medical student (who was not a doctor) had struggled to save the baby, using expensive equipment and medication. That was absolutely untrue. With good reason Tina was furious and so was I. She ripped the bill into tiny pieces and threw them away. Though we got nothing from the medical people, they had the gall to send us an itemized bill. I decided they would get nothing from me even when pestered by lawyers, and finally they left us alone. Tina suffered from a nagging pain in her back and legs and from emotional pain. When the hospital staff hesitated to help a poor woman, she lost her child. Though one of them came too late, they had the nerve to send an outrageous bill for services.

Also she had lost her job and now had to tolerate isolation and boredom. In my hours off work I tried to comfort her but couldn't. Once pliable and eager to please, she was becoming unpredictable, querulous, and quarrelsome. For reasons I could never quite understand, except for maybe losing the baby, she became rebellious and quick of temper and bitter of tongue. Sometimes in a quiet mood she would apologize for her behavior and call me a good man. Then moments later she would fly into a tantrum again. I was finding it hard to live with her and spent a lot of my time on the job just to be away from her and domestic misery.

Then I got to thinking that maybe a change of scenery would improve her temper. I had a comfortable income at last, and so I asked if she would like to live in a house for the first time in her life. I said I knew of a house for rent that seemed just perfect for us. Her eyes lit up at the very suggestion, and she seemed thrilled. She looked deep in my face, her eyes aglow, and asked if I was joking.

"You know we can't afford a house. So why do you torment me with stuff like that? I would love to live in a house, and you know it, but we can't afford it. I think you're trying to give me some kind of hope, or maybe it's just another one of your sick jokes."

"We can afford it and I'm not joking. I take home pretty good wages now. I'm making as much now as when both of us were working a while back. It's the most I ever earned, and the chief at the station is saying I'm a damn good fireman."

"Do you really think we can live in a real, honest-to-goodness house? I've always dreamed of living in my own house, my home. Even when I was a little girl that was my favorite dream. It would be neat and clean and would have a picket fence around it. My parents always laughed at me when I talked about my dream house."

"I'm not laughing, Tina. I have a good house in mind in a good part of town, and I talked to an agent about it, and he said the rent is reasonable. We can afford it and you'd be happy there."

———

We moved into the house at the end of August. It was the first time in my life I could afford to rent a house, and I breathed a great sigh of relief. When I was growing up in Kelly Junction, we lived in a poor excuse for a house. It was really a hut or a hovel, but this one was airy and spacious in a neighborhood of family homes. I felt certain we would be living there for a long time, and I felt our domestic life was back on track. Tina would look after the house and keep it orderly and no longer work at a job away from home and maybe become a mother. I would go to work as the breadwinner and come home again to a loving wife and family, and all of us would have a delicious dinner and later sit in front of the hearth and enjoy the warmth. It seemed to me our dreams were being realized, and I felt life was good. Tina really did seem happy in this house of our own, this very satisfactory house with every convenience.

As we had hoped she got pregnant again. But when her belly became big and her movements slow and clumsy, her emotional fuse became very short and her temper explosive. Again, because I dreaded the quarrels, I spent more and more time on the job. She complained I was deliberately making myself scarce, and that made the situation worse. She accused me of having another woman, a slim and attractive woman to help me forget the ugly woman I lived with at home. In a cool and rational way I tried to convince her of my loyalty, but all I got in return were emotional outbursts that somehow produced gutter language, a side of her I'd never seen. I didn't want to admit that our marriage was falling into ruin even as a child was on the way, and yet that seemed to be happening.

Justine – now she insisted I call her by her formal name – gave birth to a little boy in the middle of winter and we called him Edwin after someone she had known and liked. It was the winter that saw many fires in Baltimore. The old, jerrybuilt tenements caught fire one after another and went up like tinderboxes. Every fireman in the city had to be on alert twenty-four hours a day. Even when all the fires were out and under control, a dozen could flare up when least expected to threaten and destroy an entire neighborhood. I had to work long hours that winter, and it meant being away from Justine who was left alone and blamed me for her morning sickness.

After giving birth she began to suffer from sciatic neuralgia, as the doctor called it. It was a sharp pain that came and went, running down her left leg to her foot. It inflamed her temper and made her fiercely cranky. I tried to make light of her condition to help her cope, but she no longer had a sense of humor and believed I was making fun of her. That brought on outbursts of unrestrained scolding. She heaped upon me almost daily a torrent of verbal abuse, bombarding me with smutty language. In her anger she didn't hesitate to spit out four-letter words made sharp with shrill contempt, and she took comfort in the effect they had on me. But that's not all. Sometimes to vent her anger she lobbed crockery at me. I worried that she was losing all control, and I worried about the infant.

I was living in a genuine home in a pleasant neighborhood made bright by flowers and foliage. After many years I was no longer living in a wagon pulled by an old horse (as in the early days), and I was no longer a tenant in a squalid lodging house in a mean and noisy slum. As far as one could tell, I had realized my dream of escaping poverty to live as any decent human being ought to live. Yet in that comfortable house, now becoming unkempt and cluttered, a feeling of misery and discomfort persisted. I could see a daily increase in Justine's indifference, depression, and ferocity, and I was powerless to understand her condition or get to its cause. I inquired of doctors regarding her volatile behavior. They hemmed and hawed but eventually said it appeared she was unstable and constitutionally weak. I asked if they had some sort of cure for the condition they described. Again they hemmed and hawed and pontificated as very learned men and finally answered "no, not really."

An unreliable and tainted heredity had left its mark upon her, they said, and the result could be a gradual slipping away from sanity into a stark, unconditional madness. In time she might have to be committed to an institution, they said. The institution would have no cure for her either but would protect her from herself and not allow her to harm others. At present because of her youth and recent motherhood and lucid moments now and then, there was little anyone could do about her condition. I would have to find a way to endure her mood swings, her erratic behavior, and violent temper. She was my wife and the law demanded I support and care for her. Also I had to see to the safety of the child though working long hours away from home. Well, I don't mind telling you, I felt overwhelmed.

Every day after work I went directly home to find she had given the baby very little care. It seemed to me she stayed in bed half the day, and even when she was up and about she never bothered to bathe, or comb her hair, or dress properly. Once she took it upon herself to go shopping at the greengrocer market and left the baby in his crib to sob himself to sleep. She changed his diaper only once a day, ceased to bathe him properly, and the whole house smelled of an unattended infant. Sometimes I had to be on duty at night and went home in the morning to find her sound asleep and blissfully unaware of the little one crying his eyes out. Instead of sleeping when night came so as to go to work strong in the morning, I found myself caring for the child.

Then it happened. One morning after working the night shift I came home and found little Edwin dead. He was curled naked on the floor and she was bending over him and moaning like a stricken animal. I demanded to know what had happened, but she couldn't speak coherently. Clothed only in a flimsy nightgown, she banged her head on the floor, screamed hysterically, shrieked and sobbed. Then silence came when she began to hold her breath. As she was turning blue in the face, I scooped up the child and ran with him to the hospital. They took what seemed a very long time to examine the little body and tell me what went wrong. Finally, a fat little man in white, perhaps the lead doctor, spoke for the other two and the nurse. He said Edwin had no bruises anywhere at all to suggest maltreatment. He had not been beaten and he was not undernourished. Though his little body was unclean, in their estimation the mother had done nothing to cause his death.

I found their diagnosis hard to accept. In his sleep, they said, he had simply stopped breathing. Hundreds of babies died that way every year. They had a name for it, but it was a mystery no doctor had been able to solve. When I walked into the room and saw what seemed to be an unspeakable horror unfolding, in her own inept way Justine must have been trying to revive the infant. Some official-looking people came to our house to survey the scene and essentially reached the same conclusion. No charges were filed against her. They deemed her a loving mother who had lost her child through no fault of her own. Case studies in medical literature could prove that healthy infants died in their sleep every day. It was something the doctors were working on but didn't understand, and so the babble went on and on. I was angry and suspicious and thought simple neglect had caused my little son's death but couldn't prove it. I was tired to the bone but had to arrange for the burial of a son who lived only a few weeks, an infant I never came to know.

With the death of little Edwin a calm that soon became a paralyzing stupor swept over Justine. For days on end she made not a sound and said not a word. Every day she sat for hours by the window and stared into the street and sort of rocked her body back and forth. She ate very little, in fact would eat nothing unless I urged it upon her, pleading almost. Coming home exhausted after work, sometimes after fighting a fire and getting soaked to the skin with icy water, I found no food on the table and had to cook it myself. She spoke to me only in a dull monotone and only to answer or evade answering a direct question. She seemed to be grieving the loss of her child, and I tried to be loving and patient. Then one day out of the blue she asked if we could walk beside the river that flows into the inner harbor. I liked being near the water and was off work, and so I readily agreed. It was a long walk and a good one even though she said little. Before returning home we stopped at a little eatery for refreshment. It pleased me to see her eating. The activity that afternoon was the first sign she was emerging from the prison she had made for herself. She was free for a day, walking and eating again.

Early in the morning of a balmy day in July we went for another walk to explore the old neighborhoods of earlier days. Though littered with rubbish, the streets were fresh at that time of day, and a gray mist was rising from the water. As the sun came up the mist became a blanket of rainbow colors that sparkled with gemlike brilliance. Breathing deeply and feeling the warmth of the sun on our faces, we paused behind the walkway wall to enjoy the scene. The air was cool and clean and easy to breathe.

Briskly we strolled through the slums and passed rundown factories, quaint shops, and new construction. Men on their way to work in the early morning greeted us with a smile and a nod. In the distance we could see the stately buildings of business and commerce, and then we turned homeward. The long walk made for a keen appetite, and we ate a big, belly-filling breakfast. For the first time in months Justine seemed to be without a temper. Then one evening as I was preparing dinner she began to scream in anger. For what appeared to be no reason at all, the fury that defined her returned and made her dangerous. She became unstable and unpredictable, a danger to herself and others, and again I worried about her.

October came with bleak winds promising cold weather for November. The quiet domestic life I was seeking when I married Justine Ryan was again in raucous uproar. Her temper was back again and all my hopes when I married her – a wife and children, a cuddly pet or two, and a family hearth – were falling into little pieces. I no longer had any affection for her, nor she for me, and now instead of walking together and talking, dining and laughing, she spoke only to complain and find fault. I suffered from a persistent cough at that time and dreaded the coming of winter. She thought I had a cold she might catch and ordered me to sleep in the sitting room. I tried to convince her the cough came from breathing toxic fumes while fighting fires, but she wouldn't listen. The sitting room had no bed, not even a couch, and I refused to obey her order.

Of course she exploded with anger and played the martyr. She decided herself to sleep on a pallet in the sitting room under a thin blanket. Her breathing was labored, and she made a strange noise all through the night. Every morning when I got up before the sun for work, she complained bitterly that I was abusing her. Then for weeks she ignored me entirely and gave me the silent treatment. Even so, I wasn't about to leave my warm and comfortable bed to sleep on the hard floor and catch the cold she thought I already had and die.

I was able to go on working as a fireman, but at every fire we fought I breathed some smoke and it was affecting my lungs. I guess you can see how yellow my teeth are, and if you look into a fireman's mouth you'll see more teeth turned rotten from heat and smoke. Maybe I shouldn't say this to you, Isaac, since I don't want you to hate me as I think she did, but I had thoughts of chucking it all and becoming a vagabond. I had thoughts of simply walking away and letting her stew in her own misery. And yet I didn't. For reasons I don't understand even now, I didn't.

Every other week or so, from the time we were married, Justine was in the habit of visiting her father in the old neighborhood. He was now old and ailing and had lost his cobbler's shop but not the crude rooms he called his home. Then one day she discovered he had dissolved in the stream of humanity one sees on the sidewalks of Baltimore, and she never saw him again. The one or two friends she had while working as a waitress also moved elsewhere, and she was left feeling more alone than ever. I really believe she thought she was sinking downward while my star was rising. The chief had put in a good word for me in the department and I was promoted and given more responsibility and a little more pay. You would think hearing good news would have pleased her, but not so.

I felt pretty good about the way things were going at work, but I couldn't say that for home. Living with Justine had never been easy, but now with each passing day it was getting worse. After little Edwin died I have to say she was less bitter of tongue, but now in the middle of winter she seemed more ornery and more unpredictable than ever. The isolation she was up against, being home alone all day with little or nothing to do, wasn't good for her. I asked her if she would like a cat to keep her company, and she laughed in a kind of high-pitched hysteria until tears rolled down her cheeks. I hinted that maybe she should go back to work. That brought a furious response though no verbal abuse. She marched into the bedroom, slammed the door shut, and went to bed early.

While I dreaded sleeping in the same bed with her, I refused to sleep on a pallet and so did she after trying it. So two people who should have been worlds apart were sharing the same house and the same bed. At any time of the day or night I could expect a sudden outburst of anger, a tirade from an acid tongue. I got into the habit of spending time at the station even when I wasn't on duty. The men I worked with were the only friends I had. Justine fumed I was deserting her to be with my special friends while she had no friends at all, nothing to do but keep house for an ungrateful husband, and nowhere to go. Truth be told, she did precious little housekeeping.

Yet I guess her charges weren't entirely false. Often I played a few hands of poker with my friends and even won some money, all the time knowing she was alone and miserable at home. Her tirades bothered me because half the time her words had some truth in them. I had my faults and she was good at finding every one of them and telling me all about them. I had to take some of the blame for her misery, but how could I blame myself entirely? As time passed I had to believe in what the doctors said. If she had some kind of mental illness, and they seemed to be sure of that, then ancestry or hereditary would have to take the blame. It was all so confusing, so cold and crippling. In brooding silence I knew that I had married the wrong woman, and yet divorce was out of the question.

Through the winter and the cold spring that came after winter, I suffered from a sore throat and persistent cough. The men at work called it the fire below and said it was common in our line of work and would go away in warm weather, but it didn't. So I thought I'd take a week off and go south again and visit my relatives in Kelly Junction and try to get well again. It'd been years since I was there, and even though I had no enduring love for anybody in the village, I didn't want to lose touch with my roots either. Also I thought the milder climate might help the cough and send me back to Baltimore stronger. But I guess the main reason I wanted to go was to get away for a week or two from Justine. I mentioned my plan to her as she was washing dishes after supper. Before I could fully explain she exploded. In a rage she smashed a plate at my feet.

"I can't believe you're planning to abandon your wife and take a long trip just for your own selfish pleasure."

"I didn't say anything about abandoning anybody."

"Oh, yes, you did! You expect me to stay here all by myself while you go home to your no-good relatives in the sticks."

"You don't understand. I'm looking for a milder climate to get rid of this nagging cough that's been bothering me for months."

"You're looking for something all right, but not a milder climate. If I know you, and I do, you're looking for a dirty little slut to be your toy. Oh, I know you, all right! That's all you think about!"

It wasn't the first time she had accused me in a jealous fury of cheating on her. She cursed and shrieked and tried to strike me with clenched fists. She grabbed a broom and tried to hit me with it. I fended off the blows as best I could and said nothing. Immediately I tossed a few items into a pillowcase and left. She stood in the doorway screaming. I didn't know what I was doing at the time, but as it turned out I never returned to that house or to her. Later I wanted to believe the marriage was over, but without a divorce no marriage is over. I doubt even divorce ends a bad marriage. She was dependent upon me, and the law said I would have to support her for as long as she lived, or for as long as I lived. It was not a rosy prospect.

Chapter 15

Things Fall Apart

When I checked with Chief Huggins about taking a few days off, he said he might be able to spare me a few but wanted to know how many. After some hesitation I asked for two weeks. He was silent for a minute or two and then said I could have four days off. Though Huggins ran his department with tight reins, he wasn't a hard man, and so I guess I understood. I was a well-trained fireman by then, and he needed me on duty. That wasn't enough time even to think about going all the way to Kelly Junction and back. So instead of going home again, I used the days off to find a new place near my work. It was a poor substitute for the house I walked away from, leaving most of my belongings behind, but it was all right for one person.

The little apartment had two rooms and a kitchen. The kitchen had all the utensils necessary for a complete meal, and I could even bathe there. I was soon eating canned soup, cheese, vegetables, eggs, beef with bread and gravy now and then, and fruits. Nearby was a thriving butcher's shop and beyond that a grocery store. I liked the convenience of the new place, and my neighbors were well behaved. I never heard a sound from them, and I liked being able to come and go without bumping into them. Also I didn't have to tolerate a nosey landlady as in the early days. I was glad to be rid of those irksome women, for they reminded me too much of Justine.

When I returned to work after my short vacation, the chief called me into his office for a confidential chat. Someone had told him my wife was alarming her neighbors, and he wanted the full story. She was quarreling with everybody, venting her fury on the woman who owned the house, and threatening violence when told she would have to move. My boss was wondering why such information would be sent to him and not to me. I said it appeared my wife was trying to get me in trouble, perhaps get me fired. Chief Huggins explained the letter had come not from Justine but from another person. Then it hit me. No one in the quiet neighborhood knew my current address, and so the owner of the house wrote to my employer. Had she held off only a day or two, I would have sent her the rent and all this airing of dirty linen could have been avoided.

To the chief I had to explain I was living apart from my wife because for some time she had been behaving in the manner described in the letter, and there was little I could do about it. With some hesitation he offered his support but gave me cause to worry too. He said the department prided itself on good family values, and tales of domestic conflict were troubling to say the least. To this day I don't know if the letter from the landlady hurt me at work or not. I do know I wasn't promoted to a higher rank when the time came, and though I was commended for bravery when I dragged to safety a man who might have perished, it didn't help.

By then I was becoming confused and bitter. I didn't want to believe Justine's behavior was that of a lunatic, but what else could I believe? It seemed to me she was descending into madness, and it seemed she was fated to plunge deeper and deeper into a dark and crazy world that belonged only to her. It was clear to everybody who knew her that she was unstable and unpredictable and needed round-the-clock care. But that in itself was a problem. She was too young and too proud to be looked after by other women.

In her mind she was the victim because she believed I had reduced her life to a shambles. Too late I saw that a chief cause of her fury was alienation from her relatives and former friends. When we married she was young and lively, outgoing and gregarious, and constantly gossiping about all the people she knew. Then she quit her job and ceased to work outside the home and lost contact with those who peopled her world. She was expected to be content with no friends, no relatives, and no social life while I worked to gain a secure footing in the Baltimore Fire Department.

When months elapsed with no incident, I no longer feared that Justine would come pounding on my door with fire in her eyes. Then as I began to relax I discovered my place was located on a road well known to peddlers. At my building a man could leave his wagon, go knocking on doors, and sell his goods to several families all at once. It was a convenience for him but something of a burden for the residents. One morning near the end of June my doorbell rang. It was the kind of bell that one turns by hand to send a shrill signal through every room inside. I got up and went to the door and met a smiling colporteur. He was a young man not more than nineteen with sandy hair, pale blue eyes, thin lips under a sharp nose, and freckles.

"Good morning, sir!" he said by way of greeting. "I have in my hands a book you cannot do without. It is the King James Version of the Bible fully annotated with fine illustrations."

He paused a moment to observe my reaction. Standing in the doorway and tucking my shirt in my trousers, I looked down into his face and couldn't help being amused by his earnestness. His mission was to sell me a Bible, and he put all he had into the effort.

"I'm glad to see you love the Bible, young man, and I do wish you well. But I'm not in the least interested in what you are selling."

"But sir!" the peddler quickly replied. "This printing of the great book is far better than any of the others. They used a new process to make the print quite clear and the ink will never fade. The price is really quite reasonable. You won't find a better deal anywhere."

"It's a good book. My mama used to read it to me when I was just a little fellow, but I'm not in the market for a Bible now."

"Oh it's full of divine truth, sir! It'll make your life better. It will! If you read it carefully, every day will be as nice as today."

I shook my head slowly and said nothing. His pale blue eyes had a pleading look, like a puppy wanting a treat. I could tell he wasn't having much luck selling his product, and I felt a little sorry for him. Then he turned on his heel and walked away.

I know you're wondering why I bothered to bring this up. It's because I was beginning to think I had strayed too far from the spiritual life the church in Kelly Junction tried to instill in me as a boy. And just as I was having thoughts of how religion might improve my existence, this peddler of Bibles comes along. A colporteur he called himself, I had never heard of that word. He was only trying to make a living, you know, and maybe I should have bought his product. He was struggling like me and so I could sympathize with him, but I had no money to shell out for a Bible and no time to read it. All of us reflect at times on what we should have done.

As I think about it now, reading the Bible might have eased my mind a little as I tried to work through my troubles with Justine. I do know I needed some kind of solace and didn't have it. I heard she was looking for me and was determined to find me, and was threatening all kinds of trouble. In the warm weather she had been harassing her neighbors again and was asked to leave. Without notifying anyone she walked away one day in the early morning and found another place. I think she moved down in the scale because the rent the lawyer required me to pay slowly got smaller. Though living in the same neighborhood where she grew up, she was asked time and again to move away because of sudden and violent outbursts. Her fits of temper, set off by the smallest of incidents, were becoming so frequent and so violent that anyone who knew her was thinking she was plainly crazy. In one lodging house when given notice to leave, she attacked her landlady with a heavy stick and was nearly arrested. The next day she was on the streets again, dragging her belongings behind her in a little cart and looking for another place to live.

I was trying to persuade her lawyer to work out an agreement with her, but at every turn she stubbornly resisted. She had grown up suspicious of the law, of lawyers, and legal documents. Even though our backgrounds were different, in that one respect we were very similar. I didn't like lawyers either but felt I had to work with them if anything at all could be accomplished. I was seeking a legal separation from Justine, but she refused to sign anything. Bothered by the legal mess, she relieved her stress by venting her caustic temper on any person unfortunate enough to cross her path. Reports of her behavior clearly showed she was slowly becoming more violent. Though the lawyers claimed they had seen worse behavior, I really believed she was going insane. I feared she would come pounding on my door at any time of the day or night, demanding that I take her back, and that is exactly what happened late one afternoon just as darkness was coming. The law was on her side, she insisted, but I refused to quarrel with her. She gave me one of her dirty looks, the signal she was about to explode, but to my surprise she turned and went away without causing a scene. I never saw her again.

At that time I believed without wanting to that she would end up in a lunatic asylum. Nearly four years later I found out she had been arrested for assaulting an acquaintance. By then she was well known to the police, but instead of hauling her off to jail they took her to a hospital to be examined by doctors who specialized in emotional disorders. They judged her insane and committed her to an asylum. It surprised nobody, for any number of people saw it coming.

From the time of her commitment until the day she died fifteen years later, Justine remained in close confinement and received no visitors. She died in her middle forties, according to the death certificate, of "organic brain disease." It was a catchall term the doctors used when no real cause of death could be determined. In all the years she suffered in confinement she never revealed my name to anyone. Yet until the day she died she wore the wedding band she proudly displayed to her papa the day we were married.

Now you've heard how I lost my second wife. The first brought me joy. The second brought pain and misery. Then both of them suffered and died while I survived. After all the trouble with Justine I made up my mind to live as a solitary man and never marry again. That's how you know me now. That's how all the people in Blue Anchor have always known me. I live not exactly apart from people but not bothering any of them either. Well, sometimes people get under my skin and then I have to say something, but most of the time I mind my own business and go my own way. And I hope that's how the good folks in Blue Anchor will remember me.

———◦◉◦———

Chief Huggins was a good boss and I liked him, but after he heard reports of my unstable domestic life, he began to have doubts about my ability to fight a good fire and survive. It was a common story in the department that when a man began to have trouble at home, when his marriage was falling apart and he was in the dumps, he became reckless on the job. It wasn't unheard of for a troubled man to walk into an inferno and never walk out. And that sort of thing just couldn't be tolerated. Well, I was miserable at times and that I will admit, but I never had thoughts of self-destruction. Even so, after Justine came to the station making a spectacle of herself and demanding my address, Chief Huggins reached a decision. I would have to go. He was nice about it but adamant. He would have to let me go, and he did. I was out of work again and didn't know where to turn. Even though I had saved some money for a rainy day, I knew when my rent came due I would have to move to a cheaper place.

Down on Colchester Street near the waterfront I found two rooms for a month with an option to stay longer. It was a shabby rooming house with thin walls, and the rooms were shabby but not repulsive, and I made do rather well with them. I had a small sitting room and a slightly larger bedroom, and a tiny nook with no window where I could make coffee or a scanty breakfast. The sitting room had a large window with a view of the street below where people came and went in a steady stream. I often wondered as I sat there and looked down at them what their lives were like, where they were going, and from where did they come. What kind of bed did they sleep in at night and what kind of food did they eat to give them the energy to move so briskly. I knew I should be among them and moving at the same pace, but the difference between them and me seemed to be they knew where they were going and I didn't. For more than a week I walked the streets every day looking for work and found nothing. I passed shops with all sorts of merchandise in their windows and began to think I might find work in a store, perhaps a haberdashery.

From fireman to retail clerk would be a step downward, I thought, and certainly the wages would be lower. But had I not already moved downward from a comfortable apartment with a private entrance to two shabby rooms behind a brown and greasy door in the narrow hallway of a shabby rooming house? I couldn't be choosey, and so I narrowed my search to stores catering to men and selling men's clothing. I would become, if I could, a haberdasher, or failing that I could stock the shelves and sweep the floors after closing time. I walked until I found a store that looked as though it might be in need of help and decided to try my luck.

Before going inside I combed my hair neatly, adjusted my shirt and coat, and flicked away the dust from my trousers and shoes. Invariably, or so it seemed, the owner or manager was a dapper little man with a mustache, pallid skin, hawk eyes, thinning hair, and a superior smile. He was always standing in a prominent place near racks of clothing and spoke curtly with a show of impatience. He seemed to be saying, "I pity you, poor fellow. You would like to have my job but you'll never get it. I was born and bred for this job. You were not." I judged these arrogant little men as self-centered and displaying no humanity. With a jaundiced eye they looked down on me in my rough clothing to make themselves look bigger.

One by one they turned me down. Some bluntly said I didn't belong in the retail business. They said I looked more like a laborer or a sailor than a salesman of men's fine clothing. Maybe I should apply for work as a bricklayer or gravedigger, or maybe I could get work as assistant to a plumber or carpenter and learn a trade. To sell men's apparel one had to have a certain finesse, they implied, and that I didn't have. Eventually they convinced me I was barking up the wrong tree, and so I began to walk into grocery stores and ask for a job. One didn't have to be a fine gentleman to stock shelves in a grocery store, or create a polite stream of patter to convince a customer to buy a suit. All one had to do in a grocery store was lift heavy boxes and wait on customers and learn how to make change.

When it looked like that job was off limits too, I was hired as a helper by a small mom and pop store. The old couple went by the name of Giovanni and Gina Gabrielli, and the name of their store, naturally enough, was the Three G's Grocery. On the sign identifying their place in big red letters were some smaller words in black – Italian American Meats & Food Stuffs. A small Italian flag decorated one corner of the sign and business was good. The Gabriellis had been in the neighborhood many years, and they treated their customers fairly and with uncompromising honesty. A couple of years before I came on the scene their son had gone into the army and had become a cavalry officer. They felt in his absence they could use some help, and so on the spot I replaced him. I knew the pay would be just enough to get by but made up my mind to work for them.

They were good people and I liked being in the small store with them, though often I was called upon to visit wholesale houses to keep supplies in stock. Gina was a very talkative woman and spoke with a singsong accent. Her husband preferred to listen but sometimes told stories of life in the old country and New York. They had emigrated from Verona when fairly young and had lived in New York's Little Italy for a time. Later they moved to Baltimore where they bought their business and managed to keep it solvent for many years. In New York Giovanni worked as a barber. His father before him was a barber and taught him the art of cutting hair. So when he went looking for a job in the new world, he found one in Bleecker Street but had to prove his skill. After a trial period of several weeks, any number of people had good things to say about his work, and so his job as a barber was secure but kept him standing on his feet too many hours each day. At times when the grocery business was slow, he would relax in his easy chair and recall those days in New York when he stood eleven hours six days a week washing hair, cutting hair, and shaving beards with a blade he sharpened on a strop. He could sit only when no one was in the shop, and that was seldom.

You won't believe some of the stories Giovanni heard in that Italian barbershop. A man would come in for the full treatment lasting an hour and tell a story timed to end the moment he got out of the chair. There were stories about the Mafia back in Italy and Sicily and about men setting themselves up as godfathers in Little Italy, and the cutthroat competition that sometimes ended with a man dead in a barber's chair. And there were funny stories too, like the one he told me when they invited me up to their apartment for dinner one evening. It went like this and I laugh as I put it down:

A man walked into my barbershop and sat in my chair. Well, it really was my chair but not my shop. I worked the third chair, and that's the one that pays the lowest. I put the cape over his ample belly and asked, "How do you want your hair cut, mister?" The man says to me, "I want it short on one side, uneven on the other side, crooked in the front and a hacked up in the back." Well, that really surprised me, and I said after some hesitation, "That's a tall order for a simple haircut, mister, I don't know if I can do it." The man looked me straight in the eye and very seriously replied, "I don't know why not, that's the haircut you gave me last time."

Giovanni knew I had struggled through some hard times, and so whenever he could he tried to cheer me up with stories like that and a little off-color joke now and then. His wife would say, "Ah, Leo, don't listen to him! When anybody listens to my old man, it goes to his head and I have to live with the old fart! You will never know what I have to endure living with him." And then she would glance lovingly at him and laugh and poke him in the ribs. They were good people, those two, and they had a good marriage and it did me good to see it, coming only recently from one that lay in ruins.

In the midst of my troubles someone told me compromise is the key to a good marriage. "Learn to compromise," the all-knowing pundit said. "Compromise can settle most of the problems that arise between a man and his wife." Well, compromise didn't work for me, and this Italian couple didn't need it. They had a long, enduring love for each other and respect and tolerance. Maybe tolerance was the key factor in their marriage, but that's only speculation on my part. I don't claim to be no expert on marriage.

Chapter 16

A Maritime Hearing

Giovanni and Gina lived in a comfortable apartment above their grocery store. Evenings when business was slow, especially in winter, they would often close the shop and retire early. More than once they invited me to have dinner, and of course I accepted. Gina was an excellent cook, and I gorged on her Italian dishes. I guess you can say I liked her lasagna best of all, but her meatballs in a rich sauce were also a favorite. They joked about opening a restaurant some day and treating the community with food worth eating. Then sadly they confessed it was too late in life even to entertain such plans. One day they invited me up for what they called a musical evening.

"You will like our music," Giovanni chortled. "I play the fiddle and la mia amata, Gina, has a piano and we do canzoni di strada, Italian street songs. All very zippy, make you wanna dance."

I laughed when I heard this and readily accepted the invitation. I had a vision of an old couple raising the roof with zippy tunes while young couples abused the floor with marathon dancing. When I got there, all clean and neat in my best clothes, the first person I saw after Giovanni invited me inside was a young woman. She was slender with dark hair to her shoulders and wore a delightful smile. Giovanni introduced her as his niece and said she was visiting for a few days. The couple knew I had bouts of loneliness, and the girl was their solution. In her early twenties, her name was Angelina.

After dinner came the musical evening. It was filled with laughter and music and lively chatter. Giovanni brought out his violin and stood beside Gina's piano, and to my surprise Angelina sang the words of the tunes in a mellow and melodious contralto. Their music was as good as any I'd heard. It seemed to me I was in a theater watching and listening to professionals. Angelina was more than just a pretty young woman. She had talent, intelligence, sensitivity, and a voice reflecting her name. She was in training to sing on the stage but was having difficulty finding steady work in a music hall. Her home was in Richmond, but she was planning to move to New York to realize a dream. In a way I was smitten, and then I told myself it was too soon to get involved with another woman, and so I ran. I enjoyed that evening very much, eating their food, drinking their wine, and sharing their laughter. I am now convinced that while the Irish know how to have a good time, the Italians do it better. Giovanni and Gina hoped I would see Angelina again, perhaps take her out for an evening on the town, but I never did. I wish I could tell you what happened to her, but I never found out. I hope she had a good life and I like to think she got it all.

As warm weather flooded Baltimore, I began to get restless and wanted to be in new places. I didn't want to leave my benefactors high and dry, and so I found a boy all too willing to take my job. Good-hearted Gina shed a tear when I hugged her and said goodbye. Giovanni slapped me on the back and wished me luck. For reasons I never understood, I lied and said I would come again even when I knew I wouldn't. I drifted down to the waterfront and boarded a brigantine for New York. My aim was to go to sea again. I wanted to get away from all the troubles the land had dumped in my lap, and I wanted to breathe salt air again.

On the way to New York I got into a long conversation with the captain about my past and my years at sea. Without thinking much about it I mentioned the *Sea Cloud*. Captain Marvel Blink had heard all about the mystery ship and how she was found with not a single person on board but seaworthy and sailing with very little canvas. The saga of the *Sea Cloud* fascinated the man, and he had read as much about it as he could find. So when I claimed to be the sole survivor of the disaster, he didn't believe me and who could blame him? He was dubious and looked it but poured me another glass of brandy and urged me to tell him the whole story.

At first I didn't want to get into the details of that very bad day, but with his prodding I revealed everything I knew. I could tell him only my side of the story, saying the last I saw of the ship she was moving easterly toward the horizon. News accounts later said she was found by the crew of a British ship and sailed to Gibraltar to be claimed as salvage. Captain Blink knew more about that part of the story than I did and so began to talk. It was a good conversation and a good way to pass the time, but the next day Blink told me he had received a wire from the Maritime Commission in New York, requesting me to appear before that body at a formal meeting.

I was dumfounded to hear that because in all the years since the ship was deserted and lost no one had asked me to testify about anything. I guess that was because I didn't want to go around telling people I was the sole survivor of a maritime disaster that was in the headlines. I kept a tight lip about it, but now with brandy to loosen my tongue I was telling my story and making news. It seems Blink had mentioned what I told him to the first mate, and that worthy revealed it in a wire to a friend, and the newspapers heard about it and informed the Commission. Charged with getting all the facts, they were now petitioning me to meet with them and tell my story.

Well, I knew I didn't do anything wrong, and so I made up my mind to tell them all I knew and at the same time learn the full story. They informed me the first mate of the ship that found the *Sea Cloud* would also be testifying, but I would go first. So early one Tuesday morning I met with a dozen people in this big room and sat in front of their row of desks and answered their questions as best I could. The hearing consumed the entire day from early morning until late in the evening. I gave my testimony in the morning, and the first mate of the *Gilded Swan* gave his in the afternoon and evening. From the two of us they got the full story. The hearing went like this —

"You were an able-bodied sailor on the *Sea Cloud* when another ship discovered her abandoned on the open sea?"

"I was."

"State your name, please."

"Leo Mack"

"Your full name, please."

"Leo Tamasin Mack."

"And where do you live?"

"I have lived in Baltimore for several years. I am without a family and wish to go to sea again."

"Please tell us what you know about the *Sea Cloud*, how and why the ship was abandoned, and what happened to those on board. Spare no details and speak as long as you wish."

"I will do that. For years I've lived with this thing, and from time to time I've wanted to reveal what I know but feared no one would believe me. It's a long story with an unhappy ending."

"Proceed, please. You have an audience that will listen."

I gave them all I knew about the voyage and the bad weather and the volatile cargo and the fear the alcohol would explode, and all of us going over the side with a long tether for safety, but having the line break when the storm hit, and being dumped in the sea by a rogue wave. I told them several heads were bobbing in the water, and people were shrieking in terror, but one by one they slipped beneath the surface and disappeared. The captain's wife was the first to go. She was holding little Sophie but gave the child to her husband and went under. I don't think she could swim. Captain Spooner held the child in his arms, but she was frightened and fighting him, and then they were hit by a wave and went under and I didn't see them again. The last person I saw was Marvin Delgado holding close to his chest a big leather bag filled with the valuables he had taken from the ship's safe and hoped to get to his relatives in Spain. He might have survived too but for the weight of that satchel. I remember, however, he was bleeding from an injury to his left temple, and maybe that pulled him down.

I told them I caught hold of a pair of oars and made my way to an island and lay on the beach exhausted but managed to survive. I had nothing more to say to them, but they had plenty to say to me. At times I thought I would be arrested and tried for saving my life while all the others perished, including the captain's wife and little daughter. They seemed to think I had committed some sort of crime when I found a way to survive. Then their mood shifted as their attention moved away from me to Henry Hobbes, first mate of the *Gilded Swan*. That was the ship that found the *Sea Cloud* abandoned and sailing on her own. Hobbes boarded her and was ready to tell the Commission all that he saw on the ghost ship. At that point I began to relax and listen rather than talk. Supplying many details I didn't know about at all, he finished the story of the *Sea Cloud*. He wrote the last chapter you might say. I'm sure you know it's been called one of the greatest mysteries of the sea.

⸺⸻◉⸻⸺

Editor's Note. *At this place in Leo's narrative I must interrupt once again. The evening Leo Mack was telling me about the hearing in New York, concerning his role as a seaman on the* Sea Cloud *and the role of Henry Hobbes on finding the ship and sailing her to Gibraltar, he was drinking apple cider and consuming with gusto a plate of fried oysters at my home. He talked as he ate, chewing the oysters longer than most people because by then his teeth were bad, and he tended to summarize all that Mr. Hobbes said at the hearing. I felt that material deserved more than just a summary, and so I've chosen to let Hobbes tell his story in his own words. In my opinion, he was quite articulate in his recital of the facts and truly a brave man. He elected in the first place to board the ship, knowing he could find dead bodies on board or even live pirates. Finding no signs of violence, he sailed and navigated the one-hundred-foot brigantine, with only two men to help him and not a full set of sails, more than six hundred miles to the port of Gibraltar. She was found east of the Azores, having sailed on her own under short canvas nearly four hundred miles. The scene that follows continues and concludes the hearing in New York City. It was held to gather the facts once and for all. The leader of the group asks pertinent questions. Henry Hobbes supplies the answers. – E. Kingston*

"It is my pleasure as chairman of this Commission to begin these proceedings by thanking you for appearing here,

Mr. Hobbes. You do it of your own discretions and without compulsion."

"Yes, sir. That is correct."

"I understand you were the first mate of a brigantine sailing under the British flag and christened *Gilded Swan* when it came upon the abandoned vessel, *Sea Cloud,* some 378 miles east of the Azores archipelago in the Atlantic Ocean. Please state your name for the record and tell this commission in full detail exactly what you found."

"My name is Henry Hobbes. I do not have a middle name. I was indeed the chief mate of the British vessel *Gilded Swan* on that fateful day. I am here to tell you all I know. It will be in many respects a duplicate of my testimony before the Admiralty Court held in Gibraltar. That is because the facts as I know them have not changed."

"Please continue."

"Perhaps the best way to begin is to read out loud the captain's logbook entry of December 1, Day 17 of the voyage. I have it here word for word: 'This day begins with a fresh breeze and a clear sea running heavy but the wind moderating. To the east of us near 1400 the man at the wheel (Johnson) saw a sailing ship about four to six miles away with few sails set and steering wildly. She seemed to be in distress; I gave orders to haul up, speak her, and render assistance if necessary. An hour later, near 1500, we drew in close enough to hail her. Getting no answer and seeing no one on deck, we got one of our two boats in the water, and I sent the mate and two men to the vessel. The seas were running high at the time, but they managed very well. The mate and one man boarded her while the third remained in the tender. In about an hour they returned and reported to me. The ship was the *Sea Cloud* out of New York and bound for Naples. She was abandoned with

221

three and a half feet of water in the hold but appeared to be entirely seaworthy.'

"That log entry should tell you much, but I will add details. We left New York just nine days after the *Sea Cloud* departed with her cargo of alcohol in wooden barrels. Our cargo was a shipment of turpentine, our destination Gibraltar. In that port our skipper, Captain Norbert Jonberry, expected to receive instructions from the vessel owners as to where the cargo would be delivered. We carried eight men all told. I was the first mate. A man named Richard Coltrane was the second mate. For several days we had good weather, enduring a rather violent storm only once, even though every day the seas were running high with a brisk wind behind them."

"Please continue."

"On December 4, near two in the afternoon, Abe Johnson at the wheel thought he saw a sail in the distance. Captain Jonberry viewed the vessel through his glass and figured she was about six miles off our portside bow. He could see only two or three sails. The others were either furled or blown away, and the ship was yawing noticeably in the north by northeast breeze. Captain Jonberry summoned me to the deck – I was below and off duty – and pointed out the vessel. She was heading westward at maybe two knots, and neither one of us could see anybody on board. As the log entry indicates, we thought she might need assistance and so moved within hailing distance but got no response. That's when we hauled our wind, lowered a boat, and rowed over. Two of us climbed aboard while the third man remained in our tender to keep her safe."

"And what did you find aboard this apparently seaworthy vessel with not a living soul on board? Give us all the details, please. Take your time and be thorough. You will not try our patience."

"We were on board just long enough to determine she had been abandoned by officers and crew in some haste. We were on the ship an hour and fifteen minutes and made a thorough search and found no one, living or dead. In the mate's cabin we found the vessel's log, and that told us she was the *Sea Cloud* out of New York. We found no lifeboats. The one boat she carried was missing. We found more than three feet of water in the hold, enough to slow the vessel by two knots or more but not enough to sink her. The forecastle had too much water too. The hatch was off, and we judged maybe rain or waves had dashed inside. The unlashed wheel ran free, the binnacle was knocked over to one side, and the compass was broken."

"What about her sails? You said you could see them from a distance. And the ship was making headway with no one at the helm?"

"Yes, sir. We judged she was moving at about two knots. Her sails were self-tending, and so if she came into the wind too far, she would fall off and assume a different tack. When the wind shifted she came about and began to sail on a westerly tack, and that's how we found her. She had two small jibs and a fore topmast staysail driving her on a starboard tack. Two of her sails were blown away, another hung by its corners in shreds. All the rest were furled. The standing rigging was in good condition but not the running rigging. We could tell a storm had battered the running rigging."

"It appears you found no signs of foul play on deck or anywhere else on the ship. The first reports speculated that pirates hit the ship, or perhaps the crew got into the alcohol, went berserk, murdered the officers and passengers, and tried to escape to an island in the ship's boat. I gather that theory does not fly with you. What did you find in the cabin and elsewhere below?"

"I will tell you what we did not find. We found no signs of pirates, violence, or a drunken crew. The cargo had not been touched, had not even shifted. Inspectors in Naples found nine barrels had leaked all their contents. They were made of porous wood and unfit for holding alcohol. Their fumes could have caused the minor explosions Mr. Leo Mack described. The captain's chronometer, sextant, navigation book, and other ship's papers were missing. The ship's safe in the captain's quarters was open, and we found nothing inside. Captain Spooner must have opened it in great haste and grabbed its contents. I doubt if anyone else knew the safe's combination. We found the logbook in the mate's cabin, but some pages seemed to be missing. We found nothing to eat or drink, no cooked food in the galley or any sign of cooking, no embers in the stove, and no table set for a meal for anyone on the ship."

"Some reports said the men who boarded the abandoned ship found hot food in the galley, meals half eaten, and cups of coffee half full as if suddenly abandoned. All that was false? A fabrication?"

"Yes, sir. All that was false. Some newspapers veered from the truth in the name of sensationalism. It was a made-up fiction to add to the drama of the event. You will agree that a stirring story is more fun to read than dry facts. Some reports said we found blood on the deck and a bloody sword. We did not."

"We have read those reports. What did you find specifically?"

"We came across a full store of drinking water and enough provisions in the storeroom to last six months. We found sea chests, some of them quite dry, and women's clothing in the captain's cabin. Also we found in his cabin some clothing that obviously belonged to a little child and some toys. That evidence led us to conclude that a small child had been on board, and later that was confirmed."

"You say your inspection took about an hour. What did you and your men do after that? Did you leave the ship to fend for herself?"

"We did, sir. We clambered over the side into our tender, all this time tossing in the waves and banging against the hull of the ship in spite of Johnson's efforts to fend off. We went back to the *Gilded Swan*, and the *Sea Cloud* moved slowly in a westerly direction. Aboard our vessel again, we reported to Captain Jonberry. I wanted to salvage the boat, but our captain was reluctant to spare two or three men from a small crew."

"A prudent captain concerned with safety and up against a situation calling for a difficult decision. What caused him to relent?"

"It was my opinion I could sail the boat with a couple of men to safe harbor in Gibraltar. The captain insisted he couldn't spare three men of seven. To do so would put both ships in jeopardy. However, because the cargo of the *Sea Cloud* was of considerable value, eventually he allowed me to take two men and give it a try. Between us and Gibraltar lay six hundred miles of ocean with unpredictable perils for two small ships with minimal crews. Also I should add, both ships were loaded with a volatile and dangerous cargo."

"What you have said to this commission is most interesting, Mr. Hobbes, and certainly dismisses any number of misconceptions. We appreciate all you've told us, and we've taken careful notes. At this juncture let us take a brief recess for a light repast. Please make yourselves available in one hour for the rest of your story. Enjoy your supper and rest a bit, for this hearing could extend well into the evening."

"Welcome back, gentlemen. I think we are all here now and seated. You may continue with your testimony, Mr. Hobbes. When we adjourned, you and two men were returning to the derelict ship with the intention of sailing her to safe harbor. Your purpose was to salvage the ship and her valuable cargo. You proved your competence as worthy seamen beyond a doubt, and we commend you. Some of us contend you were foolhardy to attempt such a feat, and perhaps a little greedy as well?"

"I do not deny that greed was a motivating factor though not the most important. You must know that a sailor's life is a hard one, and any time he has the chance to fill his pockets with coin, an insistent voice within will tell him to do it. It's the will to survive and prosper. And yet I think we sailed that ship to see if it could be done. We climb mountains for the same reason. Summoning the strength to accomplish a splendid feat is fundamental to human nature."

"Your thoughts on the subject are well reasoned, Mr. Hobbes, and quite sound. Now will you please continue?"

"Captain Jonberry placed me in command and chose two men to accompany me. These were more experienced men, not the two who went with me first to the ship. He let us have one of two small boats, a barometer, a compass, charts of that part of the sea, and a clock. Also we took along some food the steward had prepared and the nautical instruments I take with me on every voyage. In the late afternoon we went about the task of putting the *Sea Cloud* in readiness for the remainder of her journey."

"Please state for the record the names, rank, and social station of the men under your command on the *Sea Cloud*."

"They were both able-bodied seamen who knew sailing ships and the sea well. Their names were Gregory Dutton and Peter Hampton. Both were and are respectable British citizens of the working class. At sea, however, we judge a man by the gumption he demonstrates, not by the stigma of social station."

"Gumption. I think we understand the word. And you speak of social station as stigma? Well, never mind. We have the names of your crew duly recorded. Please continue."

"Before night came we had pumped out most of the water that flooded the hold, reeved some new running rigging, and set all necessary sail to get underway. It took about three days for the ship to fall into her traces, as we say, and begin to pull her weight, but eventually we had her going well. Until that time we lost headway, and the *Gilded Swan* moved well ahead of us and slowly disappeared in the mist. She got to Gibraltar well before we did, and yet we managed to arrive intact just as a storm was approaching – tired in every bone and sinew but watchful and happy."

"When exactly did you drop your anchor at Gibraltar, and how long were you and your men at sea?

"Captain Jonberry and his crew got into port early in the morning on December 8 after twenty-four days at sea. We came in late in the evening of December 9. So we were not too far behind after all. We were on the *Sea Cloud*, just the three of us, for one week and one day, and to my reckoning we sailed the ship close to 600 miles in good weather. That averages to less than a hundred miles a day, but one must take into account the three days it took to set her right."

"You say good weather for 600 miles. What was the weather like as you and two men sailed that ill-fated ship?"

"We had fine weather most of the time. The wind remained in the north and never increased to high velocity. We had a good beam reach mile after mile under sunny skies most of the time in seas no more than three feet or less. But as we made landfall and approached the Strait of Gibraltar, a storm moved in from the southwest and hit us hard. We furled our sails and ran under bare poles until its fury was spent. Then for a few hours we sat in confused seas in sight of land. A confused sea is the state of the water after a storm. We could do nothing but wait for a steady breeze to correct the seas and give us power to move. The sea often requires a sailor to wait."

"Your were on the ship for more than a week. That gave you time to explore every nook and cranny. We would like to know what you came upon below, from deck to hold, during that time. Please take a moment to recollect and give us details. On second thought, why don't we take a ten-minute break for some tea or coffee."

"You look refreshed after drinking your tea, Mr. Hobbes. We can see that you as an Englishman like that beverage better than coffee, but we are now ready to hear the last of your testimony. Before the break you were about to describe what you found below decks."

"I will begin with the captain's quarters. It seemed to me everything he owned was left in his cabin. That indicated he was in a great hurry to get off his ship, or he expected to return after a short interval. I judged a woman had been on board, but the rumpled and wet bed was left unmade and wet clothing was on the cabin sole. I found a number of nautical charts and books, some wet and some dry, but no charts on the table. In a corner and on the bed were some toys made for a small child. In a chest marked with the captain's initials was more clothing, mainly for a woman, and under the berth was a pair of sea boots. An entry in the logbook dated November 8 showed they had come within sight of Sao Miguel Island in the Azores and planned to anchor behind it. The logbook, as I said earlier, was in the mate's cabin. Its last entry was brief and dated November 9. It was garbled as if written with a shaky hand very fast in heavy seas."

"Can you remember what the entry said?"

"It said they had chosen to sail north of the Azores to avoid an approaching storm. The usual route to Gibraltar would have been well south of the islands. They had anchored in the lee of Sao Miguel, and in early afternoon were on course toward Gibraltar to the southeast. Land was sighted to the southwest, which they took to be Santa Maria Island, the southernmost of the nine islands. Beyond that, as you know, is the vast and open sea."

"You explored the rest of the ship. What did you find in the mate's cabin, in the forecastle, in the galley, and the hold?"

"In the mate's cabin we found in addition to the log book a chart hanging over his bed. Sea charts are often quite big, and so to hang a chart as on a clothes line in restrictive quarters is not unusual. On the chart was the ship's track from New York, calculated by dead reckoning and other means. Clearly shown was the last position of the *Sea Cloud* northeast of the Azores. We also found some books, some clothing, and a small harmonica. Everything in that cabin was in place, but we could see it was left in haste."

"And what did you find later in other parts of the ship?"

"In the galley we found the usual pots and pans, a cold stove, and no sign of a recent meal prepared. The stovepipe was knocked askew. Other than that everything in the galley was in order. In the forecastle, or fo'c's'le as we sailors call it, we found many personal items belonging to the men who lived and slept there. Every man had a sea chest, except for two brothers who shared one. The chests contained pipes, tobacco, reading material, clothing, various trinkets like the harmonica I mentioned, and so on. In the hold we found a cargo of 1,701 barrels of raw alcohol. I found out later it was being shipped to Naples to fortify wine made in Italy. We checked the barrels carefully and found them all in place. Not a one had shifted. However, when the cargo was unloaded in Italy, the dock hands found out that nine of the barrels made of porous wood had leaked their contents."

"Other than the barrels that made up the cargo, did you find any wine, beer, or whiskey on board? During the time you were sailing the ship to Gibraltar, did you smell alcohol in the hold?"

"We checked the hold daily and did not see any barrels leaking and did not smell alcoholic fumes. Our search of the boat revealed no spirits on board whatever. The captain of the *Sea Cloud*, Captain Spooner by name, was said to be a teetotaler and did not allow alcoholic beverages, not even beer, on board. Particularly on this voyage there would have been none because his wife and child were present. I should add I saw in the captain's cabin a pair of tiny shoes with socks tucked into them. They obviously belonged to a little child."

"At the time you were exploring the ship and sailing her to Gibraltar, did you form a theory as to why the ship was abandoned?"

"I did, sir. It was apparent the *Sea Cloud* had weathered a storm, had taken on a lot of water, but had not been knocked on her beam-ends. If that had happened, the cargo would have shifted, and it did not. So I concluded the captain and crew judged the ship to have enough water in the hold to be deemed unsafe. Being near an island, they thought they could abandon the ship, which they thought was about to sink, and make it to land in the small boat. Now I know from Mr. Leo Mack's testimony that the reason for leaving the vessel in a hurry was a rumble in the hold that sounded like small explosions. That, I now believe, produced an over-riding fear of a violent explosion. Everyone knew the cargo was volatile. We saw a line trailing in the water from the transom. Mr. Mack has said it was attached to the life boat as they waited to see what would happen, but then a storm blew in and the line was severed."

"Yes, that severed line! If not for that, probably nothing untoward would have happened. Mr. Mack has said it was knotted to the life boat's painter. That in my opinion was the fatal mistake."

"We were not able to tell if the knot gave way or whether the smaller line parted and broke. All we saw is what appeared to be a halyard from the ship's rigging, and Mr. Mack confirms that."

"Yes, the facts as stated appear to be accurate. Testimony from the one survivor of the disaster, coupled with the account of the man who saved the derelict ship, seems in effect the last chapter of the saga. The mystery of the *Sea Cloud* appears to be no longer a mystery. This commission wishes to thank you both for your appearance before it and for your unstinting cooperation. For your time and your willingness to bare all, we have decided to pay you both a small fee."

Editor's Note. *As editor of this tale, I should make it clear that neither Leo Mack nor Henry Hobbes expected to receive a fee, for they believed it was their duty to testify without compensation. They were pleasantly surprised, therefore, when the commission paid each of them a generous sum for their testimony. For Leo Mack, who at the time had*

no job and dwindling resources, it was far more than "a small fee." He was delighted to have the money, for he could live on it while looking for a job. His story moves into other adventures in the next chapter.
— E. Kingston

Chapter 17

Home Again

For the second time in my life I was in New York, haunting the waterfront and looking for a berth on a boat. I was older and no longer so spry but unlike the early days I had some money in my pocket. In those earlier days though young and strong and more energetic than now, I was living from hand to mouth and often went hungry. In those days I was always in a hurry, always rushing to get somewhere as if some ogre or monster was chasing me. Now I could saunter along, spit on the sidewalk, and take my time. If I couldn't find anything to my liking, I could always travel south again. I talked with owners of vessels and skippers, but they were all looking for someone younger. A first mate on a rusty tramper bluntly told me I was too old, able bodied and experienced or not.

"You have to be young to be a sailor, Pops, and you ain't young no more! I think you gotta look for a job that don't require work."

I didn't say a word in reply to that bum. I just turned my back on him and walked away. But I can tell you I was thinking I was young enough to kick his ass, and I could have done it too. But why bother? Why bother to run the risk of a broken jaw? Why bother to get into a fight and get tossed in jail on bread and water when I had better things to do? So I walked away and said nothing, and I don't regret it either. My brother Luke was the hothead of the family, and the last I heard he was in jail for a good long time. More and more while looking to go to sea again I was thinking about the family in Kelly Junction. Ma and Pa were dead and Luke in jail, but Lena was alive and blind and probably needing my help. I kept thinking the least I could do was to see how things were going with her. But Kelly Junction was a long way from New York. I could send a wire, but probably in that isolated village they never heard of the telegraph.

So I moped around New York half-heartedly looking for a job on the waterfront and thinking of home. I don't like to admit it, but the punk who thought I was too old to go to sea again was right. I talked to a lot of people who might have hired me, but all of them said they were looking for younger men. That's when I first realized you don't have many old sailors. Some go to sea at thirteen and stay at it for thirty years or more, but when they start pushing fifty, if they didn't get to be a captain, it's back on land for them. How they manage to survive after their seafaring days I don't know. I've heard of charitable organizations that help an old sailor stay on his feet, but like a soup kitchen they can do just so much for only a short time. Then if the man don't find a job washing dishes or sweeping floors, he's on the streets and homeless with no hope and no place to go. I got to thinking that if I wasn't careful in the present, that could be my future. I didn't want to be down and out in a big city with no friends and no relatives and getting old and feeble at the same time.

I had money in my pocket and didn't have to find a job right away, but one afternoon when I was strolling down a street in the Bowery I saw "Help Wanted" in front of a business that turned out to be a bakery. I went inside mainly out of curiosity and talked to the baker's fat wife. She said her husband needed a helper, but I would have to talk with him about the job. She said he comes to work very early to do the baking for the day and then goes home for rest and shut-eye most afternoons. She said if I came back at the noon hour, I'd be able to talk with him. At that time his duties for the day would be done, and he might be in a good mood. So I went back the next day and talked to the baker. His name was Otto Preminger and he had a big neck, no chin, a baldhead, little black eyes in a fat face, and the biggest potbelly I think I've ever seen.

I don't know if it came from drinking too much beer or eating too much pastry, but that belly was just plain big. He had to be on his feet many hours every day, moving with that belly of his in the close confines of a kitchen with hot ovens. So it was no surprise to me he was looking to hire someone. He spoke with a thick German accent and I'm not sure I understood every word he said, but he needed a helper and I was there to help and so he hired me. He said he really wanted an apprentice to learn the trade, but I was too old for that. I asked him about hours and wages, and he said the workday would run from 4 in the morning to 3 in the afternoon with half an hour for lunch and Sundays off. The pay would be four dollars a week plus lunch every day. The lunch would be good German food prepared by his wife, and I could wash it down with a beer. On the job I would mix ingredients according to his instructions and bake them to produce breads and pastries. Also I would have to roll, shape, and cut dough for cookies and pies. When all the baking was done and before I left for the day, I would have to clean all the equipment, including baking pans and ovens, and mop the floor.

I don't have to tell you it was not an easy job, but I had never done that kind of work and was curious to know what it was like. I straggled out of bed at just a little after three in the morning and walked several blocks in darkness and got there near four. I had to go around to the back door to get in and found the old baker already firing up his ovens and rolling out pastry dough. His wrinkled shirt looked like he had slept in it, but he was wearing a baker's hat and a white apron that covered his belly. His fat hands were white with flour and a smudge of white was on his pink face. His little beady eyes twinkled when he saw me, and quickly he put me to work using a big rolling pin on a pile of very resistant dough.

"We make pies and pie crusts this morning," he said to me. "I have the dough ready. You roll it nice and thin and I fill with fruit and we bake. We make apple pies. You like apple pie?"

I liked apple pie and still do, and when the pies began to bake I couldn't believe how good they smelled. He knew exactly how long to bake them, and when he took them out of the oven they were golden and sumptuous. That's when I learned a baker must resist the atmosphere he creates when he does his job. He can't fall victim to the way an apple pie smells when it comes out of the oven, or to the way it looks. He can't take a knife and cut the pie in half and eat it with a tall glass of milk. That's exactly what I wanted to do but knew I couldn't. It was agonizing 'cause I got up earlier than usual and had no breakfast and was hungry. Otto could see my distress and offered me a cup of coffee.

"I make strongest coffee in neighborhood," he said. "You drink one cup my coffee and you got pep all day. It's black and thick and smells like a wet dog!"

"I'd sure like a slice of pie with the coffee," I answered slyly.

"No pie for you. No pie for me neither! Pastry chefs don't eat on job. It's first rule you remember, Leo. You drink coffee now. Pretend to chew on every sip. It calms your hunger. You eat soup and bread and strudel for lunch."

And he was right. One mug of coffee allowed me to work from four till eleven smelling apple pie, cherry pie, flakey German pastries, and loaves of golden bread fresh from the oven. For lunch Frau Preminger served a thick and tasty soup with German sausages and day-old strudel for dessert. Then it was back to work half an hour later. Otto left his domain shortly after the noon hour but required me to stay until three. After he left I had to clean up the kitchen and all its utensils and have the place prim and proper for the big man to perform his artistry the next day.

Once I got used to working in Otto's kitchen I didn't mind it all that much. It was small for two men, one big and one middle-sized, and I bumped into him several times that first week. Each time it happened he muttered something I didn't understand, something like Dummkopf! I think it meant dummy, knucklehead, idiot or fool, and of course it was just his way of letting off steam. We got along all right after I ceased to bump into him, and I noticed the longer I worked the more satisfying were the hot lunches Frau Preminger prepared. I mean sometimes her lunches were so filling I didn't bother to eat supper when I finally got off work. Or maybe I was just too tired to eat. I'd get back to my room in the late afternoon and fall into bed and sleep sometimes until dark. As I said, it was not an easy job and I never quite adjusted to getting up so early in the morning, but I worked with Otto long enough to call myself a baker even though I didn't have any papers or the like to prove it.

When fall came I began to have thoughts of moving southward again. It was already getting chilly in New York, and I didn't want to spend another winter in a cold climate. I didn't have any special love for Kelly Junction and was no longer an Irish Traveler yearning to go home again, but I remembered the climate as always good. When snow and ice were on the ground in northern states, boys in South Carolina were shooting marbles for keeps. Any time we knocked an opponent's marble out of the ring, we kept it. I was pretty good at shooting marbles and by the end of the season I always had more than when I started. When the season began in March, I had a big purple bag – I think it was made of felt – filled with beautiful glassies ablaze with color. It was a custom among the boys to trade with other shooters, and I had some aggies all of them envied and wanted. The marbles were made of agate and looked like gemstones, and they were hard enough to crack other marbles. Well, anyway, I had a hankering to go home again. I had a nostalgic remembrance of good weather as early as March and good weather for Christmas and good times mostly when I was growing up.

By the time I decided I would go home again railroads were replacing canals and even offshore ships for travel north and south along the eastern seaboard. So I was able to get on a train pulled by a steam locomotive in New York and go all the way to Columbia, South Carolina but not on the same train. Because of the different gauges, I had to change trains several times along the way and that was a headache. Even so, it was a lot better and faster than traveling by coach and less expensive too. Later they made the railroads the same gauge so all lines could be connected, and a lot of people went to working on the railroads and even made up songs about it. As you know, slave labor was used to build some of the southern railroads, and the blacks were in the habit of working to the rhythm of a good song as they pounded the rails in place. The bosses didn't mind the singing at all 'cause they worked better and faster that way. In the free states blacks and whites worked together, but I'm not sure they sang together. I do know the pay for working on the railroad was pretty good, and I thought I might give it a try, but other things got in the way and I didn't. It's just as well 'cause you have to be young and strong to lay railroad track. You sweat a lot even when the day is cold, and you eat as much as you can just to keep going.

I went all the way from New York to Columbia. That put me some distance from Kelly Junction, but there was no railroad in that neck of the woods until much later. So I had to go to Columbia and then double back to get to Kelly Junction, and it took me almost as long to get there from Columbia as it did to Columbia from New York. I couldn't afford to go by coach, and so I finally hitched a ride with a hacker traveling that way. The ride down on the train was as memorable for its discomfort as for how fast we went, and maybe I should tell you about it.

Children on the train were rowdy and unsupervised. Fat men with fat cigars filled the car with a haze of blue smoke that burned my nostrils and turned my stomach. An old man with a gray beard and a hacking cough was hugging a burlap bag filled with live poultry. A frowzy woman in clothes that looked like they were made for someone else was eating fried chicken and other goodies. She lifted each piece from a large tin bucket, gnawed it to the bone, licked her stubby fingers, smacked her lips loudly, smiled like an angel, and began on another. The odor of fried food has always made me hungry, and for an instant I thought I might ask the woman for a drumstick. She had several in her bucket and could surely spare one, but something inside me, maybe foolish pride, stood in the way of asking. I decided I would have to wait for the next station to eat.

I came into Kelly Junction late one autumn night when the town was completely deserted. None of the houses had any lights burning and nothing moved except for a stray hound dog sniffing his way down the street. Then I saw a gaslight way down near the end of the street and walked toward it. I guess you can say I was in luck 'cause that light was in front of the Volunteer Fire Department and the big door was wide open. Inside was the one fire wagon the village owned, and it looked all shiny and new. In a small room in back three men were playing poker. I said I didn't want to interrupt their game but needed a place to sleep for the night. I asked if it would be all right to drop my haversack on the floor near the fire engine and sleep there. When they said they couldn't allow no tramp to sleep in their place, not even for one night, I told them I had served as a fireman in Baltimore and was told all firemen are brothers wherever they happen to be. Well, they asked me a few trick questions to be certain I wasn't lying and gave me leave to stay there. They even brought out an old mattress for me to sleep on and put it near the fire wagon and offered me a snort of booze that I refused.

Morning came and I found myself back in my hometown after being away for a long time. I thanked the men at the fire station for letting me spend the night there, asked if any had ever heard of the Mack family, and one had a vague remembrance of my old pa. I asked if he knew anything about my older brother Luke, but nothing I said seemed to ring a bell. They insisted I have some coffee before I left, and I was glad to have it 'cause at sea I got in the habit of drinking coffee to get the day started. I really needed the big mug they gave me and thanked them again for their hospitality. Then early in the morning I went back up the street to refresh my memory of Kelly Junction and look for the house we lived in long ago. I strolled along for a block or so before I realized I was watching the homecoming of the Irish Travelers. It was fall and they were returning to the nest after being away all summer. Six or seven wagons were slowly moving into the village and down the street, looking almost like a parade. That many or more had come in the day before, and a big celebration was planned to welcome them back. The men at the fire station had talked about festivities coming soon, and now I knew exactly how soon. It was Friday morning. An all-day picnic would begin at 9 or 10 on Saturday, and the entire village would be there.

———

I hadn't lived in Kelly Junction for a long time, but that didn't matter. The saying among Travelers is "Irish forever and a Traveler for as long as you live." So I didn't feel like a stranger and no one treated me like one. I rented a room, just a temporary place, for a reasonable fee. Then I went out and found a little café on the edge of town that served good meals with big portions, and the food was cheaper than any I ever bought in Philadelphia or New York or even in Baltimore. Also the weather was better, and a good fall day was a perfect time to hold the big picnic celebrating the end of the summer season of work. No one specifically invited me to the big event, but as a native son of the village I was naturally invited and looked forward to it. So on Saturday morning after a late breakfast, I went out in the warmth of a sunny day to the picnic site. It

241

was located in a pasture just south of town, and a crowd was already there.

A group of women were working with large wicker baskets of food set up on tables under a gazebo-like shelter erected by village carpenters. Their job was to sort through the baskets and place the food on the tables. People attending the picnic could select what they wanted and take it to the shade of a tree or eat it beside the brook nearby or in the open field where cattle grazed. Although the cows had made the grasses short and neat, one had to watch where he stepped or where to put a picnic cloth. Aromatic herbs seasoning the food – thyme, basil, savory – scented the air, but anyone tromping through the meadow had to be on guard for other aromas. In the middle of September the insects that can be a real bother in the southern climate in summer were gone. The day was warm enough for no coats and even the ants were no problem.

I stood by and listened to happy, carefree children yelling and screeching at play, and I watched intently as the baskets were emptied. I have to tell you I was amazed at the variety of food people had brought to a single picnic. I guess you could call it popular American picnic food with a bit of Irish magic to make it interesting. From one basket after another they unloaded apple pies, cherry pies, peach pies, cookies, deviled eggs, fried chicken with biscuits, macaroni salad, potato salad, pickles of all kinds, summer sausage, and sandwiches stuffed with meat and cheese. To wash it all down, there was lemonade, tea and coffee, and beer.

On a little stage prepared also by the carpenters a band was playing, and on the bare ground couples were sort of jiggling to the music. I'm sure you will agree that no community picnic is worth its salt without music, or at least a bunch of fellows making a racket to simulate music and heighten the festivity. The music never has to be all that good, just loud enough to scare the livestock and with a beat people can feel, and this band was doing all right. Children were dancing in the dirt, and that attracted the teenagers who began to do rowdy jigs to the music. That took up a lot of space and chased away the couples trying to dance slowly.

Near noon the women had a little ceremony to welcome the men of the village back home. Some of the Travelers made little speeches to show their gratitude, and some spoke of their adventures during the summer, and some boasted of the money they made. When all that was over, people began to pick up food at the tables and wander off to eat it. Younger couples drifted down toward the brook or into the woods while the older people, especially the ones with children, stayed more in the open and afterwards played games with balls. The children had a potato-sack relay race and a three-legged race mainly for laughs. I roared at kids bouncing in potato sacks trying to outrun each other, but the three-legged race was even funnier. Most of the time the kids with their legs tied together never made it to the goal line and fell screeching on top of each other. It was a hoot!

The picnic went on like this into the afternoon. Then as some of the men in the crowd got a bit bored, a few brought out pocket flasks filled with gin. Slowly as the flasks were passed around with any number of men (and a few boys too) taking a swig from them, things got a little out of hand. A fight broke out between two hotheads, and they knocked each other into a barbed-wire fence and got all bloody. Their wives ran to clean the blood off their faces, but by then the damage was done and the men had quit fighting and were shaking hands. They swaggered off with clean faces but bloody hands.

As the excitement from all this was beginning to fade, the band playing its tunes even during the fight, another eruption took place. A boy and girl emerged from the woods where they had eaten their food and somehow got a heifer in the pasture all upset and bellicose. The heifer began to chase the two across the field. She had no horns and so couldn't gouge the couple to hurt them all that much, but she was doing a pretty good job with her head. The girl fell down, rolled in the dirt, and lost her skirt. In just her bloomers she sprang to her feet and ran faster than the heifer and finally got to some rocks and climbed up on them and rested all out of breath. Her young man was able to escape the heifer long enough to get her skirt and return it to her. Scores of people watched the real-life drama and breathed a sigh of relief when it was over and no one was hurt.

I talked with a few people that Saturday, but it was mainly small talk. I didn't know any of the people I met and they didn't know me, and so we couldn't get into a conversation with any real meat in it. Most of the men wanted to talk about their travels during the summer, and some of the stuff they said was interesting but most of it I'd heard before. Some of the women didn't want to chat at all, and I could understand that with me being a stranger. Then one woman came along and was open and friendly, and I found out something I wanted to look into later. She said her name was Mary Sullivan, and she told me her mother had known a family in Kelly Junction named Mack. I perked up my ears at that 'cause I really believed she was talking about my family. I asked her if the family had a girl or young woman that was blind or nearly blind. She nodded her head, gave a little thought to it, and even remembered the name.

"I think they called her Lena. My mama told me that everybody in the family had a name that started with an L

244

except the wife and mother, and I think she had a biblical name. Ruth I remember."

"Sarah," I answered. "My mother's name was Sarah."

"Sarah? Really? I'm almost certain it was Ruth. She died a few years ago. For a long time she had trouble with her joints and could just barely move around, and then my mama said she just up and died one day of pleurisy and her joints had nothing to do with it."

"You're right about the names. My papa's name was Liam and he named me Leo and my brother Luke and my sister Lena. He sometimes called my mother Laura though her real name was Sarah. You probably thought it was Ruth 'cause that's a biblical name too. Do you know what happened to Lena or anyone else in the family?"

"I don't really know about the men. I only know Lena was blind and went to live in the county home 'cause she had no one else to look after her after her mother died."

The county home the woman called it. Years ago everybody, even the county officials who ran it, called it the poorhouse. When I was just knee high to a grasshopper my old man scared me silly with threats the whole family would end up in the poorhouse, and he painted a gloomy picture of it. People went there when they were sick or lame or too old to work. It was a warehouse for the old and useless, for people waiting or wanting to die. My daddy didn't call it a prison, as I listened to his vivid description, but said it was just as bad as one. Now as a grown man necessity was forcing me to reckon with the county home or the poorhouse. Lena was there and I wondered if she was being cared for properly. She could be comfortable and content or miserable. I would have to find out, and I would have to do it without beating around the bush.

Chapter 18

The County Poorhouse

T he weather was not good the day I walked all the way to the poorhouse. Owned by the county, it was some distance from Kelly Junction. In recent years people had started to call it the county farm because that sounded better than poorhouse. Also the place had more than a hundred acres of land surrounding it, and the people sent there were required to cultivate the soil and work it. Several gardens supplied fresh vegetables in summer, and the farm had a large potato patch and cornfield. Of course some like my sister weren't able to work outside, and that placed them beneath the residents that could. On the lowest rung of the social ladder, they were pariahs in an institution that was itself a pariah. Even though the citizens of Kershaw County supported the place with their taxes, they shunned it.

From a distance as one walked up the narrow lane leading to it, the sprawling three-story building made of white stone and yellow brick looked impressive. One got the feeling it was a rich plantation owner's mansion, or maybe a country manor in the English countryside. The builders that erected it thirty years before I got there were apparently well funded and did a good job. The building looked rich and appealing, but when you got there you found out it was just the opposite of all that. It was a county-run residence where paupers (mainly elderly and disabled people) were supported at minimum public expense. It was a bureaucratic institution funded by unwilling taxpayers, and it was not a happy place.

When I walked inside I expected to be greeted by some official who would ask about my business there and try to answer whatever questions I had. In the wide, open space beyond the front door I found people shuffling about in a kind of daze and dressed in what seemed to be sleeping clothes even though it was late in the morning. I saw a counter off to one side and a desk behind it, but no one was there. So I just wandered about to get my bearings and merged with the sleepwalkers. Within minutes an old woman tugged at my sleeve and began to talk to me in a low, confidential voice as if she didn't want anyone but me to hear what she was saying. Her aggressive behavior confused me a little, but I listened to what she had to say as she pulled me to a little alcove near a window where she sat down and urged me to sit.

"I'm old and gray and sixty-seven," she began in a gravelly voice that became sort of chirpy the longer she spoke, "but I don't deserve this. They brought me here two weeks ago 'cause I was down and out with no family no more, and they called me a pauper. I asked them am I lazy or crazy, am I blind or lame? You don't see that I am, do you? I can work for a living and pay my way. Just help me find work and leave me be. They just laughed at me and hustled me to a tiny little hole they called a room."

She was intense beyond her years and struggling to understand what had happened to her. She wanted me to listen and perhaps understand and help her in some way. I began to feel sorry for her.

"What happened to your family?" I asked in the same quiet tone she had adopted. "Couldn't you go live with a daughter or a son? Are you a widow now? Do you have no friends or relatives?"

"I was married to a good man and we worked hard and raised a family, but as the years pass, you know, things fall apart."

"No, I don't know. What do you mean?"

"We had three daughters and three sons and we raised them every one, worked for them summer and winter, night and day, and then when they got grown they drifted away. Then the Lord Almighty came one day and took my John and I was alone but not for long. My son, my unemployed Charlie, came to live with me and brought with him his hoity-toity little bride."

"Well now, that's good to hear. Things must of got better then. You were not alone any more. You had another woman as your companion when Charlie had to go looking for work."

"No, things didn't get better. Charlie couldn't keep a job even when he was lucky enough to find one. And try as I might I could never please his wife. We didn't even speak the same English. We couldn't get along at all. It was fussin' and cussin' all the time, and I got bone tired of it and went to live with Susan. But Susan's place was tiny and crowded somethin' awful, what with her husband and his two unmarried sisters and three children under ten. Well, soon I could see there wasn't no room for me."

"So what did you do then?"

"I went to live with my boy Tom but that didn't last either. His children were soon all over me, and he expected me to care for every one of the five like one of my own, and I tried to teach them some manners, and he got huffy when they complained.

He made it clear he was the boss of all the children, not me. So I wrote to Becky, hoping to get away from Tom, but she said the climate up north was too cold for an old woman."

"Now I understand. None of your children wanted you 'cause you were in the way and interfered with their lives."

"I guess you can say that, but I can tell you one thing. All the time they was growing up I was never in the way. It was always 'Mama do this, Mama do that, Mama find my shoes. Mama go buy us something good to eat. We're hungry, Mama, cook us some rice and beans and feed us!' Well, to make a long story short, Charlie took steps and I ended up here, and I still say I don't deserve it. I just don't deserve it. Nobody old or not should be treated so bad."

Her name, she said, was Helen. I think I caught her last name as Hopkins but couldn't be sure. She was so slight and frail a puff of wind was ready to double her up and turn her over, ready to blow her away like a wilted leaf in a storm. Though I could see her health was not the best, her senses were keen enough and she had feelings, and her loved ones had made her suffer. She wanted to know if I was new to the place. Before I could explain I was there looking for my sister Lena and expecting to find her blind, the woman had drifted away from me and was already telling her story to a tall and lanky man who walked with a cane.

I went on down the hall into what they call the common room. All the residents who couldn't be outside and working seemed to be in that room. It was filled with a new and different race of people. In rags and tatters and nightclothes, many were short of stature and paunchy. Some were old and wrinkled and wearing on haggard faces either a silly smile showing one or two teeth or a frown. Here and there in a resounding chaos of misery I found little spots of what appeared to be happiness. However, at best it was a dull, animal happiness that seemed delusional to me.

Most of the residents in this poorhouse, this "county home" as some would have it, teetered on the brink of despair and were clearly wretched. Some of them were so emaciated they looked like walking cadavers. Here and there a tottering old man or woman in nightclothes and slippers lurched forward to accost me, and in their effort almost fell to the floor. Outside within plain view of everyone inside, a man and woman in flimsy clothing were searching through what looked like a pile of garbage. They were greedily eating whatever they could find and squabbling. The crisp air of autumn carried inside the sound they made, and it caught my attention. I stood at the window and watched with sad eyes the ruined gold of the yellowing trees drift downward, the dead leaves falling on thin shoulders.

In the common room a severe-looking woman I took to be a nurse was seated behind a counter. I believe at one time in her life she just had to be pretty, but her prettiness had no grip on time and was doomed to fade away like the colors of autumn. Her sensitive, aquiline nose and black eyes were in a cheap magazine. Looking at the pictures and flipping the pages, she didn't notice me. I stood at the counter to speak to her, expecting her to say something. She didn't. I waited for her to speak. She didn't even look at me. For her, it seemed, a magazine was more important than a living soul. I cleared my throat, hoping to get her attention, and spoke first.

"I'm here looking for my sister. I was told she's living here but I just don't know. Her name is Lena Mack and she's blind."

The woman closed her magazine, placed a thin, blue-veined hand on it, and looked at me with tired eyes. Slowly she began to speak. In the midst of a rising tide of incoherent babble, I could barely hear her. An old woman was screeching, 'You hit me! You hit me! How dare you!' An old man in the rigid stance of a preacher in a pulpit was loudly reciting what sounded like a biblical verse. A younger man was singing a throaty ballad and pretending to conduct an orchestra. All three had energy, and yet in the stupefying atmosphere that pervaded the place a poisonous torpor seemed to wrap around them, make them two-dimensional, and deaden them.

"I don't know a blind resident by that name," the nurse was saying through the din. "I work in the West Wing most of the time and don't have the records here. If you go to the main office, they might be able to help you. I've been here thirteen years and ran into several blind people, but I don't know a blind Lena."

I thanked her for her reply even though I got no help from her. She had worked there a long time, and what did she get for all the time she had put into the place? I could tell by just looking at her. She got a tired, sullen face surrounded by hair turning gray. She got a frowsy and soiled white frock they called a uniform and probably had to wash and iron it herself. She got toil and boredom and a lung condition, she told me, and also stooped shoulders and callused hands. She had spent the best years of her life in a warehouse filled with sick and deranged people. The respectable citizens and vocal politicians of her county had labeled these people paupers, had hidden them away at some expense from other people, and had hired this woman to look after them. I began to feel sorry for her.

"I'm wondering," I said, "what the rules and regulations are for this place. I hear institutions have all kinds of regulations."

"Oh, we have a long list of rules for the government and good order of the county farm," she replied. "I took the time to read through most of the rules and it seems to me they are very humane. This ain't a prison, you know. It's a home for the poor. It ain't no hotel but we try to make it tolerable."

"It seems more like an asylum or hospital or even a prison than a home," I said with some emotion. "Some of the people milling around in this room don't have their full wits about them, and some appear to be sick. And you and I both know not one, not a single man, woman, or child has the freedom to leave this place."

"Well, sir, it is the county poorhouse and it was never meant to be a resort. People sent here are maintained by public funds and Kershaw is not a wealthy county. I think I might have a copy of the rules in a drawer somewhere. Would you like to see them? Most people don't bother to ask, but every station is supposed have a copy."

She rummaged in a drawer and found the document. It had a long title I think I remember. It went something like this – *Rules and Regulations and Bylaws for the Government and Good Order of the County of Kershaw Farm in the State of South Carolina.* I read through some of the rules and they didn't seem totally harsh, but even as I read I knew many were being ignored. One rule in particular caught my attention: *When any person dies, the female assistant shall immediately take care of the clothes belonging to the deceased, cause them to be washed and mended, and deposit them in the storeroom provided for clothing.* That same rule, I knew from experience, applied to the clothing of an inmate who died in prison. Other rules said all persons who could work would work. Any person claiming to be sick to get out of work and found to be well by a physician would be sent to solitary confinement and fed on bread and water until fully compliant. Any person late for dinner without a valid excuse would forfeit the meal, and no person would talk at dinner. Any person found to have a contagious disease would be kept in solitary confinement until well again or dead. And they said this was not a prison? Many of the rules and regulations were exactly the same as for prisons.

———◈———

I wished the woman well and went in search of the main office. As I walked down the dark corridors past numerous cramped little chambers, I could tell the sanitation of the place was less than perfect. In spite of what the rules dictated, no attempt was being made to ventilate the rooms and corridors properly. I could feel a clammy dampness in the air, and strange odors merged into other odors the farther I went. The unhealthy atmosphere of the place brought on visions of my blind sister falling victim to diphtheria, croup, typhoid, erysipelas, bronchitis, pneumonia, consumption, and kindred disorders. I felt the death rate was probably quite high in this selfless, benevolent, altruistic home funded and operated by the good taxpayers of Kershaw County. It was in fact much the opposite of a refuge or home. All I had seen convinced me it was a Bastille where paupers went to die, and I feared my sister was no longer among the living.

I went through a maze of corridors before reaching the main office. As luck would have it, I got there just as the clerk was closing his operation for the day. He was a self-important little man in his middle fifties with big ears and a fringe of gray hair on either side of his head. His blue eyes above pale cheeks blinked behind little round spectacles and looked watery. He appeared to be filing some papers, and I stood behind the counter and waited for him to finish. When he turned to tell me the office was about to close, I could see his arms were long even though his torso and legs were quite short. He spoke with a southern drawl typical of the region surrounding Kelly Junction but different from the speech of Irish Travelers.

"We're closing, mister. You'll have to come back tomorrow. If you need to talk to somebody, try to get here early. The office opens at 6:30, closes at 5."

"I know you want to get home, but I'm wondering if you can tell me quickly if my sister is a resident here. I was told the county board placed her here maybe two years ago."

"Yes, I do need to get home. My old mother ain't well and I have to leave her there alone all day when I come here. As I said, mister, I can't help you today. You'll have to come back tomorrow, and the sooner the better before the work piles up."

"I've heard you have a ledger with all the names of the inmates. Will you take a few minutes to look at it? My sister's name is Lena Mack. I don't think she would have signed in by any other name."

"If your sister is living here she's a resident, my dear man, not an inmate. We don't use that word here. The rules strictly forbid it. We don't call our residents inmates."

"I meant no disrespect, sir, but I do understand that people who come here can't leave of their own account any time they feel like it. Will you see if you can find her name, please?"

I was being too pushy and knew it. I was trying to seize the chance to get information as soon as I could, and I saw no harm in that. The officious little man took me by the elbow and without saying a word ushered me out of his office. Then as I stood in the corridor bewildered and becoming angry, he seemed to take pity on a flustered visitor and spoke curtly but kindly.

"I'm not able to do that now, my good man, 'cause the office is closed and the books are put away. You walked in just as I was closing up. My advice is to come back tomorrow morning bright and early. A body will be here to help you then."

The poor farm was located at least six miles from town, and I had walked that distance for nothing. Now I would have to go back to my room and make the same trek into the countryside the next day. I was not in a good mood as I trudged back to Kelly Junction. I was asking only ten minutes of the clerk's time, but he couldn't be bothered to accommodate me. Then I placed myself in his shoes and understood he had every right to call it a day after a very long day. And he needed to get home to his mama who was old and alone and in poor health. He had come to work at six, had taken half an hour for lunch, and was determined at all costs to leave at five.

———◆———

Early in the morning of the next day I went back to the poorhouse looking for Lena. A different clerk on this day was there behind the counter, a taller man who seemed ready to help when my turn came. Already a number of people were waiting, and for nearly an hour I waited. When I informed the man why I was there, he smiled wanly and rummaged under the counter. From beneath it he pulled out a ledger bound in faded green cloth and almost as wide as a newspaper. He placed the heavy volume on the counter and opened it. Inside were many names. I asked how many but got an evasive answer. Maybe he wasn't allowed on pain of losing his job to give out any more information than necessary.

The ledger had alphabetical tabs pasted on the pages. He found the M tab, flipped the pages to that place, and ran his finger down the page. Macaulay was close to the top of the list and then Mack. His finger stopped on Mack, obscuring the name. I waited for him to move it or to speak. Then when the finger moved away, to my surprise I read "Sarah Mack, 8 mos." In smaller script beside it were the words, "Wife of Liam Mack, occupation unknown." There was no doubt about it. My old gentle-hearted mama, wracked by pain in all her joints, died in the poorhouse in winter after being there eight months. Maybe I shouldn't admit it, but I felt a little weak in the knees when I saw that. Later, thinking logically about it, I reasoned if Mama was alive in the poorhouse eight months before she died, Lena was probably there with her.

"Does this tell me," I asked the clerk, "that Lena never lived here? I have it on pretty good authority she came here too."

"Well, it don't say she did and it don't say she didn't. Just says a Sarah Mack came and went. Did you know her?"

"She was my mother, and the mother of two other children."

"I take it the one called Lena was the daughter. I don't see no Lena above Sarah on this alphabetical list, but this is an old ledger. Gimme a few minutes and I'll see if I can't find another book more up to date." He rummaged under the counter a second time and came up with a ledger looking newer.

"I think I'm gonna have to ask you to sit over there 'cause you're not supposed to be looking at the records. Rules, y' know."

I found a wooden chair beside the flyspecked window and sat down. For half an hour or more I waited for the clerk to tell me something, wondering why it was taking so long. Then I discovered he had to go off on an errand to another part of the building. Beside me in another chair was a grim-faced young woman who had come to visit her elderly parents. To pass the time we began to chat. They had a good marriage and a good living, she told me, until her papa fell off a wagon at work and broke a leg. Instead of paying for his hospital bill and waiting for him to get well again, his employer fired him. Her mother tried to keep the wolf from the door by sewing garments, but that was only seasonal work, and so with every passing day they slipped downward and deeper into poverty. When they could no longer pay their rent or buy the simplest food to stay alive, they were forced to apply for beds in the poorhouse. Because so many others were ahead of them on the waiting list, they starved before being admitted and came in as walking skeletons. By then their health was broken and the daughter didn't expect them to live long.

I asked why didn't she take them into her house and look after them. She hesitated before answering and slyly wiped away a tear. She said she lived with her husband and four children in two rooms and couldn't find the space for another bed even if they could have bought another bed. Her husband was a pipefitter, she said, and often didn't have steady work and sometimes drank too much. The woman was no older than thirty but looked fifty. She lived in another part of the county to the north of Kelly Junction, and it seemed to me her life was harder than any Irish Traveler's, even one who might have fallen on hard times. In a sad place, maybe to unburden herself, she was telling a stranger a sad story. Before I could hear the end of her tale the clerk called me back to his desk.

"I found the entry," he said. "A woman named Lena Mack came here with a woman named Sarah Mack. They were admitted at the same time nearly three years ago. The older woman was infirm with severe rheumatism but able to mop floors. The younger woman was blind and not able to do farm chores or even housekeeping chores, but we put her to hackling flax and picking oakum to help pay her way. As far as I can tell by the record here, she remained in the same room after her mother died and she's still able to work."

For years I had been a sailor, you know, and I knew all about oakum and picking oakum. Sometimes on idle days at sea, especially when becalmed, some of the crew was assigned the task of tearing apart old tarry ropes strand by strand to get a fibrous material used to caulk a vessel's timbers and deck planking. It was an ornery task that blistered your fingers and made them so black even turpentine couldn't clean them. Now I was hearing that delicate Lena, struggling all her life to see more than shifting shadows, was doing that kind of work for a roof over her head, a rickety bed to sleep in, and coarse food to stave off the hunger in her belly. Or if she was not picking oakum she was hackling flax. That too was a hard job but at least she could use a steel comb for the fibers and not her fingers. With no little misgiving I asked the clerk where I might find her, thanking him for the help he gave me as I did so.

"I'm not sure," he replied, "but I think your sister might be living and working in the East Wing of our building. Ask the nurse in charge there. She'll tell you."

I was off again, wandering with not a little agitation through dark and dreary corridors in the midst of sick and demented people. Like ghosts from another world, they shuffled along the hallway staring straight ahead, each of them wearing and sharing an unchanging grimace of pain and confusion. As if mesmerized, they moved in cloth slippers and nightclothes with stiff arms pointing downward. A tall, emaciated man with a long white beard and sparkling eyes, clearly not one of the herd, walked with arms akimbo as if daring the others to bump into him. All of them moved slowly and methodically like puppets on a string, or like lost souls looking for light. The sound they made was like the buzz or chant I had heard in my youth at church, but simplified with only a few words repeated. While some tugged at my clothing and tried to stop me, others less aggressive pressed themselves against the wall to let me pass.

I found the East Wing with no one in charge and found my sister. She was sitting on a hard chair at a table in a tiny room with no door in front of a pile of oakum. The hour was early, but her long hard day of unceasing labor had already begun. I stood in the doorway looking at her, recalling what she looked like in her youth and trying to see a delicate girl in the thin and worn woman. I couldn't.

Chapter 19

Kershaw County

I stood in the narrow hallway for several minutes, observing the figure inside the room. I'm sure my jaw was slack and I was staring in disbelief. I was looking at a scene I hoped I would never see again. My favorite person all the time I was growing up in a turbulent, uncertain household where love and affection were prized commodities had turned into a rapidly aging woman before her time. Her pallid face was drawn and pockmarked. Her frame was so frail she looked as though she would break at any moment. She sat stiffly upright with the oakum piled in front of her, her thin and transparent hands kneading the stuff skillfully and rapidly. She seemed to be looking not at her work but at the blank wall in front of her. Yet I could tell she was blind and seeing only darkness. All the time I had known her she was going blind, and now sitting straight and prim on that hard chair she was without sight but not insight. As a child she had peopled her shadowy world with sunny events, and maybe she was doing that now. A little smile flickered across the thin, cracked lips.

Sensing my presence, she turned to face the doorway, and smiled broadly. In that way she invited her unknown visitor to speak. Struggling to put down feelings that welled up inside me, I didn't know what to say. For a fleeting moment I was sorry I had gone in quest of her. Maybe I was bringing more harm to her than good. Maybe for me to come back into her life would disrupt any peace she might have found. Words of deep feeling rose up in my throat from some place deep within and poured out of my mouth.

"Lena? Your brother Leo is speaking! I'm home from my travels and have a room in Kelly Junction. I've been looking for you."

The mindless, automatic movement of her tar-blackened hands stopped abruptly. The head on the long neck slowly turned away from me, and her hands went back to her work. She was uttering softly something I didn't recognize. I think she was saying, "Billy? Billy?" That name had no meaning for me, and I repeated my name. It had no effect on her. She went saying . . .

"Billy? Billy? Is that you? I will get it done before noon, I promise. Two fingers on my left hand are blistered and hurting, and so I have to go slower than usual. But I'll make my quota. I will, I will."

And then she began to sing in a flat monotone a little song she sometimes sang in childhood . . .

> Rock a bye Billy in that old treetop,
> When the wind blows the cradle will rock,
> When the bough breaks the cradle will fall,
> And down will come Billy, Billy and all!

She had changed the words of the old rhyme and was mocking her taskmaster, predicting doom for him. A sly smile crossed her lips.

I was beside her now, lightly touching her shoulder, and I could feel a tremor running like wildfire down her neck and

261

across the thin shoulders. She reached out, caught my hand, and buried her face in the palm. Her warm affection was the signal I needed to let me know she understood. Not until later did she tell me her sense of smell let her know I was truly her brother. She held my hand to her face for a minute or two before speaking in the way I remembered.

"My prodigal brother returns! After roaming the world the wanderer comes home again! I can't believe it, I really can't believe it. After crossing the wild deserts of the world, Leo is home again!"

"No," I said to her, "no deserts unless you see the rolling ocean as a vast desert. I went to sea. In all my life I never saw a desert."

"You've never seen a desert, Leo? I see them all the time! And they're not all bad, you know. Some bad people put me and Mama in a desert, and I thought the sun would burn us to a crisp. Mama put up a fight but died all dried up in the desert. Lena found a way to survive. I can shut it all out, and then I see blue skies and feel a cool breeze on my face and hear birds chirping. I hear music too, Leo. I often hear the most beautiful music in the middle of the night."

"I can see that very active imagination you had as a child is still with you, Lena. I'm glad you never lost it."

"Oh, Leo, please understand. I'm not always a dreamer lost in a world that never was. Sometimes I think about life and the mystery that surrounds us in the here and now. Sometimes I ask myself what is the secret of human destiny. And then I say to myself, I don't even know what that means! My thoughts can be so confusing!"

She was laughing and I was beginning to laugh with her. Then as we began to talk about home and childhood and Kelly Junction, an attendant in a white coat appeared in the doorway looking perplexed. I tried to explain I was the woman's brother, absent from her for many years, but he didn't understand or care to understand.

"If you really are her brother," he said with a firmness that startled me, "you are seriously breaking the rules. You are causing trouble and must go. We don't allow relatives of residents in the workplace. How did you get here anyway? You must go now."

Without a chance to say goodbye to Lena, with no chance to assure her I would see her later, I was hustled out of the room and down the bleak corridor to the main office. The attendant was a big man, rough and strong. I was in no mood to resist him.

I could hear my sister calling, stricken and disconsolate, "Don't you hurt him, Billy! He's my brother! Don't you dare hurt him!"

She was too weak to stand up to a rabbit, and yet she was cautioning big and burly Billy to go easy on her brother. The spirit of the girl I remembered lived on in the woman who was not entirely broken. I later found out that Billy was notorious for his rough treatment of residents. He felt it was his calling to bully and brutalize paupers of both sexes. He was not confined to a specific wing of the place but had free run of the entire farm. He had misbehaved on his job for years, an ogre and a tyrant feared by all, and he remained unpunished year after year. The rules and regulations I had seen earlier emphasized in every paragraph humane treatment of residents. They didn't seem to apply to Billy.

In minutes I stood before the counter that shielded the main desk to answer charges of trespass. One of five superintendents was sent for, and the staff gathered around him. A dozen people were accusing Leo Mack of willful trespassing in a public institution supported by taxpayers but deemed off limits to taxpayers. A dim-witted clerk, conveniently absent, had given me permission to walk with the walkers, had even told me where to go, but my accusers refused to believe me. Calling themselves compassionate and humane public officials who wanted only to help the poor unfortunates who stumbled into their refuge, they wrangled with the man they called a trespasser for half an hour. Then out of the goodness of his pompous heart the superintendent decided to let me go, but only on one condition. If I ever came back to upset the smooth running of the establishment again, he would have the sheriff throw me in jail.

⸺◦◉◦⸺

I knew what sheriffs thought of Irish Travelers, particularly the sheriff of Kershaw County, and so I knew in the face of such a threat I would have to tread lightly. I knew also I would have to find a way to see my sister again, have her released from that awful place, and have her examined by a competent doctor to determine the state of her health. After making inquiries at the courthouse, I learned it was no easy matter for a friend or relative to bring about the release of any person sent to the poorhouse. Paupers who go there voluntarily may leave at will, I was told (though I doubted it), but anyone seeking the release of a person legally committed would have to go before all five superintendents with a petition. Because Lena was blind, not able to fend for herself, and had no person willing to care for her, she was committed and viewed as a permanent resident. To get her released into my custody, I would have to find each superintendent in whatever office he occupied, arrange a meeting with him, and repeat the act with all the others. I spent an entire day tracking them down and one more day working out an agreement to meet with all of them at the same time. Their names were William Smith, Jesse Wood Jr., John Wilson, Daniel Corwin, and Gilbert Holmes. All were upstanding citizens of Kershaw County.

The meeting took place in a large conference room at the poorhouse near the end of October. The weather was damp and chilly, and again I walked all the way to the county farm for a meeting that lasted two hours and then trudged homeward again. On going into the meeting I half expected I would be returning with Lena, but that was fond and foolish thinking. I should of known when one attempts to deal with self-important bureaucrats that time, though prodded with spurs, moves at a snail's pace.

Promptly at nine o'clock the superintendents filed into the room and took their seats behind a row of desks. I was required to wait outside until a bailiff, or maybe a county employee acting as a bailiff, was told to usher me inside. He walked beside me lightly holding my elbow as guards do with prisoners and sat me down in front of them. The superintendents with a lawyer among them were shuffling papers on their desks and didn't bother to take notice of me for several minutes. All five were wearing frock coats and didn't take them off in the chilly room. Then one of the men put his papers aside, looked over the rims of his wire spectacles, and spoke.

"This meeting has been called to order to decide the future of one Lena Mack, a blind and infirm resident of the county home. She has lived here for nearly three years. You, sir, are here with a petition for her release. Please identify yourself by name, state your connection to said person, explain why you want her released, and tell us what accommodations you have for her sustenance after release."

I could see only the balding head and sloping shoulders of the man as he spoke, and I knew the stilted language was a stranger to his twangy tongue. He was speaking from rote or reading a prepared text. He viewed himself as a very important man, and the language coming from his round face had to clothe his importance and make an impression. In deliberate contrast to his bombastic opening remarks, I replied as simply as I could.

"My name is Leo Mack. I am the older brother of Lena Mack. I wish to take her from this institution to live in a better place with me. I have comfortable quarters for one person in the village of Kelly Junction and will look for another place as soon as she comes to live with me. I want her released so that she may be able to live out the rest of her life in peace and comfort. I will look after her faithfully."

"You live in Kelly Junction? That's where Irish Travelers live. Are you one of them? Kelly Junction don't have a sterling reputation in this county, and you must know the Irish Travelers living there are constantly in trouble with the law."

"I was born in Kelly Junction and grew up in a family of Irish Travelers, but years ago I left the village and went to sea. For most of my life I have not been an Irish Traveler even though my father and my brother were staunchly opposed to my leaving their way of life."

"Your father and brother? Why are they not with you today? How is it your sister became the responsibility of this institution when your father and brother could have cared for her?"

"I am told my father is now deceased. My brother to the best of my knowledge is somewhere in prison."

"And you expect us to believe all this? Given the reputation of the Irish Travelers in Kelly Junction and elsewhere?"

"I speak the truth, sir. I know the Travelers take advantage of respectable but gullible people to enrich their pockets, and I know they often butt heads with the law, but though I live now in Kelly Junction I am not an active Traveler and will not be one in future."

"We are not certain that if your sister went to live in the toxic atmosphere of Kelly Junction she would be any better off than living here. You must convince us that you can provide her with food, shelter, and clothing in addition to the care she needs as a blind woman. What is your occupation, sir?"

"I am at present unemployed. I came home a short time ago. I will find steady, honest work as a tradesman and look after my sister far better than she is being cared for here. I have seen the labor she is required to do here, and it sickens me. I have some money saved from previous jobs, and we can live on that until I find work."

For several minutes the superintendents were silent. Admitting that I was unemployed seemed to startle them as birds are startled into flight by a loud noise. They put their heads together and conversed in a low murmur. Then nodding their heads, they resumed their separate seats and looked at me with pursed lips and eyes with question marks in them as if they didn't understand a thing.

"As chairman of the meeting at hand," announced Daniel Corwin, rising as he addressed me, "I must speak for all of us. Each person on this Board of Superintendents is of the opinion that you must be employed to secure the release of your sister. When you find employment and a place large enough to accommodate another person, you may petition this Board a second time for the release of Lena Mack. If at that meeting you show us the courtesy we deserve, it may go very well for you. I must emphasize, however, that you will not be able to meet with us a third time. Your first petition is denied."

"What happens to Lena if you deny my petition a second time?"

"If you are denied the second time you meet with us, your sister will remain in the custody of the county home for the duration."

"For the duration? What does that mean?"

"It means she will probably die here."

"I am not willing to sit on my hands and do nothing while my sister weakens and dies in what has become a prison for her. I will stand before you a second time, and I wish to have her present."

"Understand it is our policy never to keep persons against their will. Whatever people say about the county home, it is not a prison. It costs the county a lot of money to extend the life of just one pauper, and so we want to see people leave. If your sister truly wishes to live with you, and if you can prove to us that you are employed and capable of supporting her, you will have no difficulty securing her release. You may apply for a second hearing in one month. Please do not attempt to apply earlier. This meeting is hereby terminated."

The Board of Superintendents left me with the feeling they were all a bunch of pompous little men whose one pleasure in life was parading their power. I didn't like them and I believe they had no love for me either, but now as I think about it they were not all that bad. They had a job to do and did a good job it seems to me in hindsight. They let me know as clear as a bell that I would have to get an income before I could even think about rescuing Lena. So that alone was the prickly pear to make me find work somewhere in Kershaw County but not in Kelly Junction. Half a dozen places, jerkwater towns like Kirkland or Peckwood, might have something for me to do. If not, I could possibly work as a farmhand. But times were hard in those days, even as they are now, and a man without a job was out of luck. My luck had never been good and now the little I ever had seemed gone completely. I think I must have walked all over the entire county looking for a job and asking if anyone knew of anybody needing a hand. Most of the people I talked to were polite in their southern fashion but shook their heads. The soles of my shoes grew thin from all that walking, and I didn't have another pair. A cobbler repaired the soles for thirty-four cents, and I slyly asked if he could use a helper. He shook his shaggy, gray head and mumbled he barely had enough business to put food on his own table. Sometimes he went to bed hungry.

I could sympathize with the poor fellow but felt rather smug in knowing I hadn't gone to bed hungry for some time. Yet I knew if I didn't find a job to pull in some wages soon, I could be in the same predicament as him. Then one day before autumn was beaten to the ground by winter the Circus came to town. They organized a parade that went right down the main street of Kelly Junction and into the field they had rented from a farmer for years. It was the same place they occupied when I was a boy and sneaked into the tent and found a seat high up to see the whole show for nothing. For several years to my knowledge the Circus had bypassed the village to set up near a larger town, but now it was back again and every citizen of Kelly Junction was happy and excited watching the parade.

In the fall, after the men had returned from their summer's work, most families could afford a day at the Circus. They gawked at the fancy wagons with complicated carvings and gaudy colors, but the first thing that caught every eye was a marching band of clowns. The band tooted as they marched and did a crazy little dance and threw candy to the crowd. Behind the wagons came the animals, ponderous animals with their trainers, elephants, giraffes and bears on their hind feet. Then to their amazement came a woman in glittering riding pants straddling two white horses. She received applause as she passed. The parade with all its sound, showmanship, and color announced the amazing events that would take place under the Big Top the next day. With the rest of the town I would be there to watch.

Two or three weeks ahead of the show keen anticipation began to brew. Advance men had come to town with buckets of paste and brushes on long handles. On vacant walls they slapped gaudy, eye-catching posters. Smaller posters with the same images were placed in store windows for every villager, every boy and girl and "children of all ages" to see. They played upon fantasy, urging escape from the drabness of everyday life to a world of exciting activity and miraculous events. They advertised stupendous acts with electrifying language like *Lilliputian, exotic, strange,* and *world famous.* They promised any lucky person with the leisure to spend one afternoon under the Big Top a variety of acts, including *snarling lions from darkest Africa, ferocious tigers from exotic India, elephants from the faraway East, and lady equestrians in glittering tights direct from Paris.* In one poster a tiger with jaws wide open sprang forward to attack the unwary. In another a tall, very thin man swallowed a sword next to a squat little man of three feet who juggled skulls blazing with fire.

Even though the first show of the day didn't begin until noon, scores of people were on the grounds when I got there shortly after ten. It was a pleasant fall day, sunny and mild with a gentle breeze from the south, and people were walking about and soaking up the atmosphere of the Circus. To cater to the crowd and make money, many vendors were selling candy to the children and golden, deep-fried sausages to their parents. One little girl was weeping because her mother couldn't afford to buy her the expensive treat other children were licking, a large and sweet rainbow-swirl on a stick. A smiling old man with a gentle face, observing the little girl's distress, put a nickel in her chubby hand. Grinning from ear to ear, she gave it to the vendor for a prize she would long remember.

It was something I would remember too, and so I'm recording it here for you to remember. It seemed to me he was a man of little means and couldn't really afford to part with coins worth more in those days than now. And yet what price do you put on a child's happiness? How do you measure the joy that one over-valued dollop of candy brought? And how do you measure the satisfaction the old man got with that gesture? As the years passed I remembered "the greatest show on earth" and all the sound and fury and flashing color and fantastic activity and even the smell of the sawdust. I have to admit I also remembered how one old man came to the Circus alone, found a way to assert his humanity, and made a life-long friend.

The ringmaster had been working hard all morning to bring all the elements of the show together and have them run smoothly in a seamless production. Then as the noon hour approached he stood on a high platform just outside the tent in his top hat, red coat, and black riding britches. In his right hand he was holding a bullwhip. He paused for a moment for the crowd to settle down, cracked the whip when he didn't get silence fast enough, and announced in a mellow, masculine voice loud enough for all to hear: "Ladies and gentlemen! Children of all ages! Step right up! The most enjoyable three hours you will ever spend in all your life will soon begin! Welcome, Good People! Welcome to the Greatest Show on Earth!"

As soon as he gave the signal, beckoning the gathering crowd to enter, they began to surge into the big white tent to find seats in the bleachers. Already clowns were doing dangerous and funny stunts in one of the rings and equestrians were riding broad-backed horses in another. In the third ring were elephants ready to delight the crowd, and to one side was a trapeze artist climbing a tall pole to fly through the air with the greatest of ease. Musicians with raucous instruments were playing to make the air more festive. When the ringmaster as barker began to set forth in some detail the amazing sights the spectators would see, and the amazing sounds the audience would hear, the music stopped and for a moment there was silence. Then an elephant trumpeted notes so loud they shook the canvas and made every man woman and child shiver and laugh. It was a wonderful afternoon of one fine and fancy performance after another. I enjoyed this Circus as much as the one I sneaked into as a ragged little boy, and I know everyone else in the bleachers also had a wonderful few hours of fun and fantasy and wild excitement.

I have often thought of how the Circus assails the senses of people young and old. They drown themselves in the sights and sounds and raw smell of the animals and the sweet smell of new sawdust. They taste confections in many flavors and all the other goodies at the vendor's stand. They feel the velvet touch of a warm autumn day on shoulders free of burden for one afternoon, and they hear with a sense of awe the prattle of the ringmaster. They yearn to escape the monotony of a humdrum life, and the greatest show on earth makes good on its promise. There is nothing like a Circus to cure a person of every ill he ever had. For a few hours I was free of worry, but as I walked away I knew I had to get Lena out of that poorhouse. That was the problem I had to solve, and it was not an easy one.

Chapter 20

Dixie Furniture

Near the end of the year when Christmas was approaching I found a job in Peckwood. That's a town in Kershaw County more open to the world than Kelly Junction and not far from the County Poorhouse. The town council had managed to persuade a big company to come there and set up shop. They sold them the land for almost nothing, and within a year Dixie Furniture was a thriving factory offering good jobs to cabinet-makers and craftsmen. In a long building it made wallpaper at one end and furniture at the other. Because I was a printer at one time in my life, they hired me to work with the layout, design, and manufacture of wallpaper. Of course I had to learn on the job, and so the pay was just enough to make ends meet. As I thought about it, I knew I wouldn't be able to argue my case at the poorhouse with any real hope of winning until I was making more money. So that pushed me to learn the skills of the job as fast as I could, do whatever the foreman told me to do, and work long hours.

Christmas came and went and I visited Lena and gave her a small gift. As she ran her hands over the hairbrush and comb, I could see and feel her appreciation. Even though she didn't talk much during my visit, her health seemed better than when I saw her earlier. Maybe the word got around that her brother didn't like the conditions under which she lived and was planning for her release, and so they began to treat her better. She told me the institution feared complaints of any kind and didn't like publicity, preferring to do its work in the shadows if not in secret. If a newspaper reporter had come to them asking to see their books, asking to see facts and figures, they would have firmly refused.

That's not to say the people running the place were crooks. In all respects they seemed to be upstanding citizens of the community. However, every one of the five superintendents had a full-time job away from the poorhouse, and so the place didn't have firm and adequate supervision. That alone made for waste and mismanagement and the theft of supplies by employees. It was a known fact that low-level workers in the place were getting fat on food supplies stolen from the pantry, and even clocks and ladders and farm equipment somehow disappeared. Though rumors of dire consequences persisted, nothing at all was done about expensive losses.

The institution was unlike Dixie Furniture where a close eye was kept on every worker and every thing. Yet by the time the New Year began I was actually enjoying my job. I found I had a sort of talent for dreaming up wallpaper patterns and the best colors to go with the patterns. In those days every housewife who could afford it wanted the rooms in her home made bright with wallpaper, and so the factory had no trouble selling its product. Also we copied some of the wallpaper made famous by William Morris in England. It was never an exact copy but close enough to catch the eye of ladies wanting fashion, and it brought the business a good profit margin.

Near the end of January Gideon Graves, a jolly fellow despite his name, called me into his office and broke the good news. He had put me in for a raise. If the bosses above him agreed on the figure he recommended, I would take home at the end of the six-day week more than enough to support Lena and me. We wouldn't be living in luxury, but we wouldn't be suffering hardship either. It would take a week for them to hand down their decision. While waiting for the word, I thought I would look for rooms in Peckwood. In my imagination I could see a bedroom for Lena all to herself, a bedroom for me, an airy sitting room for us to share, a kitchen with a good stove and pantry, and good sanitation.

That was the dream but reality has a way of crushing dreams. A committee met to consider my raise and turned it down. It had nothing to do with the quality of my work, I was told, but everything to do with supply and demand. While the winter in South Carolina was fairly mild that year, in the northern states where most of our wallpaper went to be sold it was severe. In the cold and bitter weather, few women left the comfort of their homes to buy decoration. Thousands who wanted new furniture and wallpaper put off buying until the spring, and that made for a downturn in business. I was told by way of consolation that my work qualified me for a raise, but until business got better it would have to wait. When the slack season was over and commerce picked up again, Graves said, he would urge the committee a second time to give me a well-deserved raise.

Well, that was good to hear but I had to drop all plans to find a pleasant living arrangement to share with my sister. Also I had to abandon my plans to go before the superintendents of the poorhouse to petition her release. I couldn't risk being turned down a second time because, as they were careful to tell me, there would be no third time. Well, near the end of April I got what I thought was good news but decided not to get my hopes up. As I worked my usual ten-hour shift and took my half hour for lunch, Gideon Graves gave me a pat on the back and said business was picking up and within a month I should have the raise he recommended in January.

By then it was springtime in South Carolina. The skies were blue and sunny and the trees were green again, and the birds of summer were already singing their songs. In the fine air all sorts of bushes were in bloom and the grass so green it dazzled the eye. It was a time to rejoice and be happy. I had got through another winter and was looking forward to a raise. Also I could plan on getting Lena released and living comfortably with me in a new place. With just the promise of a little more income per week, life for the two of us was shaping up to be well worth living.

In the first week of May the raise came through and was more than I expected. The next day on learning the good news I went looking for rooms after work. Because I wanted to see the place I was renting in daylight, I didn't take the time to eat supper. So on a hungry stomach I went looking, and to my surprise and relief I found suitable quarters within easy walking distance of work. Now all I needed to do was contact the five superintendents, petition them to release Lena, and take her away from that dreary place. To write down these three things required only seconds. To execute them one by one took more than a week, but perseverance paid off. I met with the superintendents on a Thursday, losing time and pay at work to do it, and stood before them with Lena present. As usual, they sat behind their counter that looked like a gigantic desk and lost themselves in a pile of papers. In due time they condescended to recognize us and ask questions. The top man on the totem pole, different from the man who conducted the first meeting with its bad results, opened the proceeding. He said his name was Gilbert Holmes.

"We are here today to determine if one Lena Mack should be released from this institution into the custody of one Leo Mack, her brother. Is my statement correct? Please answer yes or no.

"Yes, sir," I replied calmly, just loud enough for him to hear. I had learned it would help my case to humbly address the chairman as "sir" and show utmost respect when doing so.

"I see here that when you met with us some months ago, you were unemployed, living in one small room, and unable to support your sister. For those reasons your petition was denied. In what way has your condition changed? Please answer to the point."

"I am now employed. I have a good job in the Wallpaper Department of Dixie Furniture. At the beginning of this month I received a handsome raise. My income now allows me to live in more than one room. A few days ago I leased for an entire year two bedrooms, a kitchen with a pantry, and a sitting room with a broad and clean window. At present, with the help of my landlord, I'm in the act of furnishing the rooms."

"Do you have papers to prove your employment with Dixie Furniture? Do you have proof of an adequate income?"

"I do, sir. I submitted written proof earlier. You have it there among the papers in front of you."

"Yes, I see. Your employer seems to regard you as a good workman, and that speaks well for you. The figures do indeed show your income is adequate for the support of yourself and one other."

"Thank you, sir."

"Ah, you must not thank us quite so soon. We must have proof that you are living at the address indicated here."

"I am not at present, sir, but will move there on Sunday, the day I hope to leave here with my sister Lena. With her belongings she will go directly home from here."

"We have a letter signed by your landlord, one Peter Bracewood. He gives us the facts and believes you and your sister will be exemplary tenants. He attaches a copy of the agreement between him and you. All that is in order."

"Yes, sir. He was kind enough to help me with the proof I need."

"Let us hear now from your sister. Is this man who proposes to take you from us your biological brother?"

'Yes, sir."

"Do you go with him willingly?"

"Yes, sir."

"Will you be ready to leave this institution in just two days?"

"I am ready at this very moment, sir."

"Please answer the question yes or no."

"Yes, sir."

"Now you will wait outside until we make our determination. After we discuss your case, you will be notified on scene whether we have stamped your file Positive Accept or Negative Reject."

In the narrow and dingy waiting room we sat on hard chairs waiting for the decision in silence. We couldn't be certain how long it would take, and we had no way of knowing whether it would be good news or bad. Lena was agitated and seemed a little depressed. She sat bolt upright in shadowy gloom, folding and unfolding her thin hands as they lay listless in her lap. Neither of us felt like talking. We would have to wait and keep our fingers crossed. We expected the decision to come quickly. It didn't.

You won't believe this but we waited in that cramped little room all afternoon, expecting them to announce their decision at any moment. Then we found out they had gone to lunch, had returned an hour later, had been urged to consider a case pending for some time, and had fallen upon it rather than complete our case. Lena equated them with wounded birds plummeting with broken wings upon a case that had dragged on for months. Near four o'clock after we had entered the room near eleven and had waited all that time without anything to eat or drink, a flunky in the service of the superintendents came to us clutching a piece of white paper tightly rolled. He stood before us, unrolled the paper, and read with blinking eyes and awkward pauses but with a sense of drama and suspense the bombastic language announcing the verdict of our judges.

If I can trust my memory after all this time, I'll tell you what we heard: "As of this date compassion for humankind induces this body of elected Superintendents to rule favorably on the petition of one Lena Mack appealing release from the Kershaw County Home into the custody of her brother, one Leo Mack. She is obliged to leave the institution with all her personal effects in two days. In one month from the date below her brother, Leo Mack, is required to inform this committee in writing of her current condition. Vade cum Deus."

We expected one or two words from them, "Accept" or "Reject." They had taken it upon themselves to record their decision not only in purple prose but in triplicate. One copy went to us, another to the Home, and the third to the courts and posterity. Even now, if you go to the courthouse in Kershaw County, you may read it.

———————◈———————

On Sunday, my day off from work, we walked out of that place together. Strange, gray, ghost-like figures stared at us in the hallway and moved in close as if to block our way but said nothing and did nothing to hinder. I carried Lena's possessions in a potato sack. Her few pieces of clothing, rolled up and tied with twine, she carried herself. Outside a man in a small cart was ready to take us to our new home in Peckwood. It didn't burden me to pay the carter for the eight miles he would take us because I feared it would tax Lena's strength to walk that distance. Frail and blind and malnourished, she had spent all her time in the poorhouse sitting at a table working long hours with her hands and seldom walking. Her slender fingers were raw from picking oakum, and her legs wouldn't allow her to walk with confidence for any distance. I made up my mind as we rode along in silence to feed her well and restore her health as best I could. Her face was thin, drawn, and pale. Her large, unseeing eyes blinked constantly, but as she breathed the fresh air deeply she began to smile.

"I'm so glad to be going with you, Leo. I'm so glad you came to rescue me. I was ready to die in that place, and then you came."

"I wish I could have come sooner. You'll have no worries now, and you'll live in a good place and eat good food and walk with me in the evenings after work, and have a good life for a long time."

"You've been very good to me, Leo. Papa and Luke were never good to me, and poor Mama was sick a lot, and I was a burden."

"You were never a burden to Mama. She loved you very much, and I'm sure she looked after you as best she could. She lived with racking pain in every joint, Lena. That I'm sure you know."

"Yes, I do know, and sometimes at night I would hear her groaning in pain and Papa complaining. He and Luke never cared about nobody but themselves. Mama ain't suffering no more and Papa neither. I don't know about Luke. I guess you know Papa got run over by a wagon not many months after Mama died, and Luke claimed it wasn't an accident and tried to make old man Collins pay, but the court commissioner said Papa was drunk and walked in front of the wagon. So when Papa died, Luke was hit with medical and undertaker expenses and didn't have no money even for food, and he robbed a granary to get it and got sent to prison."

"Someone told me Luke was in prison but I never knew why. I'm glad you're telling me this, Lena, and I want to know more. Maybe we can find out where Luke is being held and visit him one day."

I remembered Lena as not much of a talker, but on that trip to her new home she talked more than ever. I know she was grateful to be out of the poorhouse, but maybe she was nervous about going to a new place. I wish you could have seen her face when she walked into the room I said was her own. It was almost as if she could see the bed and the chest of drawers and the little table with the pewter pitcher full of water for washing her face in the morning. It was as if she could see the blush of pink wallpaper with its little blue trim that me and a friend got from Dixie Furniture and put on the walls. I have to admit the room was clean and pretty and just right for her. She liked the kitchen too and the sitting room and said she would sit often beside the window near the street. She would hear every little sound – that I knew – and each sound would be a sight.

The summer weather that year was the best I'd seen in a long time, and the two of us took long walks in the evening and on Sunday. I worked ten and a half hours a day but somehow found the strength to walk with Lena after supper, and the walking made her strong. Every day she had supper ready and waiting when I finally straggled home from work. When I was planning to have her come and live with me, I thought I would be the one to prepare the meals. A blind person couldn't be cooking on a hot stove in a cramped little kitchen. Then I found out my sister could prepare simple meals and cook just about any food that needed cooking. She even made bread and baked it, and she could put a roast in the oven and know when to take it out. I marveled at how she could do all that in blindness, but she laughed and said she had learned to cook at home, and after burning her hands a few times she learned to be careful near the stove. She could even season food with a pinch of spice dropped in her palm and measured with the tip of her forefinger.

In the evenings before bedtime we occupied the sitting room. I had some books I wanted to read, and Lena encouraged me to do it. So I read a little and dosed a little and read some more, and Lena sat primly near the window knitting a sweater for me to wear in winter. Again I was amazed she could do something as complicated as knitting, but she assured me it was not at all complicated once you knew how, and Mama had patiently taught her how. She was far more independent that I expected her to be. She looked after herself with very little help from me and was always neat and clean though simply dressed. Each day when I was away at work she performed the duties of a housewife, sweeping and dusting and keeping our rooms spic and span. I joked with her, saying if fate had not made her my sister, I would make her my wife. She blushed at that but laughed at my jokes whether funny or not. Her laughter seemed to have a healing effect upon us both. It was good living with Lena.

⟐

I urged her to eat more and gain some weight, but even though she gained more color in her complexion she remained thin as a rail. I quickly learned that while she frequently thought of others and their well-being, one or two friends in the poorhouse for example, she rarely gave a moment to herself. One evening she spoke sadly of a woman who died of loneliness because no one came to visit her. The woman was only thirty-three and healthy but died one evening and no one could figure out why, but she, Lena, knew. Then suddenly she was speaking of Luke, saying he was surely miserable.

"Luke never did have many friends coz Pa always made fun of his friends and even chased them off when they came around. Papa had only Luke as a friend, and he wanted Luke to have only him. That's what I really believe. And now Luke has no family and no friends to visit him wherever he happens to be. I'm of a mind he will die of loneliness too."

"Papa and Luke were close, I guess, but not very likable. Luke was always teasing me and trying to make me feel small. I think it was his way to make himself feel bigger. He was my brother, I guess, but not a good friend."

"He was selfish and wild, that Luke. He loved his freedom but lost it. Going off to prison to live in confinement probably hit him hard, real hard. Do you think prison changed him just a little bit?"

"Prison probably changed him a lot. It changes every man. If Pa couldn't change his ways, rotting in prison probably did it."

"Can you maybe find out where he was sent? I would like to see him before I die. After all, he's my brother."

"Paternoster Vaughan may be able to help. Yep, that's his name, his real name, but his friends and acquaintances call him Peter. Only his mama calls him Paternoster. It's the first words of the Lord's Payer, you know, and she loves the name coz she gave it to him and she's religious. He knows people at the courthouse from clerks to judges and maybe they can help."

Paternoster had a Friday off work, and so in a few days he did me the favor of going to the courthouse to check the records. The clerk told him all prison records were secure in the statehouse in Columbia. He would have to write a letter identifying himself as a relative and ask for Luke's whereabouts. An official of the system would respond in time and name the prison. Peter asked how long would it take to get that information by mail. The clerk shrugged his shoulders and said he didn't know. Sometimes when they wrote to the statehouse, they got a reply right away or none at all. At other times a brief reply could take several weeks or months.

I sent a request for information to the address the clerk gave my friend. While waiting for a reply, I repaid him for his help by taking him to a barbecue bash at the Peckwood Inn. Lena came along too. The inn cooked a whole hog outside, and we ate delicious pulled pork in a rich sauce with tough bread. It was good. Three weeks later came an answer to my letter. A man by the name of Luke Mack, according to current records, was an inmate at Broad River Penitentiary on Broad River

Road nine miles south of Columbia, South Carolina. That was more than sixty miles from Peckwood, a journey of two days by coach or wagon.

Lena got all excited when she heard Luke was alive and well even though in prison. She wanted to visit him in the fine weather of summer. I thought it over but couldn't see no easy way of getting there. Trains were running from Columbia to Charleston, but not from Peckwood to Columbia. By coach the trip would be expensive and take a long time. In the wagon of a hawker moving in that direction, it would be less expensive but would also squander time. Only good, fast horses could make the trip in a day or so, but of course Lena was in no condition to ride a fast horse. I had no particular hankering to see Luke again, but after all she had been through I wanted to do all I could to please her.

Chapter 21

Lena Sees the Light

At work I asked Gideon Graves, my foreman at Dixie Furniture, if I might take some time off. He said I could probably take a week off without pay near Christmas but not in the summer or fall because the company needed every hand to manufacture its products for the Christmas trade. Lena put on a sad face when I broke this news to her, but knowing how important it was to keep my job, she began to make plans for a visit during the holiday season.

"Maybe that will be better than going in summer," she said. "It'll give us time to write and establish contact with Luke. We can tell him we want to visit and wait for his reply and make plans."

I didn't like the idea of traveling anywhere in winter with a frail woman trying to regain her health, but what could I do? Maybe I should have said, "No, we can't do it in winter." But I was too cowardly or too weak to say that. So hating myself I gave assurance.

"December in this state ain't all that cold, you know. In fact, at Christmas time it can be downright balmy. So I guess we can go then. I can save some money for the trip. Then we can travel in style by coach, and you'll have new clothes to wear and look all pretty."

"Only if I can do some work to help pay for the clothes. I don't want you spending your money on me. I'm a burden already."

She was not a burden and she was already working as a very efficient housekeeper, and I assured her of that. But as summer slipped into fall and ran like a hare to hide itself from winter, Lena began to show symptoms of failing health. When the cold weather came, it made her joints so stiff she could hardly walk, and she also had some trouble breathing. I think she must have inherited the joint problem from Mama, and the other problem must have come from breathing the bad air at the poorhouse, or maybe catching some disease floating around that place. I tried to fatten her up, hoping that would improve her health, but she never seemed to be able to eat more than a sparrow and remained almost as thin as one.

During the month of September she struggled to have supper ready for me when I came home from work. But as October came and went a nagging and constant pain drained her of energy and left her listless in the rocking chair beside the window. I came home to a cold stove, no supper, and abundant apologies when she wasn't sleeping. Many days when I entered our place I found her sitting by the window, but on closer inspection found that she was in deep and labored sleep even while sitting. She explained that at night she couldn't sleep, and so by afternoon she was lapsing into sleep even though she was determined not to sleep in bed during the daytime. So the chair became her bed during most of the month of October.

When November came she made no effort to get out of bed in the mornings, or at any time during the day. By then she was seriously ill. The money I had saved to visit Luke at Broad River Penitentiary I spent on medicine and doctoring. In Peckwood we were fortunate enough to have an old-time physician named

Franz Switzer who seemed to know his business. He came in the midst of a blustery afternoon with his little black bag and spent an hour in her room. Without saying much he examined her carefully and then attempted to chat with her. He emerged shaking his head.

"She has severe pneumonia," he said. "She has a fever and other ailments I can't exactly determine. I don't like to tell you this, but I see little hope for any kind of recovery because her system seems to be shutting down. All we can do is keep her warm, see that she gets plenty of rest, and feed her something hot and nourishing even if she resists. I daresay she won't have an appetite, but she needs to eat. You may have to spoon-feed her. I recommend vegetable soup with pieces of meat, or some kind of stew, cold milk, and hot cups of tea. She's very weak and some food in her could help."

"Are you saying she's dying, doctor? Can't we do something to pull her through? Why, only a month ago she was keeping house for me and cooking my supper, and we planned to take a trip."

"These things appear to come on fast and for no reason. But that's only the appearance. At some time in her life she was deprived of the nutriments she needed for good health but for reasons I don't understand went on doing some kind of labor day after day even when her body lacked the nourishment and the strength for sustained work of that kind."

"Until recently, Doctor Switzer, she lived at the county poorhouse. When I found her there, she was picking oakum in a stifling little room that had no ventilation and smelled of death and disease."

"I'm willing to say that possibly explains it. That place could be the culprit. I was thinking that maybe you had neglected her and was about to scold you for it. The county home is no home at all for some people. They go there and they die there, or they die soon after. Now it seems your sister is one of its victims."

The finality of the doctor's news alarmed me. It couldn't be as bad as that. Then I remembered he had a reputation for never holding out false hope. If he said a patient would die and she didn't, everyone could rejoice. If he said a patient would live and she didn't, well it was human nature to put him under the hammer of blame. So he played his cards close to his chest, hoping secretly all would go well and vowing to do all he could to that end. He was a kind man and wanted to speak good and positive words in a tense and bleak situation, but found it safer to be blunt. His honesty brought him high respect in the community, and I was glad to have him look at Lena. Again he was speaking.

"I can't be certain but I think your sister has bronchitis, and that makes her pneumonia worse. Also she has a bad case of arthritis attacking the major joints. You must put hot mustard poultices on her shoulders, hips, and knees to ease the pain and try to keep the room ventilated. It's a pity we can't move her to the hospital. She'd get better care there. Oh, I shouldn't have said that."

He knew I had no money for a hospital. No one in my family, not even the extended family, had ever gone to a hospital for treatment and cure. Irish Travelers took care of their own, and some women among us were as good as any doctor trained in a fancy school. I assured old Doc Switzer as he was leaving that I would take good care of Lena. I went into the room and to the bed where she was propped on pillows. Her face was moist, livid, distorted, and feeble. I asked if I could do anything for her and got no response. She was wide awake but seemed not to hear me.

"How are you feeling, Lena?" I asked, approaching her bed. She turned her dull, unseeing eyes upon me, looked at me attentively, and didn't recognize even the sound of my voice. For an instant she was my loving little Caitlin, my dear innocent Caitlin immersed in romantic love for all the world but dying by slow degrees when very young. It was more than I could bear.

At work I went looking for Paternoster Vaughan and asked him if he knew of some reliable woman who might come and look after Lena for a reasonable fee. I had to work during the day and couldn't leave my sister alone. Also I needed a woman to bathe her, apply the poultices, take care of her bodily functions, and keep an eye on her. I went out and bought the biggest chamber pot I could find, but even as I brought it into her room and put it under the bed I knew she wouldn't be able to get up and use it. A kind and efficient woman could help her with that and listen to her when she felt strong enough to talk. I was really looking for a nurse but I knew nurses didn't come cheap, especially if the hours were long. Only a day went by before Vaughan revealed to me the good news. His sister Molly would take the job and would require no more in pay than I could afford. I had spoken to Molly once or twice and knew her to be a fine young woman. She was a farm girl on the heavy side but strong and healthy with a freckled but glowing face, very white teeth, and a pleasant smile. She came to my rooms the very next day as I left for work and quickly became Lena's sentinel.

I have to say Molly made Lena feel better just by being there. She made my sister feel at ease and Lena liked her.

But in a few days the tiny room without ventilation began to stink. It was the middle of November and we couldn't open the window to let in fresh air because of the cold. So I hit upon the idea of burning juniper to freshen the room. Every other day or so I put a sprig with a cone on it in a dish and burned it slowly so the aroma would mask the smell of the sickbed. It made a dreary scene more tolerable, and within days Lena was sitting up and leaning against a large pillow and eating a little and talking. Molly said she talked of the past and growing up in a world of shifting shadows in a family that always seemed too busy to remember she needed attention. Only her mother took the time to care, and by the time Sarah was of middle age she was so racked by joint pain she couldn't do much. Even so, Lena had no regrets. Her childhood in Kelly Junction had made her independent despite her handicap. She was blind but not helpless.

She was eating now with Molly's encouragement and looking better. One evening I came to her with a dish of pudding Molly had made. Lena sat up and ate the pudding slowly, savoring the taste. Her eyes sparkled and I could see she wanted to talk.

"Do you feel better?" I asked, taking the empty dish from her hands and putting it in the kitchen sink.

"Yes, I do, dear Leo, and thank you for Molly. She will make me well again very soon, and then we can see Luke. Breathing is hard and I feel sore all over, but I'm improving. Yesterday my head felt like a donkey was sitting on it and threatening to crush it, but now it's free again. Oh, the pain at night! But it will go away. Molly helped me send a note to Luke at Broad River. I hope he writes back soon. I do want to see him before I die."

"You won't die any time soon, Lena. Don't you worry about that. Molly Vaughan and Leo Mack will not hear of you dying, mind you. You will live to be eighty."

"Oh, but I can feel something is happening, Leo. I can feel it."

"You are feeling the ache of being very sick, but it will pass."

"Do you think so? Do you really think so? Last night when I couldn't sleep I tried to think of what is going to happen to me. I saw a blue light blinking at the end of a long road, and I thought of heaven. Do you believe in heaven, Leo?"

"I don't know, Lena. I don't think I do. I wish I could."

"I'm not sure I believe it either. We never got much religion growing up, but I been thinking. If I die and go to heaven, will I see my family again? Will I see Papa there, or will he be in the other place? Oh, Mama, poor silent Mama! I know she'll be there. And you will come later, Leo, and we'll be a family again. Maybe Luke will come too? He wasn't all bad, you know. Headstrong and stubborn as a mule and smelling like one but not all bad."

"Luke may not even be in the pen any more. I hear they don't keep very good records down there, and when a man leaves or dies, especially when he dies, they probably don't bother to store his file."

"Oh, I did want to see him at Christmas time. But now he'll have to come here. Will you send for him, Leo? Will you tell him I'm not feeling well? Tell him I want to see him and kiss his cheek before I die. Tell him I forgive him for calling me names when I was a child and all the other stuff he did that caused me pain. Tell him I'm dying but don't alarm him any more than you can help."

"You will get well again, Lena. You will get well and strong and forget all the bad years and live with me happily ever afterwards."

"You are weaving a fairy tale, Leo. I love fairy tales!"

"It's too bad the real world can't be more like a fairy tale, but we have to live in it and make the most of it. The real world dishes out three parts pain to one part pleasure and can be very unfair, but you will live to be a hundred, believe me."

"Oh, now you have me laughing! A moment ago you said I'd live to be eighty. Well, I do want to live, Leo. I don't want to die. You will be very sad if I die, and I won't see you any more. Do you think if I die and go to heaven, I can come back and be with you in spirit? I've heard of such things. Is it true? Is it true or just another lie the old folks tell the young?"

"I don't know, Lena, and I won't lie to you. I just don't know."

"I would like to come back and see all of us, even Papa, when all of us lived in that little house on Sligo Street in Kelly Junction. Every morning Mama was in the kitchen fixing something that smelled real good. And she would always say in that chirpy little voice of hers, 'Good morning, Lena. Now wash your face and hands, child, and sit down.' We always had breakfast together. I always liked breakfast. Oh, oh! My head! This awful pain in my head! Pain all over! It's cracking my skull, Leo. It cuts like an axe!"

"Dr. Switzer told me to buy laudanum for your pain. I'll give you a little dose. Swallow it fast and rinse your mouth. It's very bitter."

"Oh, my! It is bitter! The stuff is terrible! This is agony!"

"Its taste is awful but it will ease your pain and help you sleep."

After all the talk Lena was silent. It seemed to require her whole strength to endure the pain and the bitter drug that would kill it. She grew drowsy with exhaustion, lay quietly on her bed, and slept.

More than three weeks went by and we heard nothing from Luke. I had to believe he was no longer in the Broad River Prison or if he was, he didn't want to get involved again with family matters. Lena asked more than once if word had come from Luke, and I had to tell her there was no response. Each time she merely shook her head sadly and began humming a little tune as if to forget she had asked. As the days came and went Molly cared for her while I worked at Dixie Furniture, and I cared for her after work and into the night. Then when it seemed she was much better and perhaps out of danger, her condition suddenly grew worse.

The laudanum helped relieve her pain, but as she called for more frequent doses I began to see that she suffered from its side effects. I now believe the laudanum in spite of Dr. Spitzer's diagnosis was a big mistake. The addictive drug made her feel better for a few hours, but it also made breathing more difficult and brought on constipation, mood swings, and itching. The skin on both of her arms was raw from scratching, and her itching back caused her to writhe in agony most of the night. Each time she drank the bitter brew of alcohol and opium, she was calm and quiet for a few minutes and then began to talk rapidly and with abandon.

"When I was a little girl, I wanted to go to school and study and learn everything to be learned. I begged Mama to let me go to school. She always shook her head and said no school would tolerate a blind child. In her goodness she said she would teach me all I need to know, but I never learned much. One thing, however, I did learn thoroughly. I knew I was not wanted here on earth. I knew that some power had placed a curse on me and made me a burden. I wanted to see a flower when I smelled it, but couldn't. I wanted to see Mama smile, but I couldn't."

"Mama loved you, Lena. She brought you into the world, paying for your birth with a great deal of pain, and she wanted you."

"Mama might be the one exception. The family didn't want me. The town didn't want me. The poorhouse where I slaved at picking oakum and didn't get enough to eat and slowly became a walking skeleton didn't want me. And God? I want to believe in God. I want to love him as the one Almighty, but if the Almighty had wanted me, he wouldn't have made me blind."

"Your life was hard, Lena, and you have every right to feel bitter deep down, and you have the right to let others know how you feel. I am listening to every word you say. You will have it easier now."

"Easier now? You must know I'm dying, Leo. And it seems before I die I must suffer as never before. Tell me, Leo. What did I do to offend? No, please be silent. Let God tell me! Oh God, you know all the misery I have endured. Why did you make me suffer so today? Have I in some way sinned against you? I wanted to love you and your Son. I wanted to love a mortal man too. I wanted a family of my own, and I wanted to teach my husband and children to love you, God. But I die a virgin. Now tell me, God, is that fair? Am I to be always thirsting and never to drink? That was the life that you in your infinite wisdom gave me. Is that the work of a loving God?"

"Try not to talk any more, dear Lena. You need to rest."

"This pain! It saturates my body and mind! It grows worse and worse. Please, Leo. Fill the little glass with laudanum. It will give me some relief. I can't believe there is such torture in the world as this."

From those strange, gray, intense, and sightless eyes came a last gleam of intelligence. They looked into my face as if to see and memorize every wretched line. They burned like red-hot coals in a grate. She drank the mixture with one gulp, closed her eyes and slept. No longer did she rinse her month to get rid of the bitter taste. She liked it. It bathed her tongue with acid, but she liked it.

———◦◦◦———

I let her sleep through the night. Early the next morning as Molly came to sit with her, I went to find Dr. Switzer. He was busy with patients but assured me he would come as soon as he could. He came with his little black bag shortly before noon, hustling inside without knocking.

"I'm surprised to see you here, Leo. Don't you have work to be doing at Dixie Furniture today?"

"I do have to work but Lena is dying, Doctor. I had to be here."

"Well, let us see. The room looks clean, the bed looks clean. This young woman seems to be taking good care of Lena."

"Her name is Molly Vaughan. Molly, this is Dr. Franz Switzer."

"I know," Molly replied. "He delivered me as a baby and my brothers too. He came to my house in dark and cold, they say."

"It's a year-round job, Molly. You became a young woman fast. I must attend to my duties now. Please leave the room. Leo can stay."

Switzer bent over Lena and poked at her face and neck. She uttered a low inarticulate moan like an animal in pain. He took her pulse and listened for a heartbeat. He tapped her on the forehead between the eyes, and then he applied a cool wet cloth to her face. Her chest, so flat and skinny, heaved with a long deep sigh of satisfaction. It was something terrible to see, for it seemed to be the last quiver of life before death. Then suddenly she raised herself on an elbow and cried out, "Leo, dear Leo! Breakfast!"

She was recalling a moment of her childhood. It was horrible to hear. I wanted it to end. "Why does she go on living, Doctor?"

"To suffer," he replied decisively. "But it won't be long now." And then we heard a faint whisper: "My angels! They come!"

Old Doc Switzer had participated in scenes like this before, but not me. He took everything in stride as though expected. I was nervous and alarmed. He looked into Lena's haggard face, adjusted her pillow, and turned away. He knew her agonized murmurs, spilling from fevered lips, were trying to release her soul. He knew also she was dying but holding on. Like an apparition in a world filled with more shadow and darkness than light, she lay motionless for another hour. She died quietly at peace.

"My cup of misery is full," she had said to me when the pain was more than she could bear. Now in the late afternoon of a gray winter's day a gentle smile appeared on the thin lips.

Dr. Switzer closed her eyelids and muttered, "That's all I can do, Leo. You should find a priest and make arrangements for burial."

Even though my eyes were dry, I was too numb to answer. In my sitting room Molly sat weeping. I was beginning to like Molly, but it seemed to me any time I loved a woman bad things happened. Lena was the last, and I was not about to love another. I made up my mind to be a solitary man for the rest of my life, and I wanted to be a tinker again. I told you the story of Lena on her deathbed because I thought the least I could do was leave behind a record to show she lived and died. Too many like her, victims of misfortune we might call them, live out their miserable lives and die painfully without so much as making a ripple in the millpond we call society. I was on hand to make certain my sister would not come and go that way. I tossed a stone into the water for ripples! Anyone reading my account will remember her as I remember her. Anyone with any heart whatever will know she didn't deserve what she got out of life.

I'm a Quaker now and Quaker teachings tell me to accept adversity with fortitude and never question the ways of God to man. I try not to, I really do, but sometimes I believe the Devil works his mischief when God is asleep. Often I wonder why any loving God could make it so hard for the likes of Caitlin and Lena. A thief and a thug leads a long life without trouble or pain, but two delicate girls with the purest of thoughts are made to suffer severely. Is that God's work or the Devil's work or some fluke of chance or fate? My Quaker friends in Blue Anchor tell me the good Lord was testing them and when they passed all tests he made angels of them and took them home to be with him. Maybe so, but how can a man like me with some experience in the world reconcile himself to that kind of thinking? I can't and yet I try not to question lest I burn in hell.

Chapter 22

Sleep After Heavy Toil

I was never a truly thoughtful person, never had an education to help me shape feeling into thought or to know if education is a blessing or a curse. Even so, coming home to my sister and trying to help her survive and seeing to it that she died in dignity formed thoughts in my brain. I held them in my head without saying much about them until two of my friends, Isaac Brandimore and Emily Kingston, urged me to write them down. They wanted me to talk, saying they would polish my prattle and turn it into prose. Well, maybe they did and maybe they didn't. I can't bother my head about that. I'm rambling and so I'll come back to my story and get on with it.

I took off several days from work to pay a priest to say last rites, to pay the undertaker for laying out the body, and to pay a big and rich company for a cemetery plot. At the moment Lena was laid to rest I was anything but rested, but I also had a feeling of triumph. I had managed to defy the odds and see to it that she was not buried at county expense with no name and no marker. Even though I had come almost too late, my sister was not stuffed into a pine box and tossed without ceremony into a pauper's grave. Knowing I prevented that from happening made me proud. She was buried with great dignity even though only half a dozen curious people were present.

When the soil had settled and the mound was firm, I found a simple marker for her grave. On it I chiseled for all to see an epitaph some may view as crude but one that seemed realistic and warrantable at the time and even now as I write these recollections.

Under my stick figure of the winged angel that came to lead her to the Pearly Gates ran this inscription – *Lena Mac, dead too soon. Loved by her mother Sarah and her brother Leo. Ignored and unloved by Liam and Luke. Ever yearning for light she couldn't see. Ever thirsty she couldn't drink. RIP.* Some of the gabby women in the village of Kelly Junction said it was cruel to censure Liam and Luke so open and public on a tombstone. Then some got to thinking it preserved their names though not their absolute identities for future generations to see, and that was acceptable. To me it didn't matter.

What did matter was getting back to work and paying off my debts and looking for another place to live. Every time I found a good place to live after giving up seafaring, something happened and I had to move to a smaller, more plebeian place. We had good rooms while Lena lived and a good landlord, but the rooms were meant for two and I was now one. I went back to work and labored eleven hours every day, but less than a week later my foreman Gideon Graves came to my station at lunchtime and said he hated to say it because he knew I'd been through a lot, but the big boss – his name was J. Roland Shaw and he owned part of the company – felt I was taking off too much time from work.

To more workers than one J. Roland Shaw had made it clear that anyone's work at Dixie Furniture was always more important than any problem at home. If I had to take off another day in the next six months, he had said to Graves, the company would have to let me go. They paid me not a red cent during the time I had to be off to see Lena leave this world, but that of course was water under the bridge. I could see they were not concerned with my welfare but only with an abstract thing they called the company and something even more abstract called profit. So I got a little hot under the collar and let Gideon know it, and the next day I no longer had a job with Dixie Furniture. The hypocrites insisted they liked me and liked my work but "under the circumstances" had to fire me.

So Leo Mack, born poor and doomed to remain poor, again had no income and no hope of finding an immediate job. On top of that I was in debt up to my eyebrows and already receiving letters demanding payment. I had to make monthly payments on the cemetery plot or run the risk of seeing Lena moved to a pauper's grave. That obligation was most important to me because I was determined not to have her resting place disturbed. In the rooms I would soon leave I gathered together all the things I felt I could do without, including the stove and furniture, and put them up for sale.

I gained enough to make two monthly payments to the cemetery people, and I hoped before another payment was due I would have a job that would allow me to make the remaining payments. I wore out my shoes pounding the pavement and looking all over for a job. I followed up leads I got from any number of well-meaning people. I talked with a lot of people who might have hired me, but the talk didn't bring a job. In the state of South Carolina and particularly in Kershaw County there were no full-time jobs to be found. When spring came I was working a day or two at anything I could find, living in one room again, and thinking about moving northward.

In all the years since I was there I never forgot that little town in North Carolina that seemed to be run by Quakers. They were farmers and they were prosperous and they treated me well. I went there with money in my pocket and never had to spend a dime all the time I was there. I worked stocking shelves in the general store and even saved a little money, and I rode out of that place northward to a seafaring life on a noble mare I got for nothing. So all in all Blue Anchor, as it was called, stuck in my memory as a bountiful place where life was easier than in most other places.

As I got to thinking about it I began to have a hankering to go back. I thought I might get work on one of the surrounding farms or work in the general store or livery stable. If I could find a steady job even at low pay, I reasoned I could pay off the cemetery people. Later I might be able to buy a horse and wagon and get back to tinkering. I was thinking I wouldn't be living there for the rest of my days, just long enough to get on the road as a traveling tinker. The more I thought about Blue Anchor the more dismal Kelly Junction, Peckwood, and Kershaw County became. At a time in my life when I should have been settled with a home and family and good job, I had no money for a rainy day, no friends or relatives to offer support in distress, and no prospects for any kind of future. Every door in the whole world, open when I was younger, was shut tight and locked. Winter was coming and I was standing outside.

It didn't take me long to get out of Kershaw County and leave all the bad memories of Kelly Junction and Peckwood behind. At least I tried to leave them behind, but anyone older than a child knows a person can't escape memories good or bad. All you can do is put the bad ones behind you and the good ones in front and think on them and hope the bad ones fade into the mists. But even if the painful ones do seem to fade away, they can suddenly appear again when you least expect them and be more ornery than ever. And then what? Well, I'm not here to jabber like my old friend Isaac often did, and so I'll get back to my story.

I spent a couple days getting to Blue Anchor, and the first thing I did was go to Jacob Darboy's general store and get acquainted again. Old Jacob looked a lot older than when I first met him, but I guess I did too. He didn't recognize me but soon remembered I had worked for him for a brief time, stocking the shelves and sweeping the floor and stoking the potbelly stove with wood brought in from the back yard. The customers would have to push their chairs back from that giver of heat to let me get to it, and he remembered the time Walter Jessup fell over backwards and hit the hard floor and almost cussed even though he was a Quaker elder.

The season was sort of between winter and spring in Blue Anchor when I got there the second time, and there was a lot of hustle and bustle in the store and a lot of coming and going among the farmers. I could see that Darboy was real busy, and so I asked if he needed some help. He didn't say much in his Quaker way because he couldn't pay me much. He merely pulled on his white beard and looked at me with them little black eyes. Then I broke the hesitation and said I'd work for room and board and maybe a little pay later. His stolid expression didn't change much, but I could tell I had a job when he said he had a room in back. The room had a good bed, he said, and I wouldn't go hungry and he shook my hand.

I found things getting better for me just as soon as I got to Blue Anchor. But looking back, I can say maybe my life wasn't all that bad after all. I went hungry a few times and dealt with loss and sorrow, but with a few aches and pains from the school of hard knocks I managed to survive. The basic question really comes down to this: what more can a man ask for than to live the life granted him as long as he can and do no harm to others? The Quakers were good to me. With no pressure and no persuasion they taught me how to be a Quaker. At that time in my life, getting on in years, I needed something to believe in and their doctrine was right for me. I got along just fine with it and with them too. But when summer came, I left Darboy's place and went into the Great Dismal Swamp and lived free as a swamper. I wanted to be on my own again and outside and close to nature, and the swamp offered all of that. I lived in the swamp almost a year and didn't go hungry even once.

I was doing odd jobs in my spare time for David Kingston and other planters in the area and saving some money because I had no rent to pay. Then later with Darboy's help I bought a wagon on easy terms. As a favor to me he took no commission on it and even got me a lower price. A few weeks later I got a good horse to pull the wagon and gradually collected my tools and began working as a traveling tinker again. That's what I've been doing now for several years, and I don't owe a penny to nobody. It took some time, but I paid off the cemetery people back in Peckwood and now live comfortably. I miss old Sparky but one of these days I'll have another dog to replace him. I hope I can find one that don't eat too much and don't mind trotting beside the wagon. But maybe I'm getting too old to own another dog. They can be a bother and I'm not sure Ida Crabtree would let me keep him inside in winter as she did with old Sparky.

Editor's Note. *It saddens me to report that shortly after I set down the paragraphs you see above, Leo Mack died at 78 of what we thought was nothing more than a cold. However, Robin Raintree, our medical person in Blue Anchor, called it pneumonia. He was caught in the rain in November and was soaked to the skin coming home. Sniffles came shortly afterwards and then a cold and then pneumonia most likely. I do know that in the weeks before his death he grew thinner and thinner. His legs were shrunken and his face covered with wrinkles. Below deep furrows in a broad forehead his jawbones under brittle skin were distinctly visible. The man who had come to us with something boyish in his smile had become in his dotage a feeble septuagenarian. At this point I become the narrator of his story. — Emily Kingston*

In the Meeting House a dignified ceremony attended by many people honored Leo Mack. Several people, one after another, spoke of his conversion to the Quaker faith and his life among us. Others praised his strong will and strength of character, and his willingness to share his knowledge of current events concerning this dreadful war. All of us remembered seeing his wagon on the road in all kinds of weather going from one farmhouse to another not just to mend pots but to deliver news. He was buried in the cemetery adjacent to the Meeting House in Blue Anchor. Although he was a very private person and had few close friends, his work made him known to everyone in the entire county. Over the years he became a fixture among us. We miss him now and will miss him certainly in years to come.

The day after he died I remembered Isaac Brandimore's ultimate impression of Leo: "How green was that man's life." And I thought we might be able to use that on his tombstone. However his landlady, Mrs. Ida Crabtree, had a better suggestion. Because she knew him better than anyone else, she came up with the inscription that was later placed on his headstone – *Who among us has never dreamed of cultivating a garden?* She said that remark, posing a question about the human condition, tended to sum up Leo's existence. It put in a capsule his dreams and the hardships he faced as he tried to realize those dreams. We thought it was a most appropriate epitaph for a courageous man who embraced a hard life and made the most of it.

He himself had suggested this – *If anyone at my burial whimpers or cries, I will never speak to him again.* The man had a keen sense of humor, though you could detect it only when you got to know him. Scribbled in black ink in one of his notebooks and reflecting a more somber mood, we also found this —

> Give me sleep after heavy toil,
> Give me calm after stormy seas,
> Give me air and a patch of soil,
> And blue skies after life, please.

It was the sailor and dreamer in him that was talking and surely a verse that Leo himself had composed. In spite of what he wanted the world to believe, he was a man of intellect and humor and not a simple old man with a rough exterior. He was certainly no poet in league with Tennyson, as we all must agree when reading these lines, but at least he tried. It is my privilege and pleasure, my obligation I believe, to bring his story to a satisfactory conclusion. Cut short by his death, one or two chapters remain to make the story whole. I will try to shape them and speak them as best I can.

After he became a Quaker, Leo Mack remained something of a loner because his life had molded him that way. Even so, as far as I know, everyone in the Quaker community of Blue Anchor accepted him at face value. He never became a leader, never tried to sway opinion even when carrying news of the war to outlying farms, but he attended all the important meetings at the Meeting House. Also he went to social functions such as those of the Kingston family at Christmas. On one occasion, when Pennsylvania Quakers brought a shipment of clothes from Philadelphia to North Carolina, Leo was present to receive a new pair of trousers.

"I can sure use them," said the angular man who was by then earning his living as a traveling tinker. "These old trousers I got on will now become my working britches. Do you mind if I try on the new ones and see if they fit?"

Awkward and blinking, he asked the question shyly as if it were somehow out of line. Then when given permission he shuffled off to a bedroom, put on the trousers, and with a beaming face showed himself in them to other guests. He was pleased to learn they were tough, a good fit, warm in winter, and comfortable. He wore those green worsted trousers to social gatherings for so many years that people began to see them as a badge of the man himself. He was known to be very thrifty and to use whatever he had as long as he could, and of course the green trousers were reserved for special occasions. For work and travel he had another pair.

Whatever the weather, one could see Leo on the roads early in the morning every morning. Every tool he owned, his entire shop, he carried in his wagon under canvas made from hemp. A mongrel dog named Sparky trotted always beside the wheels. He sprawled under the wagon whenever the tinker stopped at a farmhouse but never seemed to sleep. His tail was always wagging, and his owner while mending a pot never stopped talking. The dog eventually died, but the tinker went on strong as ever. He was a purveyor of news as well as a mender of pots and kettles and pans, and that gave him a sense of purpose. It became an important function as time went on.

After he left the old shack on the East Road near the swamp and set himself up as a lone tinker, he moved into a single room in a tall boarding house of many rooms. The owner of the house, Ida Crabtree, told him he would have to get rid of the dog. Later she relented and let him keep Sparky near his horse and wagon in the stable. In winter when the nights were cold, Sparky was allowed to sleep under Leo Mack's bed. Mrs. Crabtree was past middle age, hard of hearing, and the widow of Waldo Crabtree, a scrivener who had come into a small fortune before he died. She had good silver and china and old-fashioned but comfortable furniture. She kept an orderly house, but visitors were surprised to see goods that belonged in the pantry on the bookshelves of the living room. Beside the nicknacks, doodads, gimcracks, and a few old books were jars of jam and pickled apples. When times were lean the pantry items retreated to the kitchen.

Mrs. Crabtree cared about her guests and was known to be a fair-minded woman. For the evening meal all the boarders ate at the same table and talked about the day's events. Leo was not one to chat off the cuff, as we say, but always had something worthwhile to contribute. He talked about what was happening in the world at large, and one could see he spent lonely hours reading in his room. At Mrs. Crabtree's table, instead of wasting his time in idle conversation, he decided to become a broadcaster of news. He would carry the news of current events to isolated farmhouses whenever he visited them as a tinker. The times were volatile and uncertain, and people needed to know what was going on. The South was in conflict with the North, and the dogs of war were beginning to bark. All the people in and around Blue Anchor were eager to know what would happen next and how it would affect their lives. Leo took it upon himself to keep them well informed while mending their pots.

At the boarding house most of his fellow lodgers were Methodists and given to drink but were seldom noisy or rowdy. Leo couldn't abide noise and once gave notice to leave when a young man disturbed the whole house tooting a trombone late at night. The man claimed he had been offered a job with a well-known band and absolutely needed to practice to improve his playing. The boarders with their landlady presiding held a democratic meeting to decide whether he should stay or go. Even though the vote was a tie, Mrs. Crabtree turned him out the next day. It was better to require one person to go rather than have half of her guests depart. As it turned out, it was good he left her place and Blue Anchor and went up north. Years later we heard he was hired by the Philadelphia Philharmonic and given a favored seat among the horns.

In the spring of 1860 Abraham Lincoln received the nomination of the newly formed Republican party, and before the year was out he was elected President. Leo Mack, making his rounds as a tinker in a biting wintry wind, drove through Blue Anchor with the news. In a logical, well-ordered sort of way, he thought about the events of the day and dutifully set out to report them. Few people seemed to know where the man got his facts, but most of the time they were accurate. Running against a splintered and contentious Democratic Party, Lincoln captured the election with 180 electoral votes against 123 for all of his opponents. That was the kind of news Leo was delivering to people who wanted to know. When this dreadful

Civil War began in 1861, he quickly became well known in the community as the most reliable broadcaster of war news. My parents often talked about the time he visited Isaac Brandimore to mend a pot in the dead of winter. On several occasions he had told them the story, and they passed it on to me. I will try to repeat it here.

On a frosty day in late November, Leo Mack approached an isolated farmhouse, his aging mare struggling against the weight of his wagon and his mongrel dog Sparky trotting alongside. A cold breeze was coming from the southeast, and a stinging mist was in the air. The day before had seen a mix of snow and rain, and the muddy road was frozen and smooth. In some places snow and ice lay deep in the gullies beside the road. Fall had become winter.

"Hello, Leo!" called Isaac Brandimore as the tinker pulled into the yard. "I have some pots that need mending, and you can tell an old recluse about the events of the world. You look like you might enjoy a little warmth, and that dog looks like he could use a rest."

"Well, I'll tell you this, Isaac. My feet are as cold as a well digger's butt. That raw wind gets to the bone, you know. And that dog? Oh, that dog has miles in him yet! But he won't object to resting a spell, not him."

"He sure is thin," countered Isaac, "I can count his ribs."

"Oh, them ain't ribs! What you see is muscle from all the exercise he gets trotting over creation at the wheels of that wagon. He's good company but can be kind of ornery if you cross him."

"Oh, I won't cross him, Leo. That's a promise!"

"His tongue is hanging just a little, so I guess he's warm enough. He'll rest under the wagon and be still. If you happen to have a bone he can gnaw on, he'll be even more content."

"No bones, but I'll find a couple pieces of zwieback for him. That stuff is almost like a bone, you know, and good for his teeth."

"Zwieback you say! I've heard of that. German people put a loaf in the oven and bake it twice to make it hard as stone."

"And they eat it with a draft of good strong German beer. I eat it myself to keep my teeth and gums strong, and I rather like the nutty taste. Your dog Sparky will like it too I wager."

"Well, that's mighty kind of you to share it with old Sparky. But don't go giving the dog stuff you can eat yourself. You ain't rich like some folks I know around here."

Gathering his tools to take inside, Mack waited for Brandimore to come back with the twice-baked biscuits. Then as Sparky settled under the wagon and gnawed on his treat, the traveling tinker spoke with an air of concern.

"I guess it gets lonely out here, with your man Seth passing away. I heard you were sick a while back. Nothing serious I hope."

He expected to get a reply he could carry to a neighbor as one of the tidbits he used to promote his business. The dog sniffed at Brandimore's roomy shoes, circled behind him, and walked back to his place for more hardtack. Finding none, he shook himself vigorously and lay down beneath the wagon.

"Oh, I was a bit under the weather," Isaac said, as they went into the kitchen, "but my friend and housekeeper brought me around handsomely. She's a fine woman and I'm lucky to have her. Not here at present though, went home for a few days. Now what about you, Leo? Any problems with your health or with making ends meet? It's not easy growing old, is it?"

Leo Mack had lived in the midst of hardship so long it had come to be his element. Poverty he took for granted like day and night or the sun and moon. His struggle with penury, biting at times and unceasing – a condition that might have crippled another man – he accepted without complaint. If he had been a weaker person, he would have entered a plea of indigence at a Quarterly Meeting and received assistance from the community. But to ask for help had never entered his mind, not even when his trade brought him so little he worried about paying his landlady. He knew Ida Crabtree was a generous woman, and he knew she would carry him over a few weeks if he couldn't pay. It was certain that as long as he lived in her house he would never suffer the cold in winter or go hungry.

Leo was a kind and thoughtful man but eccentric in behavior and deeply private. He was in no mood to reveal his troubles to Brandimore or to anyone else. Years of hardship had taught him to play his cards close to his chest, to keep personal matters to himself. He replied only to Isaac's last question.

"Easy growing old? Guess not, but I'm gonna work till I drop. Can't do nothing else. Getting a bit creaky in cold weather but gotta work to make a living. And you'll agree there's many a good tune played on an old fiddle."

"Yes! And that's a good metaphor, Leo. The music is plaintive and sweet in the autumn of our lives, and even the air is savory. Keats called it the season of mists and mellow fruitfulness. Pretty words, I think, but I'm finding more mists in autumn than fruit. Is that your experience?"

"Misty outside right now. Been that way all morning."

Mack grinned wide enough to show his bad teeth. A glittering gold tooth seemed to mock the others. Often in conversation with customers he covered his mouth to hide the golden tooth, dental work done long before he came to Blue Anchor. It seems plausible too he did it to block any lingering bad breath from spicy food. He seldom talked about himself, and he disliked metaphorical observation made by others. So he asked about current events.

"Have you heard the election results and all the talk of secession? A lot of people hereabouts are worried."

"And they have good reason to be," said Isaac, pulling up a chair as the tinker set up his equipment on the kitchen table. "Only a couple years ago Lincoln insisted that Pierce and Buchanan had conspired to nationalize slavery, bring it from the South to the North and the whole country. Abe Lincoln thought even the prospect of such a thing was scandalous. You remember his most provocative remarks in that speech, I guess."

Mack hesitated, furrowing his brow and looking downward. "I don't go in much for politics with these pots and all. You mean what he said about a house split down the middle falling in half like a chunk of wood?"

"That's a good analogy, my friend, a very good analogy. But I think he said a house divided against itself cannot stand."

"What do you think he meant by that?" asked the tinker.

"Well he meant these United States will have to become either all slave or all free. We can't have it both ways. And that's why the house, this nation, is gonna be split right down the middle, to use your phrasing, like a chunk of wood. I'm afraid, old friend, we're in for some hard times."

The tinker stopped his work on the pot and looked surprised. "You say the times ain't hard already? I beg to differ."

"Well, you can say the hard times are maybe getting harder."

Mack was eyeing a pot of soup simmering on the stove. The steam rose from it and filled the kitchen with a fragrance of spicy potatoes. His empty stomach wanted him to ask about the soup, but a natural delicacy made him ask about the pot.

"Is that a good, sound pot? Sure wouldn't want it to spring a leak and have that soup spill on the stove and floor."

———◆———

Isaac took the hint and filled a deep bowl for him when his work was done. He ate the spicy potato soup with a good appetite, slurping it down while talking about his trade. Leo lived alone and didn't look after himself well enough to maintain good health. His liver sometimes got out of whack, but even when he should have been in bed he made his rounds all yellow around the eyes. Though Mrs. Crabtree fed him dutifully, his stomach often growled for the kind of starchy food he had known as a boy.

"I don't charge as much as some others I know, and so maybe I don't eat as well they do. But I do good work."

"That you do," Isaac assured him, "but what else do you know about all that's happening on the political scene?"

This man who read books with wavering eyesight in a solitude thrust upon him was eager to learn from any source. He was always glad to have a visitor, and he liked chatting with the tinker.

"Can't talk no more now," said Mack. "Have to get on over to the Alston place and pay them a visit. Hannah is not well, you know, and Elmer is overworked and don't know what to do."

"I know and it's sad. I certainly hope Hannah gets better. And I did hear something about Elmer not having enough help to bring in his crop. I think our community will help him with that."

"They had a couple of younger folk, man and wife, but let them go. Jeremy Heartwood gave the couple money to buy their

315

freedom. They gave it all to Elmer and got a signed certificate, and he hired them at fair pay, I hear, but that means they can up and leave any time they feel like it."

"I suppose the couple will stay on as free laborers."

"Well, yeah, but they could leave any time they feel like it. Who knows what's gonna happen? If the Alstons have any work for me, I'm not gonna ask for cash."

Leo would barter with the needy Alston family, and with others strapped financially, but he expected cash payment from the scholarly Brandimore. If the man had money to buy books, he could pay to have a pot mended. He mentioned a fee which he said was quite a bit lower than his usual fees.

"That's because recently you lost your man Seth," he said with a show of concern, "and had to go out looking for part-time help. I'm glad you found a good housekeeper. What's her name?"

Isaac was thinking about South Carolina's threat of secession and didn't seem to hear the question. He paid the sum Mack named without hesitation and helped Leo carry his equipment outside.

Flicking the reins as the signal to move, he drove off without a word. He felt he had talked enough for one little job even when rewarded with the tasty soup. His customer stood on the porch and watched the wagon wind its way out of the yard and down the road, Sparky following behind.

"What does South Carolina hope to gain by that?" Brandimore asked himself, speaking softly to the cold air. "And my state too? Maybe our politicians in Raleigh will display cooler heads. But what if this secessionist fever mounts? If it does, I don't see how any one state can hold out for long against the others. Oh, nothing good will come of this, nothing good at all."

Editor's Note: *Some would argue that in the end something good did come of it, but before that could happen more than half a million young men in the prime of their lives would have to die in nasty, brutal, immoral combat, and President Lincoln who led the massive campaign to abolish slavery would die also by violence. The war lasted too many years, from 1861 to 1865. When the North raped the South and finally won with heavy casualties, its victory put an end to slavery in the United States. We Quakers had always spoken of slavery as an evil institution. Long before the Civil War erupted we opposed it. That's why Quakers in the South were unfairly called abolitionists when many were not, were hated by their neighbors because of the Exemption Act, and often suffered more than others when the war was raging. – E. Kingston.*

Chapter 23

Preserving the Union

I n the village of Blue Anchor in the state of North Carolina, Christmas came and went in cold weather. January and February were cold and snowy, and March with high winds came in like a tiger. The weather was anything but good, and yet Leo Mack's old wagon was on the road moving slowly from one isolated farmhouse to the next. He had said to Isaac Brandimore that he would work as long as he could because he could do nothing else. In hard times he had to make a living, and he was also a traveler. To be ever on the move was in his blood, and so he urged his old and doddering horse to trudge onward even in bad weather. The dog Sparky was becoming thinner and thinner but trotted beside the wheels wherever the wagon went and lay beneath it even when the ground was frozen. No one ever saw the dog riding beside his master.

In the first week of March in 1861, Leo went to Isaac Brandimore's cozy little cottage again. When he was there in November he ate a piping hot bowl of thick soup that made him strong for the rest of the day, and he hoped he might be just as lucky again. While eating or mending a pot, he would tell the solitary man the latest political news from the North as well as from Raleigh and points southward. It would be a fair trade.

"Hello, Leo! Come into my house, old friend!" cried Brandimore as Mack pulled into his yard. "Come in out of the cold and bring that dog of yours with you."

"Oh, I can't do that," Mack replied. "That dog is trained to guard my stuff. You wouldn't believe how fierce he can be when riled."

"Yes, I know," Isaac chuckled. "You've told me more than once that he's all muscle and fit as a fiddle and ornery when crossed. But I still say he's welcome to a little warmth."

"No, he'll be just find layin' under the wagon. No wind there and not too cold, and besides he's used to it."

By now the tinker was on the porch of Brandimore's quaint little house and heading for the kitchen. Always, in any house he visited, he went directly to the kitchen more out of habit than professional duty. As he walked through the sitting-room, he caught the scent of old leathery books and his nose twitched. He preferred the scent of something cooking.

"I don't guess you have any mending for me to do. I was here not long ago. Still remember that potato soup you gave me."

"Oh, the last time you were here I had some work for you, but don't seem to have any now. I do have a rabbit slowly boiling on the stove, and I hope you'll stay long enough to have a few bites."

"I like my rabbit fried," Leo said, "but I won't object to boiled rabbit if it's tender and tasty. Old folks like us shouldn't be eating fried rabbit anyway. My teeth ain't as good as they used to be."

Removing his coat and broad hat and sitting down in a straight Quaker chair, he flashed his bad teeth in a wide grin and chuckled. At the stove Isaac stirred the boiling pot and added more salt.

"I boil my meat most of the time these days. My digestive system won't take fried foods any more even though my taste buds cry out for them. But enough chit-chat. Tell me the latest news while I get the rabbit ready to eat."

"Well, I guess you know all about Lincoln's inauguration yesterday in Washington. A real big event it was. Hundreds standing in the cold to hear him speak. Gave a rousing good speech too."

Mack was fairly certain that Brandimore, living in isolation and not leaving the house very often, had heard little. It was a ploy to stir interest, to get the conversation started.

"Well, I did hear that Jeff Davis was inaugurated as President of the Confederacy only two weeks ago. And I heard Lincoln would have to move into Washington protected by soldiers for his ceremony because of the upheaval we're going through. Looks like secession is creating a firestorm."

"Yup, Lincoln took the oath of office on the East Portico of the Capitol. Soldiers all over the place, but he went there with President Buchanan in an open carriage. The building was covered with scaffolding, I heard, 'cause they're replacing the dome."

"What did he say in his speech? I'm eager to know all the details. These are truly the times that try men's souls, Leo. Lincoln is walking on a tightrope across a bed of fire!"

"Isaac old man, you sure do come up with some pretty images. I don't see it quite the way you do but the man does have his troubles, and things are gonna get worse before they get better."

"What did he say in his speech?"

"Well, it was a long speech and I didn't read it all but the main point he made, as far as I can recollect, is he will preserve the Union at any cost. He said the states must remain united 'cause we live in the United States. And he emphasized that word united and said no individual state, or even a group of states, has any legal right to leave the United States and go out on its own."

"What did he say about slavery? Anything about that?"

"Oh, he said he wouldn't even try to abolish slavery in the South, but he wouldn't let it get a foothold in other states or territories."

"In earlier speeches I think he said he would not rest until he saw slavery abolished. I think we are getting mixed signals here."

"In this speech they say he was calling for some sort of compromise. Said he wouldn't use force to interfere with slavery in the South as we have it now, but wouldn't let it spread into territories that wanna become states."

"Preserving the Union at any cost means war, of course. I can't tell you how much I dread the future. Oh, this rabbit's done, old friend. Pull your chair up to the table and let's eat. We have some tough, new-baked bread to go with it."

"Well, Isaac, I don't mind if I do, but I can't stay much longer. Have my rounds to make, y' know. Have to make a living even in bad times and bad weather. Me and that horse and that dog have to be on the road. We're travelers, y' know, from way back. What about that housekeeper of yours? She doing right by you? Name's Olga? Don't recollect her last name."

Isaac didn't answer the tinker's questions. His mind was on politics and the pressing issues of the day, and he stammered that he had tried to examine them carefully to reach cogent conclusions but without a favorable outcome. Digesting the fancy language, Leo couldn't resist a rejoinder.

"You think you have," he said. "You scholars with brains think you have examined everything, every visible part of everything, but maybe it just ain't so. I've examined very little except the bottoms of old kettles and saucepans, but people say I have a good head on my stringy shoulders and a good store of commonsense too."

"Indeed you do have that," Brandimore assured him, not in the least upset by Leo's view of the scholarly life. "You have a vast store of commonsense, and you make it your business to know what is happening in these dire times. I might add you have the gift of gab too. I sometimes envy you, my friend."

＝＝◦◉◦＝＝

Half an hour later the tinker was on his wagon again and steering his old horse in the direction of Darboy's General Store. He would not be going there to buy anything, for in tumultuous times goods in the store were becoming scarce. Mainly he had a hankering to chat with men more like himself and share with them the news of the day. Also he expected to pick up more news and some scraps of gossip he could pass on to others as he made his rounds. He pulled his wagon into the yard, tipped his hat to the driver of another wagon trundling past the store on his way to the mill, and hitched his old horse to a post. Entering the store, Leo Mack smiled and shook his head as he glanced at the colorful posters on the south wall. He had seen them before, a long time ago.

The eye-catching posters, now brittle and faded and tainted with dusty fly specks, advertised remedies for upset stomach, sore throat, fatigue, scrapes and cuts, grippe and pneumonia, diarrhea, constipation, joint pain, and poor eyesight. Other posters praised in flowery terms ingenious farm implements and items for the home. On one was a portrait of a pretty woman in a stupendous hat offering medicated snuff that would effectively relieve headaches, dispel melancholy, shrink hemorrhoids, calm the stomach, and improve breathing. Mack knew the general store for some time had ceased to carry the wondrous potions and grand machinery the posters advertised, for in troubled times most of those things had dropped out of sight. And yet, though old and fading and full of lies, the posters retained the power to command attention.

A yellowing broadsheet advertised in fat and bold black letters, hand-printed by the seller, a well-built open carriage with four good wheels. That was the wagon Mack had bought on easy terms to use in his business. The wagon had been consigned to Darboy who would take a share of the profits when sold. As a favor to Mack, for he knew the man was struggling to make a living, he sold the wagon without a commission and even helped the tinker get it at a lower price. The wagon had served him well, and now as he looked at the broadsheet Leo remembered the wheels were beginning to squeak. He would have to pack all four of them with grease.

The store owner was a congenial man and made his customers feel at home even when they didn't buy anything. Mack had seen the similarity between Jacob Darboy and the founder of Quakerism and wanted others see it. In the farmhouse of one of his customers he had come across an old painting of the man. He traded some work for it and soon afterwards gave it to Darboy to hang in his store. All who saw the portrait agreed that venerable George Fox in 1681 was remarkably similar in appearance to Jacob Darboy in 1861.

The proprietor of Darboy's General Store was talking to a customer about reins and a yoke, but on seeing Leo they both turned to greet him. He was a walking encyclopedia of small information and always drew a crowd when he came into the store. Darboy and his customer expected news of the outside world, something they could pass along to others, and they were confident their friend would not let them down. Leo Mack found a chair and sat down.

"Well, if you ask me, there's a flurry of activity all over," the tinker reported. "Seems to be a fiery, steadfast certainty that secession is the way to go. In the larger towns speeches on every side and people parading up and down in gaudy costume. Young men by the thousands flocking to the colors and swearing to die to preserve the Southern way of life. But signing up mainly for adventure, I hear, and no trouble at all getting plenty of volunteers."

"Flocking to the colors?" asked Alvin Atterbury. He cultivated a spread of sixty acres and was there for seed. "You mean the new flag, the one they call the Stars and Bars? I'm having trouble seeing it as a real flag, the colors of a sovereign nation."

"Oh, it's a real flag all right," countered Mack. "You can bet on that. It's flying from courthouses already, and the army's gonna take it into every battle it fights. Everybody is saying it'll be a flag to spark fear in the enemy."

"I've read about flag bearers not being armed," Darboy broke in. "If a flag bearer falls in battle, the soldier next to him must grab the flag before it hits the ground and carry it forward. Then would you believe it? That piece of cloth becomes more important than either the man or his weapon. It's an easy way to die!"

"Well, I guess it is," Mack assented, "but no unit is gonna be without a battle flag or a boy to carry it, and it's gonna be the Confederate flag in the thick of action."

"I hear there's a shortage of rifles for the infantry," said Atterbury. "And not enough uniforms to go around. And a shortage of boots and other apparel. Also chaotic distribution depots and more than enough confusion all over."

"True enough," answered Mack, who now saw himself as something of an authority on the new events. "But you know these are the early weeks of the war. Officers have to be selected and given their duties. Enlisted soldiers have to be assigned, armed, and trained. Tremendous amount of drilling already going on. The generals and senior officers are trying to find commanders for all the regiments being formed, and that's a real problem right there."

"Well, it's a big and sad undertaking," Darboy sighed, "and perhaps a misguided one too. Old Thomas Paine could have been talking about us when he wrote about the bad events of his own day. You remember what he said? Something like this: 'These are the times that try men's souls!' That sure describes us all right. A melodramatic declaration maybe, but it fits."

Mack shrugged his shoulders, sighed deeply, and looked at the ceiling. He disliked fancy quotations from people who read books, and he had heard those same words from Isaac Brandimore, a good friend but a bore at times. Jacob Darboy, the struggling merchant, he favored. Darboy, the pundit and reader of books, sounded too much like Brandimore. And besides old Isaac had used that little nugget better than Darboy, and with greater impact, way back in March.

"What I know about that," he said, scratching the bald spot on the back of his head, "is about enough to put in a thimble. We can't really say how trying things are gonna get, can we? We're just plain old humans and can't see the future. Just hafta wait."

"Well, you get the gist of what I'm saying, old friend," Darboy insisted. "I'm saying these are dangerous times. Exciting times right now for the younger folk but deadly later.

You can mark my word on that, Friend Mack. All these young men with war fever in their blood tramping off to the beat of drums will live to regret it before they die by thousands. Oh, they're eager for adventure all right, but what's gonna happen to the lot of them later?"

"What's gonna happen to any poor lad willing to fight?" asked Mack. "I heard they're marching off to war singing battle hymns written and sung by Northerners. Now that just ain't right."

"Ah, still wet behind the ears. They don't seem to know the price they'll pay for just a little excitement. In another year or two we'll see them paying and paying. Paying the ultimate price!"

Darboy was now talking like a merchant, and Mack remembered he was in the store to pick up an order he had placed weeks before. "I'm here for the solder you promised to get me. Can't mend no pots without it. You don't happen to have a pile of pots or pans or pails in your back room that need attention, do you?"

Leo had been looking for an apprentice to learn his trade and take it over when he grew too old to work. But the word had gotten around that the man was too much a taskmaster to be a good master. A couple years back he had a slow-witted boy who seemed eager to learn but could never remember the details of the trade. One afternoon when his liver was acting up, exasperated and testy but not angry, Leo lectured his apprentice with so little restraint the boy scampered away and quit. Leo was seen in the community as a good Quaker, but for reasons unknown to his friends he had never learned patience and calm, commodities prized by the Quakers. I think it had to do with his coming into our faith late in life, and I think even as an old man he never lost entirely his identity as an Irish Traveler. From what I've heard, most of them in their time had short fuses.

A few days after the Battle of Gettysburg, lasting three terrible days in the summer of 1863, the people of Blue Anchor heard all about it. Leo Mack, tinker and talker, went from house to house in his old wagon reporting news that was mostly horrific. His faithful dog Sparky, a constant companion for a decade, was now dead and the man made his rounds alone. Then summer moved into fall, and Mack reported almost no fighting going on in Virginia. With news of that sort the citizens of Blue Anchor began to hope the war would soon end. From the time it began in 1861 until it seemed to be over in 1864, Leo went from house to house in his creaky old wagon hoping to mend a pot or pan but expecting also to deliver news his customers had not heard. He had become a person of value in the community, not really loved by anyone but cherished as a capable man of strong personality performing a service above and beyond his calling as a tinker. People depended on him.

He was taken for granted by the villagers but would have been sorely missed had he gone elsewhere to live. He died near the end of November in 1864 and so was never able to report the defeat of Southern forces by the North. To the end of his life he thought the South would somehow perform a miracle and crush the North, and he wanted to be on hand to report that news. It didn't happen, and I believe Providence played a role in seeing it didn't happen. Slavery in these United States in modern times had to go, and it was time for Leo Mack to go. Though some in the village wanted to erect an elaborate catafalque in praise of the worthy man, Quaker wisdom opted for a simple ceremony in the Meeting House. When he died, as I have said earlier, just about every man, woman, and child in the village turned out to honor his memory. Of course I was there among them. He had touched the lives of us all.

Epilogue

This is the way it began: "My name is Isaac Brandimore. I am not a young man. I passed the bloom of youth sixty years ago but remain active and alive in a solitude thrust upon me." Those are the words of our village scholar, as he took it upon himself to write the life story of Leo Tamasin Mack, our tinker and traveler in Blue Anchor, our broadcaster of news in tumultuous times.

These are the words I write to end this narrative: "My name is Emily Anne Kingston. I am the offspring of strong-minded men and women of the Quaker faith who worked hard to improve their daily lives and wanted even better for their children. I do believe they were pleased to see every one of them turn out well." That is the way this book ends as I write the epilogue.

I am a college graduate at a time when few women go to college, and I have begun to teach the bright and happy children of Blue Anchor the basics of reading and writing and arithmetic. Inevitably, I tell them, a shining future lies ahead for each one of them but only if they come to school and shiver when our old stove refuses to heat a large room that lets in the cold. Their hearts alive with youthful joy in spite of these uncertain times, they laugh at me for worrying about the cold. They don't seem to mind the shortcomings of our one and only schoolhouse. It is old and run-down, and there is talk it will be rebuilt in a year or two now that the war is over.

I am not here, however, to talk about my school or my students or the ghastly civil war that laid waste to the South and severely damaged the North but finally ended. I wish only to explain how this book came into existence and why its story is told by several persons. Isaac Brandimore encouraged Leo Mack to talk about the events of his life in his own words but had to intervene at times to clarify issues for the reader or to make Leo's language more acceptable. Then after our beloved scholar died of something bad in the air, with some hesitation I accepted the project he began. I too have allowed Leo to tell his own story. I was fortunate enough to have long conversations with him, and that made the work easier. However, before his story could be fully written he died of pneumonia possibly triggered by a cold he caught when coming home soaked to the skin in late November. I wanted him to read his memoir as a book.

After Mack's death with nothing more to rely upon than the memory of his existence among us, I attempted to finish the story. I wanted it to have a strong and memorable, even a moving and dramatic ending, but it seems that achievement was beyond me. Be that as it may, the story is now told. I have called it in reference to the main character, "A Tinker in Blue Anchor." I believe, had he lived long enough to see his story complete for others to read, he would have liked the title. I know he felt himself a part of Blue Anchor, for in time our village came to be the home he had sought all his life. Of all the places where he had lived during all those years of wandering, Blue Anchor was the one place he liked the most.

Yet in a way, as I write in admiration of the man, I begin to think this narrative is about two good men. Leo Mack and

Isaac Brandimore, living among us in good times and bad, quietly proved their worth. Both were valued members of our community. Both were a credit to the species Thomas Carlyle called featherless bipeds. Both were infused and animated by blood, brain, and spirit and wondrous to behold. Dying of natural causes and going on to the next leg of their journey, their departure diminished Blue Anchor. This narrative, I fondly hope, will preserve their memory.